CHANGELING

BOOK 2 OF THE YEAR KING

MARETH GRIFFITH

PRAISE FOR MARETH GRIFFITH
REVIEWS FROM THE ORIGINAL PUBLICATION

Equal parts amusing and unnerving, COURT OF TWILIGHT is urban fantasy with a sci-fi kick, perfect for readers who are ready for a taste of something beyond angels, demons and shadow hunters.

— BOOKS BY SMITHIES

Court of Twilight's a pleasant story with some darker undertones; full of mystery and a modern-day take on the Fae world.

— KATE COE, SFF WORLD

Everything about this felt new and imaginative—the concept of the novel as a whole, the kind of threats faced by the characters, the concept of the fantastical elements. I never knew where it was going and I'm desperate for the sequel so that my questions can be answered.

— AMAZON REVIEW

THE SHADOW BY MY FINGER CAST
DIVIDES THE FUTURE FROM THE PAST:
BEFORE IT, SLEEPS THE UNBORN HOUR
IN DARKNESS, AND BEYOND THY POWER:
BEHIND ITS UNRETURNING LINE,
THE VANISHED HOUR, NO LONGER THINE:
ONE HOUR ALONE IS IN THY HANDS,—
THE NOW ON WHICH THE SHADOW STANDS.

-The Sun-Dial at Wells College, Henry Van Dyke, 1852-1933

CHAPTER 1

There must have been a noise to begin with, but the first thing Ivy was aware of was her bedside clock blinking 12:17, which meant it probably wasn't 12:17 as much as it was seventeen minutes after a power outage. Squinting, Ivy peered past the red glow of the clock toward the window. Still dark, and her alarm was on her phone, so it didn't matter what time the bedside clock thought it was. Probably it was the blinking light that woke her, or a headlight. Whenever cars turned left from Haymarket Street, the headlights never failed to shine straight through the gap in Ivy's curtains, a fact Ivy had been blissfully unaware of until after she'd already moved in. It was probably just a car that had woken her.

Or Grinch, Ivy thought, hearing the bulldog's nails clicking across the linoleum in the hallway. The clatter was immediately followed by a wet, snuffling noise. Hunzu had taken to feeding the thing after repeatedly assuring Ivy there was no chance his biscuits would turn her flatmate's dog invisible. Now it seemed the dog was forever after Hunzu (and by extension, Ivy) for tidbits.

Another sniff, and the clicking noise retreated back down

the hall, fading into the murmur of the telly in the parlor and the whirr of Ivy's desk fan. Ivy's face felt sticky with sweat, the tiny fan barely making a dent in the muggy July heat. She rolled over, rubbing at her face with the corner of her bedsheet —and saw the shadow in the corner of the room.

Ivy froze with the sheet halfway to her nose, waiting for the thing twitching in the corner to helpfully resolve itself into something that was supposed to be there. A jacket thrown over the desk chair, or a weird shadow cast from the street outside, or some other innocent thing that had every right to be in Ivy's bedroom in the middle of the night.

The shape didn't look like a jacket or a shadow. Frozen under the bedsheet, Ivy stared at it, feeling the sweat on her forehead turn cold. It was looking more and more like a person. An impatient person, at that; its arms were crossed, fingers tapping restlessly against its sleeves.

"Hunzu?" Ivy hissed, immediately wondering why she thought it might be him. Early in their acquaintance, he'd broken into Ivy's former flat twice. These days he usually texted if he was going to come over.

The shape by the chair stopped twitching its fingers. It cocked its head, listening, and Ivy was suddenly certain calling aloud had been a mistake, because now it knew she was awake.

Troublingly, this didn't make the shape any more inclined to leave. Ivy squinted hard at it, feeling more awake by the second, as though adrenaline, not sweat, were trickling through her pores. The shape wasn't leaving or becoming any more comprehensible. It wasn't hiding, either, merely standing beside the window, silhouetted by the streetlight streaming in from the gap in the curtains.

Ivy fought to keep her breathing even, as if she were still asleep. Maybe she could pass off her mumble as sleep-talk if she stayed absolutely still and didn't move. If she waited long enough, the thing was certain to turn into a pile of laundry. Whatever trick it was that made things in the corner of your eye disappear when looked at properly.

It wasn't Lauren. Her flatmate standing in Ivy's bedroom in the middle of the night would have been strange, but in a normal, explicable sort of way. It wasn't Demi, who was strange in more abnormal, inexplicable ways—but Demi would have called if she planned on dropping by in the middle of the night.

The figure moved again, shifting its weight from one leg to another.

Then it spoke, three incomprehensible syllables in a tight, female voice.

Every hair on Ivy's body stood at attention. The bedroom was suddenly cold, the thin bedsheet, conversely, smothering. The figure hadn't lowered her voice, like she didn't care whether Ivy heard her or not. Ivy could keep hiding under her sheet, or else . . .

The shape in the corner shifted again, the slightest turn of its head. It had to know Ivy was there, and if somehow it didn't, Ivy was wasting her chance to run.

Carefully not looking at the thing in the corner, Ivy pulled back the bedsheet, ignoring the tremble in her arms as she sat up. A laugh track from the telly echoed down the hall, discordant and jarringly normal all at once. Forcing herself to move slowly, Ivy threw one leg off the side of the bed, then the other, and stood up. Her legs were shaking. She hoped the thing in the corner would write off her clumsiness as a result of just waking up.

Ahead of her, the wardrobe door gaped open like a mouth. Two steps and she was past it, her eyes fixed on the doorknob, not daring to look at the desk or the figure beside it. Ivy grabbed the knob, jerked open the door, and stumbled into the hallway. The light seemed overpoweringly bright, halos and dots momentarily blotting out the greying linoleum floor, the peach-patterned wallpaper, the half-open bathroom door. Ivy yanked the door shut behind her and heard it close with a click. The hallway felt too hot and too cold all at once. She let go of the handle and steadied herself against the wall.

The telly's warble was louder out here, its murmur a bastion of all things normal and usual. Ivy swallowed and looked hard at the doorknob, as though it might start turning on its own. She pushed her hair back from her face, and her hand came away covered in sweat.

Something was inside her room. But *somethings* weren't supposed to leave dark bedrooms and come out into well-lit hallways. Ivy hoped the thing inside would be good enough to follow this rule. Maybe it didn't care about well-lit hallways. Or maybe it would do something straight out of a horror movie and cut power to the flat before lurching through the door, arms outstretched . . .

If Ivy's clock was blinking, the power had gone out once already.

A brown shape streaked into the corridor ahead of her, and Ivy jumped. Toenails clattering, Grinch ran straight into Ivy's legs, his stub tail wiggling frantically as the dog rubbed his snout into the back of Ivy's calves.

"Damnit," she hissed. Feeling like her heart was ready to lurch out of her chest, Ivy patted the bulldog's neck. Grinch's tail wiggled even faster. "Good boy," she murmured. Even though Grinch would probably run howling at the first sign of danger, Ivy still felt marginally safer with her flatmate's dog crouched between her and whatever was inside her room.

"Grinch," Lauren called from the living room. She sounded annoyed; the bulldog stopped nuzzling Ivy and looked guiltily over his shoulder. "Grinch, you better not be bothering her."

The bulldog lowered his ears and dashed back down the

hall, claws clattering on the linoleum. Alone again, Ivy looked nervously up and down the hall. Her bedroom door was closed. Everything looked completely innocuous.

Maybe there was a monster in her room. Maybe there wasn't. Maybe the shape and the voice had been some sort of night terror. That still didn't mean Ivy wanted to go back in there, not without checking the locks on the front door at the very least.

Slowly, Ivy followed the dog down the hall.

In the parlor, Lauren was sprawled across the sofa, one hand on the television remote and the other hand fending off Grinch, who was enthusiastically licking her face.

"Sorry," Lauren said, shoving Grinch off her chest and sternly pointing him in the direction of the dog bed under the window. She sounded the slightest bit tipsy; two empty cider bottles were sitting on the end table next to her mobile. "He was clawing at your door a minute ago. I'll shut him in my room if he's being a bother."

Lauren, Ivy's current flatmate, was a medical transcriptionist Ivy had met through a mutual friend. Ivy had impulsively moved in with Lauren last February after discovering that her previous flatmate was both contagiously invisible and about to be murdered by an alien serial killer. Demi hadn't died —mostly because Ivy managed to rope someone else into being murdered instead—but Ivy still ended up moving to Dartry in the aftermath. Sometimes she missed the big skylights in their old flat in Howth, and Demi's beautiful (if hazardous) copper cookware.

"It's fine," said Ivy, looking thoughtfully at the front door. The deadbolt was locked and the security chain was still latched.

"You sure?" said Lauren, looking quizzically at Ivy.

The telly's laugh track chimed in, loudly punctuating some

argument between Del Boy and Uncle Albert. Outside, a car rumbled down the street, snatches of the radio carrying easily through the open window.

"Everything's fine," Ivy lied. She came farther into the parlor and bent down next to the bookshelf. Pretending to scan the magazines on the bottom shelf, she peered back down the hallway. Everything looked normal—scuffed linoleum floors, a handful of dust bunnies, peach wallpaper marred by a water stain only partially hidden by a print of the Ha'Penny Bridge hanging opposite the door to the loo. Everything looked comfortingly boring and usual.

Wasn't there some sort of rule that monsters couldn't exist in boring, average surroundings? It wasn't like this was an abandoned castle or a deserted farmhouse. By Dublin standards, Dartry wasn't even a seedy neighborhood. Strange things were not supposed to happen here: that was precisely why Ivy had moved in, and it was terribly impolite of the strange things to follow her. The only strange things that ought to be here were the ones Ivy had specifically given a pass to—namely Demi, Hunzu, and Ambrose.

Ivy tilted her head, listening hard for any noise from down the hall. Besides the telly, she only heard the rumble of traffic on the main road, motorists making their way back from whatever dubious entertainments they'd been pursuing in the City Centre after midnight on a Tuesday. The noise grew more distinct as a lorry turned onto their street, the parlor window rattling gently as it drove past. If there were any other noises, the telly and the traffic were covering them up. Ivy felt torn between asking Lauren to turn the volume down so she could listen—or turning it up so she couldn't hear anything at all.

The laugh track chortled again, followed a moment later by Lauren, her snorting laugh turning abruptly into a hiccup.

Almost like a perfectly normal evening. Except for the thing in Ivy's room.

"Did you open the door?" Ivy asked, glancing at Lauren while simultaneously trying keep her eye on the hallway. "I thought I heard something."

"You did," said Lauren, waving the remote at Grinch. "*Him.* I told you, he wouldn't stop scratching at the door. Might be a mouse."

It hadn't been a mouse.

Maybe it hadn't been anything at all.

Or maybe it was someone Grinch had noticed, but Lauren never would have seen, even if it waltzed through the flat a dozen times. Trows like Demi and Hunzu were invisible to most people unless they were deliberately trying to be noticed. If there were trows in the house, they could easily have gotten inside without Lauren realizing.

Which also meant the people Ivy might call for help with housebreakers—the Gardaí, for instance—couldn't see them, either. She could call Ambrose, except Ivy's phone was still sitting on her desk. Possibly next to some misplaced jacket flapping in the breeze that had scared Ivy half to death.

Ivy walked past Grinch's dog bed and dropped into the chair beside it. She tucked her feet cross-legged underneath her, the draft from the half-open window pleasantly cool.

This was silly. Ivy knew what trows were, and she knew they weren't dangerous. Or they *were*, but not in the same way housebreakers or angry drunks were dangerous. In fact, when you came right down to it, Ivy was a lot more dangerous to *them* than they were to Ivy. As long as Ivy didn't touch them, everyone would be fine. Ivy would stay visible, and the trows wouldn't catch whatever it was that made humans age.

On the telly, the end credits were rolling on *Only Fools and Horses*. Lauren yawned, picked herself unsteadily off the sofa, and began gathering up the empty cider bottles. Grinch stood up from his dog bed with a shake, prancing over to Lauren and shoving his head into the backs of her knees.

"Idiot," Lauren mumbled, pushing the dog out of the way as she carried the empty bottles into the kitchen. A moment later, Ivy heard the clinking of glass dropping into the recycling bin.

Lauren would be going to bed soon, which meant Ivy would be the only one awake in the flat, and the monster-free circle of light and noise in the parlor was only going to get smaller. In a few minutes, Lauren would be asleep. Then it would only be Ivy, and the telly, and the thing in Ivy's bedroom.

Unless there wasn't anything at all. Sitting in the living room, the idea of something hiding in the shadows seemed preposterous. That sort of thing only happened in horror movies or spy novels, not in real life. Maybe Ivy dreamed the whole thing. Probably whatever voice she'd heard had come from the telly, or the flat next door.

Ivy still didn't want to walk in there empty-handed, and whatever was going to happen when Ivy opened her bedroom door, she wanted it to happen before Lauren went to sleep. Before the flat turned dark and quiet, depriving Ivy of whatever courage came from late-night laugh tracks. Whatever was in the room, Ivy was certain she'd be better off facing it with Uncle Albert genially complaining in the background.

Getting up from the chair, Ivy followed Lauren into the kitchen and opened the bric-a-brac drawer next to the dish-washer. Feeling around in the back of the drawer, Ivy pulled out a claw-headed hammer, just small enough to fit into the pocket of her shorts.

Not giving herself time to consider whether this was a good

idea or not, Ivy marched back down the hall, threw open her bedroom door, and switched on the light.

Ivy half expected to see nothing. Or a jacket sitting at just the right angle to make it look like a person standing in the corner. Or that Lauren had always kept some weird portrait in her spare bedroom, and Ivy had simply never noticed it in the five months she'd lived there.

She saw none of those things.

The figure turned as the light came on, and Ivy jumped back, grappling for the hammer, feeling the pocket tear as the claw caught on the fabric. The stranger was dressed in black, just like the thing in the apple grove last winter, and Ivy almost expected to see fire in its hand. Almost expected everything around her to turn to flames, just like Larch must have seen when he died. When the thing standing in Ivy's room had killed him.

The figure—the woman—was moving, and Ivy brought the hammer up, but the woman ducked easily under Ivy's panicked swing, a thick braid of dark hair swinging free of her jumpsuit's hood. She reached for Ivy's right shoulder with both hands, gloved fingers warm on Ivy's neck. A pinprick of pain blossomed in their wake as Ivy tried to pull free. The woman let go and stepped back. Ivy staggered, bringing the hammer up for another try, but it suddenly felt far heavier than it should.

Somewhere behind her, the bedroom door slammed shut. Ivy tried to focus on the stranger, but her eyes were stinging and everything seemed blurred. The hammer hit the floor with a clatter. Everything around her was haloed and muffled, and maybe the Enemy didn't kill with fire every time. Ivy had never asked.

Ivy lunged for the door and stumbled. Slumping against the bed, she grabbed for the mattress, only managing to pull the duvet off the bed as she slid to the floor. Her feet were tingling, her head spinning as if she'd downed too many drinks all at once.

Blearily, Ivy saw the figure kneel beside her. Her clothing was exactly like what Ivy remembered from those horrible minutes in the apple grove, but the face was nothing alike. Not the Enemy. The face wasn't the same, and it hadn't killed her. Yet. Or maybe it *was* the Enemy, and since it wasn't its designated day to kill anyone, it had simply drugged Ivy instead.

A blue light flashed near the woman's wrist, painfully bright for a moment, then gone. Ivy's eyes hurt, stinging along with her neck; it seemed difficult to properly care.

The blue light glinted again and Ivy blinked, trying to focus. A metal bracelet was wrapped around the woman's left forearm, covering it like an overgrown wrist guard, its spiral heat sinks radiating from the metal like delicate wings. A trow computer, though Ivy had never seen anyone actually wearing one before. The only one outside of Haven that Ivy knew about was the one Ivy herself had helped steal, and *that* was at the Nano Imaging Centre in Belfield. Then Ivy spotted the cord, trailing from the wing computer to something held loosely in the woman's right hand.

Ivy's own mobile phone.

The hammer was still in reach, sitting where it had fallen next to a rumpled pair of trousers, a pile of paperbacks, and the remote for Ivy's Bluetooth speakers. Ivy reached for the hammer. Her arm flopped against the floorboards like a fish, her fingers fluttering uselessly against the handle. Her lip was sting-ing, like she'd bashed it against the bedframe as she fell, and there was a coppery taste in her mouth.

The stranger turned back to the desk, still holding Ivy's phone. Looking up from the floor, the desk and the Enemy both seemed unnaturally tall. The half-open wardrobe was a mouth, gaping and cavernous. Nothing in the room seemed its proper shape or size.

Would it stop her if Ivy tried to crawl out of the room? Would it kill her? Maybe Ivy was dying already, from whatever it had injected into her neck. Maybe the thing had already killed her, it just hadn't chosen fire.

Ivy swallowed, tasting blood. Something snuffed at the door; Grinch's toenails clicked as he paced in the hall.

If this was the Enemy, it shouldn't be here. Not on this day, and not with the Year King miles away. It shouldn't be interested in Ivy, let alone Ivy's phone.

She tried again for the hammer. This time she succeeded in curling her fingers around the handle. Maybe in another five minutes she could manage to pick it up.

In the meantime, the thing was still standing by the desk, and there was no sense pretending Ivy couldn't see it. Maybe that meant Ivy could ask a few questions no one seemed to know the answers to. Like why the Enemy killed, and why it only killed one specific person, on one specific day.

Also, what the hell the Enemy wanted with her phone.

"I can see you," Ivy growled, the words slurred to the point of incomprehension.

The woman turned, then glanced over her own shoulder, as though making sure Ivy wasn't actually talking to someone else. It was a trow gesture, something she'd seen many of them do on first acquaintance.

"Didn't you hear me?" Ivy tried again, forcing out the words through numb lips. The woman's gaze flicked to Ivy, then back to the door. "You can't hide. Not from me."

From the hallway, Grinch gave a low, uncertain whine.

The stranger looked back at Ivy, and for a moment her hooded face seemed like the face of a dead thing. Ivy was certain she'd made a mistake, that she should have stayed silent and clung to the illusion she was deaf and unknowing. The thing in Ivy's room was a murderer, and if Ivy caused it any trouble, she knew exactly what it would do in response.

Ivy tried to pick up the hammer, managing only to rattle it against the floorboards before it slid out of her hands. Frantically, she snatched at the handle again.

Abruptly, the wing computer on the woman's arm gave a loud, insistent chirp, and the woman narrowed her eyes. She set Ivy's mobile on the desk and began typing something in the air above the wing with her opposite hand.

Outside, the tapping of Grinch's nails was growing frantic.

The woman was just going to ignore her, the way the Enemy ignored everyone it wasn't due to kill. If it even was the Enemy. The clothing was right, but not the face. And the Enemy never, *ever*, showed up early. In his letter, Larch had wondered whether the thing had a collaborator. Could she be it? Ivy didn't know. All she had were details that didn't make sense. The clothes of a serial killer, a computer that ought to be locked up in a scary vault on the other end of the country, an inexplicable interest in Ivy's phone—and a drug that might be meant to slow her down, or might be meant to kill her.

And then Lauren would find Ivy dead on the floor tomorrow morning and no one would know what happened. Not Ivy's mum, or her dad, or her step-mum, or even Demi or Ambrose. All so some invisible serial killer could show up and snoop through Ivy's mobile, and if it was going to kill her, Ivy at least wanted to know why.

"Will you just talk to me?" Ivy snapped, forcing the words out through uncooperative lips.

The wing beeped. "Outputting local vernacular," it said, crisply and in English. Ivy stared at it in surprise. So did the strange woman, her jaw tightening in annoyance.

"*Teik*," she chided the thing, looking a bit like Lauren whenever she caught Grinch chewing on the sofa.

"Discontinuity odds at fourteen percent," the wing added serenely.

The woman glanced from the wing back to Ivy, looking confused. The wing's light cast a sickly blue hue across her face, glinting off a sheen of sweat below the edge of her hood.

"What're you looking for?" Ivy slurred, nodding at her phone.

The woman started to say something; the wing interrupted with a cacophony of unsettling chimes.

"This is not a permitted level of interaction," it warned.

"No one asked you," Ivy snapped. The woman was glancing between Ivy and the wing on her arm, looking increasingly alarmed.

"Discontinuity odds at—"

The woman tapped something on the wing, and the voice abruptly fell silent. A red light flickered in the midst of the blue, dancing ominously between the blades of the heat sinks.

Ivy clenched her hand, feeling her fingers tighten clumsily against the hammer's grip. It felt easier than it had two minutes ago.

The woman turned toward Ivy and slowly dropped to her knees. She leaned closer, the sleeve of her jumpsuit brushing Ivy's arm. Ivy met her gaze, fighting the urge to wriggle farther away.

"Do you know Diar?" the stranger asked, pronouncing each word slowly and deliberately, as though forming the sentence was somehow difficult.

Ivy started to shake her head; the whole room spun and she stopped. The glow from the wing was painting the walls in a strange red-and-blue wash. She squeezed her eyes shut, willing the room to come back to an even keel.

"No," Ivy said. It would've made more sense if she'd asked about trows. Or Ambrose, or Haven, or Carillon, or anything else.

"You know it, the place," the woman insisted. She seemed to be struggling to come up with the right words. "Where you go. For work."

Ivy forced her eyes back open. The room felt steadier, but the red glow seemed brighter, throwing a headache-like red haze across half the woman's face.

"Never heard of it," said Ivy, and added, because it was true: "I work at a pub. You know, with beer. In Oxmarten."

The woman shook her head, not like she was disagreeing, but like the words didn't mean anything to her. The red glow was pulsing again; the woman was so close Ivy could see a blemish across her left cheek that looked like an old acne scar. The Enemy's face hadn't looked anything like that, and it hadn't tried to talk to her, either. There seemed to be something important about that, but the red light was becoming distracting, like whatever the woman had injected her with was messing with the contrast settings in her eyes.

Abruptly, Ivy realized her eyes weren't playing tricks; the red glow really was getting brighter. Between the wing's heat sinks, a red ember was pulsing like a heartbeat, glittering and impatient.

The woman followed Ivy's gaze and immediately jumped to her feet, snarling something at the wing as she hurriedly typed at its interface. Behind her, Ivy's phone was sitting on the desk, still attached to the wing by a thin black cord.

This was probably the moment for Ivy to leap up and take the stranger by surprise, but Ivy could barely force her fingers to grip the hammer's handle, let alone try to pick it up. She could scream for Lauren—and her flatmate would probably get drugged the same as Ivy, and then they'd both be twitching on the floor.

Maybe there was a better option.

Ivy let go of the hammer, feeling blindly along the floor in front of the bookshelf. She ran her fingers clumsily over the fallen duvet, a Blue Parrot polo shirt, a tangle of shoelaces. Finally, her fingers touched plastic and she snatched at the tiny remote. Feeling like her fingers were wrapped in cotton, Ivy stabbed at the large button in the middle, watching as the yellow LEDs of her desk speakers started to glow. Ivy jabbed at the remote's volume knob, spinning it to the right as fast as she could.

A Lucia Micarelli track came screaming out of the speakers, loud enough that Ivy flinched even though she knew it was coming.

The woman jumped, grabbed for something on her belt, and turned to Ivy, eyes wide in surprise. Beyond the wailing violin track, Grinch was barking, rapid-fire and angry. Ivy heard Lauren shouting but couldn't make out the words.

The woman pulled her cable out of Ivy's mobile and bolted for the door. The phone clattered to the floor as Grinch's barking abruptly changed to a yelp.

Ivy rolled onto her belly, flopping like a fish as she pushed herself to her knees, sparks flaring in her vision that had nothing to do with the light in the room. She grabbed her phone, only to feel the battery slip loose and drop to the floor. Ivy cursed and forced her fingers to curl around the remaining piece. The music was so loud it was making it hard to think. Or maybe that was still the drugs.

"Grinch," Lauren shouted from the other end of the hall. Again, louder, as a door slammed: "*Grinch!*"

Ivy grabbed the battery, clumsily trying to fit the two halves of the phone back together. If Lauren hadn't reacted to the woman running down the hall, the stranger was definitely a trow, and there was no sense calling the Gardaí. Ambrose, Demi's partner and the head of the Roinn Aduain—the group of trows who dealt with humans so that other trows didn't have to—was probably Ivy's best hope for help.

A shape moved in the doorway. Ivy abandoned the phone and lunged for the hammer, the two halves of the mobile clattering to the floor as Lauren stepped into the room.

"Ivy, Grinch's run— Jesus H. Christ, did you *take* something?"

"No," said Ivy, shaking her head. Well, she had, but it wasn't like it was on purpose.

Lauren didn't look convinced. Biting her lip, she grabbed the speaker's power cord and yanked it out of the wall. The music cut off immediately, the echo ringing in Ivy's ears for several seconds after.

"I can call the Health Services nurse," Lauren was saying, kneeling next to Ivy. "Or the hospital, or—"

"'M fine," Ivy insisted, shoving the hammer into one pocket and both halves of the mobile into the other before staggering, with difficulty, to her feet. Whatever it was the woman had injected, it seemed to be wearing off. Which was good, since Ivy doubted the Health Services nurse would be able to do anything to counteract fairy knockout drops, or whatever it was she'd used.

"Or Kyle from work, I could call him," Lauren continued, fluttering worriedly. "Really, you ought to sit down—"

"I'm fine," Ivy repeated, louder. She staggered out of the room, Lauren hovering closely behind. Why Kyle from work, whoever he was, would be of any help, Ivy didn't know, until she remembered Lauren worked for some sort of med-tech company.

Down the hallway, Ivy heard the rumble of a car going by,

the sound louder than it should have been. As she turned into the parlor, she spotted the front door, half-open and swaying on its hinges.

"And how the hell did he open the door?" Lauren snapped. "Damn dog could be anywhere by now."

"Call the Gardaí," Ivy said, staring at the door and the sliver of street beyond.

Lauren stopped short and shot Ivy a worried look.

"Someone opened that door," Ivy continued. "And it wasn't Grinch, or us."

Privately, Ivy had no expectations the Gardaí would be able to do anything useful, except possibly find Grinch. But if there were people around, and cars with lights and sirens, maybe all the fuss would dissuade the stranger from coming back.

Slowly, Lauren nodded and grabbed her phone off the side table. Her face, sallow even at the best of times, looked pale and worried.

Cautiously, Ivy teetered across the room toward the open door. The breeze tangled in Ivy's hair as she looked down the street. There was no sign of the bulldog, or the woman. She could be halfway out of Dartry by now. Or lurking in the neighbor's bushes waiting to have another go at Ivy's phone. Or at Ivy herself.

"Alright, sweetie," Ivy hollered from the doorway, and if she woke the neighbors, it would only be more lights, and fuss, and people milling about. "You've gone and made the both of us *very pissed off!*"

"Might try calling him like you're not going to skin him alive when he comes back," Lauren hissed. "Try telling him 'cheese'! Or 'baco'— Yes," she broke off, turning back to her phone. "Yes, it's Lauren Guilfoyle, I'm at Hawthorne Road in Dartry, Number 562 B."

Of course, it wasn't actually Grinch Ivy was shouting at.

In the middle of the street, a crumpled takeaway bag shifted in the wind. Nothing else.

Reaching into her pocket, Ivy pulled out the two halves of her phone. This time, it only took her two tries to slide the battery into place. She pressed the power button and the manufacturer's logo lit up the screen.

"No, I'm *not* calling about the power outage," Lauren snapped into her mobile. "There was someone outside and he opened our front door and our dog's took off after him."

Impatiently, Ivy stared at the phone's boot-up screen. Even if Demi answered straight off, the trows' enclave in the Liberties was nearly four miles away.

Behind her, Lauren was making quiet *uh-huh* noises at whatever the officer on the phone was telling her. Probably they were saying that help was coming, and everything would be fine. That wasn't true in the slightest. The Gardaí couldn't help against a threat they couldn't see.

The Gardaí couldn't see trows, and they couldn't see the Enemy, either. But Ivy could. The clothes were the same, but not the face. Then again, she'd only seen the Enemy once, five months ago, for barely two minutes. Would Ivy have seen acne scars on its face if she'd looked closely enough?

A red sedan turned down the street, a thumping bass line audible over the engine. As the headlights swept the houses, they illuminated a dark shape crouched by the rubbish bins two houses down.

"Well, what the hell is animal control going to do about it at one in the morning?" Lauren snapped.

The shape by the rubbish bins looked too large to be Grinch.

Five months ago, Ivy swore she'd find a way to kill the Enemy before it could come back for Demi. Now might be the best shot she'd ever get at keeping that promise. Never mind that Ivy wasn't certain she could walk down the front stairs without falling.

"Yes, alright," Lauren muttered. "*When* do they open? Fine."

Shakily, Ivy gripped the side of the banister, experimentally shuffling her bare feet down the first step. At least in the apple grove, Demi's friends had been with them. This time, Ivy would have to manage on her own.

"They say everyone's tied up with a transformer that exploded the next street over," Lauren muttered, slipping her phone into the pocket of her trousers as she joined Ivy on the steps. Cautiously, Lauren put her hand on Ivy's arm, an expression on her face that immediately made Ivy wonder exactly how terrible she looked. "You sure you won't let me take you to A&E?"

Maybe Ivy wasn't *entirely* on her own.

"I'm fine," Ivy insisted, pleased that at least she wasn't still slurring her words. "But I think there's something by the Lewandoskis' rubbish bins."

Lauren's head shot up and she started down the stairs before Ivy could stop her. "Grinch?" Lauren called hopefully, her shoes slapping against the concrete. "Cheese, buddy! Treat!"

Ivy followed, leaning hard on the banister. Her phone chirped. As she shuffled after Lauren, she pulled up her contacts list and tapped Demi's name. "Lauren, wait!" she hissed. Her flatmate didn't stop.

A handful of gravel at the edge of the sidewalk was almost enough to convince Ivy to drag herself back into the flat for her shoes, but Lauren was walking straight toward the rubbish bins.

"Lauren, stop!" Ivy called, mincing over the gravel as fast as she could manage. The phone's ringing was blending with the wail of an emergency siren in the distance.

In her ear, the phone chirped, followed by Demi sleepily muttering, "Hello?"

Lauren had reached the end of the Lewandoskis' driveway; Ivy couldn't tell if the shape behind the rubbish bins was still there. "Lauren!"

"Ivy?" Demi's voice sounded fogged with sleep. "It's one in the morning, this better not be a pocket dial."

"Someone was in the flat," Ivy said to her phone, stumbling as she tried to catch up to Lauren. "I don't know how, and she was looking at my mobile, but I turned on my stereo, and she ran off—"

"Get to a safe place and call the Gardaí," Demi interrupted. "Don't—"

"I think she was a trow," Ivy hissed, cutting her off. "Is Ambrose there? Tell him I need him, as soon as he can."

Ivy heard Ambrose's voice faintly in the background.

"We're on our way," said Demi.

"Not you," Ivy interjected quickly. "Please, don't ask, just don't. You can't be anywhere near this."

Over the phone, Ivy heard Demi's quick inhale of breath, followed by a long pause.

Lauren was nearly at the rubbish bins, muttering a mix of threats and entreaties.

"Alright," Demi breathed. "He's going now. But I'm staying on the line."

"Lauren!" Ivy called. "Wait for him to come out, don't just—"

Lauren stomped up to the closest rubbish bin and Ivy's stomach dropped. It was going to be like the apple grove all over again. Or else Lauren would be the one stabbed in the neck and writhing on the ground, and it would all be Ivy's fault for not coming up with a better plan—

"Ivy, what's happening?" Demi asked tightly.

Something exploded from the rubbish bins. Ivy stifled a shriek as a fox tore out from the jumble of carts. Lauren jumped, throwing up her arms as the animal darted past, disappearing under the Lewandoskis' stairs.

Trying to catch her breath, Ivy stared at the rubbish bins as though she expected something else to come barreling out at any moment.

"Ivy?" Demi hissed through the phone.

With a sigh, Ivy crossed the Lewandowskis' driveway to join her flatmate.

"Someone was in the flat," she whispered into the phone, uncomfortably aware her flatmate was close enough to overhear. Ivy didn't think she could get away with saying things like "Enemy" or "serial killer" without Lauren demanding an explanation. "Someone like . . . from back in February."

There was a long silence on the line. Beside her, Lauren looked dejectedly at the fallen bins.

"Damn dog," she muttered.

"I'm switching this over to video," said Demi smoothly in her ear, as if Ivy hadn't just told her a mass murderer with Demi's name on the top of its list was roaming Dublin a scant few miles away. Numbly, Ivy accepted the WhatsApp alert, allowing the call to drop.

Ivy and Lauren stood next to the toppled rubbish bins in silence. An emergency siren wailed from the next street, and Ivy began to be aware of the ache in her neck, the concrete digging into her bare feet, the dragging sort of exhaustion of being awake in the wee hours of the morning, and the growing sense of futility that she'd woken up her friends for no reason.

By the time Ambrose finally got here, there'd be nothing for him to see.

"Was there really someone in the flat?" Lauren asked in a small voice.

"Yeah," said Ivy, nodding. "There was."

"Shit," Lauren said fervently, and sighed.

Ivy sighed as well. Grinch could be anywhere by now, and so could the woman, if she hadn't simply vanished off the face of the earth, like the Enemy did after it killed.

"Maybe Grinch'll come back on his own," Ivy suggested quietly.

"I'm still staying on the line until Ambrose gets there," Demi said firmly. Over the screen she gave a little wave. "Hi, Lauren."

"Hey," Lauren said, nodding without much enthusiasm, fingering a piece of cheese she'd brought for Grinch. Ivy's current and former flatmates knew each other slightly through Ivy's video calls. They'd been together in the Dartry flat twice, although Lauren, understandably, was oblivious to the fact that they'd ever met in person. "They said animal control opens at half seven. If he doesn't get himself hit by a car before then."

Not an idle concern. Grinch was as oblivious to cars as he was to most things that weren't food, or Lauren, or squirrels. Dejectedly, Lauren turned back to the flat. Giving a long look down the street, Ivy started to follow her—

And froze at the distant, frantic sound of the bulldog's furious barking.

Lauren spun in her tracks and started into the Lewandowskis' back garden. Ivy grabbed her by the shoulder, nearly falling as she half-dragged Lauren to a halt.

"*Someone* opened the door and let him out, remember?" Ivy hissed. In the light of the streetlight, Lauren's face grew even paler than before.

"You still got the hammer?" she asked.

Wordlessly, Ivy pulled it out of her pocket and passed it over. Lauren could make better use of it than she could; Ivy was having enough trouble just keeping herself upright and walking. The emergency siren in the next street was wailing again, howling like the worst kind of harbinger.

"You should probably go back and lie down," Lauren added, giving Ivy a sidelong look.

"Both of you should go back and wait for Ambrose," Demi's voice crackled from the phone.

"No, and no," Ivy muttered at both of them. It wouldn't help anyone if Ivy passed out in the middle of Mrs. Lewandowski's petunias, but she couldn't let Lauren go haring off after her dog without the slightest comprehension of who, and what, she was following.

Lauren nodded tightly and they both started forward, around the Lewandowskis' hedge and toward the alley beyond. Lauren reached out and took Ivy's hand, a friendly gesture that had absolutely nothing to do with the fact that Ivy was still stumbling every few steps. Ivy held on tightly, feeling one of Lauren's rings digging into her palm. Grinch's barks had ratcheted to a crescendo, an angry, frightened staccato usually reserved for delivery vans.

The light from the street didn't carry very far into the yard. A wooden gate loomed ahead, the door ajar and hanging at an angle. Ivy swallowed. At least they were on grass now, and Ivy could almost keep up with Lauren's hurried pace.

The woman could have killed Ivy back at the flat. She hadn't, Ivy reminded herself as they hurried through the gate. Ivy didn't know if she'd extend Grinch the same tolerance.

There was just enough light in the back garden to make out a jumble of flowering bushes and the vague shapes of lawn furniture. Ivy glanced at her phone. She desperately needed a plan other than *walk into the dark alley after the dog like two girls in a horror movie.*

"It's pretty dark," Ivy murmured to her phone. "Whatever's out here's going to be *very hard to see.*"

"So tell us what you do see," said Demi, her voice unnaturally calm. "The things it's doing that affect other things. That helps."

Helps to see past the trows' veil, was what Demi meant, the protection that kept trows effectively invisible. Technically, Ivy was pretty sure that helping a human circumvent the veil was against one of the Roinn's many rules. Given the circumstances, hopefully it was one Ambrose was willing to overlook.

Ahead, Grinch yelped. Lauren's pace quickened to a run as the dog redoubled his barking. Her fingers tightened around Ivy's. Ivy staggered, barely able to keep up as they tore out of the back garden, past a fence, and into the alley behind it. The ground under Ivy's feet changed from grass to cobbles. The emergency sirens vanished into the cacophony of Grinch's barks and the low ringing in her ears, glimpses of blue and yellow flashing lights cutting through the gaps between the houses on Orwell Road.

Grinch's barks sounded close, but it was still a shock when Ivy rounded the corner and saw them. The woman was standing beneath a row of dim yellow lights mounted at the peak of a dilapidated garage; Grinch had cornered her between the garage and a wooden fence beside it. The bulldog paced and circled just out of range of a kick, barking furiously, his various shadows darting and jumping in lockstep. The woman was standing with her hands on her hips, the wing on her arm flashing red, looking more annoyed than seriously threatened.

Ivy's stomach dropped as she took in the scene. Now that they'd caught up to her, Ivy had as little idea of what to do with her as Grinch.

"The hell is he doing?" muttered Lauren, sounding exasperated. She let go of Ivy's hand and started fishing in her pocket for the dog's leash. "Grinch! Cut it out!"

Ivy grabbed Lauren's arm before she could get any closer.

"Wait," she hissed. "Don't you see it?"

"Ivy, I think you should get out of there," Demi warned.

"See that my dog has a screw loose?" Lauren hissed back. "Yeah, got that."

"No, hold on," Ivy repeated, not letting go of Lauren's arm. "Look at the shadows. Really, really look."

Lauren stopped, and for a long second, she didn't move. Tentatively, Ivy let go of her arm, remembering belatedly to tilt the phone so Demi could see what was happening as well.

Slowly, Lauren lowered the hammer, and for a moment there was only Grinch's snarling and the darting figures of the bulldog and its various shadows, blending and overlapping with the shadow of the stranger, who was trying to slip past the garage but kept being turned aside by Grinch.

"The hell," muttered Lauren, and started forward with the leash before Ivy could stop her.

Under the yellow lights, the woman's head snapped up, her gaze fixing on Lauren. She touched something on the wing computer, then raised her other hand as though shielding her eyes.

A trail of sparks exploded into the air in front of Grinch. Demi's shout through the phone was unintelligible through the crackling and Grinch's yelp. Ivy was already running toward the dog before the lights had vanished.

Not as fast as Lauren, who'd abandoned the leash and was grappling with the hammer.

"Get the fuck away from my dog!" she yelled, running for Grinch.

The stranger froze, staring at Lauren, charging with a

hammer, Ivy stumbling behind, and Grinch, hackles raised and snarling like an idling engine.

The woman bolted, dodging past Grinch in an arm-pumping sprint straight down the alley toward Orwell Road. Grinch gave chase immediately, with Lauren running after him and Ivy stumbling in their wake. Blue emergency lights were flashing at the mouth of the alley, reflecting in the mirrored storefronts across the road.

The woman ran out of the alley and started to turn just as Grinch threw himself at her back. They both tumbled into the road, dust flying, a mouthful of the woman's jumpsuit gripped firmly between the bulldog's teeth.

"Grinch, no!" Lauren screamed, sounding horrified. Ivy put on a fresh burst of speed, trying to ignore the pain in her feet and how the alley was beginning to slowly spin, a wobble timed to the pounding ache in her head.

The woman rolled, shrugging Grinch off as she aimed a kick at him. Grinch leapt back as her boot swept narrowly over his head. He hesitated long enough for the woman to jump to her feet. Her braid had come loose, and her brown hair streamed across her shoulders.

Lauren's desperate calls for Grinch were beginning to attract attention. Belatedly, Ivy realized Lauren wasn't the only one shouting; beyond the gasping of her own breaths she could hear noises coming from Orwell Road: raised voices, a vehicle beeping as it reversed, the thrum of a generator. From her phone, Demi was pleading something unintelligible.

Lauren sprinted into the road with the leash in hand, making straight for Grinch. Ivy followed her out of the alley, limping straight into what looked like the middle of a construc-tion site. *Transformer exploded a block over,* she remembered Lauren saying. Emergency vehicles with spinning lights blocked off most of the intersection, and an array of people in various uniforms and orange vests were milling about, all staring at Grinch in alarm.

None of them seemed to notice the woman in the jumpsuit. She turned as if to start down Highfield Road, then hesitated and bolted the other way, nearly colliding with a red-haired man holding a clipboard.

As Lauren bore down on them, Grinch cut in front of the woman, muscles tightened to spring. For a moment, Ivy thought Lauren might have just enough time to grab him before he pounced.

Then the dog was in the air, the woman shouted something —and everything turned broiling and red.

The fire was just as sudden and hellish as it had been in the apple grove. The heat hit Ivy's face like the open door of an oven as she staggered to a stop, fighting the urge to run the other way. A car alarm was shrieking, mixing with the screams echoing across the road. Ivy was certain the woman was already dead, that she must've been dead the instant the flame went up, until she saw her hands. Her hands were reaching out of the fire *toward Ivy*. Like she knew Ivy was the only person who could see her. Like she thought Ivy was the only one who could help.

The figure tottered, then collapsed, sparks pinwheeling up like firecrackers. A bitter, chemical smell almost like wood polish was mixing with the odor of ash and broiling asphalt. The thing in the middle of the fire didn't look like a person anymore; Ivy felt both sickened and grateful at the speed with which that had happened. She stared at the dying flames, stumbling backward as the concrete under her feet began to feel hot.

Beside her, Grinch was whimpering, and he wasn't the only one. The red-haired man with the clipboard was moaning, lying on his stomach, and a woman in an Electric Ireland vest was beating at the embers on his arm with a work jacket, and everyone, everyone was screaming.

Lauren was kneeling over her dog, beating away sparks and stray wisps of ash with her shirt as Grinch's legs kicked spastically. Ivy started toward her, then staggered out of the way of a man in an orange vest. He dodged past Ivy, then pulled the pin on a fire extinguisher, training it on the collapsing inferno that had once been a woman in a jumpsuit. The acrid smell of the chemical powder barely cut through the stench of hot asphalt and burnt meat.

A million miles away on the other end of the phone, Demi was yelling Ivy's name.

Ivy slowly backed away from the pyre, afterimages of the flames pulsing across her eyes as she looked away. Behind her, a door opened with a slam. A bearded man wearing Ballymena Rugby boxers and very little else bolted barefoot across the road, juggling three two-liter bottles of Irn Bru soda and a gallon of milk.

Ivy staggered as the man rushed past her to where Lauren huddled over Grinch. The dog wasn't whimpering anymore, and that seemed like the worst sort of sign. The man in the rugby boxers opened up the first bottle of Irn Bru and dumped the soda over the dog; Grinch jerked once, then seemed to relax. A few yards away, two people holding an orange water cooler seemed to be doing the same to the red-haired man.

People were rushing into the street from everywhere: from the townhouses in shorts and nightgowns, from the work trucks in Garda uniforms and Electric Ireland work vests. In the center of the commotion sat a crater and a pile of ash, the asphalt around it bubbling and cracked. Of the woman herself, there was nothing left. Just like Uncle Patrick in the apple grove.

Slowly, Ivy raised her mobile. Demi's face, framed by the

velvet blue curtains in Ambrose's flat, seemed like a vision out of another world.

"You okay?" Demi asked softly.

Ivy nodded, swallowing hard before she was able to reply.

"I think she was a trow," Ivy said quietly, looking from Demi's face to the pile of ash, the remaining embers flickering out one by one. "And I think the Enemy just killed her."

CHAPTER 2

For a long time after Ivy hung up, everything around her was a carnival of whirling lights, emergency sirens, and uniformed people running back and forth: Gardaí, paramedics, workers from Electric Ireland and Dublin Public Works. When Ivy was finally able to catch her breath, she found herself sitting on the curb a few yards down from a squad car, watching two fellows in yellow reflective vests wrestling a pair of traffic cones out of a flatbed truck.

Ivy blinked, trying not to look at the hole in the concrete they were cordoning off. Someone had died there, and the only memorial the woman was going to get was a pair of blinking orange traffic cones.

Carefully, Ivy stood up and minced over to where she'd last seen Lauren and Grinch, somewhere behind a fire truck that was blocking the sidewalk in front of a steakhouse patio. The whole street was looking less and less like a normal intersection and more like the site of an Incident.

As Ivy passed the fire truck she spotted Lauren, sitting on a bench next to an ambulance. Grinch was actually taking up most of the bench, his front paws splayed across Lauren's lap, his head tucked against her belly as though he were trying to burrow under her shirt. To Ivy's relief, the dog looked more or less in one piece.

Standing next to Lauren was a paramedic, braided hair spilling out of the top of a red scarf, carefully wrapping a bandage over Lauren's outstretched right hand. Lauren spotted Ivy and mustered a thin smile. Her face looked puffy, like she'd been crying.

"You okay?" Ivy asked as she came up to the bench.

Lauren shrugged. "Wouldn't let them do me up until they'd done him first," she said tonelessly, nodding at Grinch while the paramedic taped the bandage over Lauren's knuckles.

Abruptly, Ivy recalibrated Lauren's red cheeks and puffy eyes. She hadn't realized Lauren had been close enough to the flames to get burned.

Before she could reply, the paramedic let go of Lauren's hand and turned to Ivy. The woman's eyes narrowed and she grabbed Ivy by both shoulders, clucking as she steered her toward the free end of the bench in a way that strongly reminded Ivy of the Blue Parrot's weekend bouncer.

"Stay there," the paramedic said, and draped a ratty-looking emergency blanket over Ivy's shoulders. "Don't go wandering off."

She disappeared back into the ambulance, popped out long enough to hand Ivy a pair of fuzzy pink socks, and retreated back into the vehicle. Gratefully, Ivy brushed a few stray pieces of gravel off the bottoms of her feet and slipped on the socks. They felt scratchy, and the soles were covered with something that felt like sandpaper.

"He okay?" Ivy asked quietly, reaching out with one finger to stroke the wisp of fur between Grinch's back pads.

"They rang up someone to figure out what to give him," said Lauren in the same toneless voice. "They said take him to the vet as soon as I can."

Grinch stirred; his hind leg kicked once and brushed against Ivy's knee. The dog's neck, front legs, and a good chunk of his torso were wrapped in a mix of bandages and blue adhesive wrap. The fur on his head was sticking up in wet clumps, like he'd been slathered with some sort of burn gel. He smelled like a mix of burnt hair, wet dog, and Irn Bru soda. Tentatively, Ivy laid her hand over his back paw and left it there.

Among the commotion of lights and emergency vehicles, an odd-looking figure was moving through the crowd of uniforms and hard hats. Dressed in dark slacks and a frilly purple blouse that appeared to be at least two sizes too large, a dark-haired, dark-skinned man was hurrying through the crowd, turning his head like he was trying to look everywhere at once.

If Ambrose hadn't shown up with his own clothes, Ivy had a good idea how he'd gotten here, and she wondered what the neighbors were going to make of the hoofprints they'd find in the morning.

Ivy raised her arm, attempting to pass the gesture off as an expansive yawn. Before Ivy could risk a more obvious wave, the medic came hustling back from the ambulance, holding a radio in one hand and a pulse oximeter in the other. She headed straight for Ivy, clipping the device onto the end of Ivy's finger.

"What's your name, luv?" the medic asked, glaring critically at the pulse oximeter's screen.

"Ivy Gallagher," Ivy said, entirely too loudly, which made both the medic and Lauren look at her strangely. The man in the purple blouse turned around with a jerk. Ivy sagged in relief as Ambrose started to walk toward her.

"Feeling alright, luv?" the medic asked, looking sharply between Ivy and the thing on Ivy's finger. Based on her expression, the pulse oximeter appeared to be telling her that Ivy shouldn't be feeling alright at all.

The medic's radio interrupted, sparing Ivy from having to answer as it chattered out a short and unintelligible query.

"Partial-thickness burns on two of her fingers," the medic said into the radio. "No signs of smoke inhalation, thankfully. The dog took the worst of it, I think."

Lauren frowned, her bottom lip trembling as she curled herself protectively over Grinch. Ivy looked away. Grinch was an idiot, but he might not have lunged at the stranger if he hadn't been trying to protect Lauren. And Lauren had only been there because of Ivy.

Ivy gave Ambrose a tight smile as he came up to the ambulance, rubbing at his temples as if warding off a headache. The frilly shirt was plastered to his stomach with sweat, the neckline cut in a way that suggested it was meant to highlight feminine attributes. Ivy wonder if Ambrose had filched the entire ensemble off someone's clothesline, or possibly from an unlocked house.

If anyone could explain what just happened, it was probably Ambrose. In addition to being Demi's partner, Ambrose was the head of the Roinn Aduain, and as such he was Ivy's occasional boss. Her errands for the Roinn earned her easily twice what she made in her four nights a week bartending at the Blue Parrot.

One of those errands might have been the reason a stranger had broken into her flat and tried to hack her phone.

The medic cocked her head as she listened to another unintelligible squawk from the radio.

"No, the other one's pulse is forty-seven, and her lips are blue," she barked into the mouthpiece. "Are they sure it wasn't a chemical leak?"

As Ambrose approached the back of the ambulance, he held up one finger, then stepped past the medic and hauled himself into the back of the vehicle. He reappeared a moment later holding a bottle of electrolyte solution, the frippery on his sleeves flapping limply as he hopped down from the tailgate. Neither the medic nor Lauren appeared to notice him. Probably they wouldn't notice him short of the trow bursting into show tunes, and maybe not even then.

Ambrose unscrewed the bottle and brought it to his lips, gulping it down. Dehydration, as Ivy had reason to know, was a common side effect of the shape-shifting technology Ambrose had used to get here.

"Are my lips blue?" Ivy asked.

"Yes," said Lauren without looking up.

"No," said Ambrose, wiping a dribble of liquid off his chin and looking critically at Ivy. "Well, maybe a touch."

"Not as bad as they were at the flat," Lauren continued, pulling her gaze away from Grinch with an effort. "You looked like a zombie." She jerked her head at the medic. "They'd look you over at St. Luke's, if you want. Your pulse *is* really low."

Ivy shook her head. Ivy had no idea what St. Luke's Hospital would make of whatever drug she'd been injected with, and she didn't particularly want to find out. Fortunately, the effects seemed to be wearing off.

"I just want to go home," Ivy said quietly.

Lauren opened her mouth as though she were about to protest, then hesitated.

"Me too," she said.

"You alright?" Ambrose asked, closing up the lid on the electrolyte bottle and wiping his sleeve across his face.

Ivy nodded, hoping it was true.

"Well, there are about half a dozen fellows with clipboards over there arguing over whether this was a gas explosion, or an electrical mishap, or ball lightning, or a bomb," he said, nodding back down the street. "Any chance you can slip away long enough to tell me what exactly is going on?"

Ambrose looked annoyed and exhausted, probably a combination of being dragged out of bed in the middle of the night and because there were too many people in earshot for Ivy to talk to him without attracting attention. Protected by the workings of the trows' veil, Ambrose could prance naked through the middle of the street if he wanted, and no one would notice. Ivy, on the other hand, couldn't speak with him in front of Lauren and the medic without looking like a crazy person. Head nods and subtle hand gestures could only go so far.

Behind Ambrose, two Gardaí officers had broken away from the cluster in the intersection and were heading toward the ambulance with clipboards. Ivy let go of Grinch's paw long enough to nudge Lauren.

"Maybe once they've talked to us, someone can help us get him home," Lauren muttered, stroking Grinch's unbandaged ear.

"Yeah," Ivy said, instantly swearing to herself that she wasn't going to walk off and leave Lauren to deal with the dog by herself, even if it meant talking with Ambrose had to wait. They were barely two blocks from the flat, but Ivy wasn't at all sure the somnolent Grinch would be willing or able to walk that far.

Ambrose turned, following Lauren's gaze. "Damn it," he muttered as he caught sight of the two officers.

The first Garda officer, a Black woman with a name badge reading M. Adebayo, came up to the bench, a sympathetic look on her dimpled face. She looked down at Grinch and smiled.

Ivy started to smile back, then immediately bit her lip and looked away. She couldn't tell a police officer what had actually caused the explosion—namely, that an alien serial killer with a thing for spontaneous human combustion had just murdered a person that no one else could see. It would have been easier to be forgetful and unhelpful if they'd sent a gruff man with gruff questions instead.

"Your fellow there looks like a real good boy," Adebayo said. It was enough that Lauren's face started to crinkle up and she had to let go of Grinch to wipe furiously at her eyes with the edge of her shirt. Behind the officer, Ambrose sighed loudly.

Gard Adebayo pulled a small recorder out of a case on her belt and set it on the ambulance's bumper. Ambrose bit off a huff of frustration and backed farther from the bench. Though neither Adebayo nor Lauren would notice anything Ambrose said, recording devices could hear him just fine. As would anyone who listened to the recording later.

"We're trying to interview everyone who saw it, and I understand you girls were close," the officer said. "I know you've had a long night already, but would you mind telling me what happened?"

Thankfully, Lauren did most of the talking, coaxed along by Gard Adebayo's questions. Ivy limited herself to head nods and affirmative noises as Lauren described their front door somehow flying open, Grinch running off, and the two of them going into the alley to look for him.

Lauren hesitated then, glancing once at Ivy, then back to the bulldog in her lap.

"He was barking like he was chasing something," said Ivy, rushing in before Lauren could say anything about a woman you could only see if you looked at her shadow first. She was staring fixedly at Ambrose, who was staring back, listening intently. "Maybe a cat. Or something. It was dark, so it was *really hard to see.*"

By the furrowed look on Ambrose's face, Ivy's eyebrows were doing a decent enough job at telling him what parts of that sentence to pay attention to. "Just like at the house," Ivy continued. "I thought someone was messing with the door when Grinch got out. But that's silly. It's not like we have any *enemies*."

The color drained out of Ambrose's face all at once. He snapped his head around to the intersection, to the orange traffic cones marking the crater in the asphalt where the pavement had buckled.

"Who?" Ambrose asked hoarsely.

"I don't know," said Ivy, cutting off Gard Adebayo in the middle of a question. "She was dressed like *it* was," she added in a rush, and that was going to sound strange when someone listened to the recording, but it couldn't be helped.

"Who was?" asked Adebayo.

Ivy started to grope for an answer that didn't sound crazy, but Lauren spoke up first.

"The woman in the alley. Grinch was barking at someone in the alley. Chasing her."

"Was he still chasing someone when he ran into the street?" Adebayo asked.

Lauren hesitated and glanced at Ivy. Minutely, Ivy shook her head.

Lauren let out a long breath, as though going along with that fiction was easier than trying to explain the truth. Grinch *had* been chasing someone, and no one else had seen her, even when she was burning to death. Ivy wondered if Lauren herself was even sure of what she'd seen. Being completely unaffected by the trows' veil herself, Ivy had no idea what those horrible few minutes would have felt like to her flatmate.

Except Ivy knew exactly how it felt to realize there were frightening and inexplicable things in the world that most people didn't know existed.

"He just ran into the street," said Lauren, shaking her head, and there was a tremble in her voice as she spoke. "Then he was barking and then something happened . . . right next to the man they took away in the ambu . . . ambul . . .”

Lauren hiccuped her way through the last word, her face twisting as she stroked Grinch's ear. Ivy was suddenly afraid her flatmate was going to start crying.

"Everyone else saw the rest," Ivy lied, nodding to the street, and the jumble of people and trucks and emergency vehicles, and the two mournfully blinking orange cones. "And we'd really like to go home now."

It took no effort at all to add the quiver into her voice. Ivy resolutely avoided looking at Ambrose, hoping desperately she wasn't about to burst into tears in front of the head of the Roinn. Or that if she did, Ambrose would at least do her the courtesy of chalking it up to her negligible acting skills.

"We'll just need your contact details," said Adebayo, nodding sympathetically. The medic, hovering behind the officer and checking a readout on a tablet, didn't look convinced. Ivy bit her lip. The longer she sat here with her own body traitorously pumping danger signals into the ambulance's machines, the harder it would be to talk her way out of a hospital visit. And she still needed to speak with Ambrose.

As Adebayo took down Lauren's phone number and their Dartry address, Ivy looked at Ambrose. His face, in the light spilling from the ambulance's back door, looked blotchy and covered in sweat, barely concealed frustration at war with exhaustion. Sliding the hand with the pulse oximeter behind her back, Ivy crooked one finger.

Frowning, Ambrose slunk closer. The frown deepened as Ivy kept motioning him closer, only stopping when he was finally, and nervously, within arm's reach.

Pasting an innocent and suspicion-free expression on her face, Ivy unclipped the pulse oximeter from her finger and hurriedly shoved it at Ambrose.

He fumbled for it, nearly dropping it as something in the ambulance began chiming in alarm, not quite loud enough to cover Ambrose's frustrated muttering as he clipped the device onto his own finger. Ivy tucked her own hands under her thighs.

The beeping inside the ambulance stopped and the medic's expression softened fractionally as she looked back at her tablet. No matter how dehydrated Ambrose might be from his brief use of trow shape-shifting technology, Ivy was willing to bet his vital signs were a good deal more normal than hers right now.

She kept her innocent expression glued to her face as Adebayo took down her phone number and turned off her recorder. Ivy could almost feel Ambrose's tension unwind by several degrees as the Garda officer slipped the device back into its case. Her radio squawked, the same sort of unintelligible chatter it had been spluttering the whole time, but something in the tone made Adebayo pick it up and turn back to the ambulance, holding the radio to her ear.

"You think you can walk?" Ambrose muttered, not bothering to keep his voice down now that the recorder was turned off. Ivy nodded and started to slide off the bench. If she got to the other side of the ambulance, she might be able to steal a handful of minutes to talk to Ambrose without looking like a candidate for psychiatric evaluation.

"I can't carry him all the way home," Lauren said suddenly. Her flatmate was staring at Grinch, still lolled across her lap, boneless, bandaged, and very large. Ivy squashed a momentary surge of irritation that Lauren hadn't chosen to adopt a tiny, frilly dog that could be carried around in a purse. A yappy dog probably would have been content to bark at the invisible, ageless terror from a safe distance, instead of trying to tackle it. Then Grinch wouldn't have gotten burned, and maybe not the man from the power company, either.

Except they were, and maybe it was Ivy's fault. She was the one who could see it, and she'd known the woman was dangerous. She should have been able to protect the people who didn't know any better. She hadn't, and now there was an Electric Ireland worker headed off to A&E, and a semiconscious dog half-covered in bandages and burn gel.

Ivy twisted around on the bench, placing a hand on Grinch's paw. His pads felt rough like sandpaper and his skin was hot, even compared to the muggy July air.

"I have a friend who might be able to help," said Ivy quietly, looking straight at Ambrose.

"Absolutely not," he snapped. "Call an Uber. She won't be happy when her dog vanishes under her nose, and I won't be happy if she notices who's carrying it."

He crossed his arms, looking annoyed. Ambrose always looked faintly ridiculous when he was annoyed. This was especially true now, with him half-dressed in a frilly shirt, the silk well on its way to being utterly destroyed by sweat stains.

Ivy looked at the street, a conglomeration of traffic cones, headlights, and emergency vehicles. An Uber wasn't going to be getting through all that in a hurry, assuming it could get through at all.

Ivy tried to think of who she could call at two in the morning to move a semiconscious six-stone dog. Her father and step-mother would absolutely come, but they lived all the way in East Worring. Ivy's actual mother, Victoria, was closer, but due to an ill-advised affair with the trow Ivy'd been taught to call Uncle Patrick, she was no more visible than Ambrose himself. Ivy's best friend, Deirdre, didn't have a car. Ivy's on-again, off-again boyfriend, Colin, did have a car, but he was only marginally more reliable than his ancient Peugeot. Also, if

Colin came over at two in the morning, he wouldn't be satisfied with a hug and a promise to call. Ivy was certain she would literally die of mortification if she ever had to make out with Colin while Ambrose was anywhere in earshot.

"Give me your phone," Ambrose said grumpily into the silence. "I'll get someone to meet us the next block over."

Relieved, Ivy handed over her mobile. "If we can get him to the next street over, we can call a ride," she told Lauren. There were fewer flashing lights toward Terenure Road, hopefully a sign that the cross street hadn't been blocked off.

Gamely, Lauren nodded. She shifted Grinch's head off her lap with a frightening sort of delicacy, as though he might start howling, or collapse upon rough handling like a particularly flimsy custard.

"Can you get his back legs?" Lauren asked.

Ivy nodded and slipped her arms awkwardly under the dog's belly. With several repositionings and false starts, they managed to get Grinch off the bench, cradled between the two of them, and gamely set off down the street with no further interruptions from the medic or the Gardaí. Ivy wondered if it was because Ambrose was hovering. Ambrose claimed the veil didn't work that way, but Ivy swore it was harder to get counter service on the nights Hunzu accompanied her to the pub.

The sandpapery bottoms of the hospital socks weren't doing much to cushion Ivy's feet from the asphalt, and she could feel Grinch's hind leg digging into her hip.

"We'll have a ride waiting at the corner of Brighton Road," Ambrose announced, texting something into Ivy's phone. "The road's blocked off closer . . . For God's sake, Ivy, if you break your leg trying to carry that thing, I'm going to be stuck standing outside of A&E all night."

Ambrose pushed his frilly sleeves farther up his arms and stepped closer.

"Go on, then," he said, extending his arms out as far as he could, and nodding at Lauren. Gingerly, Ivy shifted the dog's weight to Ambrose, uncomfortably aware that neither of them were wearing gloves. Ivy tried not to feel guilty about that. As a member of the Roinn, Ambrose spent more than his fair share of time within arm's reach of humans, any one of which was capable of passing on the 'disease' of aging. Ivy didn't like adding to her friends' quotas any more than strictly necessary.

"I've got him. Just keep your hand on his head," Ivy told Lauren as she shifted Grinch's rear end into Ambrose's arms, giving the trow an apologetic look. "See? He's doing fine."

Grinch stirred, his tongue flicking out to lick Lauren's hand. She shifted her grip, cradling his head as Ambrose took the rest of the dog's weight.

Ivy could no longer hear the radio chatter over Ambrose's panting; beyond it were only the usual sounds of traffic. It seemed impossible that the normal world could be as close as the next street away.

"Good boy, Grinch," Lauren murmured. Grinch's tail wagged once, a wave like a signal flag, and went still.

"One of those vans back there was from the Army Ordnance Corps," Ambrose huffed from beside her. "Whatever analysis they do on that residue, I want a copy."

Lauren glanced behind her, a tiny wrinkle appearing between her eyebrows.

"He's a friend, and he's helping," Ivy said firmly, not sure if Lauren could see Ambrose at all, but keen to cut off any uncomfortable speculation as quickly as possible. "And I think our ride's already here."

A long back car sat idling at the curb next to a pair of crooked orange traffic barriers. Ambrose's usual driver, Meredith, stood next to the open passenger door, looking bored.

Lauren glanced at the car, then back at Ivy.

"I didn't see her at first, either," Lauren said abruptly, and licked her lips. "The woman in the street. The one we aren't talking about."

"Do you know who she was?" Ivy asked, glancing at Ambrose.

"No," said Ambrose, and Lauren echoed the word a second later.

"But I intend to find out," Ambrose panted grimly.

"She's dead, isn't she?" Lauren asked softly.

Ivy swallowed hard, and nodded. "Yeah," she said, glancing down at Grinch.

Meredith nodded at Ivy as the trio stepped around the traffic barrier, looking completely unsurprised to see the head of the Roinn shepherding two humans and a semiconscious dog. The agent ushered Lauren into the car, then stepped back as Ambrose deposited the bulldog on the upholstery beside his owner.

"Get in," Ambrose grunted, nodding at the open door. "We can spare five minutes to get the poor thing back home."

Ivy wasn't sure if he meant Grinch or Lauren. Relieved, she simply nodded and slipped inside, shifting Grinch's back legs out of the way as Ambrose and Meredith got into the front seats.

Grinch roused himself long enough to shove his nose under the edge of Lauren's shirt. One of his back legs was dangling bonelessly off the seat, the veins on the inside of his thigh like lines of ink. Ivy leaned her head against the window, feeling suddenly and utterly exhausted.

Three blocks and an illegal U-turn later, the car was pulling up in front of the flat. Ivy hurriedly got out of the car and went to open the door before remembering she didn't have her key, and neither of them had locked the door in the first place. When she turned around, Meredith was carrying

Grinch, the bulldog slung limply over her shoulder as she and Lauren came up the sidewalk. Meredith hurried inside, but Lauren hesitated at the door. She touched Ivy's arm, her fingers sticky with sweat and burn gel.

"Your friend, back at the ambulance. He's—"

"You won't see him again," said Ivy, interrupting before Lauren could ask any of the questions Ivy could never, ever answer, especially not with Ambrose himself standing a dozen feet away. "He was just returning a favor."

Lauren's searching look grew deeper, and she started to say something else when a whimper from Grinch came from inside the flat.

"I'll be back in a sec," Ivy told her, nudging her inside. "Just got to, em, pay the driver."

Uneasily, Lauren nodded, but she didn't take her hand off Ivy's arm. "I trust you, okay? But whenever you're ready, we really need to talk about—*that*."

Ivy would never be ready to talk about *that*; those secrets weren't hers to give away. Had it been this awkward for Demi, back in Howth? When she found out her friend had been lying to her, Ivy'd been furious. Now Ivy was the one keeping secrets, and she didn't like how that felt, either. "Okay," she said instead. "Right."

Lauren let go of Ivy's arm and disappeared into the flat as Meredith breezed out the door. More slowly, Ivy followed, joining Ambrose at the bottom of the stairs.

"She shouldn't have been able to do that," muttered Ambrose, as they watched Meredith head back to the car. "Either she was too agitated for the veil to properly handle, or . . ." Ambrose trailed off and tried again. "Whatever you and Hunzu get up to is your own concern, but—"

"The pub quiz is one night a week, and he's hardly ever at the flat," Ivy protested, crossing her arms. Leave it to Ambrose to be more worried about policing Ivy's social life than about the woman who'd just burned to death in the street. There wasn't anything between her and Hunzu, and the fact that his invisibility and her mortality were mutually contagious meant it was perpetually going to stay that way. "Also, not our biggest problem right now."

Ambrose looked away, the hint of a chastened expression appearing on his face.

"You said 'enemy,'" Ambrose said, sitting down on the very far end of the steps, steepling his hands over his knees. "Did you actually see it?"

"No," Ivy admitted, dropping onto the grass next to the stairs, a careful six feet away. "Just what it did at the end. The fire. Everyone else thinks a gas line blew up. But she was wearing its clothes—the same sort of hooded jumpsuit thing."

Ambrose's gaze whipped back to Ivy's, an expression slipping across his face that almost looked like fear. Or disbelief.

"At first I thought maybe she *was* the—the thing from the apple grove," Ivy continued, shying away from naming the Enemy out loud. "But her face wasn't the same. When she realized I could see her, she injected me with something and I couldn't move. I think she could have killed me if she wanted to. But she didn't. I think she was trying not to hurt Grinch, either, until he knocked her down."

"Did you see what she was doing?" Ambrose asked darkly. "Anything she was looking for?"

"She had one of your wing computers and she'd it hooked up to my phone," said Ivy. "And she asked about my job. I mean, all the crazy things I do for the Roinn, and—"

"You spoke with her?" Ambrose interrupted, sounding surprised. He twisted around to face Ivy directly. In the light of the streetlamp, his face looked chalky. "Did she—sound like one of us?"

Ivy shook her head. "If I didn't know better, I'd say she wasn't actually very good with English," Ivy said. Some of the older generation of trows were native Irish speakers, though Ivy didn't think any of them were so cut off from their human neighbors that they hadn't picked up English in the centuries since.

A strange expression passed over Ambrose's face, and he swallowed, running a hand across his forehead. The frilly silk sleeve came away dark with sweat.

"Bloody hell," Ambrose murmured, and abruptly stood up. "Alright. Okay. Just . . . Look, stay low for a couple of days. Away from us. Any of us."

"What?" Ivy asked, grabbing the railing and hauling herself to her feet as well, leaning the tiniest bit into Ambrose's bubble. She'd never seen him look so anxious before. "What is it?"

"I don't know," Ambrose retorted, holding up his hands. "Right now I don't know anything more than you, and our only actual evidence of what happened tonight consists of a particularly large pothole in the middle of the street." He lowered his arms, his fingers drumming nervously on the pleats of his trousers. "If we can find out who this woman is—or at least who she isn't—we're a good deal closer to figuring out why she came here."

"Pretty sure it's something connected to your lot," Ivy retorted. One way or another, trows held a complete monopoly on all weirdness in Ivy's life, and had done so for considerably longer than Ivy had been aware of their existence. "You, or Demi, or any of the Roinn's errands. Or the thing I took to the Nano Imaging Centre," Ivy added, lowering her voice and glancing warily at Meredith and the car. "My address was all over that paperwork."

It was Ivy's address, instead of the trows' front business in the Liberties, because the wing Ivy had taken to the NIC was supposed to be locked up in the trows' creepy estate in County Clare.

"Let's not jump to conclusions," Ambrose interjected hastily. "There could be a completely different explanation."

"Right," said Ivy, unconvinced.

Ambrose rubbed his sleeve across his forehead again. He looked back at Ivy, and his expression sent a trail of goosebumps down Ivy's neck. "If anyone else shows up wearing that same jumpsuit, run. Don't wait, don't follow them, don't try to be a hero. Just get out of their way."

Ivy narrowed her eyes.

"You know who she was," she said, and it wasn't a question.

"No, I don't," Ambrose insisted, holding up his hands. "As soon as I know anything, I'll call, alright? Until then, just be careful."

Ivy nodded, the chill along her neck deepening as she watched Ambrose turn and hurry toward the waiting car.

Ambrose might claim he didn't know who the woman was, but he clearly had a theory, and it frightened him. Anything that frightened the head of the Roinn scared the hell out of Ivy pretty much by default. As she turned up the stairs to the flat, the breeze ruffling the back of Ivy's neck felt as chill and bleak as winter.

CHAPTER 3

Ivy's phone was ringing and the light streaming through the gap in the curtains was headache-inducingly bright. She lunged for the phone, dragged it off its charger and pawed at the screen for the snooze icon before she realized it wasn't ringing from an alarm.

Ivy blinked at the incoming number. It had a Dublin area code but was otherwise unfamiliar. She hesitated, wondering exactly how early it was and therefore how annoyed she could be with the caller. Sighing, she accepted the call as she collapsed back onto her pillows. Memories of the previous night tottered unsteadily to the forefront of her brain, along with an ache in her neck and what felt like a bruise on her left foot.

"Hello," Ivy grunted, trying to sound as though she'd been awake for more than five seconds.

"Is this Ms. Ivy Gallagher?" said the voice. If she was addressing Ivy as Ms. Anything, she was probably trying to sell something. Ivy had too much residual sympathy left over from her time at the Eirecom call center to hang up on her right away.

"Yes," Ivy said, calculating how far into the sales pitch she was willing to wait before making her excuses and getting off the line. Now that she was awake, she needed to go check on Lauren and Grinch. And call Demi. And Ambrose. And figure out if either of them had any luck clearing up any of the mysteries surrounding the woman who died last night.

"The Ms. Gallagher who dropped off a device at the Nano Imaging Centre three weeks ago?" the voice asked.

"Yes," Ivy repeated, and immediately sat up, pushing the sheets to the foot of the bed as she tried to remember the details of the cover story she and Ambrose had put on the submission form. "Did you find anything?"

Instead of answering, the woman merely sighed, a crackle of static lapsing into an ominous silence. "My name is Dr. Eliza Bannon. I'm the director of the NIC. Look, there isn't an easy way to say this, but the item you dropped off?"

"Yes," said Ivy, trying to keep any hint of worry out of her voice even as a prickle of cold ran up her arms. Trow technology seemingly had more in common with magic than with actual human computers, and a plethora of disaster scenarios were all jostling for attention in Ivy's head. Maybe it had turned someone invisible. Or into a horse. Which was ridiculous; the wing they'd taken to the NIC was already dead.

"It's missing," said Dr. Bannon grimly. Silence hung on the end of the phone, as though she were waiting for Ivy to start shouting at her.

Ivy took a deep breath, swinging her feet off the end of the bed and trying to think. This was bad. The wings were one of the few things the trows had taken with them from Valiard, the place the trows were originally from. They weren't often allowed to leave the Haven vault. Now one of them had disappeared from where it wasn't supposed to be in the first place. Uncomfortably, Ivy remembered that Ambrose's book in the

Roinn's offices listed several gruesome penalties for stealing, as it did for most everything else.

"We've started an inquiry," Dr. Bannon continued. "We're proceeding on the theory that it, em, may have been deliberately removed from our facility."

"Stolen, you mean," said Ivy. She rubbed at her eyes with her free hand.

"We've informed the Gardaí and the University," Dr. Bannon was saying. "We're committed to investigating to the fullest extent possible. Nothing like this has ever happened at the Centre before, I'm terribly sorry . . ." The director trailed off, as though she'd run through all the prepared sentences she'd practiced in advance. "I don't know what to tell you," she finished. "I trust my staff, and most of the technicians have worked here for years. The Gardaí were questioning all of them like they were criminals."

"Sounds like maybe one of them is," said Ivy. The first thing gone missing in the history of the lab, and it had to be a wing. Not a prototype, or a metallurgic sample, or someone's graduate thesis. The wing wasn't from Earth, and it was flat-out irreplaceable. The only reason Taye Carillon hadn't missed it already was because no one kept very close track of the ones that didn't actually work.

At least, Ambrose had assumed it didn't work.

Ivy looked toward the desk, remembering the woman who'd been standing next to it last night, and shivered. She'd had a wing on her arm. A functional one.

Could it be a coincidence that one wing went missing in the NIC, and a strange woman showed up wearing another? Ivy's name was all over the NIC submission form. Could that have led the thief to Ivy's flat in Dartry?

"Yes. Look, I'm sorry," Dr. Bannon, repeated sounding

subdued. "It's a terrible thing to have happen, it's just, well, at the end of the day, it's a *thing*, isn't it, and some of the techs . . .

I just wanted to call and tell you myself," she continued in a firmer voice. "We're emailing what we did manage to get on the sample before it went missing. And the chancellor's number. And an arbitration agreement I'd like you to look over to determine, em, fair compensation. We'd much prefer to come to an agreement directly."

She didn't want the Nano Imaging Centre being sued, is what it sounded like.

"I'll pass that along," said Ivy quietly. She could hardly picture Ambrose wanting to escalate matters through the Irish courts, for the simple reason he wouldn't want to advertise that the wing was missing any more than the NIC would. There was no way any arbitrator could determine fair value, since no one—trows included—quite knew what the wings were, or how they worked. Which was one of the reasons Ambrose wanted the NIC to look it over in the first place. The veil—the machinery that kept trows (and a small number of unlucky humans) invisible—was another such device, one which Ivy suspected had no backups or redundancies. "If you haven't already looked at your security tapes, look again," Ivy added. "Even if you're sure no one was in the building. The, em, owner of the item would want to know you're being thorough."

Trows were perfectly visible on screens, so it was possible a camera had caught footage of who had taken it. If it was the same woman from last night, maybe that would help identify who she was, or why she'd broken into Ivy's flat. Or why she'd burned to death afterward—the Enemy's signature calling card.

The stench from last night came flooding back, equal parts bubbling asphalt and burning meat. Ivy swallowed hard, standing up and looking for her slippers. The Enemy, like the trows themselves, was thought to be from Valiard. Where precisely it came from, or where it secreted itself between murders, were only two of the mysteries no one seemed to know the answers to. Along with why it killed, why it only did so once a year, and why it was so amenable to killing victims the trows selected themselves.

"Give me a call once you've looked over the documents," Dr. Bannon said.

"We will," Ivy said, and started to hang up, but she stopped with her finger over the icon. "When did you first notice it was missing?"

"Three days ago."

Three days ago a dead wing computer disappeared from the NIC, and last night a trow turned up in Ivy's bedroom wearing a live one on her arm.

"Alright," said Ivy, and hung up the phone, resisting the urge to dive back under her pillows. She'd hoped to get something approximating eight hours of sleep before trying to sort through last night's disaster, let alone tackling a new one.

Biting her lip, Ivy pulled up Ambrose's name on her contacts list and pushed the call button.

Glumly, Ivy supposed the dead woman might make a convenient scapegoat, if Taye Carillon ever noticed the wing was missing. The Thane of Haven had already tried to turn Ivy invisible once, and for a considerably lesser offense than misplacing a priceless ancestral relic.

Ambrose picked up on the third ring.

"You alright?" he slurred, and Ivy felt a momentary pang at waking him up so early when he'd likely gotten even less sleep than she had.

"I'm fine," said Ivy, who hadn't actually stopped to think about it since she'd woken up but wasn't going to admit to anything less. "It's something else. The, em, parcel you had me deliver to the NIC?"

"Yes," said Ambrose, sounding immediately more alert. Ivy heard something shuffling in the background, then the sound of a door slamming shut.

"It's gone missing," Ivy said bluntly. "The director called me just now. They think someone at the lab might have stolen it."

The only sound on the line was a rush of air, as though Ambrose had taken a deep breath through his teeth.

"How long ago?" he asked tightly. "Is the Gardaí involved?"

"Three days," said Ivy. "They've called the Gardaí and their own security, but it doesn't sound like they're getting anywhere. They said they'd send over arbitration papers."

"Useless," Ambrose muttered. "Forward me a copy of whatever they send. And a staff directory if you can find one."

"Okay," said Ivy. She'd have at least a couple of hours to see what she could find on the internet before she had to go to the Blue Parrot for her shift. "And Ambrose?"

"Yes?"

"The woman last night had a wing." Ivy caught herself rubbing the bruised spot on her neck and deliberately dropped her hand. "And my address was on the papers at the NIC."

Ambrose didn't immediately reply. "We'll certainly look into it," he said after a long pause. "Though if the director suspects her own staff, she may have good reason."

Bleakly, Ivy wondered if Ambrose had had another reason for keeping his own name off the NIC paperwork. If things went badly, *really* badly, it was only Ivy's word against Ambrose's that she hadn't stolen the wing from Haven and taken it to the NIC herself.

Demi knew, of course. Demi probably wouldn't hang Ivy out to dry just to cover her partner's mistakes. Probably.

"Nothing else happened last night?" Ambrose asked.

"It was less than six hours ago, and I've been asleep for most of that," Ivy pointed out. "So, no."

"Alright," said Ambrose, though he didn't sound reassured. "If anything happens even remotely strange, get out and call me immediately."

"Okay," Ivy agreed, vaguely wondering how exactly she was supposed to parse out the unusual strange occurrences from the usual ones. Case in point: talking on the phone to an invisible man about the theft of an alien artifact that had come from some weird other dimension three hundred years ago.

"I'll be in touch," said Ambrose, and rang off.

❧❦❧

Ivy's shift at the Blue Parrot was supposed to end at five. The amount of beer steins sitting in the sink meant Ivy would probably be staying longer just to make sure Will didn't start the evening shift already in the weeds. It was almost as if the pub were conspiring to be busy enough to keep Ivy from thinking about the previous night.

Ivy cleared another round of glassware from a table of men in rugby colors and stepped past a booth of costumed Haunted Dublin guides, all of whom were hurriedly trying to eat carryout without getting curry on their puffy sleeves. As she dropped the bus bin on the bar, the jukebox in the corner sighed loudly and broke into the chorus of "*Mr. Cellophane.*"

"I can finish up the dishes, if you'd rather be off," said Will, glancing at the clock. He'd cut his hair again, the mohawk transformed into a stripe of blue stubble that made him look a bit like a cartoon badger.

"It's completely fine," said Ivy quickly. "I don't mind."

Ordinarily, Ivy didn't volunteer to stay late after her shift.

Ordinarily, Ivy's walk home didn't involve passing a crater in the street where someone had burned to death.

She went to the sink, added a few hefty squirts of dish soap into the basin, and turned on the hot water, feeling obscurely grateful that at least she'd be walking home in daylight, and Lauren would probably be back from the vet with Grinch.

Not that Lauren's presence had stopped the woman last night. And maybe Lauren *wasn't* home, because she'd mentioned something about a fancy work party this week and Ivy couldn't remember what night she'd said it was.

It didn't matter, Ivy told herself as she picked up a beer stein and began scrubbing it against the bottle brush. The woman who'd broken into the flat was dead, and the Enemy who killed her wasn't likely to be bothering with Ivy. Demi was the one who had to worry about that, and not for another seven months. She was the one next in line whenever the Enemy got back to its usual business of murdering Year Kings.

The bell jingled over the Blue Parrot's door and Ivy glanced up, blanched, and immediately turned back to the pile of dirty glassware, as if concentrating on the beer steins would make her just as insensible as everyone else to the man who'd walked through the door.

"You alright?" Hunzu asked loudly, inching past the group in rugby colors. He looked nervous, his wavy brown hair sticking up in clumps. A messenger bag was slung across one shoulder, rumpling his t-shirt, which had an expansive print of a flowering orchid. "You weren't answering your phone."

Ivy glanced up from the dishes and gave him a tight, insincere smile. *Fine*, she mouthed. *Can't talk.*

Under other circumstances, Ivy would have been happy to see Hunzu, but she didn't like him dropping by the Blue Parrot. The pub was the one part of Ivy's life that remained entirely weirdness-free, and Ivy wanted to keep it that way.

"So answer the phone," said Hunzu calmly, nodding to the register as he pulled his mobile out of his pocket and jabbed at the screen.

Ivy realized what he meant in time to yank her hands out of the soapy water and squeeze past Will to pick up the phone next to the register on the first ring.

"Blue Parrot, how may I help you?" Ivy rattled off into the receiver, locking eyes with Hunzu and turning on her artificially peppy customer-service voice.

"Are you okay?" Hunzu asked, sidestepping the rugby fans to join Ivy closer to the register.

"Just fine," Ivy, smiling through her teeth. "No, there's no pub quiz tonight. You must be confusing us with *somewhere else.*"

"I heard about last night," said Hunzu, unrepentant. "You didn't call, and you weren't answering your phone, and I just want to make sure you're okay."

"Nothing to worry about, sir," Ivy simpered into the phone. "Have a nice day."

She dropped the phone back into its cradle and went back to the sink, ignoring Hunzu's spluttering. He caught up to her a moment later, leaning across the bar, closer to her than he usually allowed himself to get.

"I can't talk here," Ivy muttered out of the corner of her mouth, glancing at the hallway leading to the back office. "Last thing I need is Roberta thinking I'm off my rocker."

Hunzu bit his lip, belatedly looking abashed.

"Outside then," he suggested, nodding at the door and patting his messenger bag. "I brought you something, and you won't want to open it in here."

Ten minutes, Ivy mouthed as Will brushed by with the rugby fans' drink orders, and pointedly nodded at the bin of dirty glassware. If Hunzu wanted to show up at her job unexpectedly, he could stand to wait until she was actually finished working.

"Fine," Hunzu sighed, glancing at the clock over the bar and crossing his arms. Ivy dove into the pile of dirty beer steins, large enough that it was going to take significantly longer than ten minutes. Rubbing another stein over the bottle brush, Ivy glanced covertly at Hunzu, wondering what on earth he wanted to give her that he didn't want other people to see.

Looking nervous, Hunzu slunk farther away from the rugby group, scanning the pub as though he were looking for a corner to lurk in. As Will came back with another bin of dirty glassware, Hunzu abruptly turned and headed down the hall toward the back office. Fine, thought Ivy, putting the stein on the rack to dry. Let him be ghostly and inexplicable around Roberta if he wanted, as long as he was out of Ivy's hair.

Hunzu reappeared a moment later, holding a pair of bright yellow washing-up gloves. He tugged them over his hands as he ducked under the pass-through, awkwardly joining Ivy next to the sink.

"You'd better dry, I suppose," Hunzu said, tugging the gloves up his arms. "I have no idea where any of this goes."

With a sigh, Ivy passed him a towel and slid down the bar to make room for him at the sink. Hunzu being nice just made it harder to be annoyed at him for showing up at her work. Still, Ivy couldn't quite shake the nagging fear that at any moment Roberta would walk out of her office and demand to know who the punter was behind the bar. According to the Roinn, a very small percentage of humans were naturally resistant to the veil's effects. It would be just Ivy's luck if one of them turned out to be her boss.

Though to be fair, Roberta probably wouldn't care if an invisible man were washing the glassware, as long as he was doing it for free.

"I heard from Cirdain, who talked with Solly, who heard it from Meredith that something from Valiard attacked you last night," he said, rubbing at his forehead and leaving a trail of soap bubbles across his cheek.

"It wasn't from Val—" Ivy started, and cut herself off. Having a conversation with someone no one else could see was exactly why she didn't want Hunzu in here. "I can't talk."

If those were the sort of rumors flying around, Ivy wasn't looking forward to dealing with the fallout when she went back to the Roinn offices in the Liberties. Glumly, Ivy wondered how many other people had tried to call her since her shift started.

"I know," Hunzu assured her. "I'm just trying to explain why I came. Demi said you were fine, but she hadn't heard from you since last night. Coming down here seemed the best way to make sure."

She glanced at him, and their eyes met for a moment before he turned back to the glass rack, blushing up to his ears. Hunzu must have been genuinely worried if he'd resorted to calling Demi, who'd named him second in line for the Enemy before ducking out of trow society last year. He seemed to have mostly forgiven her that, perhaps because it was difficult to hold a grudge against someone who only had seven months left to live.

Will came hustling back, scrawling something on a ticket as he ducked under the pass-through, stepping neatly around Hunzu without apparently being aware he was doing so. It was the same thing on their pub quiz nights at the Yukon Bar—an entire room full of people walking around Hunzu without actually noticing him.

Will whistled as he looked at the growing pile of pint glasses stacked on the drying rack.

"Fastest dish washer in Oxmarten," he said, grinning at her as he grabbed three chilled steins out of the fridge.

"Thanks," Ivy murmured noncommittally. Not that she objected to getting compliments from Will, whose cuteness factor had increased exponentially once he'd cut off the mohawk. Being around Hunzu meant frequently being credited for things she had nothing to do with, like the unwarranted reputation she'd developed on their pub quiz team for sports trivia and 80s pop culture references. Both of which were firmly Hunzu's areas of expertise—but Ivy was the one who could say the answers and have the other team members actually hear them.

Sooner than Ivy expected, Hunzu was handing her the last glass. Ivy dunked it in the rinse water and stacked it on the rack. She stopped by the till to count out her share of the tip jar —the day shift was always modest compared to evenings and weekends—and ducked under the pass-through.

She went to the back office, slipping inside long enough to clock out and grab her purse. Ivy unzipped the bag, pulled out her phone, and glanced at the screen.

You have 7 missed calls and 19 new text messages.

Ivy winced and slid the phone into her pocket. She'd have to deal with those later—after she'd figured out why Hunzu was still hanging around, and why he'd brought her something he didn't want her to open in public.

Crossing back in front of the bar, she waved at Will. Looking flustered, the bartender left the register and ducked under the pass-through, nearly banging his head as he popped up on the other side.

"Half a sec," Will said, rubbing the badger stripe on his hair, and Ivy looked back to the counter, wondering if there was a second pile of dirty glassware somewhere she'd forgotten to wash.

"Glassware's fine," Will assured her, still rubbing at his head. "I just wanted to—there's a Jimmy Buffet cover band playing at Myrna's tomorrow and it's your day off and you've been really fantastic around the place." His voice was getting faster and higher-pitched, which told Ivy everything she needed to know about what Will was gearing up to ask. She was discomfortingly aware of Hunzu, lips pressed together in a tight line, standing close enough to hear every word. "And if you don't like beach music we could go somewhere else, butI-wasjustwonderingifyouwouldgooutwithme?"

Ivy could have murdered Hunzu all over again for showing up at the Parrot. Tomorrow was their usual pub quiz night at the Yukon. Hunzu couldn't play if Ivy ditched him, since no one else on the team could hear him (or even knew he existed, let alone that he considered himself their teammate). Even worse, if Ivy ditched him to go listen to twangy beach music with a cute guy from work, he'd know.

"Tomorrow's sort of a bad time," said Ivy, resolutely not looking at Hunzu. "A friend and I do this pub quiz thing. But maybe the day after?"

Will's face fell, and Ivy remembered Will worked Friday nights.

"Or maybe your friend could come round to Myrna's as well?" Will asked carefully. "I don't mind if they don't."

"No, they mind, actually," Hunzu snapped, and Will's expression barely changed, only a slight furrowing of the eyebrows that Ivy would have missed if she hadn't been looking right at him.

Ivy only barely stopped herself from rounding on Hunzu and telling him to mind his own business. She could handle this without his commentary, and he shouldn't have been here in the first place.

One of the lace-covered Haunted Dublin guides was making his way up the bar. If Roberta caught them talking while a customer was waiting, she'd have words for both of them, even if Ivy wasn't technically on the clock.

Will was cute, and he'd been patient with Ivy while she was training. Ivy ought to jump at the chance to have more relationships in her life with actual visible people. More importantly, if Ivy turned him down now, it would look like Hunzu had talked her out of it.

"Lunchtime next Monday, it'll be before both our shifts," said Ivy imperiously. "You make sure you're free, and I'll find us something even better than Jimmy Buffet cover bands."

What exactly that would be, before two p.m. on a weekday, Ivy wasn't sure. That was a problem for future Ivy. Presently, she just needed to walk out the door without Hunzu making any more critical remarks, and maybe then she could manage not to murder him when they got to the street.

"Deal," said Will, grinning and rubbing his hand across his face as he nodded. "Monday it is. It'll be great. Whatever you pick. And have a good few days off, and I'll see you Saturday—"

Whatever else he was saying was lost in the grunting of the jukebox, which had roused itself long enough to chortle through the opening bars of "*Layla*."

Ivy nodded with more enthusiasm than she felt and bolted to the door, releasing the scowl she'd been hiding behind her pleasant expression. She shoved the door open hard enough to set the bell above it jangling wildly and shaded her eyes as she burst from the Parrot's cool interior to the heat and glare of a relentlessly warm July evening.

Ivy turned down the sidewalk toward the George's Street bus stop, not bothering to see if Hunzu was following. She reached into her purse for her phone as the trow fell into step beside her and held it up to her ear without turning it on. Pretending she was on her mobile was the easiest way to talk to Hunzu in public without being stared at.

"Not okay," Ivy snapped, glaring at him.

"No, I should have gone right on being ignored," said Hunzu mildly. "You could have asked me if I minded, I was right there."

"Right, let me check my social calendar with a guy who doesn't exist."

Ivy got about three paces past him before she realized he'd come to a dead halt. She spun back around, nearly colliding with a sweltering-looking man holding a bike helmet.

Hunzu was clutching the strap to his messenger bag, a wounded look on his face.

"You know that's not true," he said, folding his arms.

For the vast majority of people in Dublin, it was absolutely true. They couldn't see or hear Hunzu without considerable effort on Hunzu's part. Ivy was one of the few exceptions. Maybe Hunzu counted on that for more than just getting to play on a pub quiz team from time to time.

Ivy sighed, the phone sliding a few inches from her ear as she looked at him.

"Sorry," she admitted. "That was rude. But you know what I meant."

Hunzu looked away. "Well, the next time a fellow asks you out on a hot date in front of me, I'll *pretend* to not exist," he said, though it sounded like a shadow of his normal gibberish. "If it makes you feel any better."

"A Jimmy Buffet cover band is not a hot date," Ivy pointed out. "And the next time you show up at the Parrot, it had better be when I'm not working. Throw peanut shells at Roberta or something. Half the staff already think the place is haunted."

Hunzu smiled and started walking again, Ivy falling into step beside him. She glanced at her phone, unsure whether to slip it back into her bag. Even if Hunzu had no grounds to object to what Ivy did outside of their pub quiz nights, it still felt awkward to talk about her incipient date with Will. Which was exactly how it was supposed to be: awkward was the design state. Keep trows and humans far enough apart that humans stayed visible and trows stayed ageless. Just because Ivy got a pass on that with her work for the Roinn didn't mean she should be flaunting it in her personal life.

"I brought this," said Hunzu, resolutely changing the subject as he pulled a small box out of his messenger bag. "Just in case. Might come in handy."

Ivy slipped her phone into her pocket as he handed her the package. She looked curiously at the plain brown wrapping, remembering what Hunzu had said about not opening it in the pub. Stepping closer to a brick storefront advertising cigarettes and international SIM cards, Ivy slipped her thumb under the flap and ripped off the tape. She unfolded a bit of the wrapping, peered at the label underneath, and immediately flipped the paper back.

"Is this even legal?" Ivy hissed.

"Probably not," replied the trow, unconcerned. "I could ask. Or if you really don't want it . . ."

Ivy looked at the box, anonymous in its plain brown wrapper. The bruise on Ivy's neck twinged. She remembered the prick as the needle went in, the way her legs had gone clumsy and numb all at once.

Ivy stepped closer to the brick wall. Shielding the box as best she could, Ivy pulled back the brown paper covering.

The label read StunnerX2, next to a picture of something yellow that looked like a cross between a handgun and a stud finder. It had a pistol grip with an orange trigger and a fat blue cartridge attached to the business end. Below it, in bold red letters: Protection. Apprehension. Nonviolent Resolution.

Personally, Ivy thought shooting a Taser at anyone was

pretty much the opposite of 'nonviolent resolution.' At least it wasn't an actual gun.

Ivy grimaced at the box. Five months ago, the worst things Ivy had to worry about were catcalls from drunken louts outside the DART station. That had all ended in February, when the Enemy came for Uncle Patrick. Last night the Enemy had been in Dartry. A hollow feeling settled in Ivy's stomach as she looked at the box. She remembered how worried Ambrose had looked, sitting on the stairs outside her flat.

Ivy shoved the box into her purse, rooting around to bury it firmly at the bottom. "Thanks," she said, trying to sound sincere. Ivy wasn't entirely sure why Hunzu thought this might be helpful: the woman was dead, the Enemy was gone, and the problem of the missing wing from the NIC wasn't going to be solved by electrocuting people. And if the Enemy decided to show up early, a Taser wouldn't make the slightest difference. She'd seen one of Demi's friends empty a gun at it from fifteen feet away, and the thing hadn't flinched.

"There's a pair of handcuffs, too," Hunzu added earnestly. "Just in case."

From her pocket, Ivy's phone chirruped an incoming text, saving her from having to think up an enthusiastic answer to that. Ivy pulled out her phone, rubbing her hand across her face as she looked at the rows of missed calls and text alerts. Sighing, Ivy pulled up the list.

From Hunzu, seven texts and two missed calls, all of which she dismissed without reading.

From Gretchen, Ambrose's secretary. *Heard you had a close call at your flat. If you need it, there's an air mattress in the closet in the agent's half of the break room, and we're stocked up on pot noodles, I checked.*

From Ambrose himself. *In receipt of the NIC documents.*

Keep working on the staff addresses. Come by the Liberties tomorrow if you can, Solly wants to look at your phone ASAP.

And if ANYTHING strange happens, GET OUT and call me. In that order.

From Lauren. The vet's keeping Grinch overnight, they say he needs fluids and he's on an IV. He keeps trying to play with the tube, so I guess he's feeling better.

So you know, I'm staying with my sister in Kimmage tonight. Just in case.

From Demi. Hope you got some sleep after the commotion. If the spot on your neck flares up, go to St. Patrick's University Hospital, ask for Dr. Mahtab, and tell her you were referred by a friend you don't see much of. She'll know.

If you don't want to go back to Dartry, text me, no one else has been out to Howth in ages.

Ivy?

Ivy are you ok?

Why on earth did you NOT call in sick after last night? OK, text me when you get this. And if anything starts to look weird, don't wait for things to get weirder. Just run—

Ivy shut down her messaging app without reading any further and slowly lowered her phone. It seemed strangely hard to catch her breath, as though she'd just run the whole way from the Blue Parrot. Looking across the street in the early evening glare, the people on the sidewalk almost looked like silhouettes, gliding from their work to their homes, or hotel rooms, or pubs like it was a completely normal day.

"You think it's going to come back," Ivy said, and she knew she was talking too loudly even before a woman in a flower-print shirt turned and stared at her. Ivy ducked her head, ignoring her. "You all think it's coming back."

Hunzu ducked his head and started to say something before Ivy cut him off.

"Don't say, 'of course not,' you're the one who bought me a bloody T—" Ivy stopped herself from saying something that would draw even more attention, and pushed herself away from the wall.

A half-open gate led to an alley and Ivy turned into it, rubbing at her eyes. The heat and the glare dropped away as she passed under the shadow of the building, walking toward a cluster of rubbish bins underneath a spindly fire escape. The noise from the street was quieter, as though the babble of the real world hadn't followed them into the alley.

"You know you can call me, right?" Hunzu asked after a moment. "If you ever need help. Or even if you don't need help," he added, the corner of his mouth rallying toward a smile. "Call anyway."

"Yeah," said Ivy, lamely. "I know."

Through the fabric of the purse, the Taser's box jutted into Ivy's hip. She pushed it as far into the depths as she could, blinking hard and not looking at Hunzu. If it weren't for the whole no-touching business, it might have been nice to hold his hand.

Everyone thought something bad was going to happen, and that Ivy shouldn't go back to the flat. Which was nonsense, because the woman who'd broken in was dead. If the Enemy wanted, it could have killed Ivy, too. It hadn't.

If the Enemy was breaking its pattern, it might be becoming more dangerous, not less. At least back in February she'd been reasonably certain the Enemy wasn't there for her.

Ivy stopped, because she'd forgotten that in February, Hunzu hadn't had that same certainty. Demi had named him her consort, a sort of victim-in-waiting, before she disappeared because she'd been trying to protect her actual boyfriend, Ambrose. At that moment, Ivy thought she understood why he'd been in such a hurry to come down to Oxmarten, waltz into her pub, and hand her something that probably had misdemeanor charges attached to even possessing it.

"Hunzu," Ivy said, fumbling for the right words that wouldn't sound like she was taking sides. "Next February—it's still Demi, isn't it? Not you?"

Hunzu let out a sigh and ran a hand across his forehead. "Anyone's guess," he said roughly. "No one's ever survived their year before, and Demi wouldn't let them call another lottery. Hard to tell what the Enemy might think."

Across the alley, a door swung open and a woman in a grease-covered chef's coat lugged a garbage bag down to the pile of rubbish bins. A Beastie Boys track wailed out the door behind her, the guitar reverberating in the narrow alley like echoes from another world.

In February, Ivy had sworn she'd find a way to kill the Enemy before it could come back for Demi. Pretending things were normal when they obviously weren't wasn't going to do anything to help.

Also, Ivy should probably text some of these people back before anyone else got worried enough to track her down in person.

Ivy pulled her phone out and opened the list of texts. Below Demi's name was a number Ivy didn't recognize. She opened the message, frowning as she started to read it.

Dear Ms. Gallagher. In light of your recent encounter, I am requesting your presence at the Haven at your earliest possible convenience. I trust you remember the way. If you've caught Valiard's attention, it's to your benefit and ours to understand why. We are not so powerless as our unfortunate dealings with the Adversary may have led you to believe. If you could arrive before eight o'clock tonight that would be ideal. Respectfully, Thane Taye Carillon.

Ivy read it through once, then again, aware that Hunzu was

looking at her nervously. She started to say something, then sighed and held the phone up. He leaned forward, his eyebrows furrowing as he stared at the screen. Ivy could sense the objection before he opened his mouth.

"The Roinn will complain, if she tries anything," Ivy said, slipping the phone back into her purse.

"Just means she'll have to be subtle about it," Hunzu said, still frowning. "Doesn't mean you should trust her."

"Everyone else is just saying don't go home. She's at least—"

"—saying what, 'Come be bait for Valiard'?" Hunzu asked.

"You already have bait," Ivy burst out, earning a strange look from the woman in the chef's coat as she tromped back into the building. Wincing, Ivy lowered her voice. "Once a year, every year. And why does everyone think this has something to do with Valiard?"

Hunzu looked surprised.

"Meredith said the person who attacked you was wearing a Valiard scout's uniform. Dark jumpsuit and a hood. Like *it* wore."

Hesitantly, Ivy nodded. Was that what Ambrose had been afraid to say, that her attacker was someone from the trows' former home? "I thought maybe that's what she was at first," Ivy said slowly. She'd never considered the jumpsuit might have been some sort of uniform. "How could someone from Valiard come here? I thought the place didn't exist anymore."

"It's not like we've been able to pop over and check," Hunzu pointed out, looking uncomfortable. He hesitated, staring hard at the metal door swinging closed behind the chef, as though he, of all people, were suddenly worried about being overheard. "If she was from Valiard . . . that's bad, Ivy. Really bad."

Ivy pursed her lips. "Don't tell me there are scarier things from Valiard than the Enemy."

"Possibly, but that's not the point," said Hunzu, running his hands through his hair so it stood up in clumps. "Point is, Valiard's doors didn't just open at random. Most of them opened to a really bad place. They were studying a— Well, they called it speciation event, but it was more like an apocalypse. Something bad in their own history they called Event Two. Fortunately for us, Event Two hasn't happened yet, and if we're all *very* lucky, it might not happen at all," Hunzu continued briskly. "But that's where their scouts were going. And if a scout's come here—"

"Wait," Ivy said, cutting him off because what Hunzu was saying didn't make any sense. "You're saying Valiard could predict the future?"

Hunzu looked away, running his toe through the loose gravel at the edge of the pavement as he bit his lip. Ivy suddenly had the feeling she'd gotten one crucial element very wrong.

"Not exactly," Hunzu said. "I told you when we met, we're not from outer space, or some other dimension. We're . . . from here, from Earth. Or what Earth turns into, a long time from now. Valiard can't predict the future; they just . . . knew things that already happened to them but haven't happened to us."

Ivy's throat was dry. "How much farther away?" she asked, fighting the urge to dismiss the idea as too ridiculous to take seriously. Or too frightening. Valiard didn't even have *plants*. Thinking of Valiard predicting the future was bad enough. The idea that Valiard *was* the future was even worse.

"I don't know. I don't think anyone else does, either, though Angevin could probably guess," Hunzu said in a low voice. "Long enough that . . . Well, it doesn't *matter*, you know? Even as long-lived as my lot are, none of us are ever going to live long enough to come close to it, not even our next couple generations of descendants. It's like knowing the sun's going to explode into the Earth someday, or an earthquake will knock California into the ocean."

"The sun is going to do *what* to the Earth?"

"Turn into a red giant and destroy most of the solar system, in about five billion years," Hunzu said primly. "And I know that from the internet, not because I'm descended from time travelers."

For a moment, neither of them said anything.

"It's still terrible," said Ivy, rubbing at her eyes as she stared at the pockmarked wall, as though something unfathomable was nestled in the joins between the bricks. Earth changed. Earthquakes and hurricanes and disasters happened every year. Every year the world changed, and someday it would change enough that it wouldn't exactly be Earth anymore.

And somewhere in that not-Earth, people who looked more like Hunzu than Ivy were peering into Ivy's world like scientists poised over a microscope. Was *that* what had come to Ivy's flat last night?

"But if Valiard was destroyed before your people even left . . . The woman last night. Did she come from before that all happened? Before everything burned?"

Hunzu looked at his shoe again and shrugged. "Maybe. I guess so."

Ivy remembered the woman's arms reaching out from the column of fire, and she shuddered. Even if she'd made it back to Valiard, perhaps she would've burned anyway. The thought should have made Ivy feel better, but it didn't. She'd died frightened and alone, and Ivy couldn't shake the notion that if she'd done something differently—not gone back to her bedroom, not turned on the music, not run after Grinch— maybe the Enemy wouldn't have killed her.

"You said the people from Valiard, the scouts, were going back in time to study a disaster."

"An apocalypse," Hunzu corrected gently, and gestured at Ivy's phone and the plethora of texts. "You can see why everyone's worried."

"If she was looking for the end of the world in Dartry, she was *definitely* in the wrong place," said Ivy firmly, daring him to contradict her.

Hunzu only shrugged, plastering a thin smile on his face, apparently with effort.

"When I was little, my aunties used to tell me if I was bad, a scout would open a door in the back garden, whisk me off to Valiard, and bring back a nice changeling boy in my place." He turned back to the mouth of the alley and the smile slipped from his face like a doused light. "Valiard always said the Valoi were there to prevent paradoxes. Your lot would call them changelings. You know the grandfather paradox? If you go back in time to kill your own grandfather—which is beastly, by the way—a changeling appears and stops you. Or the changeling becomes your grandfather instead, which has got to be worse than letting the original grandfather live. Maybe it's all just old wives' tales, something to keep people from worrying too much about changing something important."

Ivy tapped the bruise on her neck. "Last night wasn't an old wives' tale, and it wasn't just a scout from Valiard. The Enemy was there, too. I want to find out why, and it sounds like Carillon does, too." Ivy sighed, looking back down the alley to the bustling street. "But I'm not going to make it out to County Clare in three hours."

Hunzu sighed, his lips pressed together in a thin line. Even standing in the shade of the alley, a line of sweat stood out on his forehead.

"I could help you there," he said after a moment. "If you're sure you want to go."

CHAPTER 4

Hunzu was sitting ramrod-straight in the driver's seat as they pulled back onto the motorway, his hands gripping the steering wheel at precisely ten and two. They'd switched seats outside of Nenagh; it had finally grown dark enough that Hunzu could take the wheel without alarming passing motorists. Not for the first time, Ivy wondered if she shouldn't have insisted on driving the whole way anyway, even though the dilapidated Citroen C1 was notionally his. Or at least, his by right of knowing the combination to the lockbox in the garage on Dominick Street where it was parked.

The radio station they'd picked up outside Ballacolla was disintegrating into a mishmash of guitars and static; Hunzu let go of the steering wheel long enough to hit the scan button. Shifting in her seat, Ivy pulled her purse across her lap, looking nervously at the crease where the Taser's box dimpled the fabric.

Slowly, she pulled the box out of the purse, rubbing her thumb over the concealing paper wrapper. Even in the privacy of Hunzu's car, she felt queasy at the idea of opening it. As though actually unwrapping it would be admitting that maybe she needed it.

"Do you, erm, actually know how this works?" Ivy asked, nodding at the box.

"Point it at the problem and pull the trigger, I suppose," Hunzu answered, shrugging. "Aren't there instructions?"

Ivy slid her finger under the cardboard flap. Plenty of girls carried self-defense gadgets in their purses. The Taser sitting in Ivy's bag wasn't much different. It was just a precaution.

"Have you been back to Haven since it all happened?" Hunzu asked, frowning at the static pouring out of the Citroen's speakers.

Ivy shook her head as she pulled off the rest of the wrapping.

"I only wondered if you'd ever talked to her about Larch," Hunzu said, coughing tactfully.

"No," said Ivy, aghast, wondering how on earth Hunzu thought that sort of conversation might be possible. Ivy and Larch—whom Ivy had long known as her mum's boyfriend, Patrick—had little enough to do with each other even when Larch was alive. "I didn't know him, really, and I don't know Carillon at all. He was just some friend of my mother's."

Victoria claimed she and Ivy's dad would have divorced even if she hadn't become invisible—but she'd cut Larch out of her life afterward, even though he was literally the only person who could still see her.

More static fluttered into the car as Hunzu played with the dials, eventually setting on something that sounded vaguely new-age and instrumental. Only marginally more entertaining than the shipping forecast, in Ivy's opinion, but if it took Hunzu's mind off the road, she supposed she could stand it.

"You'll probably think I was silly," Ivy continued after a moment. "But I never connected him with my parents splitting up until later on. Then I think I hated him, but by that point it'd been years since I'd seen him. I never thought I hated him enough to kill him, but I guess—"

"You didn't kill anyone," Hunzu interrupted sternly, pulling his gaze off the road to look at her. "Larch grew up knowing about the Year King. He'd have suspected what might happen if he came."

"Then why did he do it?" Ivy asked.

Hunzu, staring once more at the darkening M7, shrugged, and didn't answer.

"You think the Enemy would've had something to say about it," he said finally. "Showing up seventy years late. Sorry," he added, giving Ivy a sidelong look. "Don't mean to sound callous."

"Be as callous as you want," Ivy retorted. "I hardly ever saw him after my mum left."

Turning back to the box, Ivy opened the flap and tilted the package. A plastic-wrapped bundle slid out, along with a pair of sturdy-looking metal handcuffs. A yellow slip of paper fluttered out to land on the divider between the seats. *Caution: contents are charged.*

Hunzu leaned forward, his fingers tightening around the wheel as though he expected the car to dart off in an unexpected direction at any moment. "Did you ever wonder if he wasn't the only one invisible to absolutely everybody? Like, if there's twenty cars on the motorway, and you're seeing one car less than I am, there'd be no way to tell. There's too many of them."

"If this is a roundabout way to ask me to pay more attention to traffic—"

"Fifty-four percent of traffic accidents are caused by driver distraction," said Hunzu primly, the sort of comment that made Ivy occasionally wish she could punch him in the shoulder.

She settled for snorting, and picked up the plastic-wrapped

bundle. Carefully turning the business end so it was pointed toward the passenger door, Ivy ripped open the sleeve. The Taser's barrel was blue, and wider than Ivy had expected. The grip looked like that of the pistols Ivy had seen on cop shows, with a rounded orange trigger and a white push-button safety just above. Hesitantly, Ivy hefted it. It felt strangely light, barely heavier than Ivy's phone. The design at least made it clear how it worked. Safety off, pull the trigger, run away.

Hesitantly, Ivy uncurled her pointer finger, brushing it against the outside edge of the trigger guard. It felt like touching a prop, the sort of thing that showed up all the time in movies and never in real life.

"Do you really believe it's—what everyone says it is?" Ivy asked softly, rubbing her thumb along the edge of the grip. "Some homicidal creature from back home that wants to kill all of you, but settles for one pre-selected victim a year?"

Another thing to look forward to in Earth's distant future: no plants, a city that burns, and an unstoppable serial killer. It was easier to think of the Enemy as having nothing to do with her when she still thought it came from some weird alternate dimension. The idea of the Enemy being a product of Earth, no matter how remote the Earth it came from, felt quietly horrible. There was a picture book she had constantly read to her step-brothers when they were younger, about a monster who lived at the end of the book. Every page you turned brought you closer, and nothing you did could change it. Only in real life, the monster was nothing as innocuous as the little creature in a children's book.

"It's a little more complicated than that—"

"Just saying, it seems pretty convenient to blame all this on a mysterious villain that only shows up once a year," said Ivy. She double-checked the safety, then shoved the Taser back into her purse along with the handcuffs. "How many of the original trows from Valiard are still alive? Who are now all conveniently exempt from your lottery?"

"You need to stop watching so many crime shows," Hunzu sighed. He tapped the steering wheel cover, his fingers leaving little dimples in the suede. "Forty-some Valiard-born trows were permanently excused from the lottery back in 1821, for cultural preservation. Not sure how many of those are even still alive; Solly handles the census data and he's rubbish at it. I do know a few of them fought the decision. Angevin sends in a request for a lottery spot every year, but they've never let him do it."

Ivy sat up straighter in her seat. "Someone's willing to take the kingship?" Ivy asked. She'd never heard of anyone volunteering for the position before—at least, not counting Larch, who'd shirked the kingship's only duty for over seventy years beforehand.

"He might be, but no one else is willing to give it to him," said Hunzu glumly. "Back when Valiard fell—it was his door everyone used to get out. Was supposed to be his first mission as a scout. When the city burned, he used the door as an escape route instead, and all the survivors ended up in County Clare in 1688. No one could have gotten out if it wasn't for him. Makes him a bit of a war hero. Whatever Angevin had to do to hold the door open, they say he wasn't the same afterward."

If 'wasn't the same afterward' was a polite way to say that Angevin was a few monkeys short of a circus, Ivy had to agree. Looking warily at her purse, Ivy gingerly set it next to her feet. Now that it was out of its box, the Taser was small enough to almost blend in with the rest of the bric-a-brac rattling around the bottom. Maybe that would make it easier to pretend it wasn't there.

"Thank you, by the way," Ivy said quietly, rubbing at the bruise on her neck.

"I hope you won't need it," Hunzu replied, not taking his eyes off the road. "But I think we've all given up hoping the monsters won't come back."

◆◆◆

IT WASN'T QUITE full dark when the Citroen crested the top of the hill at the end of Haven's long driveway. As the headlights reflected off the open gate, Ivy looked out the window in surprise. Half a dozen cars were parked haphazardly along the edges of the turning circle, with more visible as a line of glimmering taillights bordering the track to the stables. The windows in the house itself were blazing, lights shining from what seemed like every turret and gable.

Ivy glanced nervously at Hunzu as he inched the Citroen to the edge of the drive and cut the engine.

"I didn't think there'd be this many people," she said quietly.

"That's life in the enclave for you," Hunzu said, pocketing the keys. "Anyone hears a choice bit of news, and twelve hours later everyone knows."

"Right," said Ivy, slipping her purse over her shoulder as she climbed out of the car. Even though the Taser wasn't heavy, the purse felt unpleasantly bulkier with the thing sitting at the bottom. For a moment, Ivy wanted nothing more than to shove it under the Citroen's passenger seat and leave it there. Instead, Ivy slammed the door and started up the turning circle to the house.

Hunzu followed her, staying his usual few steps away. A group of smokers were clustered around a small gazebo near the gate, their conversation blending with the churring of a blackbird somewhere in the bushes beyond. The presence of hair colors other than brown immediately marked the group as humans; Ivy vaguely recognized one of them from the Roinn offices in the Liberties. She nodded briefly, wondering how many trows had come here and what exactly they were planning to do.

Leaves from the lilies and irises brushed against Ivy's calves as she turned off the gravel drive and onto the narrower path to the house. A handful of low lights illuminated the luxuriant garden surrounding the house and glinted off the large sundial standing where two of the gravel paths intersected. Ivy remembered the inscription below it from her first visit to the house: *One hour alone is in thy hands—the NOW on which the shadow stands.*

Ahead, the porch light illuminated an oversized wooden door with a stained-glass transom above it, the design filled with oversized kaleidoscopic butterfly wings. Changelings, which the trows depicted as butterflies, seemed to hold a particular pride of place at Haven, all of them looking as menacing and unsettling as aliens recently hatched from a chrysalis.

The front door swung open, and a familiar figure in a green vest walked out. Ivy abruptly stopped at the sundial and swallowed hard. The first and only time they'd met, the thane had tried to poison her as carelessly as Roberta set out bait stations for the rats in the Blue Parrot's basement.

"The suggestion of the couplet," Taye Carillon said, nodding at the sundial. "Is that through the whole span of eternity, the only moment in which one can act is the moment one finds oneself in. Which is both profound and depressingly prosaic."

Carillon's expression, or what little Ivy could see of it, could have been equally suited to offering a cup of tea, or a dagger in the back.

Ivy swallowed hard, composing her face to a bland mask. "I suppose all the best poems are," she said breathily, clutching the straps of her purse. Before she could stumble through any other pleasantries, Demi hurried through the half-open door, and Ivy felt the knot in her stomach unwind several inches.

"Ivy," Demi called as she brushed past Carillon. Demi stopped a few feet away, looking as though she was debating coming closer, her braids falling across her shoulders as she peered at Ivy's neck. She was dressed uncharacteristically nicely for someone whose wardrobe skewed heavily toward sweatpants and pajama tops, wearing slacks and a grey vest over an ivory shirt that looked to have been starched within an inch of its life. "Did anything else happen? Is Lauren's dog alright? Is *that* what it did to your neck?"

"Everything was quiet after," said Ivy, fingering the bruise on her neck uncomfortably. "Grinch is still at the vet. Lauren thinks they're going to let him go home tomorrow."

"Do join us inside whenever you're ready, Ms. Gallagher," Carillon said, inclining her head in the tiniest possible nod before turning and stalking back into the house, her boots tapping against the flagstones.

"Everyone's been waiting," Demi said apologetically, nodding at Carillon's retreating back and playing with hem of her vest. "And don't look so intimidated. Taye's very by-the-book, but she's honest. If she says she won't hurt you, she won't. At least, not in front of this many people," she added, gesturing at the cars lining both sides of the drive.

"So why does Carillon want *me* here?" Ivy hissed, following Demi to the door and belatedly pulling a pair of gloves out of her purse. According to Ambrose, it was more a courtesy than any real attempt at preventing disease transmission, but Ivy didn't want to start things off with Carillon by being rude.

"She wants to hear what happened last night, and not

secondhand," Demi replied. "A good many others do, too. More than I thought would turn up," she added, sounding apologetic.

Ivy followed Demi through the door, aware of Hunzu trailing her at his usual six-foot distance. Voices were echoing from farther inside the house as Ivy walked through the entryway past more stained-glass butterflies. The long wood-paneled hallway ahead was dotted with doors, most half-open, where conversations overlapped and jumbled together. Even though it was late, Ivy was struck by how crowded the house seemed compared to her previous visit, everything full of light and voices and noise.

The crowd probably ruled out any possibility of speaking to Demi privately long enough to discuss their *other* problem of the wing disappearing from the NIC. Hopefully Ambrose had already filled her in.

Demi turned down another corridor, set not quite at a right angle to the first. Demi'd mentioned once that Haven was designed around a series of hexagons, a sturdier and more defensible shape than squares or rectangles. *Something we kept from Valiard*, she'd said. Ivy had never asked what in Valiard was so dangerous that they took to building fortresses in place of houses and wasn't sure she wanted to know.

Now that she knew Valiard was Earth's very distant future, Ivy was even less sure she wanted to know.

Demi stopped in front of a large door halfway down the corridor.

"You'll need to wait until they're out of closed session," Demi told Hunzu brusquely, the first she'd addressed him since they'd arrived. Hunzu shrugged, looking disappointed but not surprised. Ivy had no idea whether the two of them had always been so irritated with each other, or if that had only happened after Demi decided Hunzu would make a better backup murder victim than Ambrose.

Demi reached for the door, hesitated, then dove into her purse and pulled out something round, heavy, and metallic. Surprised, Ivy watched as Demi settled the tarnished crown on her head. The bright light of the corridor made the thing appear even more blackened and tawdry than the last time Ivy had seen it, and Ivy abruptly realized why Demi had bothered with posh clothes. Whatever was going on here, Demi was apparently attending in her official capacity as king.

Lifting her chin, Demi grabbed the door and wrenched it open. Ivy hurried in after her, feeling her stomach lurch when she saw how many people there were.

The room was large and might have seated twenty people comfortably. Perhaps twice that many trows were packed inside. Most were sitting in chairs around a long table, its worn surface covered with books, teacups, notepads, laptops, skeins of yarn, soda cans, and phones. Other trows were standing against the wall, or pacing around the edges of the tables, or leaning over the shoulders of the trows who were seated. Everyone was gesticulating and talking over each other, as though Ivy had walked into the middle of a lengthy and contentious meeting. Every conversation spluttered to a halt when Ivy stepped into the room.

A sea of faces turned toward Ivy, double and triple copies of the same noses and eyebrows, the same brown skin tones and luxuriant chestnut hair. Ivy swallowed, trying to look unruffled, as if she walked into shadowy staterooms filled with mildly contagious invisible people every day. Which she did, if she counted the Roinn, though they tended to manage their infrequent group meetings via video calls.

"Ivy," a voice called out cheerily. A familiar man in a yellow jumper stood up with a clatter, causing a thick skein of green yarn to go rolling across the long table. Ignoring the yarn, Angevin smiled and pulled out the chair beside him, the wooden feet squealing loudly in the silence of the room. His smile tugged awkwardly at one of the larger burn scars on his cheek as he gestured Ivy toward the chair with a flourish of knitting needles.

"Lovely to see you again," he added, with more warmth than Ivy expected given she'd barely exchanged a dozen words with the fellow.

Maybe he was being overly polite to make up for everyone else staring. With his scarred face, Angevin probably knew exactly how it felt to be scrutinized. Ivy hurried to the chair and slid into it.

Angevin dropped happily into the seat beside her, pushing a pile of books out of the way as he began rewinding the skein of yarn. On Ivy's other side, an unfamiliar trow in a blue jacket hastily scooted her own chair a few inches back. Ivy tried not to notice, setting her gloved hands on the table next to Angevin's books. Most of the trows were dressed much more formally than anyone ever did at the Roinn. Besides Demi, Angevin, and Carillon, Ivy saw no one else she recognized. She shifted uncomfortably in her chair, wishing she was wearing anything other than her Blue Parrot polo shirt.

"You didn't tell us she was a sport," a man in a pea-green suit said abruptly, resting his elbows on the table and giving Carillon an unfriendly look. Ivy narrowed her eyes, trying to figure out if she'd just been insulted.

"Please forgive my colleague's lack of tact," Carillon said loudly, cutting off Demi, who had started to say something. "I hope it wasn't a tiring drive."

"No," said Ivy quietly, finding that looking at Angevin's pile of books was easier than meeting Carillon's eye. George Orwell's *Animal Farm* and a yellowing paperback titled *Keep the Aspidistra Flying* lay on top of *Essential Mathematics for Quantum Computing*. Even the tuxedoed pig on the cover of

Animal Farm looked better dressed than she was. "The drive was fine."

Carillon nodded. "If we are quite finished with any off-the-record commentary, we may as well start the session," she said, glaring at the man in the pea-green suit. "Cassion, would you please take the roll?"

A man bent over a laptop a few seats down from Angevin nodded. "Lily?" he called.

"Present," replied a voice from the back row of the room, and Ivy caught a momentary glimpse of a willowy-looking woman in a pleated skirt.

"Tyree?"

A fellow across from Ivy raised his hand.

Ivy tried to keep track of the names, but quickly gave up after the first few. No few of the trows were named after plants, with the remainder seemingly split between traditional Irish names and completely unfamiliar ones. Partway through, Ivy noticed Demi slip out of her chair, heading for the man who'd called Ivy a sport. She bent over his chair and hissed something, a ferocious expression on her face.

Beside her, Angevin leaned closer, shoving his knitting needles into the skein of yarn.

"The feature Eithne was rather rudely commenting on," he said quietly, leaning closer to Ivy, "is that you appear to have a genetic advantage, shall we say, which allows you to more easily see through our veils. An advantage, I might add, that is shared by many of the best agents the Roinn has ever produced. Though Taye's quite right, it was tactless of him to mention it."

Ivy frowned. It was the first time anyone had suggested that her immunity to the veil was due to anything other than overexposure, first in the form of her mother's boyfriend, Larch, and later from Demi herself. She'd have to ask Demi or Hunzu what exactly it meant.

At the end of the roll call, Carillon paused and looked at Ivy. Ivy fought the urge to shrink deeper into her chair.

"Ms. Gallagher, could you please recount for the council the events you witnessed last night?"

Ivy swallowed, glancing at Demi. Her friend gave her a tight, close-lipped smile. Beside her, Angevin had gone back to his knitting, the needles clicking quietly along the edges of a thick green scarf.

"I woke up last night and someone was in my room," Ivy said, keeping her eyes on Demi and trying to block out everyone else. "I ran out into the hall. I don't think she realized I could see her until later—"

"Recounting a bloody nightmare," the man on the other side of Angevin muttered. Ivy hesitated, feeling her face turning red.

Carillon opened her mouth, but before she could say anything Demi's chair screeched across the floor as she got to her feet.

"If it is, as you say, merely a nightmare," Demi said, her voice pitched to carry to the rafters. "I still have the right to petition your attention in listening to it."

For an awkward moment, no one said a word. No one was quite meeting her eye, and Ivy understood why Demi had chosen to bring her crown. Ivy couldn't imagine anyone wanting to get into a public argument with a woman who was slated to die in seven months.

Carillon sighed, also pitched loud enough to carry. "If there's no further commentary?" she asked icily, rubbing at the bridge of her nose as though trying to ward off an incipient headache. The room was silent apart from the clacking of Angevin's knitting needles. "Might I suggest we save any additional interruptions until after Ms. Gallagher has spoken?"

Slowly, Demi sat back down. Her face was pale, the blackened circlet atop her head looked heavy and uncomfortable. Under the table, something nudged her foot; Ivy was halfway out of her chair until she realized it was Angevin.

"Go on, then," the trow breathed encouragingly, nodding at the gathering.

Ivy took a deep breath and started again.

"I wanted to believe it was a nightmare, too," said Ivy. She spoke louder, trying to match Demi's volume and confidence as best she could. They had no right to mock her when they hadn't been there themselves. They had no right to mock Demi for thinking what happened was serious enough that people should know about it. "But I took a hammer from the kitchen before I went back to my room. The hammer didn't help."

Ivy told them about getting injected in the neck. She told them what the woman was wearing, a ripple of surprised mutters flickering across the room as Ivy described the woman's jumpsuit, and the wing computer on her arm, and what she was doing with Ivy's phone.

"Do you believe the intruder you saw was the Enemy itself?"

The speaker was standing in the far corner a few paces behind Demi. Ivy's eyes widened as she looked at him, taking in the greying fringe of hair, the wrinkles around his eyes and the corners of his lips. It was as though Uncle Patrick had walked into the room from one of her mother's old photographs. Ivy swallowed. She'd known there were other trows who had caught humans' propensity to age; this was the first one besides Larch that Ivy had ever seen.

Seeing her hesitation, the man frowned at her, and the symmetry broke. Uncle Patrick had never looked at Ivy with that sort of disdainful glare.

Ivy looked down at the table, locking eyes with the tuxedoed pig and firmly putting Uncle Patrick out of her mind. "I thought she might have been, until she burned in the street. Whoever she was, I think the Enemy killed her."

The room immediately broke out into a wave of murmurs, some shocked, some disbelieving, everyone turning to their neighbors, chairs scraping against the floorboards.

Beside her, Angevin carried on with his knitting needles, the unvarying taps as even as a metronome.

"What we need to determine is whether this 'apparition' is connected to Valiard," said the trow with the wrinkles, raising his voice enough to be heard over the noise.

"Emerson, it's unlikely she'd know enough to—"

"It costs us little enough to ask her," Emerson retorted, scowling this time at the woman beside him. "If I may?"

Carillon inclined her head and Emerson turned back to Ivy as the murmurs subsided. "Ms. Gallagher," Emerson said, his voice quieter, as though he were attempting to be polite, "do you know where the Enemy is thought to originate?"

"From Valiard," Ivy said simply. It probably wasn't a good idea to bring up the fact that Hunzu had just told her Valiard was a different name for a future messed-up Earth. Given the unorthodox way Ivy had been recruited into the Roinn, there were definitely a few things about trows she wasn't supposed to know, even as an agent, and she was willing to bet this was also on that list. "The place you both came from," she added, biting her lip. "I didn't think anyone else went back and forth."

"They don't," said Emerson's neighbor.

He shushed the woman with a glare then turned back to Ivy, smoothing the frown from his face, apparently with effort. Abruptly, Ivy wondered what happened that he'd come close enough to humans to pick up their disease of aging, and whether he felt differently about them afterward.

"Did anything else . . . odd happen last night?" he asked quietly. "Before you saw the woman? Or after she—" He halted, as if he didn't want to put a name to what happened next.

"A woman dressed like the Enemy appears in my flat, drugs me, hacks my phone, runs off, and burns to death in the street, and you're asking what *else* was weird?" Ivy asked, exasperated.

Cassion, the trow who'd taken the roll call, raised his hand. "Thirty-seven instances of unexplained signal interference were documented on AM and shortwave radio bands between eleven p.m. and three in the morning," he said. "Could have been more, but those were the ones the Roinn were able to verify. And the transformer that exploded two blocks from Ms. Gallagher's flat was serviced four months ago and considered in good working order."

"Even if it did come from Valiard—" the woman began.

"How would it be different?" Ivy asked, cutting her off. "If it came from Valiard, instead of coming from here?"

"Everything would be happening at once," said Angevin quietly. Ivy turned to look at him, but he was staring at the ceiling, not looking at Ivy or anyone else. "Backscatter. Things from here and there, superimposed." He hesitated, tapping his needles together as he stared off into the rafters. The tinny sound seemed lost in the large room, the pause in conversation lasting long enough that it started to feel awkward. Ivy glanced at Carillon, then at Emerson, but neither trow seemed poised to interrupt. Ivy remembered what Hunzu had said about Angevin being a war hero.

"It's like this," he said abruptly, dropping the needles and snatching at the yarn. A row of stitches popped out of the end of the scarf as he yanked it closer; Angevin seemed not to notice. "Valiard is here, on the scarf, and we're somewhere in the middle of the skein. The usual method to get between them is traveling the whole length of the yarn. Doesn't work. *Very* slow, and you can only go in one direction."

He waggled the string for emphasis. Ivy nodded, wondering why he thought you couldn't go either way you wanted, before abruptly realizing why. Angevin was talking about time travel. She sat up straighter in her chair, looking hard at the trow.

"So we shorten the distance," Angevin continued, pinching the skein and dragging a thread out of it, then yanking it to the edge of the half-finished scarf. "You merely step from one to the other and skip all the bits in the middle. The yarn's quite good for this, the bits are actually clinging together. Things from one end of the yarn get stuck on the other end by mistake. Or things arrive on the far end before they've actually left on the near one."

"That's what happens when the Enemy comes?" Ivy asked uneasily.

"Interestingly, no," said Cassion, looking up from the laptop. "We've only been able to get RF readings relatively recently, but they weren't anything like we'd expect. Which might mean the Enemy's more proficient at eliminating backscatter than we were. Or that it isn't coming from Valiard at all."

"Which is all beside the point, given that the question is regarding what appeared in Ms. Gallagher's residence last night," Carillon interjected. "I understand your visitor spoke to you, before she left?"

"She didn't leave, she died," Ivy corrected, and Carillon pursed her lips. "She didn't want to talk to me at first, and when she did, she wasn't very good with English. She was asking where I work. And I don't think she meant the pub in Oxmarten."

Even Angevin's knitting needles were silent after that.

Hesitantly, Ivy recounted the rest of the evening—how she'd turned on her stereo and the woman bolted, how Grinch ran after her and how she and Lauren chased after Grinch. How the stranger ran into the middle of the street, and how she burned.

Although many faces appeared to be listening to her intently—Angevin and Carillon among them—no few of the strangers were scowling just as openly as Emerson. Some were fidgeting, looking impatient and bored, as though they'd already decided Ivy had nothing important to tell them.

"When she burned, it looked just like what happened to— what happened in February." Ivy barely stopped herself from saying Larch Carillon's name in front of his own mother. "There wasn't anything left, not even enough to tell it was a person."

"Nightmare and a pothole," coughed someone in the far corner of the room.

This time no one jumped in to shush the commentator, though Demi's shoulders twitched.

"Or we've hit Event Two, and the Enemy's picked a side," Lily called from the far wall. "Not surprising it's chosen to back the apocalypse."

No one said anything after that, either; everyone stared at each other and at Ivy by turns. She could feel her face turning red, coupled with a sick feeling in her stomach at the way Lily had casually mentioned an apocalypse. Ivy shouldn't have come here; she should've asked Ambrose or Demi to recount what had happened; she shouldn't have expected anyone here to believe her. Probably, Ivy should just go home and resign herself to sleeping with the Taser under her pillow for a while.

"Could you please excuse us for a moment, Ms. Gallagher?" Emerson asked into the silence, though he was looking at Carillon as he said it.

Carillon nodded curtly, and Ivy got to her feet, eager to get out of the room. Whatever goal Demi and Carillon had in mind for bringing everyone out here to listen to Ivy, Ivy couldn't help but think that it had just failed spectacularly. At least the trows were letting her leave before discussing whether she was lying or deluded.

Surprisingly, Carillon rose as well, walking briskly around the table to hold open the door. Ivy nodded uneasily to the remaining trows—Angevin grinned widely and waved his knitting needles—and followed Carillon to the door. As Ivy stepped into the hallway, the thane followed, pulling the door closed with a creak of its hinges. It wasn't fast enough to muffle the outbreak of muttering that sprang up in their wake.

Ivy blinked in the brighter light of the hallway, rubbing at a prickle of sweat on the back of her neck. Though it was a relief to be out of the room, being alone with Carillon in an otherwise deserted hallway didn't feel like a major improvement.

"I apologize for the continued imposition on your time," said Carillon gravely. Her hand was still on the knob of the door, her thumb rubbing across the raised pattern on the handle. "They may have more questions later. If it runs late, we can arrange for a cot in one of the outbuildings."

Swallowing, Ivy nodded. Even when Taye Carillon was being terrifying, she was also scrupulously polite. So much for rounding up Hunzu and driving straight back to Dublin.

"You'll find a sitting room the next door down to your left," Taye continued, nodding to the hallway behind Ivy. "The fixings for tea are on the table. I thought you might prefer to brew it yourself."

"I would prefer that," said Ivy tightly, thinking about the scones the first time she came here, when she hadn't done anything but show up with an unexpected racehorse. Carillon had casually tried to turn Ivy invisible, and in return Ivy had stolen a priceless relic and murdered Carillon's son.

Not intentionally, on either count. Ambrose was the one who'd done the actual stealing, and Larch almost certainly knew what might happen when he'd come back to take the kingship that was also a death sentence. But if it hadn't been for Ivy, Larch never would have done it.

And if Ivy knew that, she was certain Carillon did as well.

"I'm sorry he's dead," Ivy said abruptly. "I'm sorry—" She broke off, grasping for something that wasn't a lie. Because if Larch had known what might happen when he came to the apple grove, Ivy had suspected it as well. Which meant Ivy couldn't say she was sorry he'd come, or that she regretted his death. "He tried to be good to my mother," she finished awkwardly. "I think she missed him. Even after everything that happened."

Slowly, Carillon nodded, her expression opaque. "Thank you," she said, her face masked by the stony politeness that she seemed to fall back on in place of any number of emotions. Her eyes met Ivy's for a moment, looking calm and unperturbed.

"I doubt Larch would wish your memories of him to be tarnished by the manner of his passing," said Carillon softly, a tight look on her face. "He was—" She stopped, the corner of her mouth turning up in what might have been a smile. "He was like every one of our kings, doomed from the moment he was chosen. If you love them, you must at least forgive them their death. I think we'd all go mad, else."

Ivy looked away. Ivy would never admit to loving Larch; he'd been an adulterous old man who'd done plenty of tarnishing to his own memory. Still, Ivy felt that Carillon had somehow placed her finger straight on the knot of anger that had lived in Ivy's stomach since the moment she'd realized who her Uncle Patrick really was. Why did *he* have to be the only

Year King who survived? And why did *Ivy* have to be the one to give up part of her family, even as wretched a member as Uncle Patrick, so Demi could spend another year waiting to be murdered?

"I'm afraid Demi will break all our hearts, very soon," Carillon murmured.

Ivy shook her head, meeting Carillon's gaze. "Forgiving Demi's death sounds like just accepting it's going to happen. I won't do that." And then, because against every precedent Carillon was actually talking to her, Ivy said, "They don't believe me. Why?"

Carillon sighed and flicked her braid behind her shoulder. "It isn't prejudice, if that's what you're thinking," she said. "Or not entirely prejudice. Believe it or not, Emerson does have some appreciation for tact."

"Then why?" Ivy repeated, crossing her arms.

"Because everyone in that room agrees with you on one point: when the Enemy's behavior changes, it's worth paying attention to. And it is very appealing to believe that the Enemy's behavior may have altered to the point that it no longer finds it necessary to kill."

"It's killed twice in five months," said Ivy flatly. "They should be more worried, not less."

Carillon glanced behind her to the closed door. "Not everyone sees it that way. Are you familiar with the term *habeus corpus*?"

Ivy nodded; she'd gathered that much from detective shows. "If you're going to arrest someone, you have to charge them with a crime."

"And in order to charge them with a crime?"

"You have to prove a crime has actually been committed."

"Precisely," said Carillon, nodding. "Objectively speaking, your version of events fails on two counts."

The trow's eyes seemed to bore into hers, as though she were challenging Ivy to find the holes in her own argument.

"What happened last night," Ivy began hesitantly. "We can't prove anyone died, because there's no body, and no one knows who she was. There's no proof it happened."

"And?" Carillon prompted.

Ivy suddenly knew what the thane was getting at; she just didn't know how she could say it in front of Carillon.

"Last February," she began, looking at the scuffed flagstones under her feet. "There wasn't a body then, either."

Larch had died instead of Demi, but he'd been missing, presumed dead, for seventy years beforehand. There were only four other people who saw Larch in the apple grove—and Ivy was the only person who'd been able to do so without relying on a screen.

Ivy wondered if Carillon herself believed what had happened in February, or if it was better to think Ivy was lying because that meant Larch hadn't died.

"That the current Year King and the head of the Roinn both confirm your version of events ought to be enough to disprove any theories to the contrary," said Carillon, brushing calmly past the reference to Larch. "However, many on the council would like to believe the Enemy is no longer a threat."

"Except that isn't true," Ivy insisted. "And by the time they realize differently, Demi will be dead."

At best, the council would keep on ignoring the Enemy, or treating it like some terrible force of nature. *What a shame that it kills people; isn't it too bad that no one can stop it?* If another scout showed up in Ivy's bedroom with a needle, they'd probably be quite happy to ignore that, too, right up until whatever apocalypse the scouts were investigating actually happened.

Carillon nodded, and for a moment Ivy saw what might have been a flash of pity in her eyes.

"Most likely, yes. I'm sorry," she said, looking away, running her hands over the sleeves of her tunic. "I believe you, if it's any consolation. And I'm glad there is someone to miss him. Someone other than me."

She turned back to the door, holding her head up with perfect school-marm posture, ready to go inside and debate, among other things, whether her son really had died by the Enemy's hand five months before. Ivy wondered if the council was more likely to believe her if Carillon backed her account. Maybe it didn't matter. Probably the council would shoo Ivy off to sleep in the stables once she'd answered all their questions and never tell her anything about what they'd decided, either way.

Or perhaps . . .

"I can prove it," Ivy said suddenly. Carillon turned around, her hand on the doorknob, looking surprised.

"Not about Larch, but what happened last night," Ivy continued. "The woman who died had a wing. It had to have come from somewhere."

Ivy hoped what she was about to say wouldn't end up implicating someone she cared about. Or implicating herself, for that matter. Queasily, she remembered some of the more descriptive passages from the book in Ambrose's office.

Carillon merely raised an eyebrow, waiting for Ivy to continue.

"You keep wings in the house," Ivy said, not quite a question.

Carillon's eyes narrowed, not quite an answer.

"Have you checked how many are still here?"

CHAPTER 5

Apart from the keypad mounted next to the jamb, the door leading to the vault looked no different from every other door in the house. The light on the pad turned green as Carillon impatiently waved a keycard in front of it. Ivy heard the whisper of the deadbolt drawing back. Carillon wrenched the door open and hurried inside; Ivy caught the handle before it closed and followed.

The light in the tiny vestibule was dim, and it looked exactly as disused as Ivy remembered—chipped rock on the floor, rusting metal brackets and patches of water damage on the ceiling. Behind her, the door shut with a clang and the air immediately felt colder. The overhead lights hummed, their steady murmur a counterpoint to the quiet slap of Carillon's boots.

Wishing again she'd brought something other than her Blue Parrot polo shirt, Ivy started down the stairs after Carillon, thankful her gloves were at least keeping her hands warm. Above her, bare bulbs protected by a thin wire cage threw jumbled shadows against the walls. Ivy felt goosebumps rising on her arms. The vault seemed just as cold as it had in

February, as though the summer warmth above couldn't touch this place, preserving it as a tiny pocket of perpetual winter.

Ahead, Carillon disappeared through an arch with a swish of her long skirt. Ivy hesitated at the bottom of the stairs, rubbing her hands on her arms. She remembered the Haven basement as the sort of room that had eyes. Yet no matter how creepy the vault was, or what sort of strange Valiard artifacts it might contain, Ivy didn't think anything down here was likely to hurt her without Carillon's permission. Which wasn't an entirely comforting notion, now that Ivy thought about it.

Biting her lip, Ivy hurried through the arch after the thane.

The main room felt cavernous after the tight corners and angles of the descending stair. Puffs of dust rose from Carillon's boots as she crossed the room, the pitted walls and rock-hewn floor patchily illuminated by bulbs dotting the conduit-covered ceiling. Carillon went straight to the nearer of the two glass cases and picked up the padlocked hasp. She undid the lock and dropped it with a clang, the noise loud against the silence and the low hum of the lights.

Cautiously, Ivy came as near as she dared, peering into the casket as Carillon opened the glass lid. She couldn't see any telltale empty space among the jumble of heat sinks and flickering displays, but she still remembered vaguely where the thing had sat before Ambrose pulled it out, the way its heat sinks jutted out between his fingers like the wings of a captive bird.

Most of the Valiard artifacts looked dead, their cases marred by rust or verdigris, their heat sinks broken or twisted. A few still managed to produce flickers of light between their heat sinks, or across their battered screens. One was flashing a string of syllabograms in Rass, the Valiard language that occasionally cropped up in the oldest parts of the Roinn's filing system. The letters slowly appeared between the heat sinks, stabilized, then fractured into static. After a few seconds, the same letters began to form again.

Out of nowhere, Ivy remembered visiting her step-mother's mum, Kathryn, in the Kiltipper rehab center after she'd broken her hip. Every time they'd come, an old man with grey hair and lost eyes was sitting in the corner of the cafeteria, rocking back and forth. All the times Ivy had visited in the three months before Grannie Kathryn was released, she'd never seen him do anything else.

Ivy wondered how long the wing had been repeating itself like that, and how long it would keep doing it, a precious and broken thing that hardly anyone knew how to use. At least the one Ambrose had taken was completely dead, so Ivy probably didn't need to worry that it had done something impossible in front of a room full of scientists before it disappeared.

Beside her, Carillon was scouring the case, her lips moving silently as if she were counting.

"One *is* missing," Carillon breathed, staring at the jumbled devices for a long minute. "Chitna. It hasn't been live in decades. And it stopped being useful decades before that. But how—"

"It still doesn't explain why the Enemy killed the woman who had it," Ivy said quickly, certain it would be better if Carillon didn't think too hard about how the wing got out of the vault in the first place. "Or why whoever took it also wanted to hack my phone."

"No," said Carillon, looking her full in the face. "It doesn't."

A tendril of guilt rippled across Ivy's stomach. One person was already dead, and if Ivy wanted to find out why, lying to someone who might be able to help was probably not the best way to start. But if Carillon found out that Ivy had helped steal the thing, even inadvertently, Ivy didn't want to consider which clauses in the Roinn's book the thane might choose to invoke.

"What is it, Ms. Gallagher?"

Carillon's voice was somewhere between a purr and a growl, her eyes flint-like and cold and utterly focused on Ivy. The moment Ivy might have breezily said, "Oh, nothing at all," passed with Ivy still fumbling for something to say.

"I don't—" Ivy started belatedly.

"If you know something about this," said Carillon in the same dangerous voice, "I would very much like to know it as well."

She leaned against the top of the glass case, crossing her arms, something predatory and possessive in her gaze.

Perhaps there was a way to pass along the most pertinent bits without admitting everything Ivy and Ambrose had done.

"The wing was taken from University College Dublin," Ivy said in a low voice. "From their Nano Imaging Centre in Belfield."

"The Universi—" Carillon broke off, looking like that was the very last thing she'd expected Ivy to say. "Did she tell you that? The woman?"

The queasy feeling in Ivy's stomach was all for the notion of nodding emphatically and abandoning this line of questioning as soon as Carillon would let her. But if Carillon did any sort of investigating at the NIC, she'd eventually come up with Ivy's contact details buried in the paperwork. Licking her lips, Ivy chose her words carefully.

"I think it would be better for both of us if you assume that's exactly how I know."

Carillon's face went still, her lips pressed together in a firm, dark line. She opened her mouth to say something—something angry, from the look of it—and Ivy cut her off.

"I came all the way out here on three hours' notice because

you asked me to," Ivy snapped, nodding back at the stairs. "You're trying to figure out how to protect people you care about. Maybe—*just* maybe—I'm trying to do the same thing!"

Carillon shut her mouth with an audible click, and for a moment there was no sound apart from the buzzing of the lights.

"Which would either be a member of the Roinn," Carillon said quietly, her eyes intent, "or a very close personal acquaintance."

It was official—Ivy was going to get one of her friends killed. Then again, if the council upstairs decided to do nothing because they believed the Enemy was no longer a threat, that was also going to get one of her friends killed when the Enemy came back in February.

Carillon turned back to the case, staring at the jumble of broken artifacts with an unreadable expression on her face.

"Larch knew how to get into this house," Ivy said in a low voice. Even after what happened in the apple grove, Larch couldn't make up for what he'd done to Ivy's family, but maybe he could even the score a little, even though he was dead. "He came here looking for you the day he died."

Something twitched at the corner of Carillon's mouth. Abruptly, she grabbed the top of the glass lid and lowered it into place, the edges sealing against the gasket with a hiss.

"My son is, in fact, the only one of your acquaintances unable to confirm or refute your claim," Carillon said softly, her fingers stroking the glass as though she were tracing the outline of one of the dead things inside. She continued in a very different voice. "Larch never troubled himself greatly with responsibilities as a young man. I never knew if that changed after he disappeared. It . . . would be regrettable if you were one of the responsibilities he neglected."

She looked up from the case, and Ivy was startled to see

something that almost looked like sympathy in Carillon's face.

"I didn't need looking after, and no, he never tried," said Ivy bluntly. Things had been fine when Larch left Ivy's family alone. Things would have been even better if he'd stayed away from Ivy's family to begin with.

"It wasn't because he didn't love you," said Carillon, and Ivy had to squelch the urge to burst out in furious objections. "If he sent you to live with your mother's husband, he probably thought the man could do a better job than he could."

"He wasn't wrong there," said Ivy, not bothering to keep the anger out of her voice, an edge of fury like the whistle of a teakettle. That particular pot had been simmering for years. It was impossible to keep some of it from spilling out, not with Carillon standing there defending him. Acting like Larch had loved her. Like Larch had ever cared.

He hadn't. Ever. Maybe he'd tried, back when it was fishing trips to Lough Leane, and walks to look at the boats along Tolka Quay. Back then, Ivy was too young to notice that Uncle Patrick only turned up when Ivy's father was away visiting his mother in Bantry, or at the head office in Leeds.

Carillon's gaze remained fixed on Ivy, looking through her and beyond her, as though the missing wing sat on one side of a balance scale, weighed against the tangle of sacrifices and abandoned obligations Larch left behind him when he took back the kingship and died with Demi's crown on his head.

To Ivy's surprise, Carillon looked away first, pulling her hand back from the glass cabinet.

"If my son did take Chitna, we can only speculate as to his reasons," she said finally. She turned back to Ivy, an ice-calm expression falling across her face like a mask. "And in removing suspicion from your associates, he has done you a *considerable* favor. Is that clear?"

"Thank you," Ivy said, nodding her head the barest fraction

of an inch, because it still didn't make up for what Larch had done. He'd been a rotten uncle, and he was proving to be much more helpful to Ivy now that he was dead than he'd ever been when he was alive. Which was a terrible thing to think about, but that didn't necessarily make it untrue.

Wordlessly, Carillon locked the case. Ivy's shoulders sagged in relief as she stepped away from the casket. Carillon knew the wing was gone, and she didn't seem likely to immediately string anyone up as a result. Which was good, given their actual problem had less to do with Ivy stealing an alien supercomputer that didn't even turn on and more to do with finding out why the Enemy killed the person who'd probably stolen it next.

Ivy turned back to Carillon—only to find herself staring at an empty corner of the room. Whirling around, she spotted the trow leaning over the second glass case, twenty feet away from where Ivy was sure she'd been standing.

God, this place was creepy. It'd be a relief to get out of the vault.

"You quite alright?" Carillon asked without turning around.

Ivy felt her face flush, an odd counterpoint to the prickling of goosebumps along her arms.

"I'm fine," Ivy said automatically. "I just—does it really not feel creepy to you, being down here?"

"Proximity to this many wings," Carillon said briskly, closing the lid on the second case and securing the lock. "The manuals mention it occasionally. Something like *between one and four meters, operators may experience a palpable feeling of growing unease.* The effect rarely persists outside of this room."

Haven's own haunted vault is what it sounded like. Her parents' house at Trails Cross had acquired that reputation back when her parents had still been married to each other. So had the museum Larch had been living in before he died. No one knew he was living there because the docents couldn't see him. When Larch had come back to Haven in February, his fellow trows couldn't see him either, until Ivy started recording him on her phone.

Five months ago, Ivy had stood in this room and hadn't seen anything, even though she was certain something was here. It had been watching from the shadows, invisible and silent but somehow perceptible. And terrifying.

Slipping her hand into her purse, Ivy felt for the edge of her mobile. As Carillon turned away from the caskets, Ivy pulled her phone out of her purse and thumbed it on. Glancing speculatively at the thane, Ivy brought up the camera function. The screen flickered, then steadied on an image of the stone floor, patches of dust, and the toes of Ivy's own white sneakers. Then the screen went dark.

"We do *attempt* to protect what's down here," Carillon said irritably. As Ivy guiltily looked up, the thane nodded at the stairs, looking more amused than angry. "Shall we?"

It wasn't a suggestion.

Nodding, Ivy turned and slid her phone back into her purse as she followed Carillon, staying a careful few feet behind.

Knowing the vault behind her was completely empty did nothing to diminish the goosebumps running up and down her neck. Or the feeling that something in the emptiness was watching her walk away. Again, Ivy wished she'd brought a jacket, silently cursing whatever Valiard programmer had decided that low-grade terror was an acceptable bug in their hardware.

As Carillon disappeared up the stairs, Ivy shuddered and glanced behind her. The empty room looked back. Ivy shivered and started to turn away.

And hesitated.

Ivy knew a little more about how veils worked than on her first visit. The veil didn't affect the real world, only people's perceptions of the world. If something strange was inside the vault, Ivy's mobile could probably see it. And the camera on Ivy's phone might still be working, regardless of whether or not Ivy could actually see the screen. She'd already put the phone in camera mode before the screen went blank.

Impulsively, Ivy snatched the phone out of her purse, aimed the blank screen straight into the middle of the empty room, and tapped the shutter button.

Ivy held the phone steady for a long second, half expecting something horrible to appear out of the void and tell her off for it. Nothing did. Sheepishly, Ivy shoved the mobile back into her purse and hurried up the stairs after Carillon, trying to stifle the feeling she'd just done something wrong.

Probably she'd just taken a blurry picture of an empty basement. Or a picture of a room that contained a few more wing-filled glass cases than Ivy was able to see on her own.

The chill subsided as Ivy reached the tiny alcove at the top of the stairs. Carillon was already rummaging in her pocket for the keycard.

"Was it an important one?" Ivy asked quietly. "Chitna, I mean?"

"Every one of them is an important one," said Carillon, sounding irritated. "They're the only things left from Valiard, other than us."

Carillon waved her keycard in front of the pad; it chirped, followed by a low hiss as the bolt slid back. "At least poor Chitna's given us something to stir up the council."

She slipped the keycard back into her pocket as she pushed open the door. The air in the corridor felt warmer and smelled slightly of wood polish. The hallway, with its slate flooring, wood-paneled walls, and cheery electric sconces, seemed to belong to an entirely different building than the cold, conduit-studded basement below.

Or maybe it only felt that way because Ivy wasn't imagining invisible monsters lurking in the corners.

Footsteps echoed down the hall, and a moment later Angevin came hurrying around the corner, cradling his books, needles, and yarn in an awkward bundle against his chest, seemingly unaware of the half-knitted scarf dragging across the floor behind him.

Hunzu followed a few feet behind and started to make a beeline for Ivy. His eyebrows twitched as he spotted Carillon and he turned away, beginning what looked like a deep and consuming inspection of the nearby wallpaper. Ivy supposed she wasn't the only person who found Carillon intimidating to talk to.

"Emerson hasn't shouted nearly as much as I expected," Angevin said as he came up to them, flicking his long hair out of his eyes. Leaning in closer, he touched Carillon's arm. "But Eithne is going to walk out in less than five minutes unless you convince him we've more to go on than hearsay."

"Eithne'll come around quickly enough," Carillon murmured, the corner of her mouth turning up as she looked at Angevin.

Dropping his hand, Angevin turned to Ivy, cheeks dimpling as he smiled at her. "Some of our kin may actually be reconsidering opinions they haven't budged from in decades. And look, I've finished the scarf!"

The jumble of books, needles, and yarn skeins tumbled to the floor as he held up the scarf, stretching it out in front of Ivy. Angevin waggled one tasseled end, oblivious to the mess on the floor. "The color suits you. I hadn't realized."

With no more warning than that, Angevin stepped close—very close—and looped a coil of the scarf around Ivy's neck.

Ivy's polite smile froze in place as she hurriedly took a step back. He wasn't wearing gloves, and Ivy didn't even let Hunzu get this close to her unless he had a very good reason.

Ivy wasn't the only one who noticed Angevin was taking liberties. Hunzu was at Ivy's shoulder a moment later, clearing his throat and visibly bristling.

"Yes, apologies," said Angevin, who didn't look apologetic in the slightest. He dropped the rest of the scarf, leaving the free end dangling somewhere around the level of Ivy's knees, and stepped back. "Brings out your eyes."

"I really don't think—" Ivy started to pull the thing off her neck and Hunzu not-so-subtly kicked her in the shin. She remembered what he'd said about Angevin being a war hero. "It's lovely," Ivy said instead, and Angevin's smile blossomed into a grin, the burn marks on his cheeks twisting into new and unsettling configurations.

"I was cold earlier," she added, grabbing the dangling end and looping it loosely around her neck. "Thank you."

Beside her, Carillon was smiling as well. It looked nothing like the calculating expression she usually wore when she was pleased.

"We should be getting back," the thane said in the gentlest voice Ivy had ever heard her use, as she put her hand lightly on Angevin's shoulder.

"Right. Of course. Certainly," Angevin said as though he'd momentarily forgotten about the council, and crouched down to gather up the books and scattered yarn.

Hunzu joined him on the floor, wrapping up the dangling ends of the skein as he handed it back to Angevin.

"We may have more questions for you later," Carillon told Ivy. "I've no idea how long they're going to keep at it—"

"Close to an hour," muttered Angevin.

"—but if the issue becomes one of theft, it seems whoever

ended up with Chitna is beyond our ability to question. Pity. Might have settled our justice and the Enemy's at the same time."

With that, Carillon turned back down the hall, Angevin and the yarn following in her wake.

As Ivy watched them go, something in the pit of her stomach marginally relaxed. For the first time since she'd set foot inside the house, Ivy wasn't facing an inquisition. Or Carillon, which was more or less the same thing. There would probably be more questions later, but for now, maybe Ivy could sit down long enough to drink a cup of tea without having to worry that the wrong words out of her mouth were going to get someone killed.

Ivy tugged at the edge of the scarf, pulling it away from her throat. The yarn felt like some sort of chenille, softer than she'd expected. At least it wasn't as itchy as the socks her step-mum used to knit for Ivy and the twins.

"Might be kinder to leave it on," Hunzu murmured, nodding at the scarf. "If you're not sweltering, that is."

"No, it's fine," said Ivy, dropping her hand. "Does he always— I mean, is he—"

Hunzu interrupted her, sparing her from finding a polite way to ask her question.

"He's like that most of the time," Hunzu said, falling into step a few paces away as they headed down the hall. "Like he doesn't always know what's happening, or when."

"I gathered that," said Ivy, nodding. She remembered what Hunzu said in the car, that Angevin was willing enter the lottery but no one else would let him do it. Ivy was starting to understand why.

The hallway bent again, another not-quite-perpendicular angle, as they passed the bottom of the main stair. The skylight at the top was dark, the glass panes looking down on a thick tangle of flowers and shrubs spilling out of terra-cotta pots clustered at the bottom of the stairs.

"I suppose everyone feels a little guilty," Hunzu said quietly, ducking his head. "He took the worst of it, somehow, when everyone got out."

"Was that when—" Ivy broke off, gesturing awkwardly at her own face. She'd always assumed they were burn scars, but she'd never been rude enough to ask.

"That and everything else," said Hunzu, sighing.

Passing the garden at the bottom of the stairs, they turned into another hallway. Hunzu stopped at the second door and opened it.

Overstuffed furnishings and spindly wooden tables were scattered about the room, some bearing photographs or curios. By the far wall, a tea set and an electric kettle sat on a tray. The heavy curtains across the windows and the threadbare tapestries lining the walls made the room feel smaller and darker than it actually was. Ivy was relieved to see that the table was absolutely devoid of food.

Ivy pulled Angevin's scarf a little tighter around her neck, wishing again she'd brought a warmer shirt. Or that there actually was a fire in the small fireplace. From the ash in the grate, and an elaborate set of tongs and pokers on the stand nearby, the thing looked like it was still occasionally used.

Ivy dropped her purse onto one of the chairs and drifted closer to the tea tray, flicking through the array of sachets, all bearing fancy floral names written in an even fancier font. It hardly seemed possible that less than twenty-four hours ago everything had still been normal. Or at least, as normal as her life ever got, between her friendship with Demi, her pub quiz nights with Hunzu, and her side jobs for the Roinn.

Ivy grabbed something that looked strongly caffeinated and dropped it into one of the teacups. The tea set looked delicate, like the sort of cups that spend most of their time gracing the higher shelves of a china hutch. It should have felt like a nice gesture; what it actually felt like was a confirmation that Ivy was completely and eternally an outsider.

Not even a proper outsider, Ivy thought, thinking of the human agents smoking by the gazebo as she'd arrived. If she'd been a usual Roinn agent, she'd probably be off with the other drivers, trying to scrape together enough cell signal to ring for takeaway.

If she'd been a usual Roinn agent, maybe someone wouldn't have broken into her flat and drugged her.

As the water in the electric kettle began to hiss, Ivy flicked it off and filled her cup. The steam smelled like bergamot, blending with the wood-polish scent that permeated the house.

"Didn't know they'd be at it all night," Ivy murmured apologetically to Hunzu. She picked up a tiny spoon and stirred in a packet of sugar.

"Two of my aunties were on the council," he replied, examining the tapestry in front of him: a pair of red-eyed butterflies perched on a flower, the color of its petals faded to an indeterminate grey. "They do tend to yammer on."

As Ivy took her cup and went back to her chair, Hunzu crossed to the tea set, keeping the sofa between them, smoothly enough that Ivy almost didn't notice how deliberately he'd done it. Circling the furniture, as usual. Never exactly beside her, always keeping far enough away that conversational distance felt awkward—as though Ivy ought to be two steps closer, or constantly be raising her voice.

Ivy shoved her purse next to the armrest and sat down, tucking the dangling ends of the scarf out of the way. She listened to the rattling and tapping of the ridiculously elaborate china as Hunzu made himself tea.

If any of Ivy's friends had a weekly standing date with a

nice single fellow, Ivy would've assumed they were dating. In fact, if Hunzu hadn't been completely and categorically off-limits relationship-wise, *Ivy* would have assumed they were dating. They weren't. Any romantic notions of love conquering all was so much sugar-coated claptrap, covering up the unpleasant truth that sometimes people could like each other very well and the best thing to do was walk away and not ever see each other again. It was what Ivy's mother should have done. And there was no way Ivy could possibly consider the situation that didn't bring her to the inescapable conclusion that Hunzu was precisely the same sort of mistake.

A mistake she was not making, not now and not ever. They showed up for each other for pub quiz nights and life-or-death situations. They weren't a couple, and never would be, and even if Ivy ever changed her mind about that, Hunzu almost certainly had his own reservations about dating someone who could pass along a fatal disease.

Ivy pulled the tea sachet out of her cup, set it on the edge of the saucer, and took a sip. It tasted even more orangey than it smelled, and Ivy regretted not adding the whole packet of sugar after all. She cradled the cup in her hands, the china almost too warm to hold, feeling if she let herself relax into the chair she would probably fall asleep immediately.

Just as Hunzu moved to join her, the door to the hallway swung open with a bang.

Ivy jumped, sloshing half the hot tea over her fingers as Ambrose stormed into the room wearing the blackest expression Ivy had ever seen. Ivy hastily put down her cup and jumped to her feet, rubbing her scalded fingers on Angevin's scarf. Demi followed a step behind Ambrose, also looking worried, and Ivy belatedly realized what was wrong.

"If I'd known your council would tell me I was delusional to my face, maybe we could have discussed how to bring up what the dead woman was wearing on her arm," Ivy snapped as soon as the door had closed, and before Ambrose could start bellowing at her.

Ambrose snapped his mouth shut, visibly swallowing whatever he'd been about to say. Beside him, Demi put a hand on his arm, her face carefully emotionless. Ivy bit her lip. Demi might be Ivy's friend, but Ivy had a suspicion Demi wouldn't intervene on Ivy's behalf for anything short of bloodshed. Hunzu, for his part, was standing next to the tea table, looking like he was trying to blend in with the wall.

"Do you have any idea what the penalty would be if the thief were identified?" Ambrose asked in an icy voice.

"I did skim that book in your office before I signed my name," Ivy snapped. "So yes, I have a general idea. But no one in that room believed a single thing I said. Maybe now they will. Carillon does, at least."

"They don't think you're lying," Demi said gently.

"No, they just think I'm crazy," said Ivy, crossing her arms and rubbing at her fingers, still smarting from the hot tea. "I'm not lying about what happened last night, and I'm not going to lie about the wing, either. Not if it's connected to why that woman died."

"That woman died because the Enemy likes killing us, and you are very close to moving certain people to the top of its list," Ambrose snapped.

"Hush," said Demi, rounding on her partner. "*I* am next on the list and that is *not Ivy's fault*. I could have pushed for another lottery. I didn't. We'll see what the Enemy thinks of that soon enough. And you can't expect her to lie about something this important."

"She's an agent of the Roinn," Ambrose muttered, looking at his feet. "We ask them to lie all the time."

"What did they say in there?" Hunzu asked tentatively, still looking like he was considering hiding behind the nearest wall hanging. "When Carillon told them it was gone?"

"Mostly a lot of shouting and talking over each other," Demi said, shrugging. "Taye regained the floor long enough to suggest we reconvene in the morning. Which was fine as far as getting everyone to stop yelling over each other, but eight hours of chatting up and down the hallways isn't going to do anything to dispel rumors."

"Rumors about what?" Ivy asked.

"About whether the woman in your flat was a scout sent from Valiard," Ambrose said grimly.

"I thought you'd be happy to hear the place still exists," Ivy said.

"For sentimental reasons, perhaps—but for practical purposes, I for one would be just as happy to never hear from Valiard, ever. Their doors . . . They were studying a particular disaster, something I'd prefer not to experience in my lifetime. The thing they called Event Two."

Lily had also mentioned Event Two, back in the council room, and everyone had gone very quiet after that.

"Hunzu said Event Two was something that already happened to Valiard, but it hasn't happened to us yet. It's still in the future."

Ambrose shot an annoyed look at Hunzu, who shrugged and threw up his hands. Ivy wondered how long Ambrose would have dawdled about sharing that particular piece of information if Hunzu hadn't already told her.

"Our future isn't necessarily the same thing as Valiard's past," said Demi quietly. "We're pretty sure we're already changing things just by being here. We've probably been changing them since 1688. Hopefully we're changing them enough to throw us off Valiard's timeline entirely."

"Or not," Hunzu put in glumly. "That's one theory about

why the Enemy exists, that it's actually some sort of changeling." He gestured to the red-eyed butterflies on the transom over Demi's head. "Kill enough of us, keep our population down, we never make a big enough impact to alter anything, and Event Two happens right on schedule."

"Changelings have never been proven to exist," said Ambrose huffily as he turned to the tea table. "Also, one scout arriving here doesn't necessarily mean anything. She could have missed her mark. She might not have been aiming for this year at all, or even this century."

"She didn't just show up somewhere at random, she came to *my flat*," Ivy pointed out, standing up because it was too much to sit in an uncomfortable chair in a vaguely creepy house while discussing doors to Armageddon. Ivy thought of Angevin's skein of yarn, tangled and looped and inextricably connected. "How much farther along are we talking about? And is the apocalypse they were studying closer to our end, or theirs?"

"Probably closer to our end, but we didn't know that for sure until last night," Hunzu said apologetically.

"Not as though we know for sure now, either." Ambrose put in from the other side of the room.

"I feel like I need a primer on what you do know for sure," Ivy said, because sniping at Hunzu was a better option than cowering under a blanket or driving back to Dublin and cowering under a bomb shelter. Ambrose turned around, looking like he was going to object, and Ivy snapped, "My flat, remember?"

She turned back to Demi. "Just tell me what's going on."

"Okay, Event Two," Demi said, dropping into her chair and pushing her hair back from her face. "We don't know what caused it, we just know the results: humans, plants, and things like breathable air on one side, trows and a lot of big mushrooms on the other. We know it didn't happen all at once. It was gradual, but we don't know how long it took, or what the tipping point was. We know Valiard was studying it. We don't know their conclusions, or what they planned to do with that information once the study was complete."

A future civilization with an interest in apocalypses had also taken an interest in Ivy's phone. The room felt too hot and too cold all at once; her tea seemed to congeal in her stomach.

"Which means if the scout was looking for you, she was probably looking for us," Ambrose confirmed with a sigh.

"You see why some of the council would prefer to think you were dreaming," said Demi gently, taking a step closer and reaching out as though she might touch Ivy's shoulder before thinking better of it.

Mutely, Ivy nodded.

A beam of light shone across the window, accompanied by the crunch of tires on gravel. Apparently at least one of Carillon's guests had decided not to stick around for further discussion. Another murder that no one could explain, and maybe weren't even trying to understand. Chalk it all up to mysterious and terrible things from an impossibly far-off place that could never be called to account for their actions. Uncomfortably, Ivy remembered Angevin holding the skein of yarn between his fingers. A single thread connected Earth to Valiard, with an apocalypse waiting somewhere in the middle.

"So Valiard can send anything they want over here, is that it?" Ivy muttered. "Everything from their side is murder and disaster, and they're never around except when things go wrong, and no one really knows what they're doing or why. Have I got that about right?"

"It's not for lack of trying," Ambrose said testily. "The fact that this many people are here in the middle of the night on twelve hours' notice should prove we're trying." He folded his arms, glancing uneasily at Demi. "I just . . . I don't expect any decision the council makes will get us any closer to figuring out what it wants. Valiard, or the scouts it sends, or the Enemy, or any of it."

"How many of the original Valiard refugees are still alive?" Ivy asked darkly. "If this was a true crime show, one of them would turn out to be a serial killer. Just saying," she said, holding up her hands as Ambrose frowned.

"Don't be rude," he muttered, skirting around Ivy and heading to the tea set.

Demi gave Ivy a sympathetic look.

"He's worried for you, too," she said, leaning closer and trying to whisper. "Last night wasn't like anything that's happened before. I think everyone here is hoping it doesn't happen again."

Ivy started to nod, then hesitated.

"Things like what happened last night," Ivy said tentatively. "Maybe that's the only way we'll ever figure out anything about the Enemy, by trying to understand the things that are different. The bits that don't make sense."

"None of it makes sense," Demi murmured, and abruptly turned away to join Ambrose at the tea tray, not before Ivy caught her calm expression starting to unravel. Forgoing the tea, Demi went to the fireplace, looking over the pictures on the mantel as she rubbed at her face.

Ivy looked away. She remembered how Demi had looked on the day she was supposed to die, and Ivy never wanted to see that again. Not now, and not in seven months.

She sighed and went back to her chair. Exhaustion was dragging at her limbs in a way no amount of hot tea could counteract, and Ivy still didn't know where she was going to be sleeping, or when. If these meetings were going to drag into tomorrow, she should probably text Lauren and let her know she wasn't going to be at the flat tonight, either. And ask how Grinch was getting on, she thought guiltily.

Ivy slipped her phone out of her purse. The camera app opened and Ivy automatically thumbed it closed. She started to pull up her messages—and hesitated.

She had never actually stopped to check the picture she'd taken of the vault. Biting her lip, Ivy flipped back to the camera and swiped to the most recent picture.

Disappointingly, most of the picture was floor, and what wasn't floor was badly out of focus. Off to the left Ivy could make out the edge of one of the glass cases, sitting like a coffin in a mausoleum. And on the right . . .

"Demi, look at this," Ivy said suddenly. Something in her tone was sharper than she intended, and Demi immediately hurried over. Hunzu followed as well, coming up behind Ivy's chair and leaning in closer than he usually allowed himself.

The floor on the righthand side wasn't empty. Ivy switched her phone to her left hand as she peered at the screen. Her fingertips felt uncomfortably warm; maybe the burn from the hot tea was bad enough to need ice.

"It's from downstairs," Ivy said by way of explanation. She wrinkled her nose; the smell of wood polish seemed to be getting stronger. "I couldn't see the screen on my camera, but I tried to take a photo anyway, and it worked. Sort of."

Ambrose, who had started to come over, stopped and rolled his eyes. "Are you this much of a security disaster at your other job?" he asked pointedly, and turned back to the tea tray.

On the right side of the frame, a tall, vertical shape rose from the floor, out of focus and pixelated but visible all the same. It wasn't rectangular like the glass cases. It didn't seem to be any sort of geometric shape at all, instead looking curved, uneven, and studded with fins.

A breath of the vault's ever-present chill crept up Ivy's shoulders and under Angevin's scarf. Ivy had the strange sensation that even if she were seeing it clearly, it might not be a shape that made any sort of geometric sense. Maybe she was better off seeing it through a screen, where the camera's lens forced a rationality onto its appearance that might be absent entirely if Ivy looked at it straight on.

"What do you think it is?" Hunzu asked.

"That bit in the middle looks like the heat sinks on the wings," said Demi, as Ivy switched her phone back to her right hand, rubbing her fingers on her trousers. Either she really had scalded herself with the tea, or her phone had picked up another virus. It was definitely running hotter than normal.

"So what's it doing that far off the floor?" asked Ivy, rubbing at her nose as she stared at the screen. Whatever cleaning solution they used at Haven, the janitor ought to consider a weaker dilution. "Or else it's— Oh, come on!"

An error message popped up as the rest of the screen went black. *Your phone is overheating and is automatically closing this program to avoid damage.*

"Damn it," Ivy muttered. It wasn't like she was playing six different movies, or a bunch of video calls. She switched the phone back to her left hand—and dropped it with a yelp.

The phone hit the floor with a thud and Ivy jumped to her feet. Cracks spread across the dead screen. A rivulet of smoke wafted from the edge of the case, quickly turning into a torrent; the wood-polish smell was suddenly overpowering. Hunzu and Demi jumped back as well. Ambrose snatched the electric kettle off the table, sending two teacups tumbling to shatter on the floor. He hurried over and upended the kettle over the phone. A few drops of scalding water splattered painfully against Ivy's legs as a hissing cloud of steam rose from the remnants of Ivy's mobile.

For a moment, no one said anything. Cautiously, Ivy knelt, wafting away the dissipating smoke to stare disbelievingly at what was left of her phone. Ambrose slowly stepped back, still holding the mostly empty kettle as though he half-expected the mobile to ignite again.

"Did you know that would happen?" Ivy asked, looking from him to Demi.

Demi shook her head, still staring at the phone. Ambrose echoed the motion a moment later. "I don't think anyone's ever tried that before," he said.

Even if no one had tried it, someone had apparently planned for the possibility. And the smoldering lump that used to be Ivy's mobile was their idea of a contingency plan.

Ivy grabbed the teaspoon from her saucer, apprehensively poking the phone with it. The plastic seemed to give a little, as though it had gotten hot enough to partially melt. Frowning, Ivy flipped it over. On the back was a gash like a claw mark, revealing a jumble of charred innards and bits of metal flaking off like ash. Below it Ivy could see a black mark on the floor, as though the phone had gotten hot enough to sear the varnish.

"Little overdone for a do not disturb sign," said Hunzu mildly.

Ivy wasn't thinking about do not disturb signs. The little pile of ash and the acrid smell were all too close to last night in the street. Ivy looked away, feeling her stomach lurch as she tried not to think about the ash, or the burning smell, or the screams, or how the man with the red hair had been whimpering as they'd bundled him into the ambulance.

Setting the kettle down, Ambrose prodded the phone with his shoe, then bent over and tapped it with his gloved hand. Apparently finding it cool enough to touch, he picked it up, carrying it gingerly to the rubbish bin as though he were disposing of a dead mouse.

"It makes sense there's things in the house Taye wants protected," said Demi apologetically.

"But what?" Ivy asked, crossing her arms. "It's not that big a secret you keep things from Valiard here."

This time, it wasn't only a matter of altering her perceptions. Whatever brand of trow magic was responsible, it had completely destroyed her phone.

"You could try asking Carillon," said Hunzu sarcastically.

"Right," said Ivy. If this was the reaction that just trying to photograph the basement had summoned up, Ivy really didn't want to find out what might happen if she confronted Carillon about it directly. So far, nothing Ivy had done tonight had gotten anyone poisoned, though Ivy was certain the idea must have crossed Carillon's mind. Possibly more than once.

"And it could have exploded in my hand. Or yours," she added, looking at Demi. "Are all your secrets as dangerous as that?"

She hadn't meant it seriously, but Demi's face grew solemn. "Maybe they are," Demi said quietly. "Everything to do with Valiard always was life and death. The scouts, and the door that got us here, and the city burning when everyone left. And the Enemy, of course. And we know so little about why any of it happens."

"Or no one's saying anything if they do," said Ambrose darkly, rummaging through the bin like he was burying the destroyed mobile under a layer of napkins and tea sachets.

From the bleak look on Demi's face, she wasn't thinking about a dead phone. It was the sort of look Ivy had sometimes glimpsed when they lived together in Howth before she'd known anything about who Demi really was. The Enemy was life and death, and it killed for reasons no one understood. Or admitted to understanding, if they even knew.

And the Enemy burned things. Always.

With a sigh, Hunzu bent down and grabbed the edge of the nearby runner, pulling it concealingly over the scorch mark on the floor. He looked appraisingly at the result, which was off-kilter but at least not suggestive of a minor explosion.

If there was something hidden in the vault, something impossible to see and dangerous to photograph, it was going to stay covered up just like the burn mark under the carpet. The suggestive image on Ivy's phone was nothing more than another bit of trow magic with the tendency to bite back. Like the circlet that had gotten her out of Haven last winter, at the cost of spur marks on her hips, hoofprints in the back garden, and a truly ferocious headache. Or the trows' invisibility itself, an insidious and ever-present danger to anyone who ever got too close to them.

She could wonder about the picture as much as she wanted, but she couldn't get back into the vault without a keycard, and it wasn't likely she'd ever be invited down there again. Or be given the opportunity to run her hands along the walls looking for a strange, shadow-casting object even if she were.

Ivy picked up her mostly empty cup of tea, took a sip, and set it back on the table. Her face felt flushed, as though the July air had finally overcome the lingering chill from the vault. She tugged at Angevin's scarf, pulling the chenille farther away from her neck. As she rearranged the loops, something small and white clattered to the floor. Still finagling with the scarf, Ivy glanced down at it.

Immediately, Ivy bent to snatch it up, fighting the urge to shove it into her pocket, or her purse, or under the cushions of the chair before anyone saw her holding it.

Hunzu was on his feet in an instant, and Demi beside him, both coming around to the back of the chair and peering over Ivy's shoulder.

From the front of the keycard, Taye Carillon's face peered back at them.

CHAPTER 6

The keycard felt warm in Ivy's hand as she passed the jungle of potted plants at the bottom of the stairs, uncomfortably aware of how loudly their footsteps echoed down the hall. Uncomfortably aware, too, that Ambrose had grabbed the poker from the set by the fireplace before they'd left the room.

A distant voice echoed from the upper levels of the house. The stained glass bordering the stairway seemed to glow, faintly lit by the security lights outside. For a moment, the butterflies didn't look like glass at all, but like real creatures watching from beyond a barrier that could shatter at any moment.

Ivy shuddered, glad to turn away from the unblinking glass eyes. Walking past them felt too much like she was being watched.

She reached the door, and with a last glance up and down the deserted hallway, pressed the keycard against the lock. The light turned green as the bolt drew back with a faint hiss. Grabbing the handle, Ivy hurried inside, stepping quickly out of the way as Demi, Hunzu, and Ambrose followed after her.

It took a moment to adjust to the dim light, but Ivy looked

back and could see Ambrose carefully easing the door shut. The latch caught, followed by a low hiss as the deadbolt re-engaged. By the light of the bare bulbs, Demi and Hunzu's faces looked sallow, with skull-like shadows lurking in the hollows beneath their eyes. Ambrose shifted uncertainly, holding the poker as if he didn't quite know what to do with it.

"Are you sure about this?" Demi asked. It was the first time anyone had said anything since they'd left the parlor. Somehow, it felt safer to be talking behind a locked door, even though Ivy could already feel a prickle along her arms, a precursor of the spirit-haunted darkness lurking at the bottom of the stairs.

"No," said Ivy, shaking her head. "I think that's why I need to look."

Slowly, Demi nodded, and Ivy wondered if she was thinking of the charred mark under the apple trees last winter.

"But if you'd rather not," Hunzu added hesitantly, peering past Demi with hunched shoulders. "You'd be in worse trouble than the rest of us, if . . ." He trailed off, swallowing uncomfortably.

If Carillon found them down here. If the *thing* in the photo didn't take well to being disturbed. If Ivy's phone wasn't the only thing it knew how to burn.

"Angevin gave *you* the keycard," Ambrose broke in, looking hard at Ivy. Ivy remembered what Hunzu said about Angevin being the closest thing they had to a war hero. He'd been a scout once, perhaps not so different from the woman last night. Ivy loosened the scarf, rubbing at the pinprick scab underneath it. Was it possible Angevin knew something about Event Two, or why the people searching for it would be coming after Ivy?

"We'll be quick," said Ivy, nodding with more confidence than she felt. She started down the stairs.

The bare bulbs snaking along the ceiling threw jumbled

shadows against the wall, a many-headed hydra descending the stairs. Ivy slid Carillon's keycard into her pocket, gripping the railing tightly as she continued down. Demi's footsteps were a quiet comfort behind her, and for once Ivy felt no hesitation at staying as close to her friends as possible.

The arch leading into the main part of the vault opened ahead of her, the light shining through like an open mouth, and Ivy felt a draft of warm air blow past her face. She shuddered, tucking her gloved hands under her armpits, wishing again she'd brought a jacket.

Looking around the room, it seemed as bare, cold, and shadow-filled as ever. Ivy wasn't sure which was more frightening—that there *was* something in the vault, or that there wasn't. This was probably nothing more than another dead end in the strange puzzle box of the Enemy and its yearly murders. Ivy pulled Angevin's scarf tighter around her neck, taking the dangling ends and looping them a few times around her upper arms. She could still feel her skin pricking with goosebumps under the cloth. The room smelled overpoweringly of dust and wood polish.

"I don't suppose anyone else wants to try with their phone?" Ivy asked.

"Not especially," Hunzu murmured from somewhere behind her.

Stepping farther into the room, Demi hesitantly pulled her phone out of her pocket and prodded the screen. She turned, panning the phone across the room, and frowned.

"It just goes dead when I try to put it in camera mode," she said, biting her lip.

"It doesn't go dead," Ivy corrected, wondering if it was even a good idea to be discussing any of this out loud. The sense of a presence in the room wasn't as strong as before, but the room still felt unsettling, as though they were being watched. "We just can't see the screen. The same way you don't literally vanish when you're around people who can't see you."

"We also don't set fire to people's phones if they do happen to catch us on camera," Ambrose pointed out sourly.

"Mistress?" someone said.

"It'd make a good party tri—" Hunzu shut his mouth abruptly as Ivy put a finger to her lips.

For a long moment, no one said anything as Ivy turned in a circle, straining for a repeat of the voice she thought she'd heard, just for a moment, as Hunzu was speaking. The only sound was the faint buzzing of the lights, and the low whirr of the fans in the glass cases.

"What'd you hear?" Hunzu hissed, stepping closer to Ambrose.

"I don't know," Ivy admitted. A breath of hot air blew past her cheek, almost welcome given how cold it felt in the room. Maybe the noise was an echo. The corners and crevices of the room seemed just as happy to deaden sounds as to toss them back in unexpected ways. Strange noises could as easily be normal acoustics as unearthly technology.

Probably this was pointless, and she risked torpedoing the arrangement she'd come to with Carillon on little more than a hunch. The fact that her phone was currently a melted heap of plastic in a rubbish bin upstairs was a clear indication of how seriously trows took this sort of thing. It might have been completely by accident that Carillon's keycard ended up in Ivy's scarf.

And even if Angevin had intentionally given her the key, it still didn't mean coming down here was a good idea.

"Alright, how do we do this?" Demi asked, hands on her hips as she looked around the room.

"No idea," said Ivy, shrugging. "You're supposed to be the experts. How do you be invisible?"

"How do you have brown hair?" Demi replied. "It's just how it is."

"There's a few different ways to get around the veil," said Ambrose briskly. He'd switched the poker to his left hand and held the right one up, as though he were feeling for air currents. "You can prime someone to expect to see or hear us. You can try to startle them. Or you get them in a very boring room and try to be colorful and loud."

"Those all depend on the invisible person wanting to be seen," Ivy pointed out. "We need to get at it from the other side."

"Which means looking for things that aren't supposed to be there," said Demi. "Shadows that look out of place, or a book you don't remember leaving on a table. Things moving in the corner of your eye."

"You make it sound like you're all poltergeists," Ivy muttered, looking from the glass cases to the dusty corners of the room.

"Or we look for something Ivy sees that the rest of us don't," Hunzu pointed out. "Like how she could see Larch and no one else could."

"Except I'm not seeing anything here," Ivy said, sighing. Only hearing things that might have been completely imaginary. She went to the closest glass case and bent down to look underneath. Below was only a tangle of power cords and air hoses, all covered with a thin layer of grit.

"So we've got two jewelry cases and a doorway on either side of the room. Got all that?" Hunzu asked.

"Yes," said Ivy.

"A lot of conduit, a breaker box, and eight overhead lights. You're seeing all that, too?"

"*Yes*, Hunzu," Ivy replied. This whole exercise was turning out to be the world's most boring game of I Spy.

On the other side of the room, Ambrose was slowly walking a circuit, one hand lightly touching the wall, going hesitantly enough Ivy wondered if he had his eyes closed. Demi was standing closer to the doorway they'd entered by, bobbing her head and squinting her eyes as though she were trying to recreate the angle of Ivy's phone.

Ivy looked into the glass case at a jumble of dimmed screens and agitated, blinking lights, thinking hard. Humans couldn't see through veils consciously. That was why Hunzu was so cautious crossing streets—drivers wouldn't stop. Fellow pedestrians, though, usually moved out of the way. No one walked into Ambrose when he'd turned up by the ambulance last night. When Hunzu sat on a barstool at the Yukon, no one ever tried to sit on his lap.

Which meant if there was something invisible in the room, on some level Ivy might already know where it was.

She turned away from the glass cabinet, feeling another tingle of hot air across her cheeks. Narrowing her eyes, Ivy dropped to her knees, wrapping the scarf more tightly around her shoulders to keep it from dragging in the dust. She ran her hands over the rock floor, feeling the grit under her fingers. Dust rose from the floor in little puffs as Demi came closer, crouching beside her and following Ivy's gaze.

"Ivy?" Demi asked, but Ivy ignored her, holding up a hand for silence. Looking toward the arch, Ivy could see a cluster of heel-shaped outlines where the dust was just thick enough to take a track.

The thing that was down here, did it leave footprints, too?

Ivy remembered watching a Doctor Who episode on the telly, one of the scarier ones with monsters you couldn't remember unless you were looking straight at them. They were waiting, close-furled and hanging from the ceiling, as Amy

Pond struggled to get out of the room. Every time she looked away, she'd forget she was in danger.

The monsters didn't forget. They always remembered.

Ivy looked back to the floor, deliberately letting everything else in the room fade into the background. She let her gaze float over the floor instead, aimlessly following the tracks and whorls in the dust. Accept that part of the vault wasn't real and look for the seams where reality and illusion don't quite match. Something was in the room that her eyes shied away from. Something here was different from everything around it, though Ivy couldn't for the life of her say why.

"Ivy!" Demi said again, sharper. "You alright?"

Ivy let out a long breath and nodded. The odd feeling persisted, like a dozen invisible eyes were boring into the back of her neck. She stood up, fighting the urge to huddle closer to Demi. It was the same feeling as in her flat, when she'd realized the strange shape in the dark had no reason to be there and that something was terribly wrong.

Demi offered a shaky grin. Her face looked pale, sweat standing out on her forehead despite the cold. "Did you see something?" she asked, her voice low.

Ivy hesitated and shook her head. Nothing but an empty room and a couple of glass cases. Ivy wondered if she'd have better luck wrapping the scarf around her eyes and stumbling around with her arms out.

Abruptly, Ivy turned back to the arch, goosebumps multiplying on her arms. She didn't have to wrap a scarf over her head because that was *already happening*. Something was changing her perceptions, throwing a blanket over whatever it didn't want her to see.

After five months living in Dartry, Ivy could walk through her room in total darkness because she already knew what was where and how to avoid tripping over it. She walked past her desk chair every time she had to get up in the middle of the night. If the desk chair suddenly vanished, Ivy would probably keep walking around it at night, even if it wasn't really there. Ivy knew her own room, and she wouldn't expect its configuration to change while she wasn't looking.

That was the giveaway. That was the little tell. Not the things you see, but the things you assume don't change.

Ivy looked up, meeting Hunzu's eyes from the other side of the vault.

"Close your eyes," she told him.

Hunzu narrowed them instead. "Excuse me?" he asked, sounding nervous.

At the far wall, Ambrose dropped his hand, looking between Ivy and Hunzu curiously.

"Trust me," Ivy told him. "Keep them closed until I tell you."

Hesitantly, Hunzu did so. He crossed his arms in front of him, looking strangely vulnerable standing in front of the arch with his eyes squeezed shut, as though his eyes gave him an illusion of preparedness, even against something they couldn't see. As though if something came for him, he might still see it in time to run. The monsters in Hunzu's world didn't work that way. They decided when you saw them and when you didn't.

Quickly, Ivy went to the glass case, pausing only long enough to set something down on the lid. She turned and walked back across the vault, dust rising up from her feet in little puffs.

"Keep your eyes closed and turn this way," she called, trying to ignore the way the shadow-haunted room seemed to swallow her voice. Hunzu turned, eyes still squeezed shut, one hand outstretched to ward off anything he might stagger into.

"Alright," said Ivy, trying to keep her voice steady, as

though it was all a game and nothing depended on the outcome. "Are you facing the sound of my voice?"

"I think so," he said, a furrow appearing across his forehead.

Ivy thought he was, too, but if she was right about this, she couldn't entirely be sure. She could be looking right at him and still not know for certain.

"Open your eyes and tell me what you see."

Hunzu opened his eyes, started to turn his head.

"Just here," said Ivy, urgency bleeding into her voice even as she tried to sound calm. "Just over here. Don't look anywhere else."

Hunzu's eyes met her own, looking as frightened as she'd ever seen him.

"There's nothing behind you, I swear," Ivy assured him, knowing even as she said it that it might not be true. Out of the corner of her eye, she saw Demi take a step forward; Ambrose, on the far side of the vault, waved her back. "Just tell me what you see."

Desperately, Ivy wished she knew whether Angevin had really meant to give her the keycard. Maybe it was completely by chance it had ended up tangled in her scarf. Was Angevin trying to help? To show them something? Or was he simply tossing a grenade into the understanding Ivy had fashioned with Carillon for some obscure reason of his own?

"You're standing about four feet from the back wall, and there's a row of lights above your head," Hunzu said. He stopped to lick his lips. "The bulbs are caged. There's shadows."

"Just look at me," Ivy said, feeling the chill air even more keenly along her bare shoulders. "Right here. What do you see?"

"Your hair's down," he said. "You're wearing that shirt from work with the bird on the front. You're wearing gloves, and that fuzzy green scarf. Tan trousers, and—"

"Look at the glass case," Ivy said, cutting him off, the chill of the room like fingers at the back of her neck. From the far wall, she could hear Ambrose's sudden intake of breath.

Hunzu turned, and Ivy knew the moment he spotted it, because every muscle in his body seemed to tense all at once.

On top of the jewelry case, Angevin's green scarf sat in a heap, right where Ivy had left it.

Ivy was already hurrying across the vault toward him as Hunzu turned back to her, disbelief written across his face.

"Shit," he murmured, rubbing at his eyes. The moment Ivy was close enough, she grabbed the bottom of his shirt with both hands, balling the fabric between her fingers because it was the safest part of him she could touch.

Whatever was down here was real. They'd just proven that, and they still had no idea what it was.

"There was something in the way," Hunzu murmured, leaning close. She felt his hand brush lightly against her shoulder.

Ivy nodded. Hunzu hadn't really seen Ivy, only his memory of her, because something else was standing between them. For a moment, Ivy wanted nothing more than to throw her arms around him and bury her head in his shirt, just until someone told her what the hell they were supposed to do next. They didn't have time for that: the thing down here might already have worked out what they were doing.

"You saw what you remembered," she said instead, forcing herself to let go of his shirt and step back to a safer distance. "Not what's really there."

She looked at Demi and Ambrose as the pair joined them. Demi's face looked stony. Ambrose was holding the poker two-handed, like he wasn't ruling out having to hit something with it.

"Last chance," Ambrose murmured, nodding toward the stairs. Demi snorted and shook her head. After a moment, Hunzu did as well.

And even though Ivy ought to be watching for a monster in the shadows and corners of the room, she found herself instead trying to remember Angevin's expression as he'd wrapped his scarf around her neck. She could recall nothing but an impression of laughing eyes, and a wild, momentary grin.

"Let's see what's behind the curtain," Ivy said, and turned toward the thing she couldn't see. Hunzu came closer, his hand resting lightly on her shoulder, like the last bit of warmth left in the room.

Ambrose shifted the poker in his hands, staring across the room with an abstracted expression. "Assuming it's relatively stationary," he muttered, trailing off. Abruptly, he took two steps forward and reached out with his free hand.

In front of him, reality popped like a soap bubble.

Ivy jumped as Hunzu stiffened beside her, and all Ivy could do was stare. She'd never seen it before; she'd walked past it three times in the last five minutes. She never could have described it; she already knew exactly what it looked like.

Ambrose's hand was pressed against the front of tall glass case. The glass was rimed with frost, and inside Ivy could make out a wing computer perched on a metal stand above a mass of cables and circuitry. The red and orange lights on the wing's heat sinks gently flashed in a slow, undulating pattern.

"This is what destroyed my phone?" Ivy asked, coming closer. She reached for the glass, pulling away with a start as the cold bit into her fingers. The imprint of her hand lingered for a moment, the outline slowly starting to dissipate as she watched. The entire case was ice-cold and brimming with hoarfrost. She rubbed her stinging fingers against the side of her trousers.

"The hell is it?" Hunzu murmured as he came around to stand next to her.

"More importantly, what is it doing?" said Demi, staring at it as though it might vanish if she took her eyes off it. "Looks livelier than any of the others."

"Indeed," murmured Ambrose. Cautiously, he pushed at a catch on the front of the case. Ivy braced herself for a wave of cold as the door swung open, but the breeze that wafted out of the case felt warm, as though she'd walked in front of a window on a sunny day. A low humming drifted from the open door, like a distant conversation in a far-off room.

Cautiously, Ivy held out her hand, feeling a flicker of heat on her fingers as though she were standing next to the radiator in the Dartry flat. With the frosty glass out of the way, she could see the lights glinting along the metal body, as well as from what passed for a screen in the space between the heat sinks. The dimming and brightening lights seemed more numerous and more orderly than on any of the other wings locked in their caskets.

"Is it the veil?" Ivy asked.

"Easy way to find out." said Demi. Shrugging off Ambrose's belated attempt to stop her, Demi reached inside the case, spun the wing a quarter turn, and pulled it straight off its stand.

The strange murmur grew louder, no longer muffled by glass. Holding it gingerly, Demi tilted it, peering at the underside like she was looking for a serial number. Biting her lip, she switched the wing to her right hand, holding up her left wrist as though offering it a perch.

The dead woman had worn her wing on her wrist. Ivy remembered how the metal gleamed in the flames when she'd burned, and suppressed a shudder.

The pattern of lights on the wing's display shifted for a moment, then steadied.

Frowning, Demi shook it, offering her wrist again. The wing didn't seem to notice, continuing to repeat the same slow pattern of symbols.

"Or not," said Hunzu, leaning over Demi's shoulder to peer at it. "Got to be doing something or it wouldn't be putting off so much heat."

"You have a go, then," Demi told him, sounding irritated, and held the wing out to Hunzu. Eyes wide, Hunzu cautiously held up his wrist, but the thing seemed to take no notice at all.

"Shall we see if it likes you any better?" Demi started to pass the wing to Ambrose, then hesitated. Ambrose's face looked chalky, sweat standing out in beads across his forehead.

"Give it to Ivy," said Ambrose, his voice sounding like something scraped over a rock, staring intently at a point somewhere past Ivy's head.

"Why—" Ivy spoke up at the same time as Demi and Hunzu. Ambrose shushed all of them with a look.

"Prove me wrong," he snapped, looking at Ivy, his face unreadable.

Demi opened her mouth, the line between her eyebrows forecasting objections. Before her friend could say anything, Ivy slipped the glove off her left hand and reached out, offering the wing the back of her wrist the same way she'd seen Demi do.

For a moment, nothing happened.

With a clockwork shudder, the wing slipped out of Demi's hand. Ivy yelped as three bands of metal slid out from the wing and tightened around her forearm. She tried to pull back, but the wing was already firmly attached, two of the heat sinks rearranging themselves to cover her forearm like a wrist guard. Her arm sagged with the weight of it, or maybe it was only the shock of the metal against her skin, the heat only just on the near side of tolerable.

Hunzu was beside her in an instant, one hand on her shoulder, the other fluttering over the wing as though he was considering wrenching it off her arm.

From the other side of the wing's spindly heat sinks, Demi was staring at Ivy like she didn't know who she was.

Or maybe Demi was just staring at the wing. A blue-tinted display was glowing in the air between the arching metal, just like on the woman's arm last night. The display was an incomprehensible grid of Rass syllabograms. Among the unintelligible jumble, clusters of normal arabic numerals leapt out, dizzyingly familiar.

Staring at the quietly pulsing display, Ivy felt a shiver run down her spine.

"Can you read it?" Hunzu asked, glancing at Ambrose.

"A bit," Ambrose hedged, frowning as he stared at it, mouthing words under his breath.

"At least some of it's regular numbers," said Ivy, pointing at the screen. Dotted among the Rass lettering, the numerals were the one thing Ivy's eyes seemed able to make sense of, like page numbers in book written in an unfamiliar language. "Like here and—"

Ivy jumped, pulling her hand back as the number in question lit up, brightening noticeably as her finger brushed the edge of the display.

"Shit," she hissed. Her hand had gone right through the display, which didn't feel like anything. Like trying to touch the rainbows cast from the prism in her mother's kitchen window.

"Careful," Demi cautioned. "We don't know what you're asking it to do."

"Try the squiggle in the top corner," said Ambrose, pointing. "The one that looks like a rope wrapped around a traffic cone."

Hesitantly, Ivy poked the syllabogram Ambrose indicated. The display shifted, switching to what looked like a pie chart, the various slices widely unequal and slowly changing size as Ivy watched.

"It's a breakdown of what it's doing," said Ambrose. "Or rather, how many resources are being allocated toward any one particular task."

"So what *is* it doing?" Ivy asked, glancing back toward the door.

"A lot," said Demi, pointing at one of the thinner slices of the pie. "That sliver is unallocated. Should be a lot bigger. We hardly do anything with the wings that brings them that close to capacity."

Staring at the pie graph, Ivy wondered how the wing would compare in processing power to a computer. Was the thing on her wrist more like a smart phone, or a mainframe? Were wings so different from regular computers because of how they were built, or because of what sorts of programs they were able to run?

Ivy reached up and touched part of the pie, and the entire display immediately shifted, bringing up another panel of unintelligible glyphs and somewhat-intelligible numbers.

"Careful," Hunzu hissed.

"Not like you know what you're doing, either," Ivy shot back.

"There should be a way to put it in trial mode," Ambrose broke in. "Three physical buttons, at the base of the heat sinks. You'll need to press them all at once for a count of three."

Hesitantly, Ivy touched the metal surface of the wing. It felt even hotter close to the heat sinks. After a few hesitant taps, Ivy found the buttons and pushed them. The buttons sank into the metal surface of the wing with a shudder and the metal against her arm grew a fraction less feverish.

Just as Ivy was about to let go, the edges of the display flashed and something that looked very much like a warning message appeared in a box in the upper right corner.

"Trial mode," Ambrose confirmed with a nod. He reached out, tried to brush part of the pie chart, but the wing took just as little notice of him as it had before. Hurriedly, Ambrose dropped his hand and tucked it into his pocket, but not before Ivy noticed it was trembling.

"Could you pull up the largest of those allocations?" Ambrose continued, his voice not entirely steady.

"Ambrose?" Demi asked quietly, tilting her head to look at him.

"Why is it just me it's listening to?" Ivy asked, pointing at the thing with her free hand.

"It thinks you're its operator," said Ambrose brusquely, sounding fractionally more like himself. "Which I suppose we ought to be grateful for, or we could hardly do anything with it at all. If you could?" He nodded impatiently at the display hovering over Ivy's wrist.

Biting her lip, Ivy touched the largest, pulsing section of the pie chart. The section immediately expanded, the remainder of the graph falling away to be replaced by two clusters of red, angry-looking Rass text. Below it were two strings of numbers and another dense block of Rass.

"Protocol Four," Hunzu read, leaning closer to Ivy as he squinted at the text. "Iteration 328. That next string might be the build number. And a lot of warning labels. Do not something-something except when something location is . . ." He trailed off, rubbing at his temples. "Not very specific about what it's actually supposed to do."

"It's not a build number," said Demi abruptly, and Ivy's

head came up with a jerk at the leashed fury in her voice. "It's a countdown. *Look* at it."

As if on cue, the righthand number in the final string dropped. Ivy stared at it, fighting the sense that somewhere in the holographic muddle was something that could explain everything that had eluded Ivy so far. Why the wing was hidden away in the vault, veiled from other trows. Why Angevin had given her the keycard. Why the wing only answered to Ivy, and why it protected itself with fire, a move that could have come straight from the Enemy's playbook.

328, the display read. 227:11:14:06.

There was only one countdown that had ever mattered to Demi.

"Two hundred twenty-seven days," Ambrose whispered in a hollow voice. "Eleven hours, fourteen minutes, six seconds."

The wing was like a manacle around Ivy's wrist, something that might drag her down and never let go. Ivy grabbed the edge of the wing nearest her elbow and tugged on it. The metal fasteners dug into her arm, and the thing didn't budge.

"How do I take it off?" Ivy asked, hearing the panic in her voice and tightening her grip on the edge of the wing. It was Demi's countdown on Ivy's arm, and that seemed like the worst sort of presentiment. Until last night, Ivy had been certain that whatever else could go wrong with the Enemy, the trows' adversary would never target Ivy directly.

With the countdown to next year's murder ticking over silently on Ivy's wrist, that certainty suddenly seemed dangerously naive.

"We don't know anything for certain," Ambrose started, and Demi rounded on him with a glare.

"You seem to know a great deal more than the rest of us, and I am wondering why that is," she snapped, looking angry enough to pick an argument with anyone careless enough to give her an excuse.

"Take a deep breath," said Hunzu, coming closer. "There's an exit syllabogram, looks a bit like an upside-down toaster. We just have to find it."

Ivy let go of the edge of the wing, looking among the confusion of characters for anything that looked like what Hunzu had described. Not in the top row. Or the warning box for trial mode, whatever that was.

"Not in front of them," Ambrose hissed at his partner, ineffectually trying to keep his voice down.

"Then why—"

"Because we didn't have a goddamned lottery this year, that's why," Ambrose snapped, sounding angry, though Ivy didn't understand why, or why the lottery to select a Year King had anything to do with anything.

"Deep breath," Hunzu repeated, his hand fluttering uneasily over her right shoulder as though he were seriously considering touching her bare-handed. "It's in trial mode. It won't actually do anything. It can't. Not for real."

In the center of the display, the counter ticked down another number.

Two hundred twenty-seven days, eleven hours, and thirteen minutes. There might be an innocent explanation. Just because the wing was timing the intervals between the Enemy's visits didn't mean it was doing anything more sinister than acting as a high-tech stopwatch. And if there *wasn't* an innocent explanation . . .

If that terrible suspicion was true—and if Hunzu was right about trial mode—this might be Ivy's best chance to find out for sure.

Not giving herself time to reconsider, Ivy stabbed at the row of syllabograms Hunzu had called Protocol Four.

The figure was already walking toward them when Ivy looked up, and she realized she'd been wrong to think the woman last night had looked anything like it. It wore the same hooded coverall, but that mattered less than the complete lack of expression on its face. Its eyes were empty and disinterested in a way that wasn't natural.

The Enemy was saying something as it glided closer, but Ivy couldn't hear it; she was screaming at Hunzu, her fingers locked around his arm, and he was shouting, too. Ambrose had thrown himself in front of Demi, screaming at it in Rass. Demi had the poker in her hand, aiming to swing it. If none of them were running, Ivy wasn't, either, even though it was coming closer and its wing was on *her* arm and the smell of ash and wood polish was in her nose and it was all happening again.

Ivy shoved her free hand into her messenger bag, fingers curling around the Taser. A futile gesture—bullets hadn't touched it last time—but she wasn't going to let it near her without at least trying—

"Upside-down toaster!" Hunzu hissed, shaking her. "Upside-down toaster!" Abruptly she spotted what he was pointing at. Abandoning the Taser, Ivy stabbed at the icon as hard as she could, shoving her finger straight through the hologram and grazing the edge of the heat sinks, jerking back as the heat blossomed into a searing pain on her fingers.

When she looked up, the Enemy was gone. Ivy spun on her heel, gaze darting around the vault. The room was empty apart from them. She looked in horror at the wing on her arm, still quietly displaying the pie chart allocations and the countdown.

"It was in trial mode," Hunzu said weakly, rubbing at his forehead. "It wouldn't really have . . ."

He trailed off, gesturing shakily to the place where the Enemy had been standing.

Wouldn't really have killed them, was what Hunzu meant.

The equivalent of Safe Mode on a PC. Your computer slows to the speed of a garden slug, but at least it won't summon up a vicious alien serial killer to burn you to death.

Ivy felt a hysterical giggle building in the back of her throat. It burst out, dismayingly more like a sob than a laugh, and something sharp was pricking at her eyes. She reached up to wipe at her face with her free hand. Her fingers were smarting where they'd brushed against the heat sink, a red mark growing on the back of her pointer finger that looked like the beginnings of a blister.

"Here," said Hunzu breathlessly, pointing at something on the wing's side that looked like a catch. Ivy grappled with it. The display flickered out, but the afterimage of the countdown hung in the air for a moment longer. Ivy felt a wave of relief as the metal bands on her arm loosened. She yanked the wing off her arm; Ambrose jumped to catch it before it could hit the floor.

Two hundred and twenty-seven days before Protocol Four ran for real.

"It said something," said Demi breathlessly, still holding the poker and eyeing the wing in a way that made Ivy feel even happier it was off her arm.

"It said, 'Please remain calm,'" Ambrose said, staring warily at the thing in his hands.

Ivy shuddered. Uncle Patrick had tried to talk to it, Ivy remembered, in the seconds before he died. She didn't know if the Enemy had answered him. Those three words might have been the last thing he'd heard before it killed him.

"Could someone have hacked it?" Hunzu asked.

"I don't think so," said Ambrose wearily. "Whatever that was, it's something that came with it all the way from Valiard."

He took a step toward the case, gingerly lifting the wing as though he was going to put it back in.

Abruptly, Demi switched the poker to her right hand and grabbed Ambrose by the wrist.

"Put it down," Demi said quietly, nodding at the stone floor.

Ambrose hesitated. "There's got to be some reason why they've kept it. However Taye managed to keep this a secret—if it's even Taye at all—"

"What reason could possibly be worth the lives of over three hundred people?" Ivy snapped.

"What reason, indeed," said Ambrose darkly. Slowly, he lowered the wing to the floor, setting it down with a quiet clink. Sitting at their feet, it looked no more alarming than an iridescent paperweight.

"Someone's been harboring this. Asking questions is only going to give them time to move it somewhere else," said Demi, her voice hard. "We finish this now, and there won't ever be another lottery. No one ever has to be afraid of the Enemy, ever again."

Watching Demi, the look in her eyes equal parts cold and desperate, Ivy was forcibly reminded of the morning in the apple grove. When Demi first saw Larch, she'd suggested they kill him, too.

"It's not worth a person's life, no matter how rare it is," Hunzu said seriously. "Unless you think we can reprogram it?" he added, looking at Ambrose.

"Carillon could," Ivy said suddenly. "She must have done it for Larch, back in 1936."

"All the more reason not to give her any more opportunities to meddle," Demi hissed.

Ivy looked at the thing on the floor, rubbing her stinging fingers on the edge of her shirt, thinking of the crater in the street and the apple grove in February. Larch had hated the Enemy, long after he'd stopped being afraid of it. Maybe that hate was something Ivy could carry, too, like an antique neck-lace or a hand-me-down watch. His hatred of the Enemy was maybe the only thing he'd ever passed along to Ivy that she'd actually wanted. Plus, perhaps his determination to do some-thing about it, there at the very end.

Maybe it meant something, that Ivy had found the thing that had killed him. And an errant, ridiculous corollary: Larch would have been proud of her. Ivy shouldn't care what he thought—but he would have been proud, and the only reason he wasn't here to see it was because of the strange metal gadget lying on the floor.

A gadget that somehow answered to Ivy, as though it had some claim on her. *Because we didn't have a lottery this year.* Remembering the feel of the metal cuffs closing around her wrist, Ivy shuddered.

As Demi started to raise the poker, Ivy grabbed the rod, her fingers inches from Demi's. As Demi looked up, Ivy met her friend's gaze and smiled.

"Rock, paper, scissors for it?" Ivy asked.

CHAPTER 7

"Mistress?"

Ivy's head was killing her, her hands were scalded, and her left arm felt like murder. A scratching noise was drilling into her head like a saw blade, something whisking back and forth across the stone floor. Vaguely, Ivy considered curling into a ball and ignoring it, but someone was trying to get her attention—had been for several minutes, Ivy thought. Ivy didn't think feigning unconsciousness would be enough to get him to go away. She could practically feel his eyes on her already, a quiet and insistent sense of unwelcome company.

Slowly, Ivy pushed herself up from the floor, started to rub a hand across her face—and stopped short with a heat sink inches from her face. Ivy yelped, staring at the wing locked around her arm like it was the worst harbinger of disaster.

Across the room, a figure in a yellow jumper startled, a broom and dustpan hitting the floor with a clatter. Ivy took no notice, going for the wing's catch with blistered fingers as she tried to wrench the thing off her arm. Damn her mobile anyway, she hadn't thought it'd been *that* hot when she dropped it . . .

The wing wasn't budging. Her fingers felt clumsy and sweaty as she fought with the mechanism. A terrible ash-and-metal smell was filling the air, and Ivy had a horrible sense of eyes on her, a keen and smothering alien awareness.

"Mistress?" it asked again.

"Get off," Ivy snapped, not sure who she was talking to, or if it was crazy even to try. "*Now.*"

Another tug, and a catch gave way under her fingers, the bands on her wrist telescoping open as the wing tumbled off her arm.

It hit the stone floor with a clatter; the whisper of an unseen presence vanished. Ivy stared at the wing, started to rub at her left arm, and flinched. The blister on her right hand had more than doubled in size. Both her arms hurt, and so did her face, burning as though she'd stood all day in the sun. The past few minutes all seemed muddled in her head; Ivy stared at the wing, certain there was something important about it that had just that moment slipped her mind. *Dehydration is a very common side effect,* Ivy recalled Hunzu saying.

That hadn't happened here. There were no hoofprints, or none that Ivy could pick out among the jumble of dust bunnies and ash scattered across the floor. There was no sign of Demi, Hunzu, or Ambrose.

On the other side of the vault, Angevin picked up his fallen dustpan and straightened up, looking at Ivy with a pained expression.

Ivy scrambled to her feet, arms tangling in her purse straps as she yanked the keycard Angevin had given her out of her pocket. She stumbled toward him, resisting the urge to aim a kick at the wing as she passed it.

"What is Protocol Four?" Ivy snarled, waving the stolen keycard and wishing for a moment it was her Taser instead.

"It's a failsafe," said Angevin quietly, tapping the dustpan into a rusted paint can sitting at the foot of the nearest glass case. "Or it was supposed to be. A last resort for the scouts if our mission was falling apart. If someone was injured or trapped, if we had no chance of getting back to our jump site or completing our objectives, Protocol Four was supposed to bring us home. A get out of jail free card, if you will. That's what we were told."

Out of nowhere, Ivy remembered the fear on the woman's face in the street. She'd been shouting at something, right before she burned. Had she been asking the wing to take her home? And would she have been panicked enough to do that if Ivy, Lauren, and Grinch hadn't chased her down the alley?

For a blinding moment, a horrible, jumbled memory presented itself in Ivy's head, the burning, pinwheeling figure overlaid with the vision of the Enemy from the trial mode—and Demi had been screaming. For just a moment, the burned-hair smell was thick enough to gag her. She staggered and barely stopped herself from falling, her knees suddenly unwilling to hold her up.

Whatever Ivy and her friends had tried to do with the wing, it clearly hadn't worked, and she was torn between the urge to shake a sensible answer out of Angevin and the impulse to bolt out of the room and find Demi and everyone else. *They'd left her lying on the floor with a murderer wrapped around her wrist.* Her friends had better have a very good explanation for that, because otherwise—

Otherwise, something had gone terribly wrong.

Ivy dove into her purse, grabbed the Taser, and jabbed the tip hard into Angevin's chest. He snorted and let go of the broom, which fell with a clatter at his feet, sending up a little puff of ash.

"I need you to be more clear than you have ever been in your life," Ivy snapped. The tip of the Taser was dimpling the fabric of his shirt, the temptation to squeeze the trigger, to hear him screaming just like *Demi* had been screaming, was nearly overpowering. "It's the Enemy, isn't it? Protocol Four is the Enemy. Why is the wing running it allowed to exist?"

"The things aren't exactly easy to kill," Angevin snapped, eyeing the tip of the Taser with an aggrieved look. "Best we've been able to do is keep it out of the way so *heroes*"—he drew out the word as though it were a schoolyard insult—"don't get themselves killed any more often than necessary. Protocol Four triggers automatically if the wing itself is threatened or a mission is overdue. All I could do was push the mission duration back to the maximum interval the wing would allow. One year exactly, if idiots don't take it into their heads to provoke the thing early," he sniffed.

Ivy slid her finger closer to the trigger, ignoring the ache in her fingers as she tried to make sense of what Angevin was telling her. "But, if it's only supposed to bring people back to Valiard, then no one died."

If the Enemy was merely an automatic return, then Larch wasn't dead. He might be trapped, stuck in his former home, unable to leave and hating every minute of it, but he wasn't dead. And if he wasn't dead, then it wasn't Ivy's fault she'd killed him.

Angevin sighed heavily, making the tip of the Taser twitch. "You've seen it happen several times now. Do you really think that's what Protocol Four does?"

Hesitantly, unwillingly, Ivy shook her head.

"Everyone thought so at first," Angevin continued, bending to pick up the dustpan, shrugging off the Taser as though he'd decided Ivy wasn't going to use it. "They figured whoever went back to Valiard could reprogram the wing from that side. Remove the time limit entirely, let the Valiard survivors and their descendants muddle through history as best we could. Unfortunately, Protocol Four doesn't actually work that way."

He bent down, picked up the broom, and began sweeping more of the ash into the pan. A larger piece, bone-pale and uneven, struck the side of the pan with a metallic ping. Something lurched in Ivy's stomach to hear it. She switched the Taser to her left hand, rubbing her right hand against her trousers. Her fingers were throbbing, and her knees felt strangely unsteady, like the whole world had turned on its edge.

"Didn't you ever wonder why it was always the kings?" Angevin asked. "Before there was a lottery, why it was always the leaders and elders?"

"They didn't think they were victims," Ivy said slowly. "The first kings. They were volunteers."

"Even worse," Angevin said in a low voice. "Heroes."

Ivy's hand was beginning to ache from gripping the Taser. Taking a deep breath, she loosened her fingers, keeping it pointing at the trow. Angevin grimaced and continued to sweep the floor.

"I'm going to ask you again," Ivy growled. "Why didn't you destroy it when you realized what it was doing?"

"Why didn't we kill our little monster, you mean, once we realized exactly how monstrous it was?" he asked. Angevin's grin, through the fringe of hair, was almost mocking. He tapped the dustpan against the side of the metal can, sending a cloud of ash floating over the top. "Because that monster knows everything Valiard knew about Event Two. That's what it was built for, and that's still its mission. It doesn't care it's been waiting three hundred years to carry it out."

"So it's not that you can't kill it," Ivy snapped. "You won't."

All of those people who'd burned, one a year for three hundred years, and Angevin could have stopped it. He hadn't.

He'd let them die, just like Larch in the apple grove and last night in the street. The pavement buckling in the heat, hands reaching out in terror. Ambrose had been screaming and Ivy'd tried to pull her out of the fire but the heat wouldn't let her, and her hand had burned . . .

Except that wasn't what happened. Ivy was halfway across the street when the scout caught fire.

Ivy had also been six feet away, screaming her name.

Vision blurring, Ivy shook her head. Something was awake and burning in her chest, as fierce as the fire in the apple grove, something that would burn her own skin if she couldn't find it other kindling. She looked at Angevin and his dustpan full of ashes and wanted to hit him. She wanted to cry. She wanted to run up the stairs and find everyone she'd ever cared about and hug them and tell them she was sorry.

Except there was no one in this room she trusted, and it wasn't safe to fall to pieces here. Which left hitting Angevin as the only possible outlet. Ivy shifted her grip on the Taser, heading toward Angevin and his insufferably calm face.

Two steps and her boot caught on something lumpy and metallic, sending it skittering across the floor to slam with a thud into the bottom of the Enemy's glass case.

With a jolt, Ivy recognized the fleur-de-lis design from the poker set upstairs. The handle was the same as the poker Ambrose had brought, though this one must have been another from the same set. Nothing remained of it but the handle and a few inches of a misshapen rod.

Ivy bent to pick up the remnant poker—and the world slipped sideways around her as the Taser clattered to the floor, because Ivy was certain she'd already done it. The poker was already in her hand. She'd already seen the corner of the Enemy's glass case behind it, she'd already been standing in this exact spot, watching the iron tip of the poker's undamaged twin wavering between herself and the pulsing lights of the wing on the floor.

Staring at the mangled remnants of the poker, Ivy knew she'd held its twin in her hand not ten minutes ago. Ivy closed her eyes and tightened her grip on the poker, throwing herself into that blurry echo. She'd held the poker, just like she was holding it now. Then, it was complete and undamaged in her hand. Then, the wing's lights shone like a kaleidoscope, blurring out everything else in the room. *We'll see about can't or won't.* Ivy hefted the poker.

From somewhere very far away, Demi stepped out from behind the wing's glittering light and grabbed the rod before Ivy could swing it. The poker quivered under Ivy's fingers, as though Demi's hands might be shaking, but as she locked eyes with Ivy, her face was intent and fearless. She'd never looked more like a fairy king.

Ivy looked into her friend's face. The smile that tugged at Ivy's lips felt rough-edged and dangerous.

"Rock, paper, scissors for it?" Demi asked.

THE BURNT SMELL WAS EVERYWHERE. Ivy felt her stomach lurch as she looked in horror from the wing to Angevin. The trow stared sadly back, his mouth turned up in a grimace. Ivy wanted to scream at him, wanted to wrap herself in the darkest corner she could find and weep, wanted Demi to run down the stairs and burst through the door and tell her none of it was true. Instead, she shifted her grip on the damaged poker. The stubby broken end wasn't ideal but it was better than nothing.

There had to be another answer for what had just happened, but there was no time to piece it all together, not while the wing still lay glittering on the floor, surrounded by the ashes of its latest victim.

Ivy lifted the remnant poker over her head, tightening her grip on the broken fleur-de-lis.

"Absolutely not," Angevin snapped, and dropped the broom, jumping between Ivy and the wing. Ivy tried to duck past him, then went for the wing before he could grab it himself. As she yanked it away from him, the wing's metal bands irised open like an invitation.

"Mistress?" someone asked.

Ivy flinched and dropped it. Angevin snatched it up before it could hit the ground.

"Don't be an idiot," he snapped, cradling it to his chest protectively. "I just finished cleaning up the floor!"

"It killed her," Ivy said, not letting go of the poker. The handle still felt warm, like it hadn't had time to cool from when Demi had been holding it. Or maybe it had been Ivy holding it. The memory of what happened next was sliced to ribbons, nightmare flashes of heat, the smell of burnt hair, the sound of Ambrose screaming.

"I'm so sorry," said Angevin seriously, and turned back to the frosted-glass case, gently settling the wing on its stand. As if he cared about it. Like he wanted to protect it.

The damaged poker could still bash in a skull. She raised her arm; Angevin ducked past the door of the case and grabbed her wrist. He squeezed hard and Ivy nearly dropped the poker, flinching from his fingers as if from a live wire. His skin was fever-warm against hers, and neither of them was wearing gloves.

"How can you possibly be sorry?" Ivy spat, trying to wrench free. He wasn't letting her go, as if he didn't *care* they were touching, like it was another rule he dismissed out of hand. "You gave me that keycard!"

"Yes, I did," said Angevin, far too close and still not letting go of her wrist. "Listen to me very carefully. That scout last night won't be the last. Another one's coming, very soon. You have to find him, and you have to help him—"

"I'm not doing anything for you," Ivy interrupted heatedly, and finally, finally snatched her arm out of his grip, backing up as she scanned the floor for the Taser. "You're just as much of a murderer as it is."

"Well aware," snapped Angevin, sounding more irritated than remorseful. He slammed the case door closed, the Enemy's lights blurring behind the frosted glass. "If you want all those sacrifices to mean anything, right now is when it matters. Very soon, a door's going to open between here and Valiard, and we cannot waste that chance."

"Chance to do what?" Ivy asked, snatching up the Taser, safety off, finger around the trigger.

"Warn Valiard that their city is about to burn," Angevin said, and for the first time Ivy saw something that looked like real horror in his gaze. "Tell them to get everyone out before it happens, and tell them to take the one-year limit off their goddamn time machine! We both have information the other side needs. That's how we win, Ivy. That's how we change everything that's gone wrong. *We* know what happens to Valiard. Valiard needs to know what's happening to *us*. None of that happens without you."

He was completely serious. He was talking about changing the past and the future all at once, and he thought *Ivy* was the one to make it happen. The expectant, almost hopeful look on his face was just as frightening as the blurred lights of the wing locked away behind him.

"I'm *not* helping you," Ivy snapped. "You're a murderer, and they will feed you to the Enemy when they find out."

Then she turned and bolted for the stairs.

Ivy shoved the keycard against the plate at the top of the stairs, and wrenched the door open as soon as the bolt slid back. She stormed into the hallway and slammed the door closed behind her. Too much to hope that Angevin would be trapped downstairs. His pet murder computer could probably burn through the door whenever it wanted.

She hurried down the hall, through the jungle of potted plants at the base of the stairs. The house was quiet; hopefully there would be someone still in the meeting room who could help her find Ambrose and Hunzu. They'd been with her, when Demi . . .

At least, Ivy thought they'd been with her. Surely she'd know it, somewhere in her chest, if all three of them were dead?

Ivy pushed the thought away as she tore down the corridor, the red eyes of the butterflies in the transom gleaming like remembered fire.

When everyone finds out, he'll be the one to burn, war hero or not.

A bar of light from a half-open door spilled into the corridor in front of her, followed by a half-heard, familiar voice. Ivy grabbed the handle and pushed. The spindly door flew open, slamming against the wall as Ivy stumbled after it.

Hunzu jumped to his feet; everyone else was staring at her, and for a moment all Ivy could do was stare back. Everything looked normal. Every*one* looked normal, if you discounted the roll of gauze one of Carillon's people was carefully wrapping around Ambrose's right hand. It felt like looking at a funhouse mirror. How could everyone be sitting there like nothing was wrong? No one was screaming or crying or even arguing.

"Ivy?" Ambrose asked. He was staring at her like *she* was the one who didn't make sense. "You alright?"

Abruptly, Ivy realized she was still holding the Taser. She hurriedly jammed it into her purse, her finger curled so tightly around the trigger guard it took an effort to loosen it. Ambrose's eyes flicked to the bag and his frown deepened.

"Demi Gentian," Ivy said. It took effort to get the name out around the hitch in her throat.

Ambrose's eyebrows tightened, a flicker of something dark and unsettling crossing his face for the barest of moments.

"Ring Solly if you need to track down one of the other agents," he said finally. Oblivious to how Ivy's heart was splintering, he rubbed his left thumb across his bandaged palm. "But not now, if you please. It's nearly midnight."

Not trusting herself to speak, Ivy turned away, managing a few steps toward the wall. The room was some sort of library, the surroundings a meaningless wash of leather and dust covers. She felt more than saw Hunzu following her, waving his hands in the vicinity of her shoulders like he wanted to touch her but couldn't quite follow through.

"Are you alright?" Hunzu asked, his fingers almost brushing her face. And then, more sharply, "What happened to your hair?"

His fingers brushed against a lock near Ivy's cheek. It looked shorter than it ought to be. Ivy wondered, with a hopeless sort of detachment, how close she'd been to Demi if the flames had managed to singe her braid.

Something else she didn't remember, just like Hunzu and Ambrose.

Neither of them seemed to remember Demi at all, or the thing that killed her. If they didn't remember what was down in that room, then they wouldn't believe her. Or even worse, they'd believe her just enough to go looking for it, and the nightmare of the past hour would happen all over again to someone else. *Heroes*, Angevin had said, drawing out the word like an insult.

Instead of answering him, Ivy slipped her hand into her purse and grabbed the broken end of the poker. Ignoring the tempest brewing beneath her ribs, Ivy met Hunzu's worried eyes and carefully pressed the remnant into his hand. When he made to draw back, Ivy grabbed his sleeve and leaned in as close as she dared, ignoring the hitch in his breathing, until her lips were inches from his ear.

"You might not believe me," Ivy whispered, her fingers digging into his sleeve. "But we found the Enemy. Both of us. I know what it is."

Hunzu pulled back, shaking his arm free, looking between Ivy and the broken bit of metal like he didn't know what to think.

Abruptly, Carillon pushed her chair away from the table and stood up, staring at Ivy with a strange look.

"You were asking after a Ms. Gentian, were you not?" she said, raising an eyebrow, and Ivy's heart immediately lurched. Ambrose, carefully re-rolling an unused elastic bandage, didn't react to the name at all.

"Yes," said Ivy, turning away from Hunzu, who looked as though he was going to interrupt, and hesitantly stepped back to the table. Carillon's expression looked like that of a woman who knew any number of secrets, which was exactly how Carillon always looked every time Ivy had spoken to her. The Enemy lived in her own basement. It had spared Larch in 1936, and then five months ago the Enemy had killed him.

Swallowing hard, Ivy lifted her chin. "Have you met?"

"I don't recall," said Carillon smoothly. If Ivy hadn't been looking closely, she might have missed the twitch at the corner of Carillon's mouth. "But if you'd remind me of some salient details, perhaps I can be of assistance."

The Enemy lived in her basement. She had to know it was there.

The same way Ambrose had to remember his own partner, or how he'd gotten a burn on his hand bad enough to require bandaging it like a mummy.

Carillon would have to be an idiot to live with the thing for so long and not have some inkling of what it was doing, and Carillon was no idiot. Maybe she was just as complicit as Angevin.

Or else the Enemy's amnesia-inducing veil worked on her as well it did on everyone else, and she'd spent a lifetime living where its influence was strongest. How many decades might it take to pick up on the clues? The cracks and seams where one's memories had been cut out and stitched back together like a badly mended doll? Years and years of slowly building suspicions that no one else would believe, suppositions that never quite held up to outside scrutiny.

Carillon could be just as much a murderer as Angevin.

But if she wasn't, she might be more likely to believe Ivy than anyone else. She'd been the one Larch had written to, when he'd been puzzling out the mystery of why the Enemy spared him in 1936. Had Larch written to her only because she was his mother? Or did he suspect that Taye Carillon—sharp, calculating, cold, and observant—might be their best chance at unraveling the Enemy's yearly murders?

Larch had trusted her, once. Maybe Ivy should, too.

And, some cold and self-serving corner of Ivy's heart added, if revealing the Enemy's secret to someone else really could get them killed, as Angevin claimed, Ivy would much rather risk Carillon's life than Ambrose or Hunzu's.

"Join me outside?" Carillon asked, nodding to the door.

Warily, Ivy followed.

THE DOOR CARILLON opened led into a small garden tucked between the central bulk of the house and a smaller, offshoot gallery. A path laid out in white stones meandered through a group of raised beds toward a lamppost and a pair of benches. Carillon began walking toward it and Ivy fell into step a careful few feet beside her.

"Demi Gentian," she hissed as soon as she heard the door swing shut behind her. "What do you remember about her? Anything?"

"Not a thing, but you think I ought to," Carillon replied, turning the question back on itself. "Why?"

"Because two hours ago, you were arguing," Ivy snapped. "You don't remember that and no one else does, either. She just —" Ivy swallowed hard, watching Carillon's face, only just visible in the light of the lamppost as the thane waited for Ivy to continue. "She just died, and no one remembers her. Like the universe swallowed her and no one noticed. It's happened before, hasn't it? There's something evil in this house, and it's more than one a year, and I think you know it."

Carillon folded her arms, her expression sharpening. "The term 'evil' might be applied to half a dozen of the relics downstairs. Did one of them try to speak to you?"

Ivy hesitated, then nodded. "It was inside a case covered with ice. There was a timer on it and we put it in trial mode, and it was the same thing I saw in the apple grove. The Enemy is down there, and Angevin's been protecting it, and we tried to kill it, Demi and I, and now her partner doesn't even remember her name!" Ivy took a deep breath, and added, "I need your help to figure out how to destroy it before it kills anyone else."

It was too dark to make out much of Carillon's expression, only a tightening of the lips as the thane reached into the pocket of her skirt and tugged something free. Ivy tensed, thinking of her Taser before she recognized the shape as a wallet. Carillon ripped it open, tearing at something in the inner pocket with her fingernails.

"If you want to keep it from killing anyone else, stay out if its way," Carillon said quietly, holding out a small bit of paper at arm's length. The thane's hand twitched for a moment, her chin held high, as though she were glaring at Ivy, or simply didn't want to look at the paper herself. "If you haven't already figured that out, you haven't learned a thing from whatever it showed you downstairs."

Ivy took a step back, diving into the purse for the Taser. Carillon already knew. She wasn't screaming or yelling or calling for Angevin's head on a platter and *she already knew.* Which meant maybe Ivy should be the one screaming and running, going back inside to Hunzu and Ambrose—except they knew even less than Ivy about what was really going on.

Instead, Ivy reached out and took the paper. The garden was too dark to make it out right away, and Ivy turned, holding the photograph up to the light from the lamppost.

"I don't remember them and I never have," Carillon said, a hitch in her voice. "I don't know who this Demi was to you, Ivy, but if she meant anything, let her go. Or there will certainly be others."

Two faded, sepia-toned children looked back at Ivy from the crinkled photograph. Ivy could have guessed who the boy was, even without the lopsided twist to his smile. He'd worn it in the portrait in Carillon's study, and it had still been visible through the mess of wrinkles he'd carried as an old man. Larch couldn't have been more than twelve years old in the photo, looking scrawny and suspiciously respectable, with his hair slicked back and his arm thrown around the shoulders of a much younger girl in a pale dress, her wide eyes staring straight at the camera as if entranced.

"You'd know Larch, of course," said Carillon. Her voice sounded brittle as glass. "The girl shows up in pictures all over the house. Varying ages. She was grown at least, when it happened. I've never let Angevin tell me the details."

Swallowing hard, Ivy stared at the photo. The paper felt warm from sitting in Carillon's pocket, and Ivy shuddered, remembering the scorching puffs of air from the wing in the vault.

Uncle Patrick had never mentioned having a sister. He'd barely mentioned his family at all, but . . . what would it be like, to just forget you had a sibling? How long had it taken Carillon to realize she'd once had a daughter?

"I don't understand why you're protecting it," said Ivy in a low voice.

"Because fewer people die," Carillon said harshly. "Do you really think Ambrose won't try to be the hero, if you tell him? I'm sure you could convince him to believe you eventually, and what happens then? The same disaster with a new victim that everyone forgets. They're safer not knowing."

"So I lie to them instead?" Ivy snapped.

"If necessary, yes," said Carillon, unrepentant. "You know what the Enemy is, and with that knowledge comes responsibility. The wing . . . will probably protect you, up to a point. You've seen what it does to anyone else who provokes it."

"Why would it protect me?" Ivy asked, and saw something unsettling flicker in Carillon's eyes, as though the question was more troubling to her than discussing the dead child she couldn't remember. Ivy glanced down at the picture again, the almost-familiar face of the man she'd been taught to call Uncle Patrick. "There were four of us in that room. Why am I the only one who remembers?"

Carillon licked her lips, and hesitated. "One possible reason is you're too different from us for it to manipulate. You aren't like anything it was designed for." She plucked the photograph from Ivy's fingers, her thumb running over a crease in the photo as she slipped it back into her wallet. "It doesn't want to lie to us, Ivy. It doesn't even want to kill us. To the extent it can be said to want anything at all, it wants to be left alone to follow its programming. It's trying to do the same thing we are—live its way into the future. Time travel by the slowest means possible."

Carillon shoved the wallet back into her pocket, an uneasy grimace tugging at the corner of her normally expressionless mouth.

"Angevin said the wing was meant to stop Event Two," Ivy replied, unhappily. "He said that's still what it's trying to do. He gave me the key to the vault. He wanted me to see what was down there, and someone I cared about went with me and she never came out. Why?"

"If Valiard sent a scout to your flat, they likely believe you're connected to Event Two," Carillon said in a low voice, waving off Ivy's immediate objections. "Angevin thinks so, too. I've seen him ignored, or derided, or called mad, but I have never, not even once, known him to be wrong."

"I'm twenty years old and I work at a bar," Ivy snapped, gesturing at her Blue Parrot shirt. "I'm nobody. If I have anything to do with the end of the world, it's because I'm caught up in all this—your problems, and your murders, and your people!"

"Your people, too, I should think," Carillon said quietly, the corner of her mouth turning up, too hesitant to be called a smile. "Either way, if you're connected to Event Two, there's a chance, however slight, that your actions could prevent Armageddon. Or cause it to occur."

Ivy swallowed hard. The heat in the warm July air suddenly seemed just as tainted with ash and brimstone as the vault downstairs. And before Ivy had a chance to shout down that terrifying and ridiculous supposition, Carillon continued, in the gentlest voice Ivy had ever heard her use.

"The thing you saw in the basement is still alive because it's our only weapon in the only war that has ever mattered, and that war started last night. If you want to try to save the world, Salem would help you. If you let it."

"Absolutely not," Ivy hissed. Despite the warmth in the air, a thin finger of gooseflesh was running down the back of her neck. Did Carillon actually think Ivy would agree to team up with a killer computer to try and save the world? The idea was equal parts ridiculous and horrifying. "It *killed* my friend. You've hid what the Enemy really is from everyone. You've been lying and it has been *killing people.* You're so worried about the bad things that might happen in the future, you don't care one bit about the bad things that are happening right now! I won't help it. Or you."

"Not even for Garrett and Evan?" Carillon asked.

Ivy looked hard at the thane, unnerved to hear her stepbrothers' names. Carillon had nothing to do with Ivy's family, and the one person who might have thought differently died screaming in February. Carillon allowed the wing to kill both her own children; Ivy wasn't going to let her use the twins as an enticement.

"Not if it means spending another minute in the same room as that thing," Ivy said. "Find someone else."

Ambrose would know what to do about the wing, Ivy thought suddenly. He'd know if there was even a grain of truth in the idea that the Enemy might help prevent the apocalypse. Or he'd know only if Ivy could somehow convince him to believe what the Enemy actually was. If he knew, or Hunzu, or

Solly, or *anyone*, then it wouldn't only be Ivy deciding the right thing to do. But if she gave in to Carillon, never tried to make Ambrose remember what he'd seen in the vault, then she'd be entirely alone.

Apart from Carillon herself, an accessory to murder several hundred times over.

"The wing allowed you to see it," Carillon insisted, some of the steel coming back into her voice. "It might even allow you control over its interface, if you tried."

Mistress. The echo of the word seemed to hang in the air above the droning murmur of the crickets. With a feeling of dread, Ivy wondered what else the thing might say to her, if she marched back into the vault and offered it her arm.

"I won't do it," Ivy said again, shaking her head. "Find someone else."

"There isn't anyone else," Carillon snapped, frustration breaking through her ice-cold veneer. "It's already followed its goddamned protocols and too many fools on the council thought last year was a turning point, instead of an aberration. It's already chosen its current operator." Carillon came a step closer, her voice dropping to a whisper. "I swear to you, Larch never would have done it if he knew they wouldn't call a lottery."

A jumble of suppositions were tumbling through Ivy's head. Angevin called her ability to see through veils a genetic advantage. The kingship had been an inherited title once; the lottery only came later.

Which was completely irrelevant, because Ivy's mother wasn't a trow, even though she was invisible herself. And the man who made her that way . . .

"Larch isn't what you think," Ivy said, not bothering to keep the anger out of her voice. Larch never had been a father in any sense of the word, and his last-minute decision to die in place of Ivy's flatmate didn't change that.

"Mine isn't the opinion that counts," said Carillon with a shrug. "If the wing extended you such considerations, *it* believes you have a right to them. I can't think of another explanation. We didn't choose a Year King, so *it* picked the next candidate available. You."

Every drop of sweat on Ivy's neck was shot through with ice. As if from a long way off, Ivy remembered Larch's face from the apple grove, and the face of the woman in the street. Next February. She'd throw herself into the ocean and hope she didn't ignite. She'd fly to New Zealand and hope the Enemy couldn't track her across half the planet. She'd sit on her mother's porch and kiss her goodbye and walk out to the alley and away from anything flammable. She'd go to the apple grove at the bottom of the hill, and sit next to a stone with a name that no longer meant anything to anyone and scream, and scream, and scream.

At least when Larch died, it hadn't been after months of dread and goodbyes, and Ivy suddenly knew exactly why Demi had run away from the Liberties last year.

Carillon hesitated, reaching out as though she were about to touch Ivy's cheek. Instead, she grabbed the hem of Angevin's scarf, her fingers twining among the tassels.

"Something about this place and time is so critical, our ancestors bent the laws of physics to claw their way back here and change it. They failed, but we have another chance to get it right." Carillon dropped the scarf, leaning close to Ivy's ear. Her breath felt hot on Ivy's cheek, shivers dancing along her skin like a memory of winter. "And in February, I'll make sure it isn't you. I'm the only one who can promise you that."

The threat rang through the shadowed garden like a thunderclap. Demi was dust in the vault of this house, and she'd never been the one in danger. She would have lived except for Ivy, and now no one remembered her, not even the people complicit in her death. If Ivy accepted Carillon's offer, she'd be doing something even worse. Not forgetting. Ignoring. As if what happened to Demi and all the other Year Kings didn't matter.

It did matter, and Ivy had seven months to make sure what happened to all the previous Year Kings never happened to her, or to anyone else.

"I'm not helping it, or you," Ivy snapped. February was months away. She'd find a way to kill it, or reprogram it, or hurl it off a cliff into the bottom of the ocean. There had to be a way to break the yearly cycle of its murders.

Glaring, Ivy turned away and started back toward the house. She'd find a way to make Ambrose and Hunzu believe her. Ambrose had Demi's picture on the background of his phone, for God's sake. There had to be something Ivy could do to help him remember. Even if they didn't believe her, Ivy still had to try.

Two steps later, the smell of ash and wood polish was everywhere. Ivy froze, panic tightening around her throat like a noose.

Carillon wasn't going to let it wait until February.

Ivy dove into her purse as she turned back to the lamppost, latching onto the Taser and pulling it free, paper and coins scattering across the grass, expecting the garden around her to dissolve into flames at any minute.

Ivy pulled the trigger the moment the Taser was clear of her bag. It fired with a hiss and Ivy flinched, scrambling to get a better grip on the handle, already certain she'd missed.

Carillon's hand dropped to her side as she teetered, then slumped backward, collapsing in a heap like a marionette whose puppeteer had abandoned her, her head lolling against the bench's legs with an audible crack.

The smell of wood polish faded; nothing erupted into flames. For a long moment, there was no sound but the low singing of the crickets in the hedge.

Ivy ripped the spent cartridge off the end of the Taser and dropped it.

"Carillon?" she hissed, edging closer. It was too dark to see more than an outline of her body. The shape didn't seem to be moving; Ivy wondered exactly how long before the effects of the Taser wore off. Probably Ivy ought to be running before Carillon shook it off.

The thane didn't look like she was shaking it off.

Ivy automatically reached for her phone before remembering it was burnt to pieces in the parlor's rubbish bin. She crept closer, heart thudding as though her blood had been replaced with adrenaline. Had Carillon really just tried to kill her?

Ivy took another hesitant step closer and knelt. The ground felt wet with dew, soaking through her trousers almost immediately, the phantom hints of wood polish cut by a different, metallic smell. Ivy hesitated with her hand over Carillon's unmoving shoulder, two equally disastrous scenarios fighting in her head: Carillon was going to spring to life and throttle Ivy on the spot, or Carillon was never going to move again, and Ivy *wished* she'd taken more time in the car to read the Taser's instructions.

Without giving herself time to consider whether it was a good idea or not, Ivy laid her hand against Carillon's cheek. Her skin felt hot, and Ivy jerked her hand back, as though she'd been expecting sparks.

No reaction from Carillon. Ivy was certain if the thane had been capable of snapping at her, she would have.

Shit. Something had gone wrong; this couldn't be how the Taser was supposed to work. Ivy jumped to her feet, turning back to the house, her eyes momentarily dazzled by the light from the windows. Ambrose was still inside; he'd know what to do.

Ivy nearly made it back to the porch when the door burst open with a slam, and Hunzu came running out, followed by Ambrose. Hunzu's face looked ashen; he tripped on the edge of the path as Ambrose hurried past him.

"There," Ivy said, pointing needlessly at the rag-doll shape on the ground by the bench. Ambrose's eyes widened. Ivy turned to follow him but stopped with a jerk when Hunzu's fingers closed on her bare arm.

"What did you mean about finding the Enemy?" Hunzu hissed as he gingerly let go of her arm. The expression on his face was wavering somewhere between worry and terror.

"It's in the house," Ivy hissed, the shortest explanation she could come up with. "You can't go looking for it. Promise me you won't."

"Oh my God," said Hunzu, and all the color drained from his face, and maybe he believed her, if it frightened him that much. But Hunzu's eyes weren't on hers at all, and she followed his gaze down to her own shoes.

It hadn't been dew, where she'd knelt in the grass. The light from the open door picked up the color perfectly against her trousers. Ivy jumped back, as though she could get away from it, the blood covering her own clothes, and she looked back down the path in horror. The marks of her own bloody footprints were visible in the gravel. Vaguely, Ivy could see Ambrose crouching next to the bench, murmuring something to the figure on the ground.

For a moment, Ivy felt paralyzed, just as frozen and help-less as when she'd fallen to the floor after scout's injection.

Whatever she did, whichever way she moved, disaster was waiting. There was only going to be more blood, and more murders, and maybe the best thing Ivy could do was stop trying, and then maybe she'd never make any more mistakes. Like chasing the scout down the alley, or trying to kill the thing in the vault.

At least the evidence of *those* deaths weren't written in bloody footprints all over the lawn.

Ivy shuddered, forcibly shaking off the feeling of paralysis, and started to join Ambrose. Hunzu stepped in front of her, waving his hands as though he was about to touch her again.

"Ivy," he snapped, and he didn't grab her wrist but the snub nose of the Taser, and Ivy startled, belatedly realizing it was still in her hand. "You have to go."

Hunzu's face, half in shadow, was chilling in its intensity.

"Hunzu!" Ambrose's voice carried from the dark edge of the garden. "Help, if you please!"

Ivy started to turn. Hunzu stepped closer and he still wasn't letting go of the Taser. From somewhere above, Ivy heard a window thrown open with a screech.

"If she's dead, they could kill you," he hissed.

"What?" Ivy asked, and yanked her hand free, shoving the Taser deep into her messenger bag. "She's been *helping* it. She's been lying to all of you, and—"

"They won't care," Hunzu snapped. "Even if they believe you. We don't—" He stepped back, running his hands through his hair. "They would wait and let the Enemy have her, and it's a reprieve for someone else. But not if she's already dead. You just stole the only currency we have to pay the only debt that matters." His voice had dropped to a whisper. "They've killed *us* for less, and with you—"

"Hunzu!" Ambrose shouted. "*Now*, for God's sake!"

"They can't give you to the Enemy, so they won't hesitate," he hissed.

They had already given her to the Enemy. For a moment, the loathing in Emerson's face in the council seemed just as terrifying as the emotionless face of the Enemy downstairs. A furious council of trows now, or an insane alien computer in seven months. No one would believe her, and Angevin would go on feeding people to the thing in the basement in some horrible scheme to save a city that had both already burned and wouldn't exist for thousands of years.

"Hunzu!"

Another window opened with a screech. Lights were beginning to turn on in the rooms facing the garden.

"Coming!" Hunzu hollered down the path, then turned back to Ivy, pulling something out of his pocket in a quick jerk. "Get out of here," he hissed. "Steer clear of us and the Roinn, just for a few days."

"But why—"

"If she wasn't the only one protecting . . . whatever you say is down there." He shoved his car keys roughly into Ivy's hand. "If this were a novel, in chapter one the girl shows up and says something mysterious to the hero. Then she winds up dead in chapter two, and the hero spends the rest of the book figuring out what it was the dead girl already knew."

Hunzu hesitated, then squeezed Ivy's fingers, letting go almost before Ivy realized he'd touched her. "Please live long enough to help us figure this out."

Ivy nodded, swallowing hard.

"You have to live long enough to help me, too," Ivy told him, surprised to find her voice was shaking the tiniest bit. "Stay out of the basement. And think about how we met. You were looking for someone you don't remember."

Behind her, the door opened with a slam, and Ivy didn't

wait. She bolted past Hunzu and across the grass toward the drive, fingers clenched around Hunzu's keys. Haven's stone walls seemed to tower over her, lights in the windows blinking awake like unfriendly eyes. Behind her, someone called Ambrose's name. The entire house would be in an uproar soon, and Hunzu was right—trows only tolerated murder in one circumstance, and this wasn't it. And Ivy had no idea how she could prove what had happened—with Carillon or before it with the wing in the vault.

Or she wouldn't prove anything to anyone, because Emerson or others like him would take her flight as the only evidence of guilt they needed and hunt her down without bothering to listen to anything she said.

Even if they didn't, Ivy would still be dead in seven months. The idea felt too big to fathom, like trying to imagine the vastness of an ocean, or the enormity of the sun. Like the sun, it would burn her to pieces if she tried to contemplate it directly.

She reached the first group of cars in the turning circle. A voice called out from farther up the hill, too distant to make out. Crickets murmured in the grass bordering the drive; the reedy call of a blackbird sounded twice, then fell silent. Almost as if it were a beautiful evening, and the world hadn't turned upside down.

Ivy reached Hunzu's car, struggled to fit the key in the lock, and threw open the door. She glanced back at the house as she slid into the seat. Nearly every window was lit up and sparkling with light.

She shoved the key into the ignition and started the car. A hint of exhaust cut through the air, and Ivy felt tears pricking in her eyes as she threw the car into reverse. She wondered if Carillon was still alive, and if she wasn't, whether Ambrose would consider Ivy a murderer.

Ivy wrestled the car onto the gravel drive with a jerk and flicked on the headlights. The shadows in the hedgerows shifted; in them, Ivy tried not to see the rag-doll memory of the body at the foot of the bench.

Carillon was the real murderer, and Ivy shouldn't care what happened to her. She especially shouldn't care whether Carillon's theories about Larch were true, or why the Enemy, on Larch's death, might consider Ivy the logical successor to that fatal legacy.

A legacy that apparently included a massively powerful supercomputer that was built to travel in time. Ivy remembered the sundial standing before Haven's front door. *One hour alone is in thy hands, the NOW on which the shadow stands.* She imagined the beam of her car's headlights aimed at the pointer, moving the shadow's edge to whatever point she chose. Maybe that sort of power wasn't only confined to stories. Maybe, with the right sort of magic, it was possible to go back and fix everything that had ever gone wrong.

Just like Valiard had tried to do, before their city burned.

At the bottom of the drive, Ivy slowed long enough to glance up the hill. Haven shone like a beacon, every window glowing. She stomped hard on the gas pedal as she turned onto the road, throwing herself into the darkened, farm-track labyrinths of the back roads of County Clare.

CHAPTER 8

The clock on the Citroen's dash read 1:47 in the morning, and the farm track on the left looked likely. It was little more than a gap in a hedge, the start of a rutted and overgrown drive. Beyond the beam of the Citroen's headlights, the track meandered toward the faint silhouette of a half-collapsed house. Ivy slowed the car, weighing the lateness of the hour and her increasing exhaustion against the feeling she ought to get as far and as fast away from Haven as she could.

Grass was growing up between the wheel ruts, but the road didn't look rough enough to threaten the oil pan. Yielding to her bleary eyes and the pinprick headache in her temples, Ivy eased the car off the asphalt, flicking off the headlights as she coaxed the Citroen down the track. The running lights lit up a few feet of rutted ground, the bramble-studded hedge a shadowy presence on the left side of the road.

A gate materialized within a dozen yards, and a momentary flicker of eyeshine in the long grass beyond. Ivy stopped the car shy of the gate, cracked the driver's side window, then killed the engine. The sudden quiet rang in the air like a gong.

She unbuckled her seatbelt and leaned forward, resting her

head against the steering wheel. White centerline strips flickered, dreamlike, on the backs of her eyelids, as though her body hadn't quite given up on the notion that she was still driving.

Two hours, Ivy told herself, and reached into her pocket for her phone before remembering she didn't have one. If she napped in the car, there was little chance of her sleeping through the sunrise, and the sky would be light early. Pushing herself upright, Ivy reached under the seat, found the handle, and slid the seat a depressing few inches farther back.

Sighing, Ivy reclined the seat as far as it would go and twisted onto her side, wondering if the back seats could possibly be any more comfortable. She shot an appraising glance behind her—and froze.

Something small, metallic and cylindrical was sitting on the cushions in the back seat. Ivy lunged for the dome light, pawing at the roof of the car for a heart-stopping second before she found the switch.

A familiar dented paint can was leaning against the door, the edge of a torn sheet of paper sticking out from underneath. Ivy swallowed hard. Hunzu's evergreen air freshener wasn't doing a thing against the smell of smoke that had suddenly invaded the car. She could chuck the paint can into the ditch, turn the car around, and not stop until she reached the M50.

Then Demi's name jumped out from the piece of paper, and Ivy's stomach lurched. He'd labeled it, was her first sickening thought, before spotting her own name just below. Both names had been crossed out.

Hesitantly, Ivy snagged the edge of the paper and pulled it free. She held it up to the dome light, reading over the few sentences written in an unfamiliar hand.

My dear ~~Demi~~
   ~~Ivy~~

~~De~~

Your first lesson was murder. Second lesson, time travel. The next scout will be coming soon. You have to find him, and you have to help him. You have every reason not to trust ~~me~~ him. I've worked longer than you know for a chance at a solution where no one dies. None of that happens without you.

You're the only one who remembers ~~Iv~~ ~~De~~ her this time around, so it seemed appropriate to leave this with you.

Ivy stared at it, her skin turning cold in the still July air. Why had Angevin started out his note addressing it to a dead girl?

First lesson, murder.

Did he mean what happened to Demi? Or did it mean that Carillon was dead? That was impossible. Angevin had to have written the note just after Ivy ran upstairs to find Ambrose; there was no way he could have known what had happened between Ivy and the thane. Besides, the note didn't matter. Angevin was an accessory to murder as much as Carillon was, and Ivy wasn't going to help either of them.

Ivy crumpled up the note and shoved it into her purse, jerking her hand back as her fingers touched the Taser. If Angevin wanted to track down a scout to warn them about what was in store for Valiard, he could do it himself. None of this was Ivy's problem. All Ivy had to do was somehow figure out how to get Ambrose and Hunzu to believe her about what was in the vault, without them immediately doing something that would trip the wing's murderous safeguards.

Ivy turned off the dome light, a wave of apprehension washing over her as the car and everything inside it vanished in a wash of black. Ivy rolled onto her back, blinking at the ceiling and the distant, star-smudged horizon.

Following a quiet urge she didn't question, Ivy reached behind her and grappled in the back seat for the little urn. Something inside rattled and Ivy nearly dropped it, momentarily afraid that she was about to spill her best friend's mortal remains all over the back of her other best friend's car. Apparently Angevin had sealed the lid, and Ivy wrestled the can to the front seat without incident. Hesitantly, Ivy set it on the seat beside her and awkwardly patted the top. It felt cool, the edges rough with rust. Nothing about it felt the least bit like her friend.

We found the Enemy, Ivy thought. Except it wasn't the Enemy they'd expected, and maybe that was why the trows had come to think of it like some sort of unavoidable natural disaster. Most of them had given up trying to kill it, and its keepers would rather let the Enemy keep murdering their own people than relinquish a potential weapon in a war that hadn't happened yet.

If this had been the sort of fairy story that ends up in books, Demi wouldn't be dead and the villains harboring the Enemy would have ended up dying by some flaw of their own devising, and Ivy would never have had to use the Taser at all. Or even better, it could have been the kind of story where Ivy wasn't the hero at all, just someone who showed up at the right moment and helped things turn out the way they were supposed to.

In the real world, it seemed the only thing Ivy was good for was getting other people killed. Larch, five months ago. The scout last night. Demi. Maybe, just maybe, Carillon.

She rolled over, curling herself into as tight a ball as she could, and when she slept she dreamed of fire.

SHORTLY BEFORE TEN the next morning, Ivy pulled the Citroen into a fifteen-minute parking space two blocks away from the Dartry flat. She felt rumpled, bleary, and on edge, like she'd just pulled an all-nighter and followed it up with a gallon of black coffee.

Ivy hefted her purse out of the passenger seat, pulled out her keys, and gave a sidelong look at the metal can. She didn't want to leave it in the car; she wanted even less to bring it into the flat. It was impossible to treat it as both an urn and a rusted paint can, and bringing it home felt too much like inviting the problem of finding someplace acceptable to put it.

Ivy got out of the car and started down Orwell Road toward her flat. A previous stop at a Crumlin Road charity shop had gotten her a grey t-shirt and a pair of jeans going threadbare at the knees. The Blue Parrot polo and the bloodstained trousers were bundled into a ball in the Citroen's trunk.

If she could get to her computer, she could try to get in touch with Hunzu and figure out what the hell she was supposed to do next. The Enemy, Carillon, the scout who'd died, and the one Angevin claimed would be following—all were like the snarled edges of a knot Ivy hadn't the slightest idea how to unravel.

Though some corner of Ivy's heart hadn't given up on the idea that when she was able to log into her email, there'd be a message from Ambrose saying that everything was fine and it was all a misunderstanding.

The contents of the paint can proved otherwise.

Ivy shuffled her keys in her hand, so the house key was sticking out from her fist like a knuckleduster. At the corner of Hawthorne and Orwell, a woman in a green apron was arranging a cluster of tables and chairs outside a café. As Ivy passed the waitress nodded at her, and Ivy was uncomfortably aware she was holding her keys like she was walking through

Finglas at two in the morning. The ordinary bustle felt surreal, as though the traffic and the waitress and the café were painted overtop something dark, sinister, and deeply inexplicable. Ivy wondered if the traffic cones would still be blocking off the pothole on Orwell Road where the scout had died, or if someone had already sent an asphalt truck to patch it up.

As Ivy turned up the sidewalk, she fished the door key from the cluster in her fist, unlocked the door, and stepped inside. Someone bolted up from the sofa, and Ivy jumped.

"Where the bloody hell were you?" Lauren asked, hurrying across the parlor, eyes wide. "You were out all night and your door was open and you weren't answering any of my texts!"

She was shouting to be heard over Grinch's barking. The bulldog raced into the front room, his head sticking out of a cone collar like a drool-filled potted flower. Still barking, Grinch rammed the edge of the cone into Ivy's shins.

Lauren bit her lip as she looked Ivy up and down. "Everything alright? You look terrible."

"Something's come up with my step-mum," Ivy improvised, reaching down to pat Grinch on the shoulder that wasn't covered by bandages. "I stayed over to look after Garrett and Evan."

"They're seven now, aren't they?" Lauren asked, walking back to the sofa and patting the cushion. "Bloody terrors at that age. Any age, really, if they're boys. Grinch, stop that, will you?"

The bulldog looked up, claws clattering as he turned toward Lauren. Instead of retreating to his bed, Grinch scampered three steps down the hall, barked once, and bounded back, throwing himself against the backs of Ivy's knees.

Frowning, Lauren walked back to the couch and patted the cushion; Grinch continued to wind himself around Ivy's legs. Guiltily, Ivy realized she hadn't given a single thought to

Grinch or Lauren since last night. Now that Ivy was sitting in her own flat with her boringly normal flatmate and her idiot dog, everything that had gone wrong at Haven seemed ever so slightly unreal.

"How is he?" Ivy asked, bending over to gently pet Grinch.

"Clingy," Lauren said, and snapped her fingers. Grinch ignored her. "He slept most of yesterday, but this morning it's like he can't settle down. Told the Institute I'm taking a sick day. I'm going to call the vet about getting him more pain meds."

Lauren scooted a pile of papers off the far end of the sofa and patted the cleared space. Grinch considered it, then hurried back down the hall. Ivy could hear his claws clattering on the linoleum.

"Let me know if you need anything," Lauren added, slipping her phone out of her pocket. "Not that I'm offering to babysit your brothers, mind."

"Thanks," Ivy said, and walked a few feet farther into the room, staring at the pile of half-opened mail and glossy magazines as though it had come from a different universe. A bill from the cable provider. A magazine with a grinning actress Ivy vaguely recognized. A pair of fancy cards with *Gala Invitation* written across the front in an elaborate, curlicued font.

Ivy stared blankly at the pile. Something about the invitation looked strange. Or maybe staring at the loops and flourishes was easier than actually deciding what to do next, when all Ivy really wanted to do was wrap herself in a blanket and let the world go on without her for a bit.

"Work thing," Lauren said with a sigh, following Ivy's gaze. She picked up the two cards and frowned at them. "I better stay with Grinch, but you could go. Helena will be there, and her friend Devin works in HR, but don't let that put you off because he's dreamy *and* he and his ex just split up. Plus all of

Helena's friends from R&D. And there's an open bar." Lauren's eyes lit up as though she'd just thought of something, and she handed both of the cards to Ivy. "You could bring whats'er name, your friend from last night. You told me she doesn't get out much."

The world wavered on its axis and Ivy took the cards, plastering a noncommittal smile on her face because that was better than shouting or melting into a crying heap on the floor. The card stock crinkled under her fingers as she walked out of the room. It wasn't right and it wasn't fair; Demi deserved to have someone remember her, remember that she'd died fighting monsters. Ivy was the only one who remembered her properly, and she realized she was the tiniest bit jealous of the people who didn't.

Grinch bounded alongside her as Ivy went down the hall, still trying to wrap himself around her legs. He whined, shoving the edge of his cone into the backs of Ivy's calves.

"You okay?" Lauren called from the living room.

"Sure," Ivy lied, shoving Grinch away as firmly as she dared, and turned to the door of her room.

The door was shut.

Ivy stared at it for a long moment. Hadn't Lauren said her bedroom door was open, and that's how she knew Ivy hadn't come home? Maybe she'd closed it to keep Grinch out. Except they both usually kept their doors open during the day; without air conditioning, the flat needed every possible crosscurrent and open window to keep it at a reasonable temperature.

Which was probably why the door was shut in the first place. The window was open, and a breeze had blown it shut. No supernatural explanations required.

Two nights ago, it hadn't been a pile of laundry, and the burns on Ivy's hands weren't from a defective phone.

Grabbing Grinch by the collar, Ivy slowly backed down the

hallway, her eye on the closed bedroom door. She didn't need her laptop. She could pick up a prepaid phone anywhere, and anything with a data plan would get her access to her email.

Shoving Grinch in the direction of the parlor, Ivy went into the kitchen. She'd grab some granola bars and a few packets of instant noodles, and go find some other way to check her email. Or call Ambrose. Regardless of Carillon's current state of health or Ambrose's opinions about Ivy's role in that, if there was another scout inside Ivy's flat, Ambrose would want to know.

Ivy knelt and opened the cupboard door, pushing aside a box of raisins and a half-empty bag of biscuit mix. She leaned farther into the cupboard, spotted the carton of instant noodles, and reached for it. Grinch's nails scrabbled across the linoleum as he raced back into the kitchen. A low whine slipped from the dog's throat as his cool, wet nose brushed against the back of Ivy's neck. She startled so hard she smacked her head against the bottom of the cupboard.

"Grinch, damn it—" she snapped, turned around—and her heart plummeted to her stomach.

A trow stood in the kitchen, far too close, and the cold thing wasn't Grinch's nose but the barrel of a gun. The muzzle was pointed squarely at Ivy's face, so close it was weaving in and out of focus as Ivy stared at it in horror.

"Ambrose is looking for you," the trow smirked. Vaguely, Ivy recognized the face behind the gun as Maia, one of the trow members of the Roinn.

"Get up," the trow ordered, nodding at the hallway. Her stance exactly matched her voice—casual, confident, and utterly merciless. She looked like she knew what she was doing with the gun, not that she'd have to be an expert marksman to hit a target cowering at her feet.

A million miles away on the other side of the kitchen,

Grinch was pressed against the dishwasher, hackles sticking up around the bandages, growling like an idling engine.

Slowly, Ivy got to her feet and raised her hands, making sure the purse didn't slide off her shoulder. Her Taser was still in the bottom of the bag.

"Back down the hall," Maia ordered, nodding at the hallway.

All the advice on the internet said *don't let them take you to a second location*. Maia wouldn't want to shoot her here in the flat, some distant voice in Ivy's head pointed out. The veil didn't work well enough to cover gunshots, not to mention things like dead bodies, and screaming, and blood. The Roinn spent a good deal of their time trying to avoid trows being the cause of anything dramatic and unexplainable.

Ivy started across the kitchen as slowly as she dared, trying to think, while Grinch's growl deepened to a chest-rattling thrum. There'd be traffic outside, cars and pedestrians. Anywhere with a crowd, and Ivy might have options.

Maia heard the footsteps at the same moment as Ivy. The trow jumped out of the way as Lauren stormed into the kitchen, grabbed Grinch by the collar and sprayed him in the face with a lemon bottle.

"Lie down," she snapped at the dog. Grinch shook the scented water out of his face with a snort, his growl spluttering to a hesitant warble. Lauren shook his collar for emphasis and turned to her flatmate. "Ivy—shit, did he *bite* you?"

Lauren's face went chalky, as though whatever she was seeing in Ivy's expression was telegraphing the end of the world.

Uncertainly, Lauren took a hesitant step toward Ivy, loosening her grip on Grinch. Seeing his opening, Grinch lunged at the trow, baring his teeth and snarling. Aghast, Lauren grabbed Grinch's collar, jerking him back hard enough

Grinch's front paws came off the floor, his growl turning into a yelp.

"If that thing bites me, it's going to regret it," Maia said matter-of-factly. "And so will both of you."

"Just put him in your room for a bit," Ivy heard herself say, recalculating that maybe the number of bystanders didn't matter. Trows put value on their own lives, lengthy in ways Ivy couldn't quite imagine, worthy of being spared from everything but one particular kind of death. That sort of value didn't extend to people like Ivy or Lauren. Maybe the best and only thing Ivy could do was make sure no one else ended up as collateral damage.

"Okay," said Lauren, her eyes narrowing as she looked around the room, still struggling with Grinch. "I don't know what set him off. This place . . . it's just given me the creeps all day."

Ivy could see goosebumps standing up on Lauren's arms, for all that it was already warm in the room. Impatiently, Maia gestured to the hall.

"I'm going out for a bit," said Ivy, slowly and distinctly. It seemed an impossible effort of will to step away from the kitchen cabinets, as though they were the only things holding her up.

"After you," Maia said, a thin, ugly smile on her face.

"Okay," said Lauren, still looking at Ivy strangely, and at Maia not at all. Biting her lip, Lauren turned and all but dragged Grinch out of the kitchen, his nails scoring the linoleum as he tried to claw himself loose.

No one else would get hurt, Ivy told herself as she walked out of the kitchen, clutching her purse tightly against her chest. Whatever Maia was going to do, she wouldn't hurt anyone else if Ivy cooperated. From the back hallway, Lauren's door slammed shut.

"Ivy?" Lauren called, hesitantly.

Very slowly, Ivy turned around. Maia was standing just out of arm's reach, her gun pointed somewhere in the general vicinity of Ivy's belly. Beyond her, Lauren stood in the hallway, her hand on the knob of her door.

"You know if you ever—" Lauren broke off, rubbing at her forehead, and Ivy realized with a jolt that she was leaning against the wall, craning her head to see past Maia without even being aware she was doing it. "I know there's something going on with you and what happened the other night. You don't need to tell me if you don't want to, but if there's anything I can do to help . . ."

Lauren trailed off, biting her lip uncomfortably. It felt like someone holding out a hand after Ivy had already tumbled off the edge of a cliff.

"If I shoot you right now, who do you think they'd arrest for it?" Maia demanded impatiently.

Lauren shuddered and she glanced over her shoulder, as though somehow, in the corners of her mind too well-protected for the veil to play with, she knew something was terribly wrong.

"Everything's fine," Ivy lied, forcing her lips into a smile, smearing it on like a child playing with lipstick. "I'll be back soon." She turned her back on Maia, and the gun, and Lauren's disbelieving, frightened face. She grabbed the door handle, wrestled it open, and stepped through, crossing the porch and heading to the sidewalk and refusing to look back.

"What the hell is this about?" Ivy snapped as soon as she heard the front door swing shut. Maia was a coworker, for God's sake; she'd shown Ivy the Roinn's filing system and where Meredith hid her stash of coconut water and fig bars. Even if Ambrose had sent Maia to threaten her, or worse, Maia shouldn't be *enjoying* it. If Ivy could be angry about that, maybe it would cover up how frightened she was.

"Ambrose wants to see you," said Maia, and Ivy could hear the smirk in her voice. "In what condition, he didn't really specify. Left here," Maya added, as Ivy reached the sidewalk.

Ivy turned, the opposite direction from where she'd parked the Citroen. She could hear the trow's footsteps on the sidewalk behind her, staying a careful few feet away.

Ivy licked her lips. Maybe Maia really was going to bring her to Ambrose. Or maybe Maia was planning on shooting her in a back alley and dumping her in the river. Maybe what happened next depended on how badly Carillon was hurt.

"Is the thane alright?" Ivy asked.

"So far," Maia said coldly.

Ivy glanced back, then quickly averted her eyes.

"Left here," said Maia, as they approached the intersection of Hawthorne and Highfield. The tables and chairs in front of the restaurants were full and bustling, awnings and menu boards spilling onto the sidewalk. Ivy glanced down Highfield toward the intersection where the transformer had blown up, but she could see no sign of the orange traffic cones.

Ahead of Ivy, a group of tourists emerged from Dillinger's Pub, a billowing collection of sun hats, name tags, and linen shirts all proceeding down the sidewalk like a ship under sail. Ivy plowed through them, angrily pleased that Maia would have to work a bit to keep up. She knew from her experiences with Hunzu that the tourists wouldn't actually walk straight into Maia, but she would have to bob and weave a little if she didn't want them brushing up against her. Ivy risked a glance back, smiling tightly as she watched Maia do just that, hastily stepping aside to avoid a bony-looking woman with a large camera. Maia still hadn't holstered her gun.

An idea presented itself and Ivy whipped her head back to the front to keep any hint of it from showing on her face.

Maia didn't actually have to bob and weave through the crowd. She was just trying to stay away from humans the way all trows tried to stay away from humans, because the contact might start the clock of her own aging, a mechanism trows had somehow learned to stop in its tracks. Maia avoided people because the cumulative exposure might kill her.

Something like a car would do it a lot quicker.

Ivy didn't stop to consider whether it was a good idea. She simply twisted between the next oncoming couple—a man in a grey vest and a woman with a yellow flower tucked behind her ear—and darted into the road.

Maia shouted as Ivy passed the bumper of the parked car and into the traffic beyond. As the first car slammed on its brakes, Ivy belatedly realized that even with the advantage of being visible to the drivers, the cars could kill her just as well as they could Maia. Ivy bolted into the second lane, not daring to look back, car horns and shouted profanities loud in her ears. She skidded to a stop at the centerline long enough to let a white panel van scream past, passenger scowling, right hand raised in a gesture Ivy didn't linger to see him complete. She bolted again, far enough into the road that the opposing traffic seemed to have mostly seen her coming, everyone shouting, braking, and honking accordingly.

Almost braking accordingly. A truck went past so close to Ivy's heels she felt the edge of her shirt ruffle in the draft. Ivy leapt onto the sidewalk and headed down it at a run, glancing over her shoulder, half expecting to see Maia behind her, or the barrel of Maia's gun.

Ivy didn't see the trow, either in the road or the opposite sidewalk, only four lanes of traffic coming back up to the speed Ivy's mad dash had interrupted, and the crowd of tourists, now looking ruffled and excited. Ivy tore her gaze back to the sidewalk ahead of her, as close to a run as she could manage in the crowd. Maia would be after her as soon as the light changed, if not before, and Ivy wanted as much of a head start as possible.

Her purse flapping against her ribs, Ivy turned off the street and into the alley, skirting past a series of puddles rank with the stink of pigeon droppings. She slowed as she approached the row of rubbish bins near the far end of the alley, peering past them into the next street. There was only the normal, flowing mass of people: tourists clutching oversized cameras, businessmen with their ties loosened and sport coats pushed back, students in short trousers actually dressed for the weather in a way most of the businesspeople probably envied.

Three more blocks to the Citroen. Hurrying out of the alley and into the street, Ivy clawed the elastic out of her hair, shaking her head to hurry the disintegration of her braid, the only thing Ivy could think of that might quickly change her appearance. She kept her head down, looking for signs of pursuit in quick, nervous glances. Reaching into the purse, Ivy nervously fingered the Taser.

She was still gripping the Taser when she finally reached Hunzu's car. She opened the door, threw herself inside, hit the locks, and slammed the key into the ignition. A moment later, the little car tore away from the curb, careening deeper into warren of Dublin's streets.

❧❧❧

LUNCH-HOUR PEDESTRIANS CROWDED the sidewalks as Ivy came to a stop at the traffic light near the harbor. Out the window, she watched a stream of tourists in sunglasses and office workers with blazers unbuttoned and jackets thrown over their shoulders, soaking in the unseasonably warm weather.

Ivy wondered, if things had gone differently last year, whether one of those women might have been her, living a life with more briefcases and sensible shoes, and fewer invisible people and unexplainable murders. It felt like taking Ivy's actual life and looking at it through a funhouse mirror, the kind that exaggerates some parts to monstrous size while other bits are hardly visible at all.

Biting her lip, Ivy hurried through the intersection and passed the turnoff to Thormanby Road, coaxing the Citroen down a narrow alley running behind the rows of back gardens. She stopped next to a familiar garage, leaving the car idling as she hopped out and peered through the dirty windows. Apart from a rusting collection of rakes and shovels, the garage was empty. Ivy grabbed the handle, wrestled the door open with a screech, then quickly pulled the car inside.

Ivy shut the garage door behind the car, then collected her purse and the green scarf. She hesitated, then picked up the paint can as well, cradling it in her arms as she crossed the back garden, passed the hawthorn bushes, and climbed up the back stairs.

Ivy hesitated at the door for a long minute. No lights were on; the warbling murmur of one of Mr. Abernathy's smooth jazz albums was the only sign of occupancy from either side of the duplex. Taking a deep breath, Ivy yanked her keys out of her pocket, got the right one into the lock on the third try, and opened the door as quietly as she could. She stepped through, peering cautiously into the flat. The hallway looked dim and deserted and smelled slightly of dust.

Ivy tossed the scarf on the coat rack and set the paint can on the table beside it, then locked the door behind her and turned on the lights. Even with the dust and the quiet, the flat felt like home—the sort of place where her hands automatically knew the location of the light switches, even after five months away.

Ivy started down the hallway, hesitated, then went back for the paint can. The door to Demi's old bedroom was shut. Goosebumps prickled on her neck as she walked past, not looking at it.

A floorboard squeaked as Ivy passed the bottom of the stairs and stepped into the parlor. She slipped her purse off her shoulder, automatically setting it on the very edge of the end table, making room for a potted plant that wasn't there anymore. There used to be dozens of plants in the parlor alone, their pots studded with hygrometers, pH strips, and labels from the greenhouse in Dún Laoghaire listing everything the plant needed to keep it alive. It was usually a substantial list, as though Demi took a particular interest in plants that needed special attention, things that were certain to die if left entirely on their own.

Still clutching the paint can, Ivy made a slow circuit of the room, stopping at the bookcase, which was covered in circles of dust and dirt. The shelves had held considerably more plants than books; now the bookcase was empty apart from a handful of battered paperbacks and grey stains in the wood outlining the spaces the pots once occupied.

"I'm sorry," Ivy murmured, relentlessly keeping her eyes on the bookshelf, even as she felt the edge of the paint can digging into her stomach. It felt silly saying anything out loud, as if she could have another go at the Last Conversation Ever. There had almost been one of those in February, and she hadn't found the right words then, either. "We cheated it once. I'm sorry we couldn't do it again."

Even stripped of the houseplants and much of the furniture, the flat still felt like Demi, a presence hanging in the air like the scent of old perfume, or newly baked cookies.

Slowly, Ivy set the paint can on the middle shelf of the bookcase. The can rattled, and Ivy flinched hard enough to set the jumble of yellowing paperbacks sliding across the shelf. A few of them Ivy recognized as old Ray Bradbury collections, the remainder looking equally pulpy and vintage: *The Silent Tower. 1984. Dragonflight. The Time Machine.* Absently, Ivy picked up the copy of *1984*, the cover showing a Picasso-like cityscape in garish reds and oranges. She flipped it open, running her thumb over the edge of the pages. Many of the pages had sentences heavily underlined, with illegible comments scrawled in the margins, as though the book had been required reading and the student had actually bothered to take notes. The highlighted sentences jumped out at random. *Who controls the past controls the future. We shall meet again in the place where there is no darkness . . .*

There was no such place. If there wasn't darkness, it only meant someone was working very hard to make sure you didn't notice the shadows.

Ivy closed *1984* and slid it back onto the shelf, mechanically grabbing the next book and flipping it open as well. *All the old constellations had gone from the sky,* mused H. G. Wells's time traveler. *Beyond these lifeless sounds the world was silent.* Ivy shut the book, glowering at the author photo on the back. Real fairies weren't anything like what they said in books. Real time travel was probably different, too.

Ivy shoved *The Time Machine* back onto the bookcase, feeling something light and crumbling brush against her fingers. Frowning, Ivy grabbed it, pulling out the desiccated remains of a brown, crumpled leaf. She ran her finger along the edge, feeling it disintegrating under her touch.

"I'm glad we got to be friends," Ivy told it softly. "I'm sorry—"

There weren't enough words to cover everything she was

sorry for, so Ivy turned away, hurrying out of the room and quashing the impulse to either take the paint can with her or say goodbye to it. It was nothing more than the dirt stains on the empty bookshelf, leftover marks where a living thing used to be.

It still felt like a goodbye. By the time Ivy reached the top of the stairs, she was crying, holding on to her purse like it was the last real thing in the world. She opened the door and threw herself onto her old bed, giving herself over to the scratchy, impersonal comfort of a bare mattress. The air felt warm and heavy with dust. She rolled onto her side, away from the yellow light streaming through the window, and curled into a ball.

Her room in the Dartry flat would just be starting to cool off, the breezes slipping through the window along with the droning noise of traffic on the main road. Ivy didn't want to think about how long it might be until she could go back there. Or anywhere else with people who might be vulnerable to trows. Her mother, Victoria, living alone with too many cats. Her friend Deirdre, in her flat in Glasnevin. Her dad, step-mum, and Garrett and Evan out in East Worring. Any of them would take Ivy in without question, even if they knew she was in terrible trouble, which was why Ivy absolutely couldn't go anywhere near them. Not if people like Maia would be next to show up at their door.

Ivy wondered morosely if Maia would have been as quick to pull her gun if Ivy told her Carillon's theory—that Ivy was the one the Enemy would come for next.

Slowly, she pulled the Taser out of the purse, set it on the corner of the bed, and laid back down, the bare mattress rough against her cheek as she stared at the cracks in the ceiling and wondered what came next.

Ivy woke slowly, gathering herself in bits and realizing she was back at the flat in Howth without quite knowing why. She reached to pull her bedsheets closer to her nose, realized she was sleeping on a bare mattress, and everything from the past two days came back all at once.

Ivy sat up immediately, biting back Demi's name just before she said it out loud. Demi was dead, everyone else was angry at her, and she'd been ambushed in her own flat twice in three days. Howth was safe so far, but this was a temporary reprieve. She'd have to go back to work at the Blue Parrot at some point, and even if she didn't Ivy was certain Ambrose would figure out some other way to track her down, given time.

Unless the scouts from Valiard beat him to it. Or Angevin—he'd been here at the Thormanby flat in February, looking for Demi. It wasn't impossible he'd decide to come back to talk her into saving a place that wouldn't exist for centuries.

Ivy rolled over, burrowing her face into the scratchy mattress. *First lesson, murder. Next lesson, time travel.*

Time travel ought to be impossible, just as impossible as fairies, but Valiard had discovered how to do it. They'd created a door that could open anywhere in history. So why had they chosen to come to south Dublin? Which only led to another question, equally puzzling: why go to all that trouble to visit the past? Creating a door that bridged time had to be dangerous, difficult, and expensive. Were the scouts meant only to document a disaster, or had Valiard been planning to change something?

Ivy looked up from the mattress, her gaze flicking from the Taser beside her to the empty closet, the coat hangers lying jumbled on the floor.

Was it possible to change the past? The Taser, unused. Her flatmate, still alive.

Or farther back—Ivy's mother and father still living

together. A world where Larch had never waltzed into her mother's life. A world where Ivy never met Demi in the first place, and Ivy had never gotten her killed. A world where Ivy never met the monsters, even the ones she'd grown to call friends.

The scout who burned in Dartry had risked her life to travel into the past. Had *she* been trying to change something?

Slowly, Ivy pushed herself up to a sitting position. If a scout could travel centuries back in time to change something, wasn't it possible that Ivy could do the same thing on a smaller scale? One tiny push in the fabric of the universe, so that Ivy had never gone into the vault, never fired her Taser—so Ivy could solve the puzzle of the Enemy and its clockwork murders without anyone having to die.

The entire idea was mad. Even if time travel actually existed, that didn't necessarily mean the time travelers could actually change the past. If they did, then according to Hunzu the scary, red-eyed changelings would show up and change things right back.

Instead of thinking up wild plans involving alien technology, Ivy needed to take a shower, walk to the marina, and find somewhere to buy a burner phone. If she could just get a few minutes to talk with Ambrose, maybe she could convince him to at least listen to her about Carillon and what she was keeping in the vault. And what happened to Demi. Ivy owed that much to her flatmate, to try and tell Ambrose the truth.

Even if Ambrose didn't believe her, maybe Ivy could at least convince him to get the Roinn agents out of the Dartry flat. Lauren didn't deserve that—*she* wasn't the one involved with trows, time travel, and alien serial killers.

Ivy slid off the bed and went to the bathroom, looking uneasily into the mirror over the sink. Her face looked as rough as she'd expected: dark circles under her eyes, a pinprick scab on her neck surrounded by an ugly purpling bruise. The left side of her face had turned pinkish like a sunburn, the hair on that side singed and noticeably shorter. A shower wouldn't help any of that, though perhaps she could find some scissors to even up her hair.

Ivy opened the cabinet under the sink and pulled out a crusted bottle of shampoo. Poor Lauren. She didn't deserve to have Maia camped out in her parlor. Lauren was friendly, and cheery, and completely, boringly normal, which was why Ivy had moved in. Now Ivy was the one with the secrets. Setting the shampoo bottle on the counter, Ivy turned on the taps, feeling a sudden rush of sympathy for Demi. Five months ago, Ivy'd been the one who didn't understand what was happening, furious at the depth of the secrets her flatmate had been keeping from her. Ivy never would have gotten any of those secrets from Demi herself. It was all because of Angevin, turning up looking for Demi, and then Hunzu right after. Neither of them had explained anything, either, not at first, because Ivy wasn't important. She was just someone they'd run into when they were really looking for someone else.

Ivy stopped with her shirt halfway over her head.

Five months ago, Hunzu and Angevin were looking for Demi, and they'd ended up finding Ivy instead. They'd both been looking for someone else all along.

The skin on Ivy's neck prickled as she tried to think. There was something she'd seen in the Dartry flat, something important. Two nights ago, the scout had broken in and tried to hack Ivy's phone. But Ivy wasn't the only person who lived there. The scout had even told Ivy what she was looking for and Ivy hadn't known what it was. She squeezed her eyes shut as she tried to remember the exact words.

Do you know Diar? You know, the place where you go for work.

Ivy opened her eyes and bolted out of the bathroom, tugging her charity-shop t-shirt back over her head. She grabbed her purse and turned it upside down, the contents dropping onto the bed in a shower of lip gloss, euro coins, and pens. Ivy spotted the thick creamy paper and grabbed it, spreading it out on the bare mattress.

Gala Invitation; the card read. *The Dublin Institute of Anti-Aging Research is pleased to welcome employees, spouses, and friends to our gala event, Thursday, July 23, from 7–10 p.m. Appetizers complimentary, cash bar will be available at the main DIAAR lobby. CEO Mr. Winston Smith Brothers to give an address at half eight.*

DIAAR. Lauren always referred to the place as the Institute, which always sounded like she was working for a gaggle of Victorian inventors instead of a biotech firm. The scout had known someone at 562 B Hawthorne Road worked for DIAAR, but she hadn't known which one of them it was.

The scout hadn't been looking for Ivy at all—she'd been looking for Lauren.

Ivy stopped herself from reaching into her pocket for a phone that wasn't there, and shakily lowered the card. A spy from the future had traveled through time to investigate a Dublin biotech company that possibly had something to do with the end of the world. And Ivy was holding an invitation to their company party.

Ivy crumpled up the card and shoved it back into her purse. She shouldn't go anywhere near the DIAAR campus. Stick to Plan A: get a burner phone, call Hunzu, and tell him everything that happened last night, whether he would believe it or not. Call Ambrose and arrange a way to turn herself in that didn't involve herself or any bystanders getting shot. Tell the Roinn about the connection between the scouts and the Dublin

Institute and leave it up to the trows to figure out what to do about it.

Which might be nothing, if Ambrose didn't believe her. And the door from Dublin to Valiard—the door Angevin claimed was the key to saving the present-day trows and the future city both—would open and close without anyone noticing. Whatever Valiard was setting in motion at the Institute, no one here on Earth would ever know.

First lesson, murder.

Next lesson, time travel.

If there was one thing Ivy had learned in the past six months, it was that impossible things happened. Even the impossible world's own rules didn't apply to everything. She'd changed those rules once before when she'd walked into the apple grove alongside Larch, and the old rules, the ones that said the king had to die every time, bent just enough to let Demi walk away.

Demi hadn't walked away this time. Ivy didn't know how far the rules of reality might be willing to bend to save a girl who was currently a collection of ash in a paint can in her own front parlor. Ivy didn't know why Angevin had written the name of a dead girl atop the note he'd left for Ivy, beyond the tantalizing hint that somewhere, there existed a world where Demi had been alive to read it.

If Ivy walked away now, she'd never know what might be possible. She'd never know why DIAAR was so important to the scouts, or whether Valiard really could reprogram their murderous computer. If Carillon was right, Ivy would die in February, never knowing what might have been possible.

Ivy thought of the paint can sitting in the parlor among the ghosts of Demi's own orchids. She remembered the cold iron of the poker as she'd picked it up in the vault.

"You'd go," Ivy whispered under her breath. If their positions were reversed. If it had been Demi reading the note in the car, and Ivy's was the name crossed out. If it had been Ivy who'd swung the poker and died screaming in the vault, Demi would have gone hunting for a way to make it right. She wouldn't have given up, or tried to pass the task on to someone who wouldn't believe her.

"Right, then" said Ivy, as though that was all the answer she needed.

Ivy went back to the bathroom, pulling her shirt over her head and trying to think of everything she needed to do before seven o'clock—and the start of a company party that might be the beginning of the end of the world.

CHAPTER 9

Dithering in the parking lot of the Nano Imaging Centre, Ivy tugged at the sleeves of her charity-shop jacket and looked in the rearview mirror—hair loose and finger-combed, face made up with the eyeliner and lip gloss she'd found in the bottom of her purse. Ivy hoped it was enough to spackle an appearance of severity onto her rumpled, sleep-deprived face.

Ivy opened her purse, slipping in the new phone she'd picked up at a Tesco. She looked at the Taser sitting at the bottom, pulled it out, and shoved it under the driver's seat with a sense of relief. No telling if the NIC was the sort of place that rummaged through people's bags, and Ivy didn't want to risk bringing anything in there that might prompt a phone call to the Gardaí.

Squaring her shoulders, Ivy locked the Citroen and went up the sidewalk toward the glass-fronted doors of the University's Nano Imaging Centre. At least the Roinn had no reason to think she'd be here, Ivy thought, remembering the cold touch of Maia's gun on the back of her neck. No reason to think a scout would turn up here, either, not if the woman two nights ago had really been looking for Lauren—which was why Ivy had decided to come here in the first place. If the scout hadn't been looking for Ivy, she probably didn't have anything to do with the missing wing from the NIC. If that was true, Ivy had a very good idea of where the missing wing might actually be.

Whether finding the wing would do anything to smooth matters over with Ambrose, Ivy had no idea.

Ivy opened the front door and stepped into an airy, carpeted lobby. The air conditioning was fierce enough to raise prickles on the back of Ivy's neck, even through her jacket. She fixed a disapproving expression on her face, summoning up all the rudest and most horrible customers from her stint at the call center, and went straight to the front desk. A young man with wire-rim glasses and a pencil-thin mustache looked up from his computer.

"Ivy Gallagher, to see Dr. Eliza Bannon," Ivy said crisply. "She'll know what it's about."

Either Ivy had overdone the look of displeasure and impatience, or the receptionist had already heard enough to know who Ivy was and why she might be pissed. His eyes grew very wide and he nodded mutely, turning to his phone and hurriedly dialing an extension.

Moments later, the door at the far end of the lobby swung open, and Dr. Bannon herself walked out. Ivy vaguely remembered the bright-eyed woman with greying brown hair from when she'd brought the wing to the lab several weeks earlier

"Ms. Gallagher," Dr. Bannon began uncertainly, and held out her hand. A set of large red bracelets clattered at her wrists. "I hope you've had a chance to look at the documents we sent over—"

"I'd like to see the room where the device disappeared," Ivy said, cutting her off, her fingers gripping the strap of her purse.

It was harder to act haughty and annoyed when the person she was supposed to be angry at looked like she ought to be someone's grandmother.

"Of course," Dr. Bannon said, with only the slightest hesitation. Nodding at the receptionist, she turned back to the interior door, holding it open for Ivy.

Ivy followed the director down a beige-colored hall, passing a glass-walled conference room, then a cluster of cubicles and a drooping potted palm. Coming to a metal door at the end of the hall, Dr. Bannon punched a code into a keypad. The door opened with a hiss, revealing another beige hallway with a gleaming linoleum floor.

"The main door is locked with a key code, as are the individual labs," Dr. Bannon explained as she stepped through, gesturing at the doors leading off the hall. The air was colder, and Ivy fought the urge to pull her jacket tighter around her shoulders.

"There's the University's security guards doing rounds overnight, plus cameras in the front lobby and the loading dock," the director continued. "And before you ask, we've reviewed them and we haven't found anything unexpected."

"No cameras in the lab areas themselves?" Ivy asked.

"We've never needed them before," said Dr. Bannon quietly.

She lifted her hands in a helpless sort of shrug, and for a moment Ivy felt a twinge of sympathy. The director was caught up in something strange, and whatever had gone wrong here, it hadn't been her fault. Maybe the fault was Ivy and Ambrose's, bringing a dead artifact here and assuming it was harmless.

"I'd like to see the room, please," Ivy repeated again, folding her arms over her purse.

"Of course," said Dr. Bannon, and went to the third door on

the left. She typed another code into the keypad and pushed open the door.

The room inside looked cramped, oppressive, and very clean. A large metal worktable dominated the center of the room, and a row of computer screens and chairs lined the far wall, flanked by metal cabinets and a row of gas cylinders. The table and counters were cluttered with lab equipment, some looking like oversized versions of the microscopes at the Clarence Monaghan Day School chemistry lab, others resembling odd and futuristic-looking kitchen appliances. The air smelled faintly of bleach.

"We used the AFM on three areas of the item's casing to get a map of the surface textures. Atomic force microscope," Dr. Bannon explained, gesturing at a gleaming machine that looked like a cross between a record player and a pneumatic drill. "And then the nano CT for a better look at the interior."

The slap of Dr. Bannon's shoes against the floor sounded loud above the hiss of the ventilation system. "It's a more sensitive version of a CT scanner in a hospital," she added, seeing Ivy's blank look. "It bombards the item with X-rays and creates a 3D model of the interior based on how the X-rays are deflected. Well, not a 3D model exactly, more of a series of 2D models that the computer layers together. Anyway, Getty started the scan, and then went back to the cubicles to let it run. He didn't come back until a few minutes after it should have finished."

Ivy frowned. She hadn't realized the lab had actually done anything with the wing before it disappeared. "What did the scan show?"

Probably too much to hope that Valiard's wings came with a helpfully labeled off switch. Or even better, a self-destruct button.

"That's just it," said Dr. Bannon, the red bracelets clattering as she crossed her arms. "The scan didn't finish. Or it did, but the last half was rubbish."

She crossed to a computer screen on the central table, shuffled through a stack of papers, grabbed one, and handed it to Ivy. The printout felt thick and glossy; Ivy ran her thumb along the edge as she stared at the page.

"You can see where the scanner misfired," Dr. Bannon said, pointing.

The top right corner of the paper showed the wing's arching heat sinks, crisscrossed with hatches and lines that hinted at some sort of structure. The rest of the page looked like something spat out of a malfunctioning printer—squares of solid black, groups of fine lines curving into spirals that abruptly stopped, random starburst patterns all jutting against each another. Ivy frowned at it.

"This bit here is normal. Normal-ish," Dr. Bannon corrected, tapping at the upper section of the printout. "The crosshatch pattern is microcircuitry. Pretty standard. But where it turns opaque here, either the interior components are smaller than seven microns, which isn't possible, or there's no interior components at all."

She raised an eyebrow at Ivy. Hurriedly, Ivy looked back at the paper. She had no idea if circuitry smaller than seven microns (whatever that meant) really was impossible. Even if it was, things from Valiard, trows included, tended to break the rules about what was and wasn't possible on a somewhat regular basis.

"What happened with the rest of the scan?" Ivy asked, pointing at the bottom of the page.

"Disrupted," the director grunted. "Badly, given how corrupted the imagery is. It's almost like the detectors were receiving more X-rays than the machine was generating in the first place. That's probably when the item was stolen," said Dr. Bannon with a sigh. "And before you ask, no one should have been able to open the machine while a scan was still in progress."

"So what happened when the technician came back to check the machine?" Ivy said.

"It was gone," said Dr. Bannon simply, bracelets clattering as she rubbed her hand across her face. "The scanner was empty, the scan data was gibberish, there was no sign the machine or the lab door were forced, and no one recalls seeing anyone in this part of the lab who wasn't supposed to be here."

Her explanation had the monotony of a worn-out record, as though the director had recited the same litany of impossibilities several times over the past few days.

A scout who'd broken in might have been able to jimmy open a locked scanner. They could have been inside the lab with the tech the whole time, then made off with the wing as soon as he stepped out of the room.

Except if Ivy was right about DIAAR, a scout probably hadn't been involved in the theft at all. Which left two possibilities. Possibility one: something else had taken the wing, and Ivy was as much in the dark as anyone else. Possibility two: the wing hadn't actually been stolen.

"Starting to sound like an inside job," said Ivy quietly. It was certainly the possibility Ambrose was considering. She felt a brief, uncomfortable twinge in her belly when she remembered she and Ambrose weren't exactly on terms where she could pass along information.

"The Gardaí certainly think so," said Dr. Bannon, the wrinkles at the corners of her mouth drawing tighter. "Getty's worked for this department for six years. The Gardaí have been all over his bank records, calling his girlfriend, his mother. . . I cannot believe he would steal from this lab," she said, looking at Ivy steadily. "And I think it would be difficult for anyone to prove motive when no one on your end has seen fit to tell us what your sample actually was."

Ivy felt a shiver along the back of her neck, even under the itchy collar of the jacket. For a moment, she had a wild impulse to blurt out, *My boss thinks it's part of a network of time-traveling supercomputers that were sent here to study the end of the world, which unfortunately is going to happen soon.* Which, while perfectly true, would only result in Ivy getting tossed out of the lab.

"Can you show me the machine that ran the last scan?" Ivy asked, ignoring the lab director's implied question.

The furrows in Dr. Bannon's face deepened, but she led Ivy to the far side of the large table and nodded at a sleek, oven-sized machine.

"That's the nano CT," she said, a note of pride in her voice. The thing looked beige and roundish, with a cluster of thick cables leading off the back. The metal door was secured with four thick bolts that looked vaguely like something from a bank vault. "The door to the scanning chamber locks automatically when a scan is in progress. There's no sign the door was forced."

"It's unlocked now?" Ivy asked, and grabbed the handle without waiting for a reply. She tugged hard; the handle turned easier than Ivy had expected, the bolts smoothly retracting as the door swung open with a hiss, not quite loud enough to cover Dr. Bannon clearing her throat.

Ivy craned her head as the door swung open, forcing a bored look onto her face, angling her body so she could slip her left hand inside without Dr. Bannon noticing.

She stopped with the door half-open. The interior was dim, the inside glossy, studded with sensors, and completely empty.

Ivy tried to hide her disappointment as she closed the door. So much for the wing invisibly waiting exactly where it was supposed to be. Clearly, it wasn't there, and it didn't matter because the whole mess ought to be Ambrose's problem now. He was the one who'd stolen it from Haven in the first place. Ivy shouldn't care if he got into trouble now that it had disappeared from somewhere else.

Except Demi would have cared, and Demi would have wanted *Ivy* to care. Ivy had to turn away from the scanner, rubbing hard at her eyes with the edge of her sleeve.

Behind her, Dr. Bannon reached over to lock the nano CT, the bolts engaging with a hiss. Everything in the lab looked as though it had been cleaned within an inch of its life, the machines and counters gleaming. Entirely devoid of anything interesting. Just the way the vault at Haven had looked at first.

"Since your Ambrose Wells has been extremely tight-lipped about where his missing device originated, we've very little information to pass along to the Gardaí," Dr. Bannon continued, an edge to her words that immediately put Ivy on alert. "Other than what you might call speculation, that is. When there's no hard facts concerning its provenance, speculation can hardly be avoided."

"Speculation about what?" Ivy asked cautiously, gripping the straps on her purse.

"You'll recall from our contract that analysis for the purposes of reverse engineering is specifically prohibited," the director said tartly. "As is the analysis of stolen property. I have a difficult time understanding how a failed start-up could've produced the type of nano-circuitry that showed up in the first section of the scan. Seems more likely this came from an outfit with a substantial R&D budget—governments, militaries, multi-national companies. And if this device was indeed stolen, which of course is not what I'm suggesting at all, the thieves would hardly want to have it analyzed in its host country. Far better to bring it off to a backwater," she added with a touch of bitterness. "Someplace where the lab receiving it might not recognize what they've been handed."

In fact, Ambrose had chosen the NIC because it was reputed to be the best materials analysis lab in Ireland; apparently Dr. Bannon had something of an inferiority complex about how the Centre compared on an international stage.

"Mr. Wells is the only person who knows the details of how the device came to Dublin," Ivy said, which was both perfectly true and completely unhelpful.

Not my problem, Ivy repeated to herself. If the Gardaí investigation concluded that the wing had been stolen to begin with, that was up to Ambrose to deal with, or Carillon. Ivy bit her lip, wondering who might take charge of the Haven vault, and the monsters inside it, if the thane were injured—or dead. How many of those grim faces around the trows' council table knew the truth about what their Enemy really was?

Dr. Bannon crossed her arms, frowning. "I'd hoped this would've turned out to be an enlightening visit. For both of us," the lab director added, suspicion heavy in her voice. "If you wish to see anything further of our facility, Ms. Gallagher, I suggest you return with a lawyer. And a warrant."

"I understand," Ivy said crisply, looking uncomfortably at the rest of the room. Had anyone taken photos of the room as part of the investigation? Ivy suspected the conversation with Dr. Bannon would have gone in quite a different direction if anyone had discovered that their missing item showed up on film but was impossible to find in person.

Biting her lip, Ivy started toward the door, taking a last glance over her shoulder. The lab gleamed with plastic and chrome, the machines were silent, everything was sterile and empty, and there was still one obvious place Ivy could look.

As Ivy came around the edge of the table, she let herself stumble, dropping quickly to her knees and out of Dr. Bannon's line of sight. She leaned forward, peering into the gap between the table's lower shelf and the floor.

A cluster of dim red lights shone back at her, the shape behind them vaguely cylindrical. Ivy froze, then hurriedly reached for it. Ivy's very first flat, a horrible place out in Finglas, had some kind of ultrasonic rodent deterrent under the kitchen sink; it had red lights, and hadn't it had some sort of mouse-killing electrical pad? Ivy stretched her arm as far as it could go, wriggling closer, half dreading an electric shock.

"Ms. Gallagher," Dr. Bannon called, sounding halfway between concern and irritation. Ivy's finger brushed metal, something smooth and feverishly warm. Shoving her shoulder against the table's bottom shelf, she snagged a viciously warm metal flange, started to drag it closer—and the metal slipped out of her grip entirely. Something hot, clinging, and terrible wrapped itself around Ivy's wrist.

Ivy snatched her arm back as if she'd been burned, scrambling away from the table and staring in disbelief at the wing, wrapped around her arm like a gauntlet. A wailing siren cut through the silence of the lab like a foghorn. Ivy glanced at the ceiling, certain she'd set off some sort of alarm, but the only flashing lights were those on the wing itself, the space between the heat sinks lit up with a mix of regular numbers and Rass characters. All of them were red and most of them were flashing, like every warning light on her boyfriend, Colin's, shoddy Peugeot going off at once.

Horrified, Ivy shoved her arm under her purse, the spines of the heat sinks digging into her belly as she jumped to her feet, her jaw tight to keep her panic out of her expression.

"Ms. Gallagher?" Dr. Bannon asked, sounding confused.

"Yes, I think I've seen everything," Ivy stuttered, and

stopped, because Dr. Bannon wasn't even looking at her. The director was staring blankly at the far side of the lab, a frown pulling at the corners of her mouth. Dr. Bannon tapped her foot and looked back to the door, her gaze sweeping past Ivy without the slightest change in her expression.

The sweat on the back of Ivy's neck turned instantly to ice. She ducked back below the edge of the table, clawing at the edge of the wing for its catch.

"Off," Ivy hissed at it, feeling something give under her fingers. "Now!"

The clasps came loose all at once, and the wing dropped off Ivy's wrist. The screeching alarms went silent. Ivy barely caught the thing before it hit the floor. She threw it into her purse, tugged the cover into place, and leapt to her feet.

Something unsettled flicked across Dr. Bannon's face as she turned to Ivy, her expression wavering between anger and disbelief. Ivy felt flushed, her hair was mussed, there was dust on her jacket where she'd been grubbing about on the floor, and her right sleeve was covered in a grid-like pattern of wrinkles.

"I think I've seen everything I needed to," said Ivy, her voice sounding too fast and too loud, and she forced herself to take a deep breath. She was upright, and visible, and nothing had exploded. *Yet,* Ivy amended, thinking of the alert siren and the array of incomprehensible warning messages.

All Ivy needed to do was to get out of the lab. Conveniently, Dr. Bannon looked like she wanted to kick her out.

"You've been very accommodating," she added, heading to the door. "I'll certainly pass that on to Mr. Wells."

Dr. Bannon stared at Ivy, not saying anything for a long moment. Finally, she turned to the door.

Ivy took a deep breath as she followed Dr. Bannon into the hallway, glancing surreptitiously at her purse. The wing's warning lights were bright enough Ivy could see them through the fabric. She shifted the bag uncomfortably.

They passed the row of lab doors in silence and turned back through the cubicles. Ivy felt some of the tension dropping from her shoulders. She had the wing, and no one had gotten hurt. While the fact that it was working again would likely be a pleasant surprise to Ambrose, for Ivy it only meant the thing was probably a lot more dangerous to carry around. Ivy wondered if it was another of the things that might make her permanently invisible if she spent too much time around it. Maybe the thing had its own version of Protocol Four.

Crossing into the reception area, Dr. Bannon turned back to Ivy.

"James will need to inspect your bag before you depart," Dr. Bannon said, gesturing to the receptionist.

Ivy stopped dead, fighting to keep a pleasant expression on her face, not looking down at the pulsing red lights leaking through the canvas.

"Is that really necessary?" she asked tartly, channeling the attitude of the Blue Parrot customers who whined about setting up their tabs. "Seems a bit like locking the barn after the horses have left."

"It's a very new policy," said Dr. Bannon blandly. "We're taking the security of our lab extremely seriously in light of recent events."

Ivy slowly slipped the purse off her shoulder, her hand lingering next to the flap. If she let the wing clamp itself to her arm again, she'd almost certainly be able to run out of the building in the resulting confusion. Except vanishing in front of two people who knew her name and address wasn't a great option.

Ivy looked down at her faintly glowing purse. The wing

had managed to keep itself hidden inside the lab for five days. Could she trust it to do the same thing now?

"Of course," said Ivy, forcing her mouth into a polite smile. "Not like I have anything to *hide*," she said loudly to the purse as she placed it on the table. "Seeing as how the thing we're looking for has *completely vanished.*"

Ivy stepped back and folded her arms nervously. She had no idea if the wing understood English, and even less of an idea if it would understand her suggestion. Or feel itself inclined to follow it, even if it did.

Frowning, Dr. Bannon gestured to the man behind the desk. Adjusting his glasses, the receptionist grabbed the purse's flap and flipped it back. The wing's light brightened, covering James's face in a red wash, Rass characters reflecting dizzyingly across his glasses. Ivy froze—then the receptionist grabbed the wing by its heat sinks. Ivy jumped as James shoved it roughly aside, steeling herself for the thing to fling itself around his wrist just as enthusiastically as it had hers. But the wing only continued its agitated blinking as Dr. Bannon leaned over the table and peered inside the purse. The director frowned, looking unimpressed with the collection of makeup, receipts, coins, and alien technology at the bottom of Ivy's bag.

The receptionist flicked the cover back over the purse. Hurriedly, Ivy gathered it up and threw the strap over her shoulder, feeling the spiky outline of the heat sinks warm against her stomach.

"Thank you for your time," she managed to murmur, and bolted for the door before Dr. Bannon could think up any more questions Ivy couldn't answer. She pushed open the door, the muggy air a welcome warmth. At least the wing hadn't latched onto the receptionist.

What the wing sensed in Ivy that meant it was willing to jump *her* bones, she didn't much want to think about. Carillon was terribly, murderously wrong about a lot of things. Her theories about Ivy's parentage, and her connection to the homicidal wing in the vault, were just more things to be wrong about.

Heat pounded on the back of Ivy's neck as she hurried across the asphalt, pulling Hunzu's keys out of her pocket as she went to the Citroen. If she wanted to be on time to her date with the apocalypse, she didn't have much time to spare.

CHAPTER 10

The DIAAR campus was larger than Ivy had expected, a complex of brick and concrete buildings scattered across the slopes of a low, tree-covered hill. Ivy clutched her purse tighter as she followed a cluster of people headed from the parking lot to the closest building's glass-fronted lobby. The bright lights and orange-toned walls inside seemed to light up the room like a stage. The rest of the complex was reduced to a suggestion of darkened outlines broken here and there by a lit window.

The wing's heat sinks were pressing into her stomach. Ivy shifted her purse to a more comfortable position, then ran a hand over her shirt to smooth out any wrinkles. A second charity shop visit had resulted in an appropriate outfit—a shimmery grey blouse and a pair of black slacks that looked dressy while still managing to have functional pockets. Completing the outfit was a pair of black zip-up boots, posh enough for a formal occasion but functional enough that Ivy could still run for her life while wearing them. She wished that last consideration was only a theoretical concern.

Ivy slipped one of Lauren's invitations out of her bag, gripping it tightly as she walked up to the door. Guests were already scattered across the lobby; Ivy's heart sank as she took in the tailored suits and strapless dresses. Surely not everyone would be kitted out in evening gowns and tuxedos? Ivy was fairly certain Lauren didn't own anything like what was parading about on the other side of the glass.

Ivy reached the door, the glass throwing back a blurred reflection of herself. A clunky metal necklace gleamed at her throat, a collection of oversized metal squares that fit snugly against her collarbone. Ivy hoped the thing would be good for deflecting needles aimed at her neck. With her hair pinned up, eyes rimmed with mascara, and ears flaunting green faux-emerald earrings, her reflection looked like the sort of person who belonged at a fancy gala. Ivy looked away, plastered a pert expression on her face, and opened the door. It was hard to shake the notion that she was slowly becoming a person who could look like she belonged anywhere, while not actually belonging anywhere at all.

Ivy crossed the lobby with her head up, trying not to look intimidated by the evening gowns, and headed for a woman with a clipboard standing in front of the main stairs.

"Lauren Guilfoyle's plus one," Ivy said, holding out the wrinkled party invitation, keeping a pleasant smile glued to her face. She could feel the wing's heat sinks digging into her stomach through the sides of her charity-shop handbag, her second, infinitely more dangerous option for getting inside.

The woman glanced at the paper briefly and Ivy not at all before marking something down on her sheet and waving Ivy toward the door at the far end of the hall. She was already turning to the next guest as Ivy hurried away, thankful that no one wanted to search her bag. Even assuming the wing could keep itself invisible, the Taser was another matter entirely, and Ivy didn't dare leave it in the Citroen after what happened the first time she'd crossed paths with a scout.

Ivy rubbed at the bruise under her necklace as she walked further into the lobby. The charity-shop necklace was probably meant to look avant-garde, but it actually looked like someone had attacked a dog collar with a hacksaw and glued it back together using rhinestones.

Protection against scouts, Ivy hoped. And possibly vampires.

Ahead of her stood a pair of tall, frosted-glass doors. Ivy came closer, nodding cordially at a woman in a stately black dress, keeping a disinterested smile on her face. She wasn't doing anything illegal, and no one was going to kill her if they found out why she was here, which was already better than she'd managed visiting Haven, or even stopping by her own flat. She was just attending a fancy party she hadn't actually been invited to, hoping to run into a time-traveling spy who thought this company was somehow connected to the end of the world. Nothing to worry about.

Ivy grabbed the handle and opened the door. The music inside was louder than she'd expected, fighting with a roar of people attempting to talk over it. Silver and gold party streamers dangled from the ceiling, brushing against Ivy's arms as she walked into the room.

The place already looked crowded, or perhaps it was only the lighting that made it look that way, everything dim, patterned, and full of shadows. Scattered racks of theatrical lights were clustered along the walls, casting squares of blue and magenta light across the room. The center of the room was a muddle of suits and dresses, coiffed hair, glimmering jewelry, and people gesturing with champagne flutes, everyone drinking and talking and nodding all at once.

Ivy stepped away from the door, hugging the lefthand wall. This looked nothing like any office party Ivy had ever attended, more like one of the pop-up concerts Colin occasionally took her to. Biting her lip, Ivy pulled her burner phone out of her purse, pretending to look at it while she scanned the room. At the far end was a small stage with a podium, the looping infinity symbol of DIAAR's logo projected in silver across the back wall. Below it, emblazoned in a bold red font: *And death shall have no dominion.*

Ivy shuddered, biting her lip against the scent of ash that suddenly seemed to waft from the stage. Death had a dominion, and an exact date of arrival, at least as far as Ivy was concerned. That date was still seven months away. Anything could happen in seven months.

She slipped her phone into her purse and slowly walked past the podium. The speakers were blaring out the opening bars of Cliff Richard's *"Devil Woman."* Besides a few committed wallflowers standing as far away from the speakers as possible, most of the guests were clustered together in groups of six or eight, leaning in close, shouting and gesturing to be heard over the music, all the conversations only adding to the impenetrable wash of noise. At least her weird necklace wasn't going to stand out, Ivy thought, stepping aside from a woman in a lavender dress decorated with what looked like actual peacock feathers. It looked less like Eirecom's Christmas party and more like the opening few hours of a rave.

At least with the music as loud as it was, Ivy could simply pretend not to hear anyone who tried to talk to her.

Avoiding the crowd milling at the bar, she angled toward a long table covered in tiny plates and chafing dishes, her stomach reminding her she hadn't eaten since the granola bar and packet of crisps at the Tesco where she'd picked up her new phone. She helped herself to a few tiny sandwiches and a bowl of cocktail sausages swimming in some sort of brown sauce, retreating back to the wall that seemed to have the best view of the main door. Ivy popped one of the sandwiches in her mouth, scanning the room as she chewed.

It was a distinct possibility that free food was the only thing Ivy was going to get out of the evening—at least, if she didn't count a headache from the noise, and blisters where her charity-shop boots were starting to rub against her heels. Even if Valiard was interested in the Institute, their scouts didn't exactly need the pretext of a large party to wander about the building unnoticed. If a scout did come, it was probably going to be at two in the morning on a Tuesday or some other time when the place was completely deserted. Which meant Ivy was probably going to spend the evening awkwardly eating too many finger foods, learning nothing of importance, and trying to avoid thinking about what she ought to do next. At least no one was waving a gun in her face.

Morosely, Ivy speared another tiny sausage with her toothpick and popped it into her mouth. She looked up just in time to see someone who didn't belong walk into the room.

HE WAS DRESSED IN BLACK, the same close-cut, hooded jumpsuit that Ivy remembered from the apple grove, and he was moving through the crowd in fits and starts, stepping and turning and stopping short, as if he still hadn't learned that people would mostly stay out of his way if he let them.

Ivy abandoned her half-eaten plate at the edge of the buffet, staring at the scout. His hood was down, his hair a closely cropped fuzz nearly the same shade of brown as the skin below it. The wing on his arm glittered in the muted lights, the tips of its heat sinks gleaming like knives. He was turning his head like he was trying to look at everything in the room at once.

For a moment, the blaring music and the crowd dropped away, as though that upturned face and the gleaming wing were the only things that mattered in the whole world. A fizz of triumph roiled in Ivy's belly, only to curdle moments later. She'd tracked down the scout. He was really here. Ivy had actually found him.

Which meant somewhere in the lumbering complex of offices and corridors beyond the colored streamers and the party lights were the beginning stirrings of the end of the world.

Ivy took a deep breath and slipped her hand into her purse, her fingers brushing against the Taser as she pulled out her mobile. She hurried back to the main door, giving one last glance over her shoulder and catching a glimpse of a thin, wide-eyed face before the door swung shut behind her, muffling the noise. Ivy's ears rang in the sudden silence.

First step: don't be the girl who dies with a secret.

Ivy dialed the number as quickly as she could and put the phone to her ear, wondering how long she had before the scout left the main room to explore elsewhere in the complex.

"This had better not be a telemarketer," muttered Hunzu by way of hello.

"Retired, thank you," Ivy snapped, and cut off the beginnings of a startled apology. She glanced up and down the hall—deserted for the moment, but not likely to remain so for long. "I can't talk long. I'm at the Dublin Institute for Anti-Aging Research, and there's a scout here. He's wearing a wing, and he's dressed like the one from two nights ago. Barneville Park West and Lavery Street."

"Get out," Hunzu's voice hissed in her ear, pitched low, as though he thought the scout might hear him over the phone lines. "Right now. If he's from—from *there*, he's dangerous. And why are you even—"

"Because it's what *she* was looking for," said Ivy, cutting him off. A trio of women were approaching from the end of the corridor, sequined tops reflecting in the glass wall like rhinestone ghosts. She stepped closer to the wall, lowering her voice. "The scout, two nights ago, she wasn't after me, she was after Lauren, and Lauren works here. This is what they're after. They think Event Two starts somewhere in this building. And Angevin thinks one of them can reprogram the wing in the vault."

"What wing in the—" Hunzu abruptly cut off his own question. "Just get out and explain it to me later."

"Angevin thinks we can stop the Enemy through them," Ivy hissed. "So no one else gets killed. Find a scout, get them to take a message back to Valiard and change things from that side."

"How does Angevin know—"

"He's been helping the Enemy and you can't trust him," Ivy hissed. "But he's also the only person who has any idea how to get it to stop killing people. If a scout's here, Angevin needs to know. Or tell—if she's still—" Ivy broke off, at a loss for how to even ask the question.

Angevin and Carillon had both abetted murder, and Ivy shouldn't have anything to do with them, except they were the only ones who knew what the Enemy really was. Even if Angevin had been shielding the Enemy, he also had a plan to defang it, and maybe that plan was better than Ivy hitting it with a poker. Angevin had been right about the second scout. Maybe there was a way to change things so no one else had to die.

The group of women passed Ivy and opened the door, sending a wave of music and loud voices sweeping into the hall.

"Carillon's alive," Hunzu confirmed softly. "We keep an agent at Saint Pat's, for emergencies. I'll call Angevin. Now please tell me you're walking away."

"I won't take any stupid chances," Ivy told him. "There's about a zillion people at this party, I'm just going to keep an eye on him. Promise."

Hopefully Angevin wasn't still out in County Clare. Hopefully he'd get here soon, and talk to the scout, and get Valiard to take the Gruesome Firey Death setting off their computer. He could warn them that Valiard was about to be destroyed. Ivy just needed to make sure the scout didn't leave before Angevin got here.

Ivy heard Hunzu sigh over the phone. "If you absolutely insist on staying, can you get me a photo?" he asked.

"I'll text it. And call Ambrose," Ivy added, before she could think better of it. "Tell him . . . tell him the Roinn needs to know about this."

"Okay," said Hunzu. "I'll see you soon."

Ivy hung up the phone, wondering if Hunzu deliberately hadn't said goodbye. Another group of guests was coming down the hallway; Ivy glued a carefree expression on her face, then followed a man in a pea-green coat back through the door.

The noise seemed even more oppressive as Ivy plunged into the middle of the room. The lights playing against the ceiling shifted and danced, the room a glittering maze of sequined dresses and unintelligible chatter. She squeezed through a gap between two groups of people, craning her head, then abruptly turned and veered for the far door beside the podium. If the scout wasn't here, he might have already gone deeper into the building.

Ivy walked past a woman in a turquoise dress, stepped around a table full of mini quiches, and spotted his jumpsuit out of the corner of her eye. She hurried after him, pulling out her phone, then abruptly stopped when she realized he wasn't moving. The scout's head was craned toward the ceiling, like he was looking at the lights. Ivy lifted her phone, her gaze darting between the screen and the scout, all thumbs as she pulled up the camera app on the still-unfamiliar screen. The image was dim and pixelated, the partygoers little more than pale impressions of faces and bodies. The scout shifted and his wing glittered, a constellation of light and color cradled against his chest. Ivy pressed the shutter button; the screen froze on a completely unhelpful mishmash of colors and silhouettes.

The scout turned his head. Ivy immediately dropped her gaze, head down, eyes on her screen, another distracted twenty-something permanently attached to their mobile. Nothing in the photo was in focus; the wing's lights looked indistinguishable from the decor in the rest of the room. Ivy felt a knot of tension winding tight in her belly as the bass pulse of the speakers echoed through her chest as though it were her own heartbeat.

One more try. She just had to get a little closer.

Ivy dodged past a busboy with a tray of glassware, lost the scout behind a crowd of men toasting to something with half-full red cups, then circled around an intensely gesticulating woman in a blue dress. The scout was straight ahead, ten feet away, still looking up at the lights.

Ivy wrenched her eyes back to her screen, fighting a sudden conviction that if she raised her head, somehow he'd know that she could see him.

Four feet away. The party lights cast a yellow wash across his face, and Ivy pressed the shutter button. The screen flashed silently, and Ivy kept walking straight ahead, eyes on her phone, oblivious, not looking up. Something clinging and black brushed against her arm; Ivy forced herself not to jump as she hurried past. Biting her lip, Ivy closed the camera program, fumbling to bring up the messenger app—

And walked straight into a silk-clad torso, sending his wineglass flying.

"I am so sorry," Ivy said, taking a step back, looking up at a red-faced man, blond hair clinging limply to his forehead, a sour expression on his face.

"I should think so," the man snapped, the words only barely audible over the thump of the music. The whole room seemed to grow warmer, as though the heat from the wing in Ivy's purse was radiating outward. Drawing attention to herself was exactly what Ivy shouldn't be doing. She didn't dare turn around to see if the scout had noticed. One wrong move with him and he might decide to activate his recall, and everything around him would go up like a bonfire. Or he'd go after Ivy with a needle and she wouldn't be able to talk or move her legs. She'd be another drunk girl at a company party, fighting off an attacker no one else could see.

The red-faced man handed his now-empty glass to a woman in a gold dress and ran a thumb along the reddish stain on his shirt.

"Get you 'nother glass?" Ivy shouted, leaning too close, adding the hint of a slur. "I'll pay," she added, deliberately fumbling with the catch on her purse.

The woman in the gold dress gave Ivy a withering look as she handed her date a fistful of cocktail napkins.

"It's fine," the man mouthed, his expression making it clear that it wasn't, and dabbed at the stain on his shirt, dismissing Ivy with a flick of his fingers.

Shouting apologies, Ivy minced away, not looking over her shoulder and trying to keep clear of anyone else. She dodged around two more clusters of drinkers and stopped by an appetizers table, ignoring the feeling of eyes on her as she turned back to her phone. She typed Hunzu's number into the messenger program, then attached the photo to send.

From the screen, the scout gazed back at her. He looked thin, the bones of his face exaggerated by the light. The wing on his arm was blazing like a firework, and his eyes looked yellow in the glow of the party lights, like the coals from a banked fire, waiting to spark an inferno.

Out of nowhere, Ivy wondered if he'd known the scout who'd died, the scout who'd tried to talk to Ivy and whose questions Ivy hadn't understood. Had her disappearance been two days ago, for him? Or was he coming from months or years away, when the scout who'd burned in the street was little more than a memory and a dust-covered plaque on a wall?

Ivy bit her lip as she hit send.

She swallowed hard, looking across the room at the infinity logo behind the podium. A handful of couples were dancing in front of the small stage, heads thrown back, drinks still in their hands. For a moment, Ivy wished she could throw herself into the crowd, find Lauren's hot guy from HR and dance with him, and forget all about time-traveling spies, or the dying supercomputer in her purse, or the woman who'd burned in the street. Forget about Demi and Uncle Patrick. Forget that Uncle Patrick's own mother was harboring the thing that had killed him.

Maybe that was the worst thing—not only could Ivy see monsters, she could even see the ones other monsters refused to believe existed. And it was long past the time Ivy could walk away and pretend none of it was real.

Ivy looked away from the dancing couples, swallowing hard as she caught sight of the scout. His wing lit him up like a flare as he wove through the crowd, brighter than it was when Ivy first spotted him. Perhaps he'd finally grown comfortable with the notion that no one was going to pay him any attention, no matter how out of place he looked.

He skirted the edge of the stage, walking slowly but purposefully toward the far end of the room. Ivy followed, trying to keep him in sight—and jumped as her phone buzzed in her hand.

Ivy flipped it open and brought up the text.

The cavalry's coming, so you should get out.

Before Ivy could text back a reply, the phone buzzed again.

But if u aren't going to do that Angevin says keep him close.

Scowling, Ivy shoved the phone in her purse, feeling the heat from the wing against her fingers. The scout was definitely heading toward the door behind the podium, his own wing shining like fire, one of the Four Horsemen seeking an apocalypse.

Walking faster, Ivy skirted a drinks table, dodging behind a woman in a red dress holding a paper fan. She caught sight of the scout again just as he reached the door. He grabbed the handle, paused, then threw it open. The light from the hallway outside spilled into the room, silhouetting him for a long moment. When the door swung shut, his afterimage glowed in the darkness for several seconds after.

There was something inside this building that meant the end of Ivy's world and the beginning of something worse, and whatever it was, the scout was probably heading right for it.

Before the afterimage faded, Ivy was hurrying after him.

❦

Ivy slipped through the door behind the podium just in time to see the black-clad shape disappear around a corner at the far end of the hall. The hall was unexpectedly crowded. A group of men were standing together, one gesturing wildly with a half-empty Guinness bottle. A few yards away, two women were standing with their backs to each other, both talking into their mobiles. As the door swung shut behind her, the clamor of the party dimmed to a muted hum.

Ivy hurried down the corridor, fumbling with the flap on her purse, feeling the wing brush against her fingers. If she put it on, she wouldn't need to worry about anyone asking if she was lost, or hauling her back to the party, or calling security. She'd only be running the risk of becoming invisible permanently, just like what happened to her mother.

Ivy left the wing in her purse. She passed the women on their phones as she turned down the hallway where she'd glimpsed the scout. Frosted-glass doors gleamed from both sides of the hallway; the air seemed cooler here. The tapping of Ivy's charity-shop boots sounded louder the farther she got from the party, and she wondered if the Institute had security cameras. She almost hoped they did, just to level the odds a bit. Between his funny-looking jumpsuit and the light from the wing on his arm, there was no way the scout could be mistaken for a wandering party guest.

The breeze from the air handlers felt cold as she reached the end of the hall, which dead-ended at a set of double doors. Ivy tentatively tried the handle, half expecting to hear the wail of an alarm.

The door opened silently into a long, dimly lit hall. Halfway down, a door was swinging closed, a familiar silhouette momentarily visible before the door shut entirely.

Ivy eased the door shut behind her. The remnant thrum from the party vanished entirely as it closed, leaving nothing but the low whirr of a fan. Ivy slipped her hand into her purse, pushing past the wing to grab the Taser as she hurried down the hallway. The darkened glass doors on either side reflected her own shape back at her; small signs next to the doors displayed names and numbers, the words illegible in the dim light. If Ivy could just stay close enough to the scout, maybe she could figure out what inside the building he was trying to investigate. Ideally without being noticed by DIAAR's security, or the scout himself.

So far, improbably, that plan seemed to be working.

She kept her gaze fixed on the door she'd seen the scout disappear through. Coming closer, Ivy's heart sank as she spotted a keypad next to the handle. She looked hard at the door, biting her lip. The lock hadn't engaged; the latch was merely resting against the jamb.

Ivy drew even with the door. Was the scout trying to preserve an exit route? Or was it something else? The hallway suddenly seemed very cold, very quiet, and very far away from anything else.

Ivy pulled the Taser out of her purse and undid the safety. With her finger on the edge of the trigger guard, she slowly pushed open the door. The handle felt cold; a breath of warmer air drifted in as the door swung open, and Ivy's stomach clenched as she remembered the vault at Haven.

A patter of footsteps carried down the darkened hallway. Halfway down the corridor, another door swung shut.

Swallowing hard, Ivy eased the door closed behind her, letting it rest on the latch. She held tight to the Taser, walking as quietly as she could, staring hard at the door the scout had entered. At the far end of the hallway, an emergency exit sign glowed green. The place reminded Ivy of the boiler room at Clarence Monaghan Day School, the walls covered in pipes and shadows all overlaid with the smell of mold and chemicals. Frosted-glass doors alternated with bulky fire extinguishers mounted on the walls. Farther down the hall a cheap vinyl curtain screened off what looked like an emergency shower next to a strange-looking sink that Ivy recognized as an eyewash station.

Through the purse, the wing's heat felt uncomfortably warm against her stomach. The door the scout had entered didn't look big enough to lead into another hallway. Could this be his destination?

Ivy shifted her grip, holding the Taser two-handed and inching nearer. A faint light glowed on the far side of the frosted-glass door. Ivy leaned closer. The light shifted; that was Ivy's only warning as the door wrenched open.

Ivy threw herself backward as the scout leapt through the doorway, one arm raised. The tip of a needle gleamed, slashing past Ivy's face and slamming into the rhinestone necklace. The blow knocked Ivy off-balance; she squeezed the Taser's trigger as the scout's needle caught on the collar of her shirt, tearing it with an audible rip.

The needle wavered and dropped, hitting the floor with a ping. A moment later the scout crumpled to the ground, twitching. Everything was silent apart from the thumping of the scout's boots against the floor.

Swallowing hard, Ivy patted at her necklace. Something gelatinous was smeared across the metal plates. She shuddered and wiped her hand against the side of her trousers. The body at her feet was still twitching, sporadic jerks like a broken marionette, which was maybe even worse than if it hadn't been moving at all. On his arm, the wing pulsed a dim, agitated orange.

The half-open door of the darkened room loomed empty in front of her, and according to the Taser's instructions Ivy had about forty seconds to figure out what to do next.

Quickly, Ivy yanked the leads out of the nose of the Taser and shoved the thing back in her purse. Stepping over the scout's body, she grabbed two fistfuls of his jumpsuit. Pushing the lab door farther open with her hip, she pulled as hard as she could. The scout slid a few inches, the wing's heat sinks squealing against the floor. Hurriedly, Ivy grabbed the scout's left arm at the elbow, draping his wing-covered arm awkwardly across his stomach. She started tugging again. His head flopped forward bonelessly as Ivy hauled him into the darkened room, and the door swung shut with a creak.

A large, sturdy table was the first thing Ivy could make out; a hard shove confirmed it was bolted to the floor. Ivy lugged the scout another few feet, dropping him next to the closest table leg with more haste than care, and dove into her purse for Hunzu's handcuffs. She opened one cuff and locked it around the scout's right wrist, then grabbed his left hand, awkwardly tugging it behind him. His fingers were damp, warm from the wing and his own body heat, his arm heavy and awkward. She yanked it closer to the table leg, realizing abruptly she wasn't wearing gloves. Ivy snapped the cuff over his wrist as quickly as she could, shuddering as her fingers brushed the edge of his wing.

Ivy hurriedly stepped back, rubbing her hand hard against the side of her trousers, glancing back at the door to make sure it was shut.

Somewhere in the room, a clock was ticking, sharp and precise. Through the dim light of the exit sign behind her, Ivy could make out two long counters, rows of shelves and drawers, and bundles of metal conduit snaking along the walls and the ceiling. The air smelled faintly of bleach.

Following the scout without being noticed had obviously been a failure. He must have realized he'd been followed and decided to jump her instead. He could have dragged her into any of these disused labs, leaving her trapped and helpless until the paralytic in his needle wore off. Assuming it was a paralytic, and not something worse.

Taking a deep breath, Ivy bent over and peered at the scout. He'd stopped twitching; under the dim light, she couldn't tell if he was breathing and wasn't about to get close enough to check. Even handcuffed to the table leg, he still had his wing, currently glowing a subdued red. Ivy wondered if it was possible to take the thing off him, but dismissed the idea almost immediately. Provoking *it* was likely just as dangerous as provoking *him*.

The scout's eyes flickered. Ivy waited a long moment, but he didn't move. Slowly, she dropped to her knees, trying not to loom over him as she tried to make out something of his expression. His face looked oddly familiar: his nose as broad as Ambrose's, a hint of Demi in the curve of his eyebrows. Mostly, with the jumpsuit, he looked like the woman who'd burned.

"Hello," said Ivy quietly. The scout didn't move. Biting her lip, Ivy continued, hoping he had enough English to understand what she was saying. "If you haven't already figured it out, I can see you. I know I'm not supposed to—"

"I am already aware of both things," the scout said, slowly and distinctly. His voice was harsh and heavily accented, the words slow and carefully pronounced. He lifted his head to look at Ivy; the wing rattled against the floor as he flexed his hands.

"Who are you?" he continued in the same carefully precise voice. The scout pulled his legs closer, like he was trying to make himself smaller. A thin holster was strapped to his thigh, the half-open flap revealing a row of familiar-looking hypodermic needles, making Ivy even more grateful for the handcuffs. His face, as he peered over his knees at Ivy, didn't seem frightened or intimidated, holding only a cautious, wary sort of anger.

"I'm Ivy," she said, and added hastily, "and if you're thinking about using your emergency recall, don't. It isn't going to do either of us any good."

The scout glanced at the wing, then back at Ivy. Ivy wondered if he didn't understand her, or just didn't believe what she was saying.

"Who are you in this place?" he clarified, nodding his head at the rest of the room.

"With the Institute?" Ivy asked, surprised. "Nobody. I don't work here, so I don't know what they're doing, or why your lot think that's so important. Your turn. What's your name?"

The scout's mouth quirked as though she'd said something amusing. He pushed himself up straighter against the table leg, the handcuffs rattling against the metal as he pulled his hands one way and then another.

"What happens if I don't say?"

"Well, if I walk away, you could be stuck here a very long time," Ivy said, trying to not sound irritated. "You can shout as much as you want, and I'm probably the only person in the building who can hear you. I'd say that means you might have an interest in talking to me."

In response, the scout stretched his legs out in front of him, wiggling his toes as though he were making himself comfortable.

"No interest at all," he said simply.

Ivy glanced at the door, then back at the scout. He was the one tied up, wasn't he? Ivy had the Taser, and the handcuff keys, and the ability to communicate with other people in the building. The trow had none of those—just a wrist-watch supercomputer that seemed equally likely to murder him as help him.

For a minute, Ivy considered texting another picture to Hunzu, giving him the room number, and walking away just like she'd threatened. Leave the mess behind for other people to sort out. Or Ivy could stay and try to fix things. Warn Valiard about their impending disaster, get them to reprogram their wing, find out what was about to go wrong here on Earth, and maybe, how they could stop it.

Small chance of that if she couldn't even convince the scout to tell her his name.

The fallen leads from the Taser glimmered as the scout shifted position, and Ivy automatically bent to pick them up, winding the wires around her hand.

He shuddered, something raw and uncomfortable flickering across his face as he looked at the wires in Ivy's hands. Ivy's skin went cold all at once.

"I'd rather not do that," she said evenly, continuing to wrap up the leads. She couldn't fire any more projectiles, but the manual had mentioned the Taser could still work without them. She'd just have to push the metal contacts against his skin and hold down the trigger.

Except Ivy really, *really* didn't want to do that. Not up close, not just to hurt someone, not when she wasn't actually in danger herself. Not to someone who might be able to save the world.

Just like Ambrose probably didn't *want* to send an agent with a gun after Ivy, but he'd done it. Carillon probably hadn't *wanted* to see Ivy burn to death in front of her.

Ivy tucked the leads into her purse, shifting to a cross-legged position, very aware of the Taser next to her knee, the nose not quite pointed at the scout.

"Will you at least tell me what you're doing here?" she asked.

The scout raised his eyebrows, somehow managing to look down his nose at Ivy even though he looked shorter than she was. "I shop for pepper and aubergines," he said brightly. "I take over the world and I start with boring party. Maybe I come from the government. Maybe I am a space alien."

Ivy took a deep breath, forcibly relaxing her jaw. "I know you come from a place in the future called Valiard." The scout's eyes narrowed sharply at the name, and he twisted his head to glance at his wing, murmuring something in an unintelligible cascade of vowels. "You came to the past because Valiard is interested in something that happens here, in my future."

"Not interested," snapped the scout. "And not talking." He hesitated for a moment, hunching his shoulders. "That is the problem with threats. You ask questions with your hurt gun, and I talk nonsense. And even if I hurt enough to stop with nonsense and start with true things, you will not know what is what."

He said it all matter-of-factly. Ivy didn't know if it was due to his stilted English, or that he'd already thought through the implications of being tortured. Despite his calm words, Ivy could see a line of sweat glimmering on his forehead.

"I train for this," the scout continued. "Go back to the party, little girl. Don't get blood on your pretty clothes."

No matter how bad his English was, the scout had to know that calling her a little girl was an insult. Which meant if he said it, he was trying to make her mad. He wanted her angry and off-balance, acting impulsively and making mistakes. And Ivy was angry; he'd gotten that part right. She'd been threatened, drugged, chased, and saw her best friend die in front of her. One handcuffed scout with lousy English was hardly the scariest thing Ivy'd had to deal with this week.

He probably made the top three, but there was no sense in letting him know that.

Slowly and deliberately, Ivy picked up the Taser, watching his face, making sure he saw her do it. Very deliberately, Ivy slid it back into her purse.

Something flickered across the trow's face, as though he hadn't expected that.

"I am not going to hurt you just to get you to talk to me," said Ivy simply. "I can't vouch for anyone else here, but for me, that isn't an option. But look, will you at least tell me your name?"

The scout arched his eyebrow, something very like a smirk appearing on his face as he nodded at Ivy's purse. "I just prove I don't have to," he said.

"Fine," said Ivy, through gritted teeth. "If you won't tell me your name, I think I'll call you Pepper."

"Good," said the trow, his smile growing wider. "And I'll call you Crazy Girl, yes?"

"I am trying to be polite," Ivy pointed out, scowling at him.

"This isn't polite," Pepper snapped, shaking his handcuffs so they rattled against the table leg. "You deciding you are not evil does not mean we're friends." He leaned back against the table, unfolding his legs as though getting comfortable. He stretched just close enough to brush the tip of his boot against Ivy's knee.

"Maybe you try sexy time now?" he asked brightly. "Or you don't know how to do that, either?"

"That's disgusting," Ivy snapped, scooting back another few inches. Her face felt red; she hoped it wasn't obvious in the dim light. The thought of walking back to the party and leaving Pepper chained to the table seemed more and more appealing.

Instead, Ivy grabbed her ridiculous rhinestone necklace and pulled it up toward her chin. She tapped her finger just below the sore spot on her neck.

"This isn't the first time this week I've run into one of your lot," she said, turning her head to show him the bruise, and the pinpoint mark from the hypodermic in the middle of it.

Pepper actually leaned forward, the handcuffs rattling against the table leg as he squinted at Ivy's neck. For the first time, some of the maddening arrogance dropped from his face.

"What did—" he began, then stopped and turned away, catching himself before he actually asked the question. He took a deep breath, bit at his lip, and snapped a few incomprehensible words to the wing.

Ivy let the necklace drop back onto her collarbone and settled into a more comfortable position on the floor. "Since you aren't going anywhere for a while, I'm just going to chat," she said. "You don't really have the option not to listen, and if you decide you have anything to add to this conversation, feel free to chime in. Alright?"

Pepper raised an eyebrow. "Still think sexy time is best option," he said amiably. He was smirking, but he was also leaning forward, as though the bruise on Ivy's neck had actually caught his attention.

"Two nights ago, a woman dressed in those same clothes and with one of those damned wings, or whatever you call the thing on your arm, showed up in my room in the middle of the night," Ivy said. "She tried that same trick you did with the needle and it almost worked. Almost. My flatmate's dog chased her down the street and I think she tried to use her recall. Protocol Four. You know, the thing that's supposed to take you home? She went up like a torch in the middle of the street. She hardly had time to scream."

"You say you are not interested in threats," Pepper said, staring hard at her. The smirk was still hovering at the edges of his mouth. Ivy wondered if he was keeping it there to cover up something else.

"It isn't a threat, it's what I saw," said Ivy. "Look, how many of your fellow scouts have used their recall to actually get home?"

Pepper didn't answer. The drops of sweat on his face glimmered in the green light of the exit sign, standing out against the dark fuzz of his hair.

"The person you saw," he said guardedly. "How does she look, please?"

"Brown hair, done up in a braid," Ivy said, gesturing at her own braid, trying to think of something more distinct than *she looked exactly like all of you do, and she was wearing the same clothes.* "She had an outfit like yours and a wing on her arm. It was in Dartry. I think she was trying to hack Lauren's phone—my flatmate, she works here—but she ended up with mine instead."

"And what next?" he asked.

"She stabbed me in the neck is what happened next," Ivy said. "I couldn't move, and I tried to talk to her but her English wasn't as good as yours, and I didn't know if she was trying to kill me so I turned on the stereo, and she ran out of the flat, and Lauren's dog chased her, and we went after the dog and she ran into the street and—" Ivy stuttered to a halt, aware she was probably speaking too fast for him, but at least he was listening. At least he was trying to understand, rather than glaring at her and refusing to say anything at all.

"And she burned," Ivy finished, swallowing hard. "Look, if Protocol Four works the way it's supposed to, *someone* should have come back to Valiard and reported they'd used it to get home."

Pepper glanced his own the wing, the display still glowering red. When he looked back at Ivy, an answer showed itself in the sudden troubled look in his eyes.

"Has *anyone* come back and said their recall worked? Even one?" Ivy pressed, leaning forward. "How many of your scouts haven't come home at all?"

"Seventeen percent," Pepper snapped. He blinked hard for a moment, dropping his head, then looking cautiously back at Ivy.

"Seventeen percent?" Ivy repeated, wondering for a moment if he meant seven percent, or zero point seventeen. Pepper hesitated, then nodded.

"You signed up for something with a failure rate of almost one in five?"

Pepper lifted an eyebrow, a gesture Ivy was beginning to interpret as something like a shrug. "Better than your fighting planes, in big second war," he said, tossing his head like he wasn't horrified by the number. Like he might even have been the slightest bit proud of it.

Ivy swallowed hard. She vaguely remembered reading that the average life expectancy of a British fighter pilot in World War II was a little over a month, and people had still signed up to fly. But that had been in wartime, with the immediate threat of a German invasion. What could Valiard want, that they were sending their own people to Dublin with a nearly one-in-five chance they wouldn't return? What was it about this time and place that could possibly be that important?

Was Valiard trying to fight a war against its own past?

Something of Ivy's shock must have shown on her face.

"I know when I come here, maybe I will not go home," Pepper said, as lightly as if he was discussing the weather. "Like your woman. And you do not know if it was Protocol Four, with her."

"No, I have a pretty good idea it was," Ivy snapped. She hesitated, then pulled her purse into her lap. The handcuffs jingled as Pepper shrank against the table leg, but the look of apprehension faded from his expression as Ivy gingerly pulled the wing from the NIC into her lap.

Pepper's eyes went wide, and he murmured something that sounded suspiciously like a curse.

"Where do you get that?" he demanded.

"From the basement of a very creepy house in County Clare, five months ago," said Ivy, settling the wing into her lap, happy it wasn't trying to latch onto her wrist like a remora. "It's not the only one they have, either."

Ivy took a deep breath. Was there some sort of cosmic rule about not revealing too much about the future? Ivy hoped not; otherwise this seemed like exactly the sort of conversation that would call down one of the red-eyed changelings from the stained glass and tapestries in Haven.

"Quick history lesson," Ivy said, crossing her arms. "Three hundred years ago, a group of refugees from Valiard showed up in Ireland. They were trying to get away from something terrible that happened in your world, some kind of attack. The wing that got them here won't let them go. Three centuries later, Protocol Four is still activating. It doesn't bring them back to Valiard. *It* just burns them up so nothing is left. Once a year, every year, and no one knows how to stop it from this side. Last February it was someone I knew. I saw it happen."

Pepper was staring at Ivy with his mouth partway open. Ivy rushed on, grateful that at least he was no longer mocking her.

"He didn't walk away, or step through a door, or disappear, or however it happens when you move between two places that shouldn't touch. He was screaming, and he burned."

"It was the same with the woman you saw?" Pepper asked. Ivy nodded. Under the muddled light of the wing and the exit sign, his face looked chalky and shaken. "And Valiard? You tell me in my future, it will be hurt?"

"They think it might have been destroyed altogether," Ivy admitted in a low voice, leaning forward. "I think we can help each other. You're here because your bosses in Valiard are trying to change something in my world," she hedged.

Pepper's eyes narrowed for a moment. "Yes," he said, after the briefest of hesitations.

"Maybe I can help you. And in return, when you go back to Valiard you can warn them about the attack. *And* change the programming on Angevin's wing. Disable the recall, make it so it can't kill anyone else."

Pepper swallowed hard and he glanced again at his wing, twisting his head far enough Ivy could see the pulse jumping at his throat.

"Who is Angevin?" Pepper asked in a monotone, not looking at her.

"The trow that brought everyone here from Valiard, three hundred years ago," said Ivy. "It was his jump, when everything went wrong."

Pepper looked back at Ivy and stared at her for a long moment, his face expressionless and remote.

"If you want me to help you, free my hands. Please," he added, almost as an afterthought.

"No more needles?" Ivy asked pointedly.

"Yes," said Pepper, though he sounded unhappy about it. "And no more hurt gun."

"Fine," said Ivy, pushing away the thought that letting him loose might be a very quick way to find herself handcuffed to the same table. But she couldn't very well ask Pepper to trust her and also keep him handcuffed. At least if they were talking, he probably wouldn't try to drug her into paralysis. Or worse.

She pulled the keys to the handcuffs out of her purse, and gently set the battered wing on the ground as she crawled hesitantly over to Pepper. Ivy felt along the table leg to find the chain, then ran her fingers over the cuff itself, feeling for the keyhole. Pepper turned toward her, close enough she could hear the quiet hiss of his breathing. It took a moment for Ivy to realize why that felt so unsettling.

"You do know we shouldn't be touching each other, right?" Ivy asked as she slipped the key into the base of the cuffs. "And you shouldn't eat any food?"

Pepper snorted, like he might have been rolling his eyes. "They tell me you have strange culture," he muttered.

"It's not my culture, it's an actual thing," Ivy corrected. She turned the key in the lock and the cuff opened with a quiet click. Pepper snatched his hands back, the now-open handcuffs smacking into the table leg with a clatter that made Ivy jump. Pepper immediately brought up his left arm, the handcuff still dangling, and began typing something into the wing's interface with his right hand. Between the heat sinks, the display was flashing a single angry-looking red character.

"You won't use the recall, right?" Ivy asked nervously, looking at the display. Something queasy rippled through Ivy's stomach at the thought of seeing that terrible fire again. Even if Pepper was an arrogant and condescending ass, even if Hunzu said scouts were dangerous, she didn't want to see him burn.

"I don't use recall because I am not going home," said Pepper, still typing. The wing chimed once, and Pepper frowned. "I finish work here, then go home. If you are even right about any of these things."

"For God's sake," Ivy snapped, and grabbed her own battered wing, holding it up for emphasis. "I'm not lying. Exhibit A, I can see you. B, I know exactly where you come from. And C, I have one of your own bloody supercomputers. Doesn't that mean maybe I have some insight into this?"

Pepper broke off from his own wing, looking at the scratched metal and the illegibly flickering display of Ivy's, something like regret stealing over his face. He reached for it, then hesitated.

"All this tells me is someone like me was lost once," he said coldly. "And they never came home." He held out his hand palm up and Ivy realized he was asking for the key to the handcuffs. Gingerly, Ivy dropped it into his palm.

Pepper set his left hand on his knee, working awkwardly to get the key wedged into the gap between the handcuff and the edge of the wing. "Also, Salem is still waking up," he added, biting his lip as the cuff rattled against the edge of the wing. "It doesn't like hurt gun, either. And it doesn't like to open doors inside. A large door in a small room makes a big mess."

"So does a large explosion," Ivy snapped.

"You want leave, you leave," said Pepper, glancing at her long enough to give her an eyebrow-shrug. "Or you want to stay and help?"

"I'll help you," said Ivy warily. "*If* you tell Angevin he has to take the recall off his wing when you get back. Can you do that? Do you even know who he is?"

If Pepper was too far removed in time from Angevin's disastrous mission, maybe he hadn't even joined the scouts yet. Maybe he was still a child, where Pepper was coming from. Or he hadn't even been born. How would it work, if the message about the murderous wing had to wait decades before reaching its intended recipient?

"Yes, I—" Pepper started, and his eyes flicked to the floor. He started again, and Ivy had the feeling it wasn't what he'd intended to say. "I will tell Angevin," he said finally.

The handcuffs dropped off his wrist; the scout caught them before they could hit the ground. Quickly, Pepper relocked both cuffs, then handed them and the key back to Ivy. Surprised, Ivy took them, the metal still warm as she slid them back into her purse.

"His jump is soon, in my time," the scout added, looking grave. "I need to do something here before that happens."

The scout dimmed something on his wing's display, then got to his feet. He held out his hand, looking at Ivy expectantly. Ivy hesitated, then surprised herself by taking it, allowing Pepper to help her up. His skin felt warm, and the slightest bit damp with sweat. Discreetly, Ivy rubbed her bare hand against the side of her trousers, hoping Pepper wouldn't notice as she followed him out the door.

CHAPTER 11

Pepper seemed to know where he was going, and Ivy stayed close as he turned down the darkened corridor and back through the unlatched door, typing intermittently on his wing. The scout turned right down the corridor, hesitated for a moment, then pushed open a metal door leading to a stairway.

"Where exactly are we going?" Ivy hissed at the scout's back as she followed him up the stairs.

Pepper looked over his shoulder long enough to glare at her and tap his lips. In the silence, Ivy heard the murmur of voices somewhere farther down the stairway.

"You should put on the computer," he said, nodding at Ivy's purse. "The hiding part still maybe works."

Ivy didn't particularly want to wear it, or risk becoming invisible permanently, but if they were going to be sneaking around the building, Pepper had a point. She slipped her hand into her purse, picked up the wing, and diffidently offered it her wrist. The metal sleeve slid open, tightening around her arm suddenly enough that Ivy flinched. The display between the heat sinks flickered unintelligibly; the alarm was keening again, though not as stridently as before. Tentatively, Ivy tapped at what she hoped was an acknowledgment, and the thing fell silent. The metal bands on her arm felt feverishly warm.

"How can you tell it's working?" Ivy hissed.

"No one points and shouts," Pepper said over his shoulder. Reaching the landing, he glanced at his wing's display, then went for the door. As he reached for the handle, Ivy grabbed his shoulder. The fabric of his jumpsuit felt cool and oddly metallic.

"Will you at least tell me what we're doing?" Ivy asked, frowning.

Pepper shrugged off her arm and opened the door. "They make something here, and there is a war about it," he said, stepping into a grey-paneled corridor. "Long war. And after, everything not like us is dead. Not even the people who—"

Pepper came to a sudden halt, staring hard at the wing's display.

"You say you do not work here," he snapped, angry for no reason Ivy could detect.

"I don't," Ivy said. "I told you, my flatmate does. Lauren. She's the one who got me a party invitation."

"The name Ivy Rene Gallagher is on the list of staff. Section Seven. Explain, please," he said, staring at her with an expression like a thundercloud.

"Yes, that's my name, but I definitely don't work here!" Ivy insisted. "I work at a pub. You know, serving beer? And occasional side gigs for your own bloody descendants." As Pepper's face darkened, Ivy added, hesitantly, "What's the date, on the staff list you have?"

Pepper's gaze flicked back to the wing and he typed something into the interface. "Now. Sort of now. Approximately contemporaneous," he added, in a way that made Ivy suspect he was reading a translation the wing was providing.

"Well, it's wrong," Ivy insisted. "If we finish this tonight, I'm never coming back here again."

Pepper stared hard at her for a long moment, long enough for Ivy to think uneasily of the Taser, and of the array of needles strapped to his leg. His staff list was wrong. It probably wasn't even a staff list. Maybe he'd gotten ahold of the roster of party attendees, or Lauren had put down Ivy as an emergency contact, or Ivy had gotten herself signed up for an Institute mailing list by accident.

"I think we both learn things about the future we don't like," Pepper muttered, and swiped at something on the wing's display. He nodded at the corridor, and Ivy uneasily fell into step beside him.

She wasn't coming back here. If everything worked out tonight like Ivy hoped it would, she'd never need to.

The hallway curved again, and as she stepped around the corner Ivy saw a flurry of movement in the darkness ahead. She hesitated, then hurried to catch up with Pepper when she realized she was seeing their own reflections in glass. A great deal more glass; it looked like a raised walkway connecting two different buildings in the DIAAR campus. The glow of the streetlights in the car park glimmered faintly to the right.

As she followed Pepper into the walkway, Ivy glanced at her wing's spluttering display, wondering how visible she might be to anyone in the parking lot who happened to look up. Or even worse, any security guard who happened to look at a camera. The trows' veil didn't do anything for screens or telephones; Ivy wondered if Pepper knew that.

Beside her, Pepper abruptly plastered himself to the wall, close enough that his nose was almost touching the glass. Ivy froze, looking around in confusion for whatever threat must have entered the walkway, when she realized Pepper was actually looking at something outside.

Shading her eyes from the overhead lights, Ivy leaned closer to the glass. She saw nothing but the half-full parking lot, a handful of figures still streaming into the party, the trees and manicured lawns of the Institute campus, and the faint outline of cranes at the Dún Laoghaire port silhouetted low on the horizon.

Pepper cupped his hands to his face, stared for another long moment, then turned to Ivy.

"There are plants out there," he said, sounding bemused. "You let them grow outside?"

"They pretty much grow on their own," said Ivy, frowning. According to Hunzu, trows were so obsessed with plants here on Earth because Valiard mostly didn't have any. "It's nothing fancy, just grass and trees."

"The trees are very large," Pepper commented vaguely, looking back out the window. Then, hesitantly, he turned back to Ivy with a hint of that same bright look she'd first seen on his face under the party lights. "When we finish here, will you show me one?"

Ivy looked away and nodded.

"Yeah, we can go look at a tree," she said, something uncomfortable twisting in her belly. Knowing the trows came from somewhere with barely any plants hadn't been disturbing until she found out their home was a future version of Earth. "You've never seen—"

Something clicked into place, and Ivy realized what he'd just given away. By the look on Pepper's face, he'd realized it as well.

"You've never been here before," Ivy said, crossing her arms. "This is your first trip!"

The bright look dropped from Pepper's face like a shuttered window. "I study very and I am much trained," he snapped, not looking at her, though the comment must have rattled him if his grammar had devolved that much. "Trees don't matter."

Pepper wrenched himself away from the glass and started down the walkway, pointedly not looking out the window.

"They do matter, or you wouldn't be here in the first place," Ivy pointed out.

Pepper didn't look back at her; he simply slipped a plain-looking security card out of his pocket as he hurried to the door at the end of the walkway.

"Isn't that why you're here?" Ivy pressed. "To change the future so you actually *have* things like trees and grass? Why else do you bother?"

Pepper held up the card to a panel beside the door, shouldering it open as soon as the panel turned green. Ivy followed him down a hallway that looked considerably newer and more modern than the building they'd just left.

"Maybe it still will not work," he snapped, shoulders rounded, still not looking at her. "Things go very wrong, very fast. Maybe not enough time to fix."

He slowed and jabbed something at the wing's display. He looked at Ivy, almost speculatively, and started to say something —then both of them jumped as an alarm over their heads began to shriek.

Ivy looked back at the door they'd entered, certain Pepper's key was somehow wrong. Above them, lights in the overhead panels were flashing like a strobe, which seemed too much even for an alarm on a very important door. Wincing, Pepper started to unfasten one of the needles from his holster.

Ivy leaned closer, bellowing in his ear to be heard over the cacophony. "Fire alarm!" she shouted.

Pepper nodded, though Ivy wasn't sure if he'd understood her or not, and took off down the corridor nearly at a run. Ivy tore after him, the wing an unfamiliar weight on her arm, as

Pepper skidded around the bend in the hallway and threw himself through another metal door with a crash that was completely drowned out by the wail of the siren. He hurried up the stairs. Ivy followed behind him, uneasily aware that if there really was a fire, running deeper into the building was *not* what they were supposed to be doing.

If anything, the alarm was louder in the stairwell, echoing like it was shaking the metal treads under Ivy's feet. Ivy felt her boots digging into her heels as she hurried after the scout. Pepper reached the next landing and hurtled through the door; Ivy caught it before it could slam shut, and slipped through.

Two steps later she nearly collided with Pepper, who had stopped dead in the middle of the corridor. At first the shapes in front of them didn't make any sense: the proportions were wrong, the heads round and cartoonish, the limbs sticklike in comparison. Then Ivy realized what she was looking at and grabbed Pepper, hauling him out of the middle of the hallway as she flattened herself against the wall, hardly daring to breathe.

A half dozen figures in hazmat suits were hurrying down the hall toward them. They all wore yellow coveralls, with a transparent window in the center of their helmets, their faces hidden behind the glare. Several carried what looked like brief-cases; one had a clipboard. Ivy took a deep breath as they came nearer, glancing at the wing on her arm, still flickering gibber-ish, then at Pepper. The scout looked back, his expression more confused than frightened, and Ivy wondered if, where he came from, it was normal to see people in hazmat suits. *Everything not like us is dead.*

A smaller figure tottered in the middle of the group, swaying as they grappled with their helmet, as though they hadn't gotten it aligned to their face properly. The figure stag-gered; their left arm was clutching a bundle of bright, colorful papers, which looked so out of place among the yellow suits and oversized helmets it took Ivy a moment to realize they were comics. The figure's insistence on holding on to them was at least half the reason why their helmet wasn't on straight.

"Pepper," Ivy hissed, "if it wasn't an alarm for a *fire*—"

Pepper's eyes widened and he snapped an order to the wing, staring intensely at the display.

The man with the clipboard stopped, turned to the smaller figure, and impatiently grabbed the helmet as the entire group came to an uneasy halt barely ten feet away. Beyond the ringing alarm, Ivy could hear static-filled bursts of muffled voices, as though their helmets had some sort of comms. The shadows cast by the strobe looked eerily similar to the theatrical lights downstairs, though the hazmat-suited figures didn't look like they belonged to the same universe as the sequined party-goers, let alone the same building.

Ivy pressed herself more tightly against the wall. No one was shouting, pointing, or trying to shove a hazmat suit in her direction, so the veil on the questionable wing was probably working. Did Ivy *want* someone be shoving a hazmat suit her direction?

Beside her, Pepper's shoulders visibly relaxed. "Computer thinks no problems with the air," he said, shouting to be heard over the alarm.

Ahead of them, the helmet on the smallest figure finally dropped into place. The face behind the vinyl shield was just visible behind the glare, and the figure was looking straight at Ivy. A head of brown hair framed their wide-eyed expression, their mouth opening to shout something unintelligible.

Pepper dove for something in his pocket at the same moment the figure's taller companion grabbed them by the arm and hauled them down the hall with a force that brooked no argument. A handful of comics pages went flying; no one seemed to notice. As the whole procession hurried past, the smallest figure was still turning their head—staring straight at Ivy and Pepper as the group rushed down the hall and through the door leading back to the narrow stairs.

For a long moment, the hallway was empty save for them and the screaming alarm. As Pepper stepped away from the wall, the alarm cut off mid-squeal. The silence rang in Ivy's ears like an echo; above them, the flashing light continued to strobe. Not the end of the emergency; someone had simply silenced the alarm.

"Did they see us?" Pepper demanded, turning to Ivy with an affronted look.

"I don't know," said Ivy. Maybe their helmet still hadn't been on right. Maybe the figure was one of the tiny fraction of humans who could see through veils without any of the desensitization measures trows employed. Or maybe they were what Ambrose called a sport—and after her little chat with Carillon, Ivy had a much better idea why some people considered the term rude. "Are you sure the air—"

"Salem says is all fine," Pepper said, hefting his wing and giving Ivy another eyebrow-shrug. "It will tell me if that changes."

Ivy bit her lip and nodded, looking at the incomprehensible characters flickering between the heat sinks. The idea of the wing having a name felt wrong, somehow. They weren't people, or pets, or things that ought to have names. The wing computers seemed to exist somewhere on a continuum with Ivy's smartphone on one end and Skynet or the Matrix on the other. If things like the wing in Haven's basement had enough autonomy to be granted a name, how far did that autonomy extend?

Would it kill Ivy in February because it had to, or because it chose to?

Ivy kept close beside Pepper as they continued walking, the scout's eyes darting between the deserted hallway and the wing display.

"What exactly are they keeping in here?" she hissed at him. In the now-silent corridor, the words seemed louder than they ought to be, echoing in way that seemed unnatural for such a small space.

"The beginning of my world," said Pepper quietly. "Some good things. Mostly bad things."

The stories said the same thing about Pandora's box.

Reaching the far end of the hall, they turned the corner, passing more half-glass doors. Light shone from one of them, casting a reddish square on the floor in front of it.

Pepper started walking faster.

"Hurt gun ready, please," Pepper said, reaching into his holster and coming up with one of his needles.

The intermittent flashing of the strobe seemed to hang a film of unreality over the entire hallway. Ivy shouldn't be here. She still had no idea what was inside the building, or what Pepper was planning to do about it, and she really, *really* didn't want to hurt anyone. Pepper seemed to have a plan . . . but Ivy had also thought Angevin had a plan when she found the keycard in his scarf, and look how that had turned out.

Ivy slipped her hand into her purse and grabbed the Taser. She pulled it out, eyes flicking from the door ahead to the back of Pepper's head, the tiny v where his hairline brushed the edge of his collar. The plaque beside the door was visible—Room 101. Something about that name felt ominous, like it was something Ivy had already seen somewhere, something frightening. As Pepper reached for the handle, a nonsensical thought shot through Ivy's head: if whatever on the other side of the door wasn't anything like Ivy expected, she could use the Taser on Pepper instead.

Then the door was swinging open, and Ivy was rushing into the room after the scout, and she was holding the Taser up without any clear idea of where to point it.

Pepper staggered to a halt inside the door; Ivy pulled herself up short to keep from running into him, eyes widening as she realized they'd run straight into the middle of an argument.

✦✦✦

THE ROOM they'd walked into wasn't a lab at all. Not like the labs on CSI, or even like the room at the Nano Imaging Centre. Room 101 was large, with a row of tall chain-link fencing, dividing half the space into kennels like Ivy remembered from the humane society where they'd adopted her childhood cat. It smelled a bit like the humane society, too, and as Ivy took a deep breath, she corrected that. It smelled worse. Like a litter box that should have been changed last week, overtop a rotting smell that reminded Ivy of the alley behind the Blue Parrot: a mix of piss, spoiling food, and old garbage.

She hesitated, trying to breathe through her mouth, still holding the Taser, waiting for something to come rushing at them from one of the chain-link runs. Beside her, Pepper was wrinkling his nose, looking around with an expression of dismay. He murmured something to the wing, and his frown deepened.

"Does anyone actually know what the hell is going on?" someone snapped from the other side of the room. Ivy's head shot up, looking across the large room to a half wall opposite the kennels.

Glancing at Pepper, Ivy slowly walked toward the end of the partition, and cautiously peered into the gap.

On the other side of the half wall were several long metal

tables, a utility sink, two large refrigerators, and a handful of desks. Three people were gathered around the closest desk, the computer monitor in front of them giving their faces a blueish cast.

Ivy froze, not entirely trusting that her wing wasn't about to drop its veil at the most inconvenient moment.

"I'm supposed to be speaking in ten minutes," said the man on the right, the same voice that had been speaking earlier. "And why the hell hasn't someone done something about the smell?"

The man was leaning over the desk, the lenses of his glasses reflecting blue in the light of the computer monitor. The fellow seated beside him was half-hidden by the monitor, visible only as a thatch of grey hair sticking up from behind the screen. A third man was standing a few paces back, his dark turtleneck doing nothing to hide the breadth of his shoulders or the hints of tattoos at his wrists. He looked like a security guard, or one of the Blue Parrot's bouncers, and he kept tapping at something strapped to his belt. Ivy glanced nervously between the group and Pepper, who was stalking the line of empty cages. The chain link rattled as he touched one of the latches; the people across the room didn't notice.

"All the fire alarms around the south stairwell went off within ten seconds of each other," said the man at the desk, sounding more annoyed than worried. "Caspar's taking a look."

"If it's another tech smoking weed, I want him fired," murmured the man with the glasses, rubbing at his nose as he craned over the other man's shoulder.

As he turned, the light from the monitor angled coolly across his face and Ivy realized she'd seen him before. Not in person, but in on the glossy paper in the flat in Dartry, and the banner downstairs in the lobby. The grey-haired man rubbing at his forehead as though warding off a headache was CEO Winston Smith Brothers.

Why hadn't he left the building when the fire alarm went off? Ivy glanced nervously back at Pepper, a cold prickle on the back of her neck. Whatever the scout was planning to do to the lab or its contents, it seemed incalculably riskier to pull it off under the Institute director's very nose.

"No sign of smoke, but something's blocking the ground-floor door," said the man behind the computer screen.

Ivy hurried back to Pepper, who was standing in front of one of the cages, one hand gripping the chain link. She wrinkled her nose; the smell was even stronger over here, even worse than the vomit-and-piss combination ringing the bus stops in Oxmarten on the mornings after rugby matches.

"Pepper," Ivy hissed. "We should come back later, there's—"

The scout whipped around to face Ivy, his face strangely lit. "There's nothing here," he said. "I am late. Or too early. They were supposed to be here."

"What was supposed to be here?" Ivy asked. Pepper's fingers were clenching the mesh wire tightly enough his hand almost seemed to be trembling. Behind him, in the back of the empty kennel, a pile of dirty grey rags was lying in the corner. Maybe left over from the last time this place was cleaned, which wasn't recently, given the smell. Or maybe a rat had crawled down one of the drains to some inaccessible corner of the building and died.

"First animal tests," Pepper said quietly. "This room. This month. This place. *He* says it, in the book he writes later." Pepper cocked his head at the other side of the partition.

So apparently Ivy wasn't the only one to recognize the Institute's CEO. She took a breath to reply, and nearly gagged on the stench. It was definitely stronger on this side of the room.

"So he had a senior moment about the date when he was writing his memoirs," Ivy said, throwing up her hands. "Send a scout to check back next month. Or *last* month. You travel in time, right? How hard can it be to pin down the right date?"

Pepper didn't answer, but he slowly let go of the chain link, his shoulders slumping. He started to take a deep breath, then appeared to think better of it and reached for something belted at his waist.

"Why they don't just smoke in the parking lot I will never understand," Mr. Brothers sniffed, checking the time on his watch.

Suddenly, the terrible smell and the pile of grey rags at the back of the kennel combined into an awful sort of explanation.

"Pepper," Ivy said again. "That thing at the back of the cage. Is it—"

"Long time dead," Pepper agreed tonelessly. "There was supposed to be something here. Something important. So we have to do this another way."

Ivy followed his gaze uneasily to the group of men clustered around the computer terminal. The tuft of hair behind the monitor was nodding back and forth, murmuring something too quietly to make out; Mr. Brothers watched with crossed arms and an unpleasant expression.

Beside her, Pepper pulled out one of his needles, slowly easing off the safety cap. Unlike the others, the lid on this one was red. Ivy swallowed hard.

"Is that what you were going to use on me?" Ivy asked very quietly.

Pepper turned and looked at her for a moment without answering.

"No, it isn't," he said in a low voice, his face calm and unfathomable.

"Then go home, tell your bosses their intel was wrong," Ivy hissed. This couldn't have been part of the original plan. The woman's wing two nights ago hadn't even wanted her to talk to the wrong person, much less . . . whatever Pepper thought he was going to do. And none of this was getting Ivy any closer to fixing her own problems with the Enemy. "Tell them to try again later, or earlier, or however that works! And tell Angevin to take the recall off his wing. If you do something dumb here and you can't get home, none of that gets fixed."

Beside her, Pepper pressed his thumb lightly on the plunger. Something grey and oily beaded at the top of the needle, hanging at the tip like a tiny, swollen balloon. He looked at her; Ivy tore her eyes away from the grey drop at the end of the needle. Very slowly, Ivy reached out and put her hand on his arm. He didn't shrug her off. His skin felt warm through the fabric.

"I knew things will go wrong even before you tell me," he said, and again, Ivy heard a hint of a strange, unfathomable pride in his voice. "Before I left, when the door was open but before I walk through. They block off the other side, so you don't see yourself come . I could still hear things. Someone on the other side was screaming."

He licked his lips, eyes flicking from the liquid at the tip of the needle to the men on the other side of the room.

"I knew I was probably the seventeen percent, even before you tell me everything is burning when I go back."

Ivy tightened her grip on Pepper's sleeve; the fabric felt slick, almost oily between her fingers. Why would Pepper think it was too late to save Valiard, or warn Angevin about what was going to happen? "It's not burning, and you can still change it."

"Yes, I can," Pepper breathed. "I can change it here. Stop

Event Two before it starts. You've already told me what happens next."

In the pulsing light of the strobe, the chain-link fences seemed to flex in the light, as though the world itself was rippling, waiting for just the right moment to transform into something else. Ivy felt every hair on her neck stand at attention as she realized what Pepper meant.

"You're Angevin," she breathed, staring at him like she'd never seen him before. They looked nothing alike, at least, not any more alike than all trows looked alike. Had she never looked past the scars on his face, or the way his hair always hung in front of his eyes? They couldn't be the same person.

"I'm sorry," said Pepper in the same soft voice. "If Valiard is burning, no one else will come. I am the last one, and this is the last chance to fix it. If it works, maybe the rest doesn't matter."

He started to walk toward the group clustered around the computer. When Ivy tightened her fingers around his sleeve, he shrugged out of her grip. Instead of pulling away, he grabbed her hand. His fingers felt warm and slick with sweat, and the alarm bells sounding in her head, reminding her she was touching a trow, seemed quiet, or else very far away. Too much else had already gone wrong, and Ivy was already invisible. Maybe this time the effect wouldn't end when she took off the stolen wing.

And Pepper—Angevin—wasn't going to catch the disease of aging from Ivy, because he was still alive three hundred years into his own future. He could still fix everything. Maybe this was the first step. Maybe it only looked like cold-blooded murder if you weren't looking at the whole, millennium-long picture.

Ivy's stomach lurched, the smell from the dead thing in the cage pairing with a feeling of dread deep in her guts.-

"Is this like—like killing Hitler?" Ivy asked in a small voice.

She tightened her grip on his hand, their paired shadows jumping and leaping in the lights. Maybe where Pepper was coming from, Mr. Brothers was a war criminal. Or a mass murderer, or he knocked down orphanages to build chemical weapons factories, or something so terrible that history was going to judge him in the harshest way possible.

Mr. Brothers was talking again, pointing at something on the screen as he adjusted his glasses, and for a moment Ivy didn't think Pepper would answer her.

"It would be easier, yes," Pepper said in a cold voice. "If every necessary thing was also clean."

Ivy stumbled on the linoleum floor; Pepper didn't stop, just tightened his grip on her fingers and kept walking. Murder wasn't ever a necessary thing. Not even when everyone insisted the alternative to murder was worse. Like Carillon and the older Angevin, hiding the Enemy away, concealing the truth about what it was and why it killed. If Mr. Brothers died tonight, no one except Ivy would know it was murder. She'd be the only one who knew that someone from the future had walked down the long, cold hallway of history to throw one particular man across the railroad tracks of time.

Pepper's history books were already wrong about the animal trials. Maybe they were wrong about this, too. No one had asked Demi if she wanted to die to save the future. No one was asking Ivy if she wanted to die next year so the Enemy could go on murdering its way to the beginning of Event Two. And no one was asking this man, either.

Ivy wrenched her hand free, dodging past Pepper. He lunged at her, but she was already running. Ignoring Pepper's shout, she tugged at her wing's catch, struggling to force it open.

"Run," she shouted, as loud as she could, and the man in the turtleneck looked up, staring past Ivy as he struggled to pull something free from his belt. The catch popped loose and the wing slipped off her wrist; Ivy grabbed it before it could tumble to the floor.

"You have to run!" she shouted, and the three men were staring at her as if she'd just appeared from thin air. Mr. Brothers was goggling at her, his mouth open like a fish. He wasn't moving, and Ivy knew Pepper had to be wrong, because it was impossible that the fate of the world could depend on someone who looked so usual and ordinary.

Pepper shouldered her aside, his wing a constellation of blinking red lights as he bolted toward the desk. Ivy tried to grab the back of his jacket and missed. The light from the wing glinted red on the tip of the needle; she tore her eyes away from it long enough to see the man in the turtleneck pulling something free from his holster—and the entire world contracted to the gun in his hands.

Ivy ducked, cradling the wing and flinching as her finger brushed the blistering edge of the heat sink. The sound was like the crack of a switch, quieter than anything she'd seen heard on the telly, and she jumped back, raising her free hand. Two paces away, Pepper staggered to a stop, his breathing loud in the sudden silence.

"What the hell, Wayne," Mr. Brothers snapped, rounding on the man in the turtleneck—a security guard, Ivy belatedly realized. He was still pointing his gun alarmingly close to Ivy's head.

"There was something— I swear to God," the man muttered, his eyes darting between Ivy and the place where Pepper might have been standing a moment ago. A line of sweat gleamed on his forehead.

"You have to go," Ivy repeated. Between the gun, Pepper's needle, and Wayne's strangely out-of-focus stare, Ivy felt dizzy, as though all the oxygen had been sucked out of the room.

Pepper might decide the needle was for her next, or the guard would actually hit what he was aiming at. Everything could go to pieces in the next five minutes and none of the bad things would change. "And whatever you're working on, stop," Ivy added, knowing it sounded ridiculous. "Please."

As Mr. Brothers stared at her in shock, Pepper took one step forward. The hypodermic needle hit the floor with a ping. Pepper dropped to his knees a moment later, one hand pressed tightly to his belly.

"Ivy," he whispered.

Everything in the room went cold, as though the wing cradled under her arm was the only bit of light in a universe turned cold and utterly distant. The guard *had* seen something, and he'd hit what he'd been aiming for. And it was all Ivy's fault.

Ivy dropped to her knees beside Pepper, hoping it looked like a natural response when confronted by a man with a gun and seemingly few compunctions about firing it. She put her hand atop Pepper's; he hissed, looking at her with frightened eyes. Under her fingers, his jumpsuit was covered in blood.

"Stop what?" Mr. Brothers asked, leaning over her even as Wayne hesitantly held out an arm to keep him back. "Who let you in here? Run from—oh my God!"

He stepped back, recoiling, and Ivy threw herself in front of Pepper, certain he'd seen the scout—but Mr. Brothers was staring at the ground, at the blood soaking the tips of his neat, white shoes.

"Call an ambulance," the man with the grey hair barked.

"Not in here," Mr. Brothers retorted, then to Ivy. "You need to come with us. We'll get you to a hospital."

He held out his hand. Beside her, Pepper slumped to the floor, curling into a ball. He was hissing in Rass to his wing, his voice shuddering, his face ashen.

This was exactly the sort of scenario that Protocol Four was meant for. Ivy could take Mr. Brothers's hand, and go downstairs, pretend she'd gotten lost and had terrible nosebleeds, and meanwhile Pepper—Angevin—would bleed to death. And Angevin wouldn't be alive to return to Ireland with several hundred innocent refugees and one time-traveling murder computer.

Except Angevin *did* live, and he *had* come back to Ireland in the Middle Ages, and they were all still standing on the edge of an apocalypse no one knew how to prevent. Everything was tied together, knitted up across centuries with the shadowy threads of death, secrets, and war.

Maybe there was still enough time to unpick the knot.

"Give me a moment," said Ivy breathlessly, opening her eyes wide, trying to look like a traumatized maybe-gunshot-victim. She tore her hand away from Pepper's blood-covered fingers, clawing at her wing's catch. A drop of blood splattered on the heat sink, sending up a smell like burning metal. As if sensing what she wanted, the wing wrapped itself around her forearm. Ivy flinched at the heat; it felt as if her arm were inches away from a bonfire.

Mr. Brothers's face went slack. Behind him, the guard shouted, his gun back in his hand. Leaping to her feet, Ivy bolted away from Pepper and toward the line of cages. She ran past the partition, wincing as the smell from the dead thing in the cage hit her full force. She skidded on the floor and grabbed the fence to steady herself. The chain link rippled, rattling like thunder, and Ivy grimaced at the noise. She turned back to see Wayne step past the partition, holding his gun like he wasn't sure where to point it.

At least she was leading them farther from Pepper, Ivy thought, seeing Mr. Brothers emerge from behind the half wall.

Even injured, Ivy was certain the scout had other things in his pockets that were just as lethal as his needles.

"There," said Mr. Brothers, pointing at Ivy. Ivy froze, grappling with the wing, ready to rip it off her arm because it wasn't working. But the director's hand was pointing lower than it should have been. Following his gaze, Ivy's stomach clenched when she saw the line of bloody footprints on the floor, leading right to where she was standing.

The guard grabbed Mr. Brothers by the arm. "Sir, we need to go, we'll send someone—"

"She could be anywhere by then," Mr. Brothers snapped, shrugging off Wayne's arm. Pushing up the sleeves of his jacket, he headed straight for Ivy. Ivy bolted farther down the row of cages, a cacophony of surprised shouts making it obvious that her bloody footprints were still visible behind her. She passed the edge of the partition and turned, following the line of chain link. Ivy could hear the slap of Mr. Brothers's shoes behind her as she bolted down the line of runs.

Ivy tripped over something that clattered like metal. She landed hard on her knees, scrambling to her feet as something behind her snatched at her hair. Ivy bit back a yelp and ducked. Mr. Brothers staggered past, half tripping over Ivy, his arms spread wide like a scarecrow.

He started to turn around, arms waving wildly. Ivy jumped onto the fence, climbing up the chain link as quickly as she could. The fence shuddered under her weight, the noise rippling the length of the room. Her bloody hands slipped on the metal links; her ridiculous metal necklace jingled like an echo of the shaking fence. Ivy threw herself over the top bar, her purse swinging wildly as she straddled the rail.

Mr. Brothers stepped up to the fence, inspecting the flecks of blood on the chain link. His glasses shone in the light as he looked right, then left, the straight up toward Ivy.

As quietly as she could, Ivy pulled her feet as high as she could manage, frighteningly aware Mr. Brothers could still reach her ankles if he figured out where she was. The director took a deep breath, and for a long moment nothing moved. Not Ivy, balanced on the top rail. Not Mr. Brothers, or the two men staring around the room in fear and confusion. Not the black-clad shape on the floor, the pool of blood by his hip visible even from Ivy's perch on the fence. Ivy wondered, horribly, how large a pool it would have to be before the veil could no longer keep it hidden.

"Mr. Brothers," said the guard, as though he couldn't quite make it an order, but devoutly wished he could.

In the silence, the door leading back to the corridor opened with a bang. Ivy jumped, tightening her grip on the top rail because the shape standing open-mouthed in the doorway was impossible. It was wearing a bulky yellow jacket, padded like a fireman's suit, thick enough to obscure anything about the stranger's body. But the wisps of brown hair escaping from their braid framed a face stolen from a funhouse mirror, and the rhinestones from Ivy's own necklace gleamed on the figure's neck.

The changeling hesitated in the doorway, and its eyes locked with Ivy's in a moment that seemed to leave no room for anything but horror. *If you go back in time to kill your own grandfather, a changeling appears and stops you. Or the changeling becomes your grandfather instead.*

"How'd she—" Mr. Brothers started to say.

"Please stay where you are, ma'am," said Wayne to the figure, holstering his gun and hurrying toward the door as Ivy tried to remember everything she had ever heard about changelings.

The figure looked away, seemed to take in the three men

hurrying toward it, and bolted out of Room 101, back down the corridor.

Wayne, shouting, tore after it, with the grey-haired man following behind. The security guard caught the edge of the door just before it closed and both men disappeared through it. Mr. Brothers took two steps toward the door, then stopped. He turned back, the light flashing on his glasses, his gaze lingering on the bloody footprints leading back to the cubicles. Ivy flexed her hands against the rail where the wire was digging painfully into her palms. She could hear Pepper whispering to his wing, but couldn't make out the words.

Something rang, shrill and demanding, and Mr. Brothers dove into his suit pocket, pulling out his phone and barking out a greeting as he turned to follow Wayne and the changeling out the door. With a last glance toward the cubicles, he turned away, letting the door slam shut behind him.

Ivy squeezed her eyes shut, fingers curled tight against the top rail, feeling like reality was rippling around her like a mirage. The scout who was supposed to save Ivy's world and his own was bleeding on the floor, and a changeling wearing Ivy's face was somewhere inside the building.

That last thought was too much to think about; Ivy pushed it away. Shakily, she threw one leg over the top of the fence, the chain link catching at her shirt as she started climbing down, trying to keep her wing's heat sinks from tangling on the wires.

Step one: Pepper couldn't die. He had to be wrong about it being too late to warn Valiard and change the recall on the wing. He had to be alive to carry that message. If he never made it back to Valiard, nothing would change.

A gunshot sounded from the hallway outside and Ivy flinched, half-falling the last few feet to the ground and staring wildly at the door. Wayne couldn't be shooting at anything, Ivy thought desperately, because all the monsters were already in here. Except for the changeling wearing Ivy's face.

Tearing herself away from the door, Ivy ran toward Pepper as she ripped the wing off her arm. Pepper hadn't moved from where she'd left him, curled into a painfully small bundle, a thick bandage belted across his stomach. Below it, the fabric of his jumpsuit was dark and wet. His eyes were half-closed, lashes flickering as he murmured something to the wing too faintly for Ivy to make out. Shuddering, Ivy dropped to her knees beside him and hesitantly reached for his shoulder. Pepper's hand shot up, his fingers slick as they tightened around hers. The blood was so thick Ivy could smell it, mixing horribly with the stench from the dead thing in the cage.

"Pepper?" Ivy asked, but the scout merely shifted his grip to Ivy's wrist, and without warning, pulled her hand palm-first into the center of the wing.

Ivy yelped, yanking her fingers back from the wave of heat that coursed through the metal. Pepper let go of her wrist, his hand dropping limply to the floor.

"You have to stop it," said Pepper, biting out every word as though it cost him something to do it. "The thing that happens here. The thing they make. Salem will help you."

"No, you'll help me," Ivy snapped, shaking her fingers, trying to dispel the tingling sensation where the wing had touched her. "You have to go home first. Somewhere with doctors, or a hospital."

Pepper shook his head, the corner of his mouth twisting up. "It will help you," he repeated, running his finger along the edge of the wing's metal sleeve. "It doesn't have a choice."

"Well, neither do you!" Ivy snapped. "You have to go home or you'll die here, and I don't know how to help you!" She leaned forward, trying to meet his gaze. "Go home and warn

Valiard, and I will do everything I can to fix things here, I swear."

There wouldn't have been so much blood, if Ivy had turned her back on Pepper and the needle and not watched. There wouldn't have been blood pooling on the floor, or covering her own hands. Would she still have torn the wing off her arm, if she knew she was only exchanging one murder for another?

Pepper made a choking sound deep in his throat. He reached for Ivy's hand again, and with a grunt, dragged it back to the wing. "Take Salem. *Help* it."

His eyes fluttered closed. Ivy stared at his bloodless face, again feeling as though reality were nothing more than a soap bubble, liable to pop at any moment. He'd called his wing Salem.

So had Carillon, last night in the garden. Salem was Angevin's wing, the wing running Protocol Four, the Enemy who'd been killing Year Kings for three hundred years.

"Pepper," Ivy hissed, flinching away from the blood-spattered wing and grabbing his shoulder. "Pepper, I can't do this! That wing—it comes back with you, and it kills people! That's all it's ever done, I can't—"

Pepper grabbed Ivy's hand again, drawing her fingers back to the catch on the wing. "Something inside this place starts a war that never ends," he said, gasping out each word. "Burn it down. Please."

This couldn't be how everything happened. Pepper had to get home, either to warn Angevin or because he *was* Angevin. It hardly mattered which.

"Pepper," Ivy hissed, and when he didn't answer: "Angevin?"

The scout shuddered, his gaze flicking to Ivy even as his eyelids flickered, then closed. There was a rasping note to his breathing that was like a knife in Ivy's belly, as she searched his face for anything that might connect him with the Angevin she knew. The scout who saved Valiard's refugees, only to kill them by inches over the next three hundred years.

If they were both the same man, what did it mean that he was dying on the floor in front of her?

If Angevin died, the trows would never come to Ireland; they'd all die in Valiard and no one in Ivy's world would notice. Larch and Demi would never have existed. Which meant it shouldn't be possible for Ivy to be here at all, chasing after a time traveler and trying to save two worlds.

Except if Ivy *wasn't* here, no one would have stopped Pepper from killing Mr. Brothers. It was all tied up in a paradox, and Ivy had the chilling sensation that the next few minutes would see the final strands of the knot looped into place.

With a shudder, Ivy thought of the changeling standing in the doorway, wearing Ivy's own face. Maybe that was how the paradox resolved itself. Maybe Mr. Brothers was already dead. Maybe that was the universe's answer, sending a Murder Ivy to snip the loose ends, wearing Ivy's face all the while.

The idea seemed equal parts implausible and terrifyingly real. She'd seen its face. And if Ivy didn't trust whatever answer the changeling might come up with, she needed to come up with her own answer to the paradox. And soon, she thought, looking at Pepper's chalky face.

Biting her lip, Ivy looked at his wing and slowly reached for his arm.

The thing had spoken to her, back in the vault. It might have spoken to Larch, in the moments before it killed him. Pepper trusted it.

He'd also agreed to take a job with a one-in-five fatality rate, but right now Ivy was running out of options.

Ivy pulled Pepper's arm closer, the heat sinks fever-hot

against her fingers. His body felt boneless and heavier than it ought to, like it was already part of something no longer alive. Ivy shuddered and went for the catch. Something gave under her searching fingers, and the two halves of the wing hinged apart, the display shifting and reforming as the heat sinks rearranged themselves.

Without giving herself time to reconsider, Ivy slapped them over her left wrist.

The metal irised closed around Ivy's arm, and where Ivy had braced for it to be hot, the bands against her skin was cool, though she could still feel the warmth from the heat sinks on her face.

"Salem," Ivy shouted, "you aren't finished!"

Something flickered in the corner of her eye. Ivy looked up, across Pepper's motionless body and straight into the brown, untroubled eyes of the Enemy.

"*Rith shaharet,*" said the Enemy, reproachfully.

"In English," Ivy snapped, reaching for Pepper's fingers and holding them tightly as she stared at the wing's interface. It was squatting beside the scout, legs tucked grasshopper-like beneath it. Looking at its face felt like a memory of fire.

The Enemy spoke again, a jumble of nonsense words lilting upward at the end, like a question.

"It's got to be in English or I can't understand you," Ivy insisted, gesturing at Pepper. "Your scout needs help. You have to get him home. Or else the men that shot him are going to come back, and they're going to find me, and him, and you. Is that what you want? The people you're trying to spy on, investigating you instead?"

"Outputting local vernacular," Salem said cooly. Its face was serene and untroubled, the same expression it had worn in the apple grove while Larch had still been screaming. She shuddered, trying not to think about whether the wing was more likely to kill her now that she was actually talking to it.

"You need to take him home—and not with Protocol Four," Ivy added hurriedly. "Actually home. There's not a big open space for you to spontaneously combust, and Angevin told me you don't like collateral damage. You have to get him home."

Behind her, Ivy heard a creak. A square of light hit the metal wires of the cages, and she heard the wail of the fire alarm, sounding as distant and inconsequential as a tin horn. Ivy hunched her shoulders and leaned closer to Pepper. If no one was yelling, then the veil was still working, and hopefully whoever it was would leave before the pool of blood around Pepper got any bigger.

"Mission objectives remain incomplete," Salem said primly. "Returning to Valiard is not advisable. Additional advisement: this unit does not spontaneously combust."

"If you don't get Pepper back to Valiard, he's going to die!"

"The survival of this unit's operators is not a primary objective."

"No, of course it's not," Ivy snapped. It was ridiculous to think she could talk the wing into helping her. Carillon had three hundred years to try talking it out of killing people, and how well had that worked out? The best anyone had managed was convincing it to take a substitute victim.

The wail of the distant fire alarm cut off with a whisper as the door swung closed, followed by the slow pacing of foot-steps. The presence felt like an itch at the back of her neck; Ivy kept her gaze on the interface.

"The people from Valiard," Ivy began hesitantly. "They talk about you like you're more than a computer. You and the other wings. They talk about you like you can think."

"This unit is considerably more sophisticated than the

computational devices produced in this timeframe," said the Enemy, raising an eyebrow.

"So *think*," Ivy snapped at it. "Even if you don't care about him, don't you care about what you were trying to do? Your primary objectives? What do you think's going to happen when those men come back and find him? Or you?"

Salem cocked its head, as though it were considering. The gesture should have made it look more like a real person, but it didn't. The footsteps were growing louder; Ivy desperately hoped she wasn't about to run up against the limits of what the trows' veils could actually conceal. Even without a wing on his arm, Pepper ought to be covered by the same veil that covered every other trow on the planet . . . but this would be a very bad time to find out otherwise.

"A finite number of outcomes proceed from such a scenario," Salem said smoothly. "This unit remains undetected in seventy-four percent of calculated scenarios. This unit completes mission objectives in four percent," it added, almost sounding annoyed.

"And what about him?" Ivy snapped, gesturing at Pepper. "What are his odds?"

"Previous operator's vital signs are currently unavailable," it said, gesturing at the wing on Ivy's wrist. This time it definitely sounded annoyed.

"He was shot, and he's unconscious," Ivy snapped, glaring at it. "You can extrapolate from that, can't you? If he doesn't get back to Valiard, you're creating a paradox. I'm only here because he *did* go home."

The footsteps were growing louder; coming too close, too fast. Belatedly, Ivy grabbed her own wing's scorched casing, started to press it to Pepper's limp arm—right as a figure dropped to his knees beside her, still wearing the same yellow jumper, and for a moment Ivy couldn't move.

"It's alright, Ivy," Angevin said, spreading his hands in what he obviously felt was a comforting gesture. One corner of his mouth turned up in a smile; nothing about his face looked even remotely like Pepper's.

"How can it possibly be alright?" Ivy snapped, suddenly feeling as though she were about to cry. She threw up her hands to encompass Pepper, the puddle of blood, the Enemy's interface, and the wing latched to her own arm.

Angevin settled himself more firmly on the floor, sliding a large, awkward-looking duffel bag off his shoulder. Leaning closer to Pepper, he brushed his fingers across the scout's cheek lightly, almost reverently. Pepper didn't react and neither did the Enemy, merely staring at Ivy as though nothing else in the world existed.

"Is this what you wanted?" Ivy shouted. Tears were beginning to well in the corners of her eyes, but she wouldn't let go of Pepper's hand to wipe them away. "For someone else to die because of that *monster* you keep hidden away?"

"It's not my monster yet," said Angevin, gesturing to the wing on Ivy's hand. "Right now, it's listening to you."

He leaned closer, bending over the motionless scout, his long hair brushing across Pepper's face as he gently kissed the scout's forehead. "Take us home, Ivy," he said, his eyes glittering through his bangs. "I've seen you do it before."

Ivy looked from Pepper's clammy, still face to Angevin's scarred one, trying fruitlessly to see anything in their features that might tie the two together. Angevin believed she could do it. Angevin believed she could take Pepper home because he'd already seen her do it.

Holding on to Pepper's fingers as tightly as she could, she turned back to the Enemy.

"If he dies here, you've just created a paradox," Ivy continued, staring straight into the Enemy's brown, untroubled eyes.

"And I don't care what kind of apocalypse starts in this building. I'm not going to help you kill anyone else, so don't even think about it."

"You are designated as the primary operator," it said quietly. "Yet you do not support the mission objectives."

"Not if it means murder," Ivy told it. "If you can't get Pepper back home, you're useless to me."

The Enemy pursed its lips. "You lack the proper context to appreciate this unit's value," it said coldly.

"Your value is nothing," Ivy snapped. "You came here to kill someone because that's all you know how to do. And now you're going to let him die because saving him doesn't fit into your objectives. He's your partner. You're supposed to be helping him. You prove to me you understand that, or your objectives can go to hell."

The Enemy cocked its head again, a jerky, angular movement more suited to the gibbet or the guillotine than to any living creature.

"Do you require this unit to demonstrate regard for his life before proceeding with mission objectives?" it asked.

"Yes," said Ivy, without hesitation.

"And you will assist in securing these objectives so long as lethal force is not used?" the Enemy pressed.

Ivy hesitated and looked at Angevin. His face gave nothing away. Ivy wondered if he could even hear what the interface was saying, but there was something troubling in his expression, and for a moment Ivy had a wild urge to rip the wing off her arm, refuse to say another word to the interface until Angevin—*her* Angevin, the one who'd saved Valiard's refugees only to murder them bit by bit over the next three centuries—explained to her exactly what was going on.

Pepper wouldn't survive that. It was only the flutter of his chest under their clasped hands that told Ivy he was even still alive to begin with.

Slowly, Ivy turned to the interface and nodded.

"Please stand by," said the Enemy.

The display at Ivy's wrist flashed red, and everything around her turned bone-chillingly cold. Across the room, the interweaving strands of the chain link were suddenly racing toward her. Ivy tried to take a breath and couldn't. Grappling for the catch on the wing, Ivy tried to stagger to her feet. A jolt in every bone in her body threw her back to her knees.

Below her, the ground wasn't there to catch her.

CHAPTER 12

There was a light shining in Ivy's eyes, and something fuzzy brushed against her cheek as she stirred. For a moment she was certain she was back in Dartry and a lorry had just turned down the street. She reached to pluck the bedsheet away from her face. It was only when her fingers touched an unfamiliar fabric that Ivy realized where she was.

Or rather, where she wasn't.

Ivy bolted upright, shoving away the jacket that had been tucked over her shoulders, and leapt to her feet. The air felt bitterly cold, the room low-ceilinged and windowless, the dark walls polished and strangely reflective. A round-shouldered figure was bent over a console, both wing computers on the floor at his feet, the display in front of him lit up with an incomprehensible mix of numerals and Rass syllabograms.

"Pepper," Ivy started to say, cutting herself off as the man turned around. The display's lights glinted off Angevin's face as he stared back at her through the dark curtain of his hair.

Angevin nodded his head toward the corner of the room behind Ivy.

"I'm terribly sorry," Angevin said, nodding apologetically, and Ivy whirled around before he could say anything else. She stumbled when she spotted him, arms crossed over his chest like a mummy, lying motionless by the far wall. The front of his jacket was dark and stained with blood; his left arm looked strangely bare without the wing. His hood was pulled over his face, and the chill in the air seemed to cut straight to the center of Ivy's heart. She dropped to her knees next to him, gaze flicking from his chest to the edge of his uncovered jaw, looking for any sign that he was still breathing. He didn't move, and Ivy was terrified that she would have to touch him, his terribly still fingers, to know for sure.

She started to reach for the edge of his hood and hesitated, feeling deep in the pit of her stomach that she already knew for sure.

"You did everything you could," said Angevin gently from behind her. It was the sort of platitude that meant nothing, and it rang in the alien room like a lie. "He never manages more than a few minutes after we come through."

The dead scout on the floor drew her gaze like a magnet, as though Pepper, motionless under his own cowl, was everything that had gone wrong over the past three days—past, present, and future. For a moment, Ivy felt a wild inclination to throw back the cowl anyway, to see if his face looked any more like Angevin's, like the murderer he would grow up to be were it not for the inconvenient fact that he was dead. Ivy had been trying to save him, and through him, everyone else. If he died, it all fell apart—starting with the man behind her.

Ivy turned back to Angevin, feeling like she was caught between two funhouse mirrors, each reflecting a distorted version of reality. He was standing at the console, his fingers dancing among the blue sparks of the display as he typed. As though whatever was on the screen was more important than Pepper. More important than his own younger self being dead.

Slowly, Ivy got to her feet, shivering with more than just

cold. Bits and pieces of the strange room were starting to jump out at her whenever she dragged her gaze away from the scout—the white-blue light of the console, the rubbery floor under her feet, a tall, translucent panel at the back of the room, the smell of dust and ammonia in the air. It was not a large room to be sharing it with a dead scout and a live murderer. And the dark, mirrorlike walls gave Ivy absolutely no sense of what might be beyond them. It didn't look like the DIAAR building at all. Wherever Salem had taken them, Ivy didn't think she was in Dublin any longer. Maybe she wasn't even on Earth.

"He's dead, and you don't care," Ivy snapped, crossing over to the console. It made no sense. If Pepper was dead, then Angevin—*her* Angevin, the one who helped the trows escape the fall of Valiard, the one who sheltered a murderer for three hundred years, the one who hid among the flower boxes in Howth last year and started everything—shouldn't exist. "He's dead and you're still alive. Why?"

Angevin sighed, propping his elbows on the console and rubbing at his temples as though to dispel a headache.

"I won't apologize for the name," he said, glancing at her through his fringe of dark hair. "It's the only thing anyone's ever called me."

"I told him he wasn't going to die," said Ivy, refusing to look back at the still, bloodied shape on the floor behind him. "He was the one who was supposed to save everything!"

"And he decided to do something else," snapped Angevin, turning away from the screen. The polished walls on either side caught bits and pieces of his silhouette, the reflections shifting in tandem. "*Your* Angevin chose to go after Mr. Brothers instead of ending his mission and returning to Valiard, so now *I* go back instead. *Again.*"

Ivy started to ask him *go back where*—and hesitated. If Pepper was dead, there was only one place Angevin could mean. Only one place with a grip on time so absolute it would steal Angevin's future and weave it inextricably with his own past.

"That's what changelings are, Ivy," Angevin added quietly. "We're the things the universe uses to fix its own paradoxes. We're what happens so that other people have free will."

"You're going back to Valiard," Ivy breathed. "To Valiard in Pepper's time. And then to Ireland with the refugees, with everyone who makes it out."

Angevin nodded. "Yes," he said bluntly, turning to look at the closed door at the far side of the room, staring at it like it was the edge of a cliff.

Ivy looked back to the wing on the floor, a whirling loop of symbols slowly rotating in the display between the heat sinks. If Angevin was taking Pepper's wing back to Valiard . . .

Ivy snatched up the wing, wincing as the cold metal bands locked around her arm.

"Salem?" she snapped.

The shape slipped into the room out of what Ivy had sworn was an empty corner. Its scout's uniform was perfect, all knife-pleat creases, and Ivy remembered Pepper's jacket, and the midnight color it had turned, soaked with Pepper's blood. Blood that was still covering a good portion of Ivy's own blouse. Ivy blinked the image away.

"Salem, I need you to disable Protocol Four," Ivy told it urgently, meeting the interface's calm stare, aware of Angevin watching her from his station at the console. "The emergency recall, whatever you call it. Whatever brings the scouts back to Valiard when they reach the time limit for their mission. I need you to turn it off. Permanently."

"If it was that easy, someone else would have done it by now," Angevin said quietly.

"This unit cannot disable Protocol Four," said the Enemy, unperturbed.

"Well, who can?" Ivy asked it, looking from the wing's interface to Angevin.

Grimly, Angevin pointed to the far door as the interface cocked its head.

"Alterations to root-level commands are not permitted," the interface told her.

"Not permitted by whom?" Ivy snapped.

The wing didn't answer. Slowly, Angevin got up from the terminal, the sound of his boots on the floor strangely muffled.

"By whoever originally programmed the Valiard mainframe, I imagine. It's like I told you before, we can't fix it from this side. We can only fix it from theirs."

"So that's your plan," Ivy snapped. "Go back to a city that's on fire, and somehow reprogram the wing before you have to use it to evacuate a couple hundred refugees to Earth?"

Abruptly, Angevin looked away and gestured to the duffel bag on the floor. "I'll have twenty-seven minutes with the mainframe before we have to leave."

"You and everyone you're going to let it kill," Ivy added, glowering at the interface and its serene face, exactly how she remembered it from the apple grove. She wondered if Pepper had seen that same ice-cold look when he was bleeding out on the floor of the lab, and it was suddenly too much to keep staring at it. Ivy clawed at the catch on her arm, dropping the wing onto the console beside her. She rubbed her hands across her arms. She could still feel where the metal had wrapped around her wrist.

"Only until I get it right," Angevin muttered, dropping to his knees next to the duffel bag. "I'll have twenty-seven minutes to try and scrub the—"

"You think you'll be able to reprogram it in twenty-seven

minutes?" Ivy challenged, folding her arms. Pepper might have managed it. He knew Valiard, and its systems. Even that might not have been enough if the city was already burning when he got back. "You're not even a real scout!"

Angevin opened the duffel bag, the zipper making a snickering sound as he pulled it. He lifted out a heavy fireman's helmet, the kind with a wide brim and a clear plastic face shield.

"Not the first twenty-seven minutes," said Angevin, shaking his head. "Or the second, or even the one after that. But eventually, one of these times, yes. Then maybe I won't have to do this anymore."

Ivy froze, staring at the reflection of Angevin's face in the face shield. It came together in her head all at once, and Ivy realized everything she'd told Pepper about his own future was a lie.

"You've done all of this before," she breathed. Angevin looked at her under the fringe of his hair, ducking his head like he was embarrassed. "It wasn't enough to let it murder everyone once," Ivy snapped, looking at the wing, seized by a wild urge to batter it against the floor until either it broke or she did. "You'll go back and do it again, won't you? Just sit back and let everyone die? Demi, and Larch, and all of them!"

"Only until I get it right," Angevin told her and got to his feet, the fireman's helmet under one arm. He touched Ivy lightly on the shoulder. She flinched; Angevin didn't seem to notice. "And I *will* get it right," he repeated firmly. "Twenty-seven minutes with the Valiard mainframe, every three hundred years. Eventually it'll be enough." He hesitated, then slowly dropped his hand. His eyes, staring at Ivy, were wide and earnest. "One day soon, we'll meet and none of it will have gone wrong."

Back in Haven, Angevin told her he could fix everything if

he got a message back to Valiard. He hadn't told Ivy that he'd already gone back in person, more than once.

"How many times has it already gone wrong?" she asked.

"Not everyone's like you, you know," Angevin snapped, turning back to the duffel bag. "You're the only one I've ever seen even come close to getting a wing to alter its objectives simply by talking to it. I suppose that's one of the advantages of a dying scout giving you user privileges. The rest of us have to work with what we've got."

"You aren't answering the question," said Ivy, staring hard at him as he pulled a second helmet out of the duffel and set it on the floor. Beside him, the console's display flickered, hints of yellow and orange creeping into the impenetrable blue sea of numbers and characters.

"Eleven times, at least," Angevin said in a low voice, not looking at her. "Possibly as many as sixteen. Or nineteen. Twenty-four, at the absolute outside. I'm certain of that much."

Staring at the door at the far end of the room, he didn't sound certain at all.

Angevin had already gone back to Valiard at least a dozen times. He'd lived through everything that came after, and he hadn't been able to change the most important things. The Enemy still murdered people. Demi was still dead. And a terrifying computer no one was willing to destroy was still sitting in a vault in Haven, counting down the days until it was allowed to kill someone else.

"So you lied to me," Ivy said quietly, balling her hands into fists at her sides. "You didn't care about what happened to Larch, or Demi, or me. None of it was about helping us."

"*All* of it is about helping you," Angevin snapped, grabbing a thick tan jacket out of the duffel bag and shoving his arms into the sleeves. "I go back every time because I can make it better. I'm sure of that."

Angevin looked at the door as he zipped up the jacket, a flicker of apprehension crossing his face.

"I'm afraid of what happens if I stop," he continued in a quieter voice as he picked up the helmet. "Maybe the universe finds another changeling, someone willing to run a three-hundred-year relay race with themselves. Maybe it doesn't." He stopped abruptly and turned to the console where Pepper's wing was sitting. "Which means I need to borrow this one more time."

"You gave me the keycard and you knew Demi was going to die," Ivy shouted, her voice cracking, stepping between Angevin and the wing. He'd known what was in the basement, and he'd known what was going to happen. Demi was dead, and it was Ivy who had taken her into that horrible room—but it was Angevin who'd given her the means to do it.

"Because you don't go to the Institute unless you think you can change things," Angevin said. "Either of you." He hesitated, biting his lip as though he were debating saying something else.

"Just say it," Ivy snapped. "Leave off the secrets, for once."

"It isn't always Demi that dies in that house, and you're not always the one that makes it here," he said, turning back to the door, resting one hand impatiently on the frame. "I think I prefer it when it's Demi. She doesn't ask so many questions."

Something cold draped itself around Ivy's shoulders. She looked away, as though somewhere in the room she might see her friend, ready to slip the bonds of reality to trade places with Ivy. It could have been Demi who made it this far. It could have been Ivy who burned to death in the vault under Haven. The idea was horrifying, and she squinted her eyes shut against welling tears, because just for a moment, Ivy felt relieved. Somewhere, in an unknowable version of reality, Ivy had done something right: she'd died in the place of a friend. Even if that shadow Ivy never meant to. Somewhere, in another place and time, there existed an Ivy who saved Demi's life, even at the cost of her own.

So that Demi could be standing here instead, next to a changeling, a murderous wing, and a door to an apocalypse. And suddenly Ivy realized why Angevin had brought the second helmet, and why he hadn't offered it to her.

"Demi goes with you," Ivy murmured, looking past Angevin at the door. Wordlessly, he nodded.

"And me?" Ivy asked.

The changeling shrugged. "If I told you, it wouldn't be your choice," he said.

That wasn't good enough. Stepping past the chair, Ivy grabbed him by the arm, pulling him around to face her. "For once in your life, don't lie," she snapped, letting go as soon as he was looking at her. "An honest answer. Please."

Angevin glanced back to the circular display. Only a sliver of yellow remained; the reflection shone in the face shield of the helmet under his arm.

"There's people there who'll need you," he said, which still wasn't an answer. "You speak the local language, and you know about the rules. You'll be an agent before we even have a word for the job, when it matters more than it ever did since. You want to keep people from dying, here's your chance. You could help them."

He nodded at the door, slipping the helmet over his head and tucking the flaps into his jacket collar casually, almost jauntily, as though he hadn't just suggested traveling through time. Ivy's breath caught in her throat, the cold air prickling along her neck. If she followed Angevin, she'd have half an hour in the terrifyingly far future followed by a lifetime living in the past. She'd be three hundred years safely away from Ambrose and his gun-toting agents, and from Carillon and the thing in her basement that thought Ivy was its next victim.

"If you go back to Dublin, I can't help you," Angevin added, nodding at the translucent panel at the other end of the room. "It's outside of my loop. If you come with me, I can protect you."

Just like you protected everyone else, Ivy didn't say.

If she followed Angevin, she'd be three hundred years away from pub quiz nights with Hunzu, and hen nights with Deirdre, or watching telly with Grinch drooling on her lap. Three hundred years away from her mum, who only had her cats to talk to, and her step-brothers, growing up on the threshold of the end of the world.

She started to look back at the figure at the far end of the room, and hesitated. Pepper had gone to Ivy's Dublin because that was where the end of the world started. Not in the far future, or the distant past. It started somewhere in the Institute, and Pepper thought he could change it. At the end, he'd thought *Ivy* could change it.

"There's people who need me here," Ivy said quietly, folding her arms. And added hesitantly, gesturing at the console, "This thing works in reverse, right?"

Angevin nodded, his fingers playing with the toggles on the fireman's jacket, his mouth turning up in a sad sort of smile. "One of these times, I'll find the right words to convince you to run away with me," he said, turning to the console and picking up Pepper's wing, slipping it neatly into one of the large pockets on his jacket. "It's easier with someone who doesn't think I'm completely mad."

The floor shivered, and Ivy grabbed for the console to steady herself. Angevin braced himself against back of the chair, though Ivy couldn't quite shake the notion that he'd reached for it a moment before the ground started to shake.

"If you have more questions, best ask quickly," he said, turning back to the door. "When the door opens, I won't wait."

Ivy nodded, her fingers digging hard into the metal of the console. The circle hovering over the console was almost entirely blue.

"He told me the end of the world starts in that building," Ivy said, speaking around a lump in her throat, resolutely not looking at the body behind her. "I want to go back and change it, but I don't know how."

"You'll have help, if you want it," said Angevin in a low voice, and to Ivy's quiet horror, he gestured to the lump in the pocket of his coat. "It doesn't care how long it's had to wait. If you want to change the future, it can help you. If you let it."

Ivy had wanted to change the future, when she walked into the Institute lobby two hours and three hundred years ago. Before she realized Pepper's plan was nothing more than cold-blooded murder, and she'd gotten Pepper killed instead.

Only the smallest sliver in the loop remained empty. Ivy glanced from the console back to Angevin. And then, because when Angevin walked out that door she'd never see him again, she said, "I haven't done a very good job so far."

Angevin smiled at her, and Ivy was struck by the strange notion that his was the kindest smile she'd ever seen.

"The universe doesn't need perfection, Ivy," he said, settling the helmet more firmly on his head. "All it needs is persistence."

With his long hair hidden by the helmet, he ought to have looked more like Pepper, but Ivy saw nothing but a face mottled with old scars, like a toy assembled in haste. Nothing about him looked like Pepper at all, except perhaps a hint of the same cool determination in his eyes. He glanced to the screen, then back at Ivy, smiling with a face that was and wasn't quite his own.

Something rattled, and Ivy grabbed for the chair again, but the sound was coming from the door. A rapid-fire series of pops rang out, like a hatch opening. Angevin's hands dropped to his sides; he was murmuring something under his breath, fingers twitching as though he were already going over numbers and formulas in his head.

The entire room seemed to lurch, and Ivy's ears popped as the door swung open. The smell of smoke came with it, sudden and strong. Ivy could see tendrils of it drifting through the door, and there was a strange light blazing somewhere beyond the threshold. It took Ivy a moment to realize it was fire. Distantly, she could hear someone screaming, the words impossible to make out.

Angevin bolted toward the door and through it, one arm raised as though to shield his eyes. Ivy dashed to the threshold, the heat on her skin like the open door of a furnace. The passage beyond was all flame and smoke, billows of it; part of the wall was so hot the skin of it was melting, coming apart in rivulets and dimples like old glass. An alarm shrieked from behind her, loud enough that Ivy jumped, and she grabbed the door's handle, tugging on it.

In the corridor, a shape in the smoke hesitated, looking back with one hand raised. Like he was waiting, despite what he'd said, just in case Ivy was mad enough to grab the spare helmet and follow him. This was why he had burn scars on his face, Ivy realized dully as she struggled with the door. From facing down *this*, every three hundred years, trying to save a world he may or may not have actually been born to.

The handle under Ivy's fingers was beginning to grow hot, the alarm behind her a desperate wail.

"Good luck," she called, but the vague shape was already lost in the smoke, or maybe he hadn't stopped in the first place. Ivy took a breath, coughed hard, and pressed her shoulder to the door. It started to swing as she tugged on the handle. The door slammed closed, then it shuddered as the latches slipped into place one after another like gunshots.

Before the last echo died away, her ears popped again. Every light in the room went out at once, and the handle under Ivy's fingers turned as cold as ice.

CHAPTER 13

Ivy let go of the handle, then immediately grabbed it again, pulling it even though she already suspected it wouldn't open. It didn't. She took a deep breath, the air still carrying hints of smoke, and leaned her head against the locked door. The cold felt soothing, but only for a few seconds, the metal rapidly becoming bone-chilling against her cheeks.

Ivy straightened up and tried the handle again; it still didn't move. Whatever Angevin had done to allow this tiny pocket of space to connect with Valiard, that connection seemed to be gone. Possibly a good thing, given that Valiard was apparently in the process of burning to the ground. All Ivy needed to do now was to get the time machine to connect to somewhere else.

Ivy turned back to the console. The display was pulsing yellow, a half dozen incomprehensible alerts jostling for space on the screen. Tentatively, Ivy tapped at a small, boxed squiggle at the bottom of the alert. The console chimed, and the alert vanished.

"Any chance you could show me these in English?" Ivy asked the screen. The console didn't react, continuing to pulse the same unintelligible messages. Biting at her lip, Ivy dismissed them one by one. As the yellow alerts disappeared, the room seemed to grow dimmer and colder around her.

As Ivy dismissed the last window, the display shifted, bringing up four blank boxes, gently flashing in blue, with a numeric keypad—thankfully all recognizable numerals and not the unfamiliar Rass syllabograms—below it. Beyond it, Ivy could dimly see the blurred reflection of her own face. She looked away from the troubled expression she saw there.

Was it a log-in screen? Was it asking her for a destination? Four numbers didn't seem nearly enough to specify where and when Ivy wanted to go. She took a deep breath. Angevin had gotten the computer working; Ivy just had to figure out how to do the same thing.

Hesitantly, she tapped the *one* on the screen, watching as the number appeared in the lefthand of the four blocks. Hurriedly, Ivy deleted the entry—the backward arrow at the bottom of the keypad doing exactly what she'd hoped. If it was a log-in, Ivy had no idea what the password was.

"You're going to have to give me a hint here," Ivy said pointedly, looking around the small room. Somewhere above her head a fan was whirring; she heard nothing else. "Hello?"

Slowly, Ivy walked to the other end of the room, not looking at Pepper, though she shuddered as she walked past that particular place on the floor. "Angevin?" Ivy added hesitantly. Her breath hung in the air like frost; she wrapped her arms closer around her chest. "Anyone?"

Shivering, Ivy dropped next to the duffel bag and gingerly picked up her battered wing. She waved her hand cautiously over the heat sinks, feeling nothing. Ivy offered it her wrist; the wing didn't move. The thing seemed as silent and dead as anything else in the room, and Ivy quickly set it back on the floor.

The translucent panel at the far end of the room was still

shut, its surface opaque and tinged blue. The whirring noise was louder here, a faint muttering almost like words. Ivy put her ear to the panel, listening hard, but the noise was no louder or clearer than it was anywhere else.

Even the cool voice of the Enemy might have been better than the indifferent muttering and the cold. Had Angevin known the system was going to lock her out? If she'd known she was choosing between a one-way trip to 1688 or freezing to death in the control room of a password-protected time machine, spending the rest of her life in the Middle Ages would have been considerably more appealing.

Ivy cupped her hand around her ear and leaned closer to the panel—and pulled away with a start. The cold where her finger had brushed the glass was fierce enough to hurt. She stepped back, cradling her hand as an angry string of Rass characters erupted onto the surface of the door.

"Sorry," Ivy muttered, tucking her hand under her armpit to warm it up. "I get it, don't touch. Look, any chance you could switch to English?"

She frowned at the door, and the incomprehensible characters didn't change. They probably spelled out something like *you need to log in first,* or *this unit is down for maintenance.* Or maybe *you're trapped here and you're going to die.*

Maybe Angevin hadn't known about this. It was outside of his loop, and he never saw the consequences. He could have been cheerily waving Ivy off to her death every time, and never realized.

Squeezing her eyes closed, Ivy turned back to the room, all glossy, black, and featureless. The whole place looked like a tomb, a sealed-in mausoleum for the seventeen percent of scouts like Pepper, the ones who never made it home.

The cold was starting to raise goosebumps on Ivy's skin. She went to the pile of Angevin's cast-off gear. The fire helmet she set aside, gratefully shrugging into the thick coat below it, zipping it up to her chin. It felt a little warmer, at least.

She picked up the duffel bag itself and turned it out onto the floor next to the dead wing. A thin paperback book dropped to the ground with a thunk, followed by three sachets of burn gel, two knitting needles, an empty crisps bag, and a single purple sock. Ivy set the bag aside and picked up the book, her hopes of a title like *Introductory Trow Language* or *Time Machines 101* fading as she took in the battered cover. *Keep the Aspidistra Flying, Classics to Go Edition* read the title, the cover depicting a large and rather unwholesome-looking houseplant.

Numbly, Ivy flicked it open, flipping through the pages long enough to see if there was anything written on the flyleaves or scrawled in the margins. There wasn't.

Ivy was trapped with a dead person inside the control room of a time machine, with what appeared on first inspection to be a deeply forgettable period novel, and somehow that felt like the very last straw.

Ivy dropped the paperback next to the duffel, kicking the crisps bag aside as she went back to the console. The display was still showing the four empty boxes, the keypad below it patiently blinking, which meant Ivy needed a number. Just four digits, and if she guessed it right she'd have a chance at convincing the time machine to let her out of the control room. No telling where she'd end up, but even a burning city or a sheep field in the Middle Ages would be an improvement on staying here and freezing to death.

Four digits could specify a year, and the year Ivy was trying to get back to was at least something she actually knew. Carefully, she typed it into the console, watching closely as the numbers appeared in the boxes above the keypad. As soon as the last box was filled, the keypad shifted to grey, leaving the two arrows as the only symbols blinking. Biting her lip, Ivy pushed the forward arrow

A harsh double chime sounded from the console and two lines of angry, incomprehensible red text appeared below the keypad, surrounded by a heavy red border. Above it, the keypad was still there, and the four blank boxes. A wrong guess, but at least the terminal hadn't locked her out.

Apparently this was going to be trickier than simply telling the time machine where she wanted to go. Ivy leaned over the console, trying to take advantage of the faint warmth seeping up from the surface.

If this were a story from one of her dad's old sci-fi novels, the password would turn out to be pi, or the Fibonacci sequence, or the atomic number of carbon, or something else basic and essential to the fabric of the universe. Pi would be three-one-four-something. Maybe seven? Or one? Fibonacci would be one-one-two-three. That seemed like one of those easily guessed passwords that security experts warn against using, which meant it was probably too simple for the security code on an impossibly complicated time-travel computer system, and Ivy had no idea what the atomic number of carbon was. She bit her lip, wondering how many wrong guesses the console would tolerate before locking her out entirely.

Fibonacci was as good a guess as any, and Ivy wouldn't know whether it was wrong unless she tried it. Taking a deep breath, she typed in the numbers, watching them appear in the boxes above the keypad with a mix of hope and trepidation. She hesitated with her finger over the enter button.

If the system locked her out after only two wrong guesses, she was dead. Or the next best thing: trapped in a very cold room with a dead body and a terrible book, no food or water, and no way out.

And if the password wasn't pi, or a Fibonacci number, Ivy

didn't want to think about the odds of correctly guessing a random four-digit number in however many tries the console might allow. Pepper's seventeen percent was beginning to look like considerably better odds than Ivy's.

Ivy started to glance behind her and stopped herself. Pepper couldn't help her, just like she hadn't been able to help him. She couldn't prevent the universe from tossing him aside like a cast-off toy, discarded by a timeline that didn't care whether the Angevin who walked out of this room really had a right to that name.

Before she could follow that thought any further, Ivy pressed enter.

The annoyed double chime rang out again, and the red text at the bottom shifted to an even longer incomprehensible message. Ivy sagged back against the chair, realizing dully that she hadn't actually been expecting the console to accept the number.

She tucked her hands under her arms, flexing her fingers against the chill. No Fibonacci number, then. The tips of her fingers were starting to tingle with cold.

"If there's something you want me to do in Dublin, just tell me what it is!" Ivy announced to the console, trying to keep any quaver of fear out of her voice. "You want to stop the end of the world? Great, so do I, we're on the same page. But I can't do anything about that if I'm stuck in here!"

The console was silent. The red letters continued to shine their incomprehensible warning. Either it couldn't hear her, or it didn't care. Or it was another computer built like Salem, determined to follow its objectives no matter how many people died as a result.

On impulse, Ivy reached into her purse and pulled out her phone. The service indicator was showing a full five bars of signal, and a Wi-Fi connection as well.

Hurriedly, Ivy pulled up the Wi-Fi menu, her fingers feeling numb and clumsy as they worked their way through an unfamiliar series of screens. As Ivy pulled up the list of available networks, the screen blossomed into a long series of gibberish network names. Ivy clicked on one at random.

Unable to connect to network j9^di#%7409#&

Ivy tried another one, then a third, with the same result.

Abandoning the Wi-Fi menu, Ivy went back to the contacts screen and pulled up Hunzu's number. She pushed the call button, and cautiously lifted the phone to her ear. There was little enough chance of being able to call Earth from here, wherever here was, but it would be sillier not to try.

The line rang twice. Ivy jumped as the phone erupted into squeals and static, a cacophony of clipped and distorted noises nearly drowning out a low tone rising and falling in the unmistakable cadence of speech. It sounded like the noises she'd hear from the conference room in Eirecom whenever someone called into the fax line by mistake.

"Hunzu?" she shouted, listening for anything in the garble that might indicate the voice on the line could hear her. "Hunzu, it's me!"

The squeals didn't change, continuing in the calm cadence of a weather report or a particularly dull local newscast. "Hunzu! Hello, anybody?"

The phone took no notice. Ivy kept it tight to her ear anyway.

"Hunzu," she hissed again, squeezing her eyes shut and telling herself she was not going to cry. "I don't know if anyone can hear me. Actually, I'm pretty sure you can't. But just in case . . ."

Ivy trailed off, opening her eyes to look again at the small, dark room, the duffel bag and the knitting needles scattered on the floor.

"It's cold here," she said, tucking her free hand under her arm. "There isn't anyone else, and I don't know where I am."

When the door had opened to Valiard, for those few seconds she'd been hundreds of years in the future. Hunzu and her mum and everyone else she'd ever known was already dead. They'd been dead for a very long time.

"I might have just saved your grandparents, or something," she said, trying to hold Hunzu's image in her mind, to let it blot out everything else. "I mean, I don't know who they are. Maybe they haven't met yet. I should have given Angevin a letter, got someone to pass it down like an heirloom to give it to you later. When I don't come back . . ."

Ivy leaned forward, burying her face into her knees as the voice in the static droned on unperturbed. Hunzu seemed almost too distant to be crying over, irretrievably lost somewhere in the unknowable reaches between Ivy and the real world, the one she'd stumbled out of twenty minutes ago. Nobody could hear her, and Ivy was going to be another one of Pepper's statistics, another traveler who never made it home.

But something had made it back. Ivy remembered the face at the lab door, the funhouse-mirror image of Ivy's own face wearing a fireman's coat, its stunned expression before Mr. Brothers took off chasing it. Warily, Ivy lifted her head, staring at her own reflection in the black, glossy wall. Ivy was already wearing its coat. Or maybe it was already wearing Ivy's face.

Pepper hadn't gone home, but something else had, bearing his name and a bit of his appearance. Something had walked into the burning halls of Valiard calling himself Angevin and making himself a hero, and no one noticed that he wasn't who he claimed to be.

If Ivy didn't get home, somewhere in a pocket of emptiness where the universe kept things it wasn't using at the moment, maybe something *else* would wake up and think she was Ivy.

Hunzu would think she was Ivy. So would Ivy's mum, and so would her dad and Shannon, and her step-brothers, and no one would tell them differently.

"If I don't come home," Ivy whispered into the phone, "you have to find out what's in the Institute lab. Maybe *she'll* help you, even if I can't."

In her ear, the warbling voice continued its unchanging monologue. Slowly, Ivy brought the phone away from her ear and ended the call. The silence as the voice cut out felt like the deepest, most suffocating stillness Ivy had ever known.

"I hope you don't ever know she's a lie," Ivy whispered, tucking the useless phone back into her pocket and slipping her hands into the opposite sleeves.

It was terrifically ironic. Ivy was sitting in the middle of some of the most advanced technology that had ever existed, and she couldn't make it past the log-in screen. She was going to freeze to death inside an actual bloody time machine all because she couldn't guess a four-digit password. If this were one of her dad's sci-fi novels, she ought to be able to hack it with her phone, or reprogram it, or hot-wire it and go off and save the day. Or go off like in the H. G. Wells book, find the fucking Eloi, and hope they made better neighbors than trows. All she needed was a number.

If Ivy had that number, she could go back and try to change things. This was one of the computers responsible for everything that had twisted Ivy's life away from what it should have been. She could go to Portrush in 1989 and make sure her mum and Larch never met. Or go back to last summer and warn herself never to move to Howth. She ought to be able to go anywhere she wanted. Mostly, Ivy wanted to go back to Dublin, to the July evening that she'd so recently left behind.

Absently, Ivy rubbed at her trousers. There was still a brown stain on the left knee from the miniature sausages she had been nibbling on an hour ago. None of that should be so far away.

He who controls the past controls the future, just like it said in the book back in the flat in Howth. From here, Ivy could reach back to any point in time she wanted, if only she could figure out how to make the time machine do it.

She'd already convinced Pepper's wing to open a way back to Valiard. The dead woman's wing had spoken to her in the Dartry flat. The Enemy in Carillon's vault had called her *mistress*.

Ivy glanced at Pepper, shuddered, and fixed her gaze firmly on the gravy stain on her trousers. Someone had died in each of those instances. No one was going to die for Ivy this time; there was no one here who could force the console to listen to her.

Ivy shoved her hands back into the ends of her sleeves and got to her feet, pacing in the little space beside the console, hoping it would help her stay warm.

Maybe it was simply a matter of odds. Out of Angevin's eleven or nineteen or twenty-six times, maybe only one Ivy had ever stumbled on the right combination. The rest of the time, she'd be a second dead body on the floor, and Ivy's mum and step-brothers and everyone Ivy cared about would keep on walking blindly toward the end of the world. Ivy was never getting the number right. Never going home. Never leaving this room.

Ivy would never get a chance to find out what Mr. Brothers was doing at the Institute. Or what happened to the dead animal in Room 101, or why they'd left the poor thing in its cage ...

Ivy stopped abruptly, pulling her right hand out of the opposite sleeve. 101 was a number, even if it was one digit too short. Slowly, Ivy typed it into the blinking keypad, hesitated, then added another zero at the end. 1010. It was too repetitive to make a good passcode, but Ivy didn't have any better ideas. She hesitated, finger hovering over the back arrow, her breath steaming in the air between her and the display.

Anything was better than sitting in the cold trying to think up a number. If she made too many wrong guesses and the console locked her out permanently, at least she'd know she'd done everything she could.

Taking a deep breath, Ivy pressed the enter key. The red box around the display grew larger as the console chimed disappointingly, and a few more incomprehensible words added themselves to the warning plastered across the screen. Ivy slowly lowered her hand.

"You're going to kill me if you don't let me out," Ivy told it. The display didn't even flicker.

She slid off the chair and picked up the duffel bag, shoving *Keep the Aspidistra Flying* out of the way with her foot. Awkwardly, she wrapped the bag over her shoulders, pulling it as snug as she could. It didn't feel even the slightest bit warmer.

Room 101. The number wasn't the password, but Ivy was certain she'd seen that phrase somewhere before. She remembered how she'd shivered when she'd first seen the sign on the door at the Institute, like it had reminded her of something.

It didn't matter. Ivy was never going to get home. DIAAR already felt impossibly far away, like thinking of Macau or Rio de Janeiro, some distant place she'd heard about but had never actually visited. Like walking back into the flat in Howth, everything stripped away or covered with sheets, all of it either abandoned or unrecognizable.

Swallowing hard, Ivy raised her head and looked back at Pepper, grateful for the hood covering his face. Pepper had trusted her to continue his mission. Swallowing hard, she looked away, tucking her hands back into the sleeves of her borrowed jacket as she looked over the rest of the useless detritus Angevin had left behind.

The abandoned book was upside down; the titular aspidistra looked even shaggier from that angle. Something about the cover seemed odd. Ivy had the strangest urge to shove the thing under the console or toss it into the farthest corner of the room.

Instead, Ivy picked it up, turning it the right way round and staring at it as though she'd never seen it before. At the bottom of the cover, the author's name was listed in bold, red letters. George Orwell. She'd seen that name before, too; she remembered it from the jumble of books left behind in Demi's old flat in Howth.

Ivy flipped open the book, her fingertips tingling, thumbing clumsily past the copyright page and a dedication. She flipped through another few pages, landing on an introduction, then thumbed her way back to the first handful of pages.

The list jumped out as she flicked toward the front of the book.

Other Works by this Author:
Animal Farm
Burmese Days
Inside the Whale and Other Essays
Then at the very bottom of the list: *1984.*

Ivy stared at the page, feeling like a corner of reality was peeling away like a scab. The universe was giving her a number. Not just giving it to her, repeating it several times: first in Demi's bookcase, then in Angevin's bag, and on the door sign at the Institute. Room 101 was something from *1984*, Ivy was almost certain. Even the Institute CEO's name, Winston Smith Brothers... Big Brother—and wasn't *1984*'s narrator called Something Smith?

Hidden in the pages of a horribly dull novel that no one

read anymore, something had given her a number. Something *wanted* Ivy to get out.

Ivy whirled back to the console, fingers digging into the book's spine, staring at the Rass display even though she had no idea what the console was trying to tell her. *Last try*, probably. *No more second chances.*

Ivy entered the numbers carefully. She could barely feel the console past the numbness in her fingertips.

One. Nine. Eight. Four. Holding her breath, she pressed enter.

A brash chime rang through the room as the display erupted into a jumble of numbers and unfamiliar characters. The light in the room was growing brighter; Ivy could feel the faintest hint of heat rising off the console.

She jumped off the chair, letting the duffel bag fall from her shoulders and turning in time to see the translucent panel at the back of the room begin to slide open. Ivy's ears popped; she grabbed for the back of the chair, the tiny room seeming to spin for a moment. A bright, amber-toned light was shining from the open panel. Beside it, a blue arrow on the wall was pulsing gently.

"Any chance you're willing to talk *now*?" Ivy asked, looking back at the console.

She tapped the screen; it didn't respond. Ivy turned back to the newly opened panel. If it was flashing blue, at least it wanted her attention. Maybe it would be more willing to communicate.

Rubbing her hands across her sleeves, Ivy went to the open door. The amber glare seemed brighter, making it difficult to see exactly what was inside. Raising her hand to shield her eyes, Ivy slowly stepped over the threshold. The light seemed even more intense, reflecting off a small space lined with metallic walls, etched with complicated designs that looked more like circuitry than anything else.

Something hissed from behind her; Ivy's ear popped again as she turned around in time to see the translucent panel sliding back in place.

"Wait!" Ivy yelped, turning from the closed door to the rest of the room, the amber light leaving streaks across her vision as she moved. There had to be some way to stop it, at least until she knew what the machine was actually doing. She staggered toward the translucent panel; it felt strangely difficult to walk the few steps, like she was pushing through taffy. She reached out to touch the panel and immediately thought better of it— and blinked hard, because she was seeing the frosted panel *through* the space where her hand was supposed to be.

Ivy snatched her hand back, holding both hands palm up, but the amber light was so bright she could barely see anything beyond the glare. The light held her, pinning her in place like a shadow puppet against a wall. She squeezed her eye shut; it didn't seem to help. The light grew brighter and brighter, burning away the walls, and the shadows, and the chill in the air, and Ivy crouched until even the light itself burned away, taking everything in the world along with it.

CHAPTER 14

Something hard and uncomfortable was digging into her hip, and Ivy was staring at her own outstretched hand, as though the lines on her palm contained some vastly important secret she'd never before understood. Ivy blinked, wrinkling her nose. Beyond her fingers was a cinderblock wall, its beige paint scorched and cracked, and the uncomfortable thing Ivy was lying on was a stairway, all metal and open slats. The stairs were quivering rhythmically, as though someone else were coming down them in a hurry.

Abruptly recalling herself, Ivy bolted to her feet, stumbled, and caught herself on the handrail. She looked up at the same time the footsteps skidded to a stop, and gasped.

"Holy mother of . . ." A man's voice trailed off, accompanied by the static-filled murmur of a handheld radio.

The section of stairs directly above Ivy was completely destroyed, the treads looking like they'd been ripped apart with a can opener. The paint on the walls was blistered and cracked, the pattern reminding Ivy of the circuitry on the walls of the room she'd just left. Distantly, Ivy could hear the blaring of the fire alarm starting up again.

Or maybe the fire alarm was sounding for the first time.

Again.

"No, it looks like some sort of bomb went off," the voice above said, his voice echoing in the tight confines of the stairwell. "Hey, wait— Hey, miss, stay where you are!"

Ivy bolted down the stairs, ignoring the surprised shout from behind her. If she didn't want to spend all night being questioned by the security team, she needed to get out of sight and into less conspicuous clothes. At least the fireman's coat, striking as it was, was hiding the bloodstains on the rest of her clothing.

Ivy tore through the first door she came through, immediately slowing her steps to a fast walk, trying to look as though she had every right to be here. Wherever, or whenever, here was.

Automatically, Ivy glanced at her watch, which blithely informed her it was 1:46 in the morning. Which was completely useless; it wasn't as though the watch would be able to tell Ivy whether she'd time traveled.

The corridor was beige and windowless, a succession of DIAAR's usual frosted-glass-fronted doors. The fire alarm wasn't as loud here; the echoes, muffled and tinny, were fading the farther she got from the stairwell. Ivy turned into the first hallway she passed and nearly jumped. A man in a partially unbuttoned blue shirt was enthusiastically kissing a woman in a green dress; two red Solo cups sat abandoned on the floor a few feet away.

Ivy hurried past, pointedly not looking at them, hoping they were distracted enough to do likewise. Fancy dresses, red Solo cups: still the night of the party.

But *when* on the night of the party? If it were early enough in the evening, Pepper might still be alive. If she could get to him before he was shot, maybe it was still possible to change things.

Which meant Ivy had to get to them before they got to Mr. Brothers. If the fire alarm was already going off, that meant they would already be on their way to Room 101.

Lab 21 read the sign on the closest door. Ivy was probably on the ground floor. Of which building in the campus, she didn't know. She hurried down the hall, turned into a wider hallway, and spotted another set of stairs. Ivy shoved open the panic bar, taking the stairs two at a time, hurrying up as quickly as she could.

Ivy passed the landing, then hurried to the next floor. She slipped through the door, scanning the plaques over the glass-fronted doors as she hurried down the hallway.

To her left was a long stretch of empty wall, broken by two fire extinguishers, a black vinyl curtain shielding an emergency shower, and an eyewash station. Ivy's heart sped up, but she couldn't make out the name on the plaque until she was almost on top of it.

Room 101.

Ivy threw open the door, started to step through—and froze. She could smell the blood, even over the stench from the cage; the jumpsuit-clad body was already on the floor, the blood pooling around him a brilliant red under the harsh overhead lights. His feet were pedaling uselessly against the floor and Ivy felt her last, remnant hope flicker to ash somewhere in the pit of her stomach. She was too late, and Pepper was already dying, and even traveling through time hadn't been enough to change it.

Ivy tore her gaze away from the dying scout—and looked straight into the face of Mr. Brothers. Sweat was standing out on his forehead, his mouth set in a grim line. The security guard behind him still had his gun in his hands. Mr. Brothers shouted something and started for the door at a run; the man with the gun followed. Just like he'd done before, when he'd fired at something in the hall; Ivy remembered flinching when she'd heard the shots. She grabbed the door, wrenching it back open—and hesitated long enough to look for what she already knew she'd see.

Clinging to the top of the chain-link fence was a girl in a bloodstained shirt with a Valiard wing gleaming on her arm. Her face, down to the expression of horror and confusion, was the mirror of Ivy's own.

She couldn't save Pepper. She couldn't even save herself from what was going to happen in the next five minutes. The best she could do was play the part that her own past and the damn time machine had already chosen for her: drawing Mr. Brothers off.

Ivy bolted out the door and ran back down the hallway, furiously trying to calculate how long it had been until she'd heard the gunshot. She didn't have a wing to hide her, and what the hell were all the George Orwell references about if the only thing she'd come back to do was get shot in a hallway five minutes after she'd arrived?

Unless the only thing she was meant to do was what she'd just done—get Mr. Brothers out of the room so Angevin could go back to Valiard and start everything all over again. Maybe, as of ten seconds ago, Ivy was expendable.

Ivy guessed she only had seconds before the gun went off. Assume the guard had worse aim if he was shooting at a moving target? Or don't become a target in the first place?

She skidded to a stop next to the emergency shower, threw back the flimsy curtain, and pressed herself against the wall. It was a terrible hiding place and she knew it; the curtain didn't touch the floor, and there was a gap between it and the lefthand wall. She reached to pull it closed, then froze as a door flew open with a bang. Footsteps pounded in the hallway; Ivy shuddered and tried not to move. The gap was facing the opposite way down the corridor, toward the glass door leading back to the offices and smaller labs. The footsteps were drawing closer. The gunshot had to be soon; maybe hiding had been enough to throw things off-kilter. Both men would run past, and Wayne wouldn't fire the gun at all.

Ivy held her breath as the footsteps drew even. The curtain swayed as one of the men brushed against it; Ivy tried not to flinch. A moment later, she was looking at their backs as the men approached the glass door. The security guard was pointing the gun vaguely at the ceiling, like he hadn't quite given up on firing it again.

The silhouette appeared in the frosted glass a moment later. As the door opened, the outline transformed into a familiar shape. Ivy's stomach wrenched; Mr. Brothers gasped. The security guard shouted something as he stepped in front of his boss, and with a jolt Ivy realized what was about to happen.

"Get down!" Ivy screamed. Ambrose jumped back from the door, plastering himself against the wall as the shot rang out. Ivy flinched.

"The hell is going on here?" Mr. Brothers snapped, rounding on the man beside him, his fist clenched. The flimsy curtain wasn't going to be enough to hide her if the men lingered in the hall having an argument. Ivy glanced through the gap in the curtain at Ambrose, still pressed against the wall. He was staring back at her with a grim expression.

Ivy bolted out from the emergency shower, ignoring Mr. Brothers's shout, hoping desperately she wasn't about to get both of them caught. Hunzu had told her once that this was possible; Ivy deeply regretted never requesting a demonstration. Even if it worked, she was doomed if Ambrose chose not to help her.

Ambrose realized what Ivy was doing a second before she plowed into him. Wide-eyed, he stepped away from the wall;

Ivy had to turn sideways to wriggle into the gap. She felt Ambrose lifting his arms. Ivy raised her head, her heart dropping to her stomach as she saw the look of anger on Mr. Brothers's face. The director was staring right at her.

"Keep your head down," Ambrose hissed, slipping farther in front of Ivy, leaning close enough she could feel the edges of his collar brushing against her cheek. "Don't look at him."

Ivy lowered her head, her cheek uncomfortably close to the sweat stain covering the back of Ambrose's shirt, forcing her gaze to the floor. She tried to focus on her breathing, keeping it as slow and even as possible though her heart was thudding like a jackhammer.

Two white shoes sidled closer, red stains darkening the tips. Ivy stared at Mr. Brothers's shoes and forced herself not to look up. Beside her, Ambrose was as motionless as a statue, hands spread wide, face turned carefully away. Ivy had no idea if the veil was strong enough for this to work, if the Ambrose-shaped hole in Mr. Brothers's perception would be enough to hide her, too.

Mr. Brothers let out a long sigh and the pointed leather shoes shuffled. Distantly, Ivy could still hear the faint wail of the fire alarm.

"Get Colliers up here and sweep the rest of the floor," Mr. Brothers said, and the pointed leather shoes finally turned away. "Without any more dramatics, if you please. I need to check on Gwendolyn."

The footsteps continued down the hall. Beside her, Ambrose let out a slow breath. Ivy cautiously lifted her head, peering past Ambrose's shoulder in time to see the door to the offices swing shut.

Ambrose stepped away abruptly, wiping his hands on his trousers as he turned to Ivy, an unreadable expression on his face.

"How much of it's yours?" he asked quietly, nodding at the blood-soaked blouse under her fireman's coat.

"Very little," Ivy said, certain it would have been better if he'd started off shouting at her. Then at least she'd know how things stood. "Sorry to disappoint."

Ambrose pursed his lips and looked at the floor.

"And the scout?" he asked in the same too-careful voice.

Pepper was bleeding to death in a lab thirty yards down the hallway. Ivy had no idea what the universe might do if she charged back into the lab to confront Angevin alongside the Ivy of an hour ago, but whatever she did, it wouldn't be enough to save Pepper.

Ivy looked down at the bloodstained hem of her shirt and shook her head. Ambrose let out a sigh that almost sounded relieved. As Ivy looked up, he crossed his arms, eyes narrowing as he met her gaze.

"You have two options," Ambrose said tightly. "The first is that the Roinn and I somehow fail to find you before you leave the building. You'll find a ticket in your name at the Qantas counter of the Dublin airport, for a flight to Sydney leaving at seven-forty tomorrow morning. I recommend not using the return half. You won't outlive our statute of limitations if you run."

Ivy swallowed hard. She'd risked her life and traveled how many centuries into the future to try and save the world, and apparently that didn't deserve so much as a thank you. At least it was a better escape that the one Angevin had offered. She'd still be able to call her mum. She could settle down on the other side of the planet, pretend the world was just as normal and uninteresting as most people supposed, and stay as far away as she could from whatever was going to happen here. And everyone Ivy cared about would still be living on Armageddon's doorstep, with no idea that anything bad was about to happen.

"What's the second option?" Ivy asked quietly.

"That would be up to Thane Carillon," said Ambrose crisply. He added, seeing Ivy's horrified look, "She's the aggrieved party, you know. Could have been killed. She's expected to fully recover, and that *considerably* increases your options."

A chill ran down Ivy's spine at the thought of ever having anything to do with Taye Carillon ever again.

"So why give me an option at all?" Ivy demanded.

"It's up to Carillon—"

"Not her," Ivy snapped. "You. The ticket to Sydney. Would you do that for every agent in the Roinn?"

"No, I wouldn't," Ambrose said, looking steadily at Ivy, and his mouth twitched.

"Why?" Ivy asked again, coming a step closer. A hint of warmth seemed to seep into his expression.

"Someone told me once that you were more valuable on your side of the veil, rather than ours," he said quietly. "I'd like to think that's still true."

Demi had been the one who told him that. He remembered, if only that much. But before she could say anything, Ambrose frowned, his expression hardening.

"If we really are on the edge of Event Two, it's going to be just as bad for my people as it is for yours. I want agents in the Roinn I can count on. I rather hope you're still in that category."

Very slowly, Ambrose extended his gloved hand, holding it out to her palm up. An uncertain smile slipped across his face, gone before Ivy could decide if it had really been there or not.

"What'll it be?" he asked. In the quiet that followed, it seemed as though the building itself was leaning closer to listen to the answer.

Something had given Ivy the password she needed; something had smeared George Orwell's bibliography across the past three days of Ivy's life. That had happened for a reason, and if Ivy walked away she was giving up on her chance to find out why. She'd go off to Australia knowing that some unfathomable bit of the universe thought she was important, that she could do something that mattered, and that she had refused to play along.

Pepper and Demi had tried to do things that mattered, and look what happened to them.

Slowly, Ivy nodded and stepped forward, and for the briefest of moments Ambrose's smile was in full evidence as she slipped her bare hand into his gloved one. He squeezed her fingers briefly, then made as if to pull back, but Ivy didn't let go.

"One condition of my own," she said.

Ambrose merely raised an eyebrow, his face unreadable.

"There's a reason your census has never been accurate" she told him. "It's the same reason there's Maeve Binchy books on your nightstand, and soy milk in your fridge. Don't argue," Ivy snapped, dropping her hand at his exasperated glare. "Just look. Will you do that? Please?"

Ambrose opened his mouth, his eyebrows already telegraphing the answer, but whatever he saw in Ivy's face brought him up short. He turned away abruptly, staring down the corridor toward the offices where Mr. Brothers had disappeared.

"Fine," he said, and continued with a forced sort of cheerfulness. "Always heard it was wretchedly hot in Australia anyway. And do cover up that shirt, it looks like you've been party to a murder."

Ambrose was already shrugging out of his vest, and he handed it to Ivy. He tapped his foot as Ivy took off the fireman's jacket, kicked it behind the emergency shower curtain, and pulled the vest over her blouse. Buttoning up the vest, she got a whiff of equal parts cologne and sweat, and Ivy wrinkled her nose. At least it covered the bloodstains on the hem of her shirt.

Ambrose stepped carefully up to the office door, opened it a sliver, then motioned Ivy to follow. "Besides the building's security and the entirety of the Roinn, is anyone else looking for you?" Ambrose asked.

"I don't think so," Ivy said, following Ambrose as they hurried down the hall. She almost ran into him as he turned to stare at something behind Ivy.

"Don't look behind you," Ambrose said crisply. "Two of your friends from security are following us."

Ivy shifted closer to the wall, her shoulder brushing against the paneled walls, forcing herself not to speed up.

"Keep walking," Ambrose called, and darted across the hall to a fire pull. He grabbed the handle and tugged it; the plastic cover fell to the floor with a clatter. Behind her, someone called out.

The shriek of the alarm was sudden enough that she jumped, even though she'd been expecting it. As Ambrose fell into step behind her, Ivy hurried the last few yards to the stairway, threw open the door, and hurried through—and walked straight into a woman in a green sweater.

Ivy stumbled back, trying to hold open the door for Ambrose, bleating out an apology that was certain to go unheard. The woman merely looked annoyed, mouthed something equally unintelligible back to Ivy, then continued down the stairs, trundling along with a singular lack of urgency.

As Ivy started down the stairs, a group of men holding red plastic cups walked into the stairway from the floor below. Ambrose shifted a step closer to Ivy, who fell in line behind the woman with the green sweater, everyone clumping down the stairs with the same morose demeanor Ivy remembered from fire drills back at Clarence Monaghan Day School.

She allowed herself to be swept along with everyone else, shoving her hands into the pocket of her borrowed vest. Beside her, Ambrose kept closer than usual, the thin line of sweat across his forehead the only sign of his discomfort.

Another landing, then the woman in green turned down a short corridor and out an unmarked door, shoving at the panic bar. Ivy felt the warm summer air a moment before she stepped over the threshold. The air felt clean, smelling of asphalt and recently mown grass.

In front of the building, two Gardaí squad cars were parked in the loading zone, their flashing lights reflecting against the glass. A small crowd of people were gathered by the smokers' pavilion a few yards beyond, but the majority of people leaving the building seemed to be drifting toward the car park. Either the party was over, or the attendees had decided to find somewhere to drink with fewer life-threatening emergencies.

Ivy headed for the parking lot, Ambrose walking silently beside her. The trees Pepper had seen from the walkway were somewhere on the far end of the parking lot; Ivy couldn't see them from here and didn't want to look. She could still hear the alarm, keening urgently through an open window. Even that faded as Ivy reached the bottom of the hill, and for a moment it felt as though Ivy had been granted some coveted and highly unusual pass: escape from the apocalypse.

Hesitating, Ivy looked back, watching as a fire truck and a third Garda car came hurrying up the road, their lights reflecting on the glass like a memory of fire.

Burn it down, Pepper had told her.

Ivy turned away from the lights as she followed Ambrose down the hill, wondering how long they had before something inside that building started them all on a long, slow fall straight to the end of the world.

ACKNOWLEDGMENTS

Thanks to everyone who read and commented on the manuscript that turned into *Changeling*, most especially Teresa Whipple. Thanks also to my Labyrinth Room beta readers Mike Justa and Tim Morrow - everything I write is better thanks to folks who take the time to read and comment on early versions. Thanks to A. L. Collins for helping this Alaskan writer make Ivy's world feel as authentically Irish as possible, and for your continual concern for Grinch. Thanks to Rachel Oestreich of Wallflower Editing for her world-class assistance catching typos, cleaning up the text and various and sundry improvements. A big shoutout to Paul J. Nahin and his book *A Writer's Guide to the Real Science of Plausible Time Travel* for an accessible and curious look at a fascinating topic.

Big thanks to artist Kaitlynn Jolley for the cover design, giving us a literal and figurative window into Ivy's world. Thanks to Heather Gallagher, for your continuing contribution to the Fictional Character Name Donation Program. Thanks to Colin, Year King's original publisher, for being willing to take a chance on an unknown author with a weird, genre-bending manuscript. You still should have taken me up on my offer to change Ivy's boyfriend's name.

Thanks to everyone at UnCruise Adventures for their continual willingness to pay me to go on other people's vacations. Thanks also to all my friends and fellow shipmates from boat life, most especially the captains and crew of the *Safari Explorer*. Thanks to everyone at the Seward Harbor, for the best pandemic office job a gal could ask for.

Thanks to Seward institutions Resurrect Art and 13 Ravens Coffee for keeping our little town lively, friendly, weird, and well-caffeinated. Thanks to the good folks behind National Novel Writing Month, for everything you do to encourage engagement with books, writing and creativity.

Thanks to friends and family in West Virginia and Alaska: Gina, Donald, and Emily; Kate, Mike, Marion, Jesse, Everett and Violet; Jolie, Dan and Stella; and Sarah and Ben, also Ben, Rebecca, Stephanie, and Nancy. As always, thanks to Dan and Penny of the Contemporary Youth Arts Company, for giving me the tools to imagine worlds different than the one I happened to be living in. Mark, you gave your time and talent to basically every arts organization in Charleston, and you left us way too soon.

Hugs and smooches to my foster dog and editing buddy Puka, who in her younger days would definitely have chased down invisible time travelers in the street, most likely for the purposes of making friends with them.

To everyone who has been waiting patiently for more of Ivy's adventures, thanks for hanging in there.

Ivy reached into her purse and pulled out her wallet. Her own face, unsmiling and awful in the way all ID photos are awful, stared back at her from her Institute key card.

Ivy's adventures conclude in *No Dominion*.

Follow Mareth on Facebook, Amazon, or Goodreads for news about the sequel.

ABOUT THE AUTHOR

Mareth Griffith bounces between the Pacific Northwest coast and various warmer locations. She mostly lives in Seward, Alaska, and assures you winters there aren't as bad as you think.

When she's not writing, she works as a naturalist and wilderness guide, leading adventurous souls on epic quests to seek out glaciers, bears, and whales in the wilds of coastal Alaska. She's also lived and worked in Scotland, Mexico, Antarctica, Hawaii, New Zealand, and Northern Ireland—where her nearest neighbors included two thousand puffins and the ghost of a spectral black horse.

Originally from West Virginia, Mareth attended Smith College in Massachusetts, studying music and theatre. Mareth plays classical violin well and rhythm guitar badly.

Follow Mareth on Amazon, Goodreads, or Facebook for news about future books.

THIS PAGE INTENTIONALLY LEFT BLANK AS PART
OF A VAST TROW CONSPIRACY...